LAST
REFUGE

LAST REFUGE

ELIZABETH ANN SCARBOROUGH

  Bantam Books
New York Toronto London Sydney Auckland

LAST REFUGE

A Bantam Spectra Book / September 1992

Published simultaneously in hardcover and trade paperback

All rights reserved.
Copyright © 1992 by Elizabeth Ann Scarborough.

BOOK DESIGN BY GRETCHEN ACHILLES

Library of Congress Cataloging-in-Publication Data
Scarborough, Elizabeth Ann.
   Last refuge / Elizabeth Ann Scarborough.
      p.   cm.
   ISBN 0-553-08961-7 (hc) ISBN 0-553-37031-6 (pbk)
   I. Title.
PS3569.C324L37   1992
813'.54—dc20   92-6177   CIP

Published simultaneously in the United States and Canada

───

Bantam Books are published by Bantam Books, a division of Bantam
Doubleday Dell Publishing Group, Inc. Its trademark, consisting of
the words "Bantam Books" and the portrayal of a rooster, is Regis-
tered in U.S. Patent and Trademark Office and in other countries.
Marca Registrada. Bantam Books, 666 Fifth Avenue, New York,
New York 10103.

───

PRINTED IN THE UNITED STATES OF AMERICA

RRH   0   9   8   7   6   5   4   3   2   1

FOR BETTY LOU SCARBOROUGH,
CHIEF PUBLICIST, CHEERLEADER,
CONFIDANTE, READER, CRITIC, AND MOM.

LAST
REFUGE

(HAPTER
1

Section One
K A L A P A

On the morning of the last birthday Mike would ever celebrate, the first changeling was born.

That day, Mike was officially twenty-one years old and an adult. He awoke before dawn and slipped out of the communal housing compound. The soft gray light of morning outlined the onion-shaped dome of the chorten against the snowy backdrop of the horned peaks of the guardian mountain, Karakal.

Prayer flags fluttered from lines strung between the chorten's dome and nearby buildings, the wind carrying the prayers to the heavens. Mike bowed to the chorten, in memory of the heroes it represented, and turned to walk down the steep path winding from the uppermost point in Kalapa—the chorten—through the compound built on the ruins of the ancient mystic city. The old city and the current compound were located on a small mountain set within a valley ringed by ranges of larger mountains, the largest of which was the horned guardian Karakal.

From the dining hall and kitchen issued muffled cooking noises and the aroma of baking bread and yak butter tea. Farther down the path the open walls of new stone buildings being constructed from the boulders of the Great Avalanche waited for the day to begin and workmen to come and add more of the raw-cut boulders and boards lying nearby. Beyond the buildings, the lushly planted terraces of the communal garden stepped down the mountainside.

Mike loved this time when the moon, as if waiting for the sun to give it permission to set, hovered just above the mountains. Even on ordinary days, when he was not having a birthday and had no momentous events to look forward to, Mike usually rose early to enjoy this quiet time and take long walks before the paths were thronged with people. He loved feeling the wings of Karakal rising behind his back, even when he was not looking at the mountain. He savored the sweet damp smell of the mist rising from the waters of Kalapa's sacred lake, the sight of the lake's blue-green waters lapping the lower garden and nourishing the roots of the rhododendron jungle.

Mike stood by the lake for a moment, watching the water shimmer and listening to the breeze in the branches of the rhododendrons, making them clack softly like tiny looms at work. The lake was fed by artesian springs and hot springs, and bled off down the valley in a pretty stream winding through the grove. The trees foamed with pink, purple, and white flowers snowing petals into the stream and carpeting the ground beneath whenever the softest breeze tickled the air.

His ears picked up the cry of the eagle owl and the distant grumbling of one of the snow lions musing to itself as it retired to the den for the day. And always, any time of the day or night, if you listened closely you could hear the cracking and creaking of snow and ice shifting on mountainsides, punctuated every so often by the boom of an avalanche.

This morning there was another sound as well, a low murmuring that had a distinctly human note to it. Rounding a bend in the stream, Mike saw the source, sitting cross-legged by the bank, dark fingers describing little O's as they poised against bony knees, tight black curls thrown back as the childishly rounded golden-brown face sought the dawn through the upper branches of the trees. "Ooooom," she said one more time, closed her eyes, lowered her head for a moment, then calling him by his childhood name said, "Hi, Meekay," and sprang to her feet, brushing away petals that had fallen onto her face. "Happy birthday. Are you on your way to see Nyima too?"

"Yes, of course. She's supposed to give birth to her new baby any time now. Have you heard anything, Chime Cincinnati?" he asked, hiding his dismay at her unexpected interruption of his journey.

"Not yet," she said.

He accepted her company with as good a grace as he could muster. She was a weird kind of girl, but his sister Nyima seemed to like her, and more important, so did her beautiful friend Isme. Thoughts of Isme had kept Mike lying awake nights, thinking of things he could say or should have said, things he could do or should have done, presents he might yet offer to convince her that she should take him as her first husband.

Although Isme and Chime Cincinnati were the same age, both nearly eighteen, they were as different as night and day, and not just because Isme was gracefully tall and blond like her mother, the mountaineer Tania Enokin, while Chime was short and dark. Isme was already a desirable grown woman, with gentle, womanly ways, and Chime— well, Chime just got odder all the time. She didn't go to school with the other kids, or play the same games. Instead, she studied and meditated and mumbled to herself and made odd remarks.

The other kids had not ever been unkind to her, but they hadn't wanted much to do with her either. Mike, who was three years older than Chime, had tried to look after her when they were both younger, before he went to work with his father in the underground excavations of the buried portions of Kalapa. He'd always felt kind of sorry for her, but he'd felt perplexed too. How could anybody grow up in such a great place as Kalapa, lucky enough to be one of the last surviving people on earth, and seem so—well—unsettled? Dissatisfied. He couldn't figure her out.

"I didn't know you meditated here," he said.

"I don't usually," she told him. "My favorite place is just beyond the chorten, facing Karakal, but I thought this morning I'd wait and walk with you to Nyima's. I knew you'd want to check and see if the baby might be coming in time to share your birthday."

"Yes, she promised to name the baby for me if it's born today," he said, pleased but a little daunted by the thought of having a niece or nephew born on his birthday, carrying his name. This child would have a special bond with him and would require a special gift from him. The only thing he possessed that was special enough was the set of hand-copied books he had hoped to trade for a bride gift, a certain silver necklace with blue enameled birds, and a length of blue silk that would reflect blue eyes.

"Isme's already there . . . " Chime teased, with a sly note in her voice and laughter in her sideways glance up at him.

"What are we waiting for?" he asked, prodding her to her feet. "They'll be needing someone to help keep my other nieces and nephews out from under foot."

"It's good to see so many new babies after all the years of destruction," Chime said, falling in beside him though he had quickened his pace a little to keep the heat in his own face from betraying his thoughts. She sounded as if she personally had witnessed the world's destruction, although he knew she had lived her whole life in Kalapa, as he had. It was one of the things that he and everyone else found so strange about her. Some of the adults, including his own parents, treated such remarks with respect—but then, his father at least treated every utterance of every resident of Kalapa with respect. Other people found Chime's pronouncements strange and a little frightening, sometimes annoying. Mike tried not to be annoyed, to ignore the implication and just respond to what she actually said.

"Yes, and more are being born all the time. It's a very good thing, of course, all of this new life, but I'm worried about the haphazard way new families are filling up the valley. We need to make plans so that people don't cut into the rhododendron grove to make room for more houses. After all, people can live in the next valley over too, can't they? Everybody doesn't have to live right here in Kalapa."

"The elders were so busy coping with having our generation," Chime mused, "that they didn't think ahead enough to what would happen when their children grew up and started having children. Since any woman who comes to Shambala before her childbearing years are ended may continue to have children here, between our mothers and ourselves we have been doing a good job of repopulating at least our small corner of the world." She took his hand and swung it back and forth in hers, as if they were still children. "Don't worry, Meekay. I remember when Kalapa was much more crowded than this."

Oh boy. There she goes again, he thought.

His thought must have showed on his face because she quickly added, "I mean, I don't remember exactly, but that's what your father tells me that my previous incarnation told him anyway."

"Chime Cincinnati, you're just thinking of the story Auntie Dolma tells the children."

"You'll hear a different version tonight, Meekay, at your birthday celebration," she said, suddenly very serious. On a person's twenty-first birthday, after the general festivities were over, the adults held a private initiation ceremony. During it, Mike knew, the elders retold the story of how Shambala, Kalapa, and the world came to be as they were now. In the ceremony, however, they added all of the personal memories, histories, predictions, and insights that pertained particularly to the person being initiated into adulthood, sharing all of the information they possessed about his or her heritage and the circumstances of his or her birth. More than the presents or the special meal, Mike was looking forward to this ceremony.

What would they add about him particularly to the basic story?

Know, O best beloved, that you are privileged to be the children of Shambala, which connects heaven and earth and which is located at the precise joining of the two.

Auntie Dolma, who was the one who told the story best and who loved the works of Rudyard Kipling, insisted on the "O best beloved" part. Mike thought it added something reassuringly cozy to the story, which was otherwise rather too sweepingly grand and timeless for comfort.

Long ago the realm of Shambala and the city of Kalapa were much different than they are now. At that time, our sacred mountain Karakal was capped with a snowy cone, perfect in its symmetry and bright enough to outshine the moon. Shambala was a mighty and prosperous realm, and Kalapa was its principal city. This was a kingdom without a king, a land filled with kind and wise people dedicated to learning, to beauty, to the accumulation and creation of knowledge, of science and art. Around Shambala ranged the mountains. Beyond lay the country of Tibet. People from Shambala visited the people of Tibet, bringing many of the attributes of Shambala to that country, but still keeping the location of Shambala a secret.

This was not, as you may suppose, to protect the material treasures within the realm, or even the lives of the wise and kind living treasures who governed the land with grace and joyousness. Oh no, my children, the real secret of Shambala is its timeless nature. We here in Shambala do not age in the way of the outside world. Those of us who live here age very slowly. You may expect to live to be more than two or three centuries old, and you will remain youthful and healthy until almost the ends of your lives so long as you remain within the borders of Shambala. Outside, even before the End of the World, people lived very short lives, for time is different out there. When I was a girl in Tibet, people counted each and every birthday as precious. Here, life as a whole is precious and only childhood is measured and celebrated by birthdays.

For thousands of years, life in Shambala was relatively untouched and unobstructed by events in the outside world. Occasionally, straying travelers would find their way here by accident, but usually newcomers who would become a part of Shambala were guided here by the Terton, a saintly being or bodhisattva, as such people are called in the Buddhist faith. The Terton travels beyond the boundaries of Shambala, and so ages and dies more often than most of us, but he or she is always reborn within Shambala and always remembers enough of previous lives to fulfill the task of guiding to Shambala those who belong here.

Inside Shambala, it had always been peaceful, but such was not the case in the outside world. Wars became so big, with such ferocious weapons, that eventually even the mountains of Tibet were broached.

Mike remembered asking Auntie Dolma if she had seen the invasion, for her face was very sad then, but she said, *No, I did not see the invasion. It happened slowly and treacherously, over a period of time. Your father saw it, Meekay. For a time he worked as an interpreter for the Chinese. That is when I met him. He quit when the government doctors killed the baby I was carrying and made me barren. Many terrible things were happening all around us, and neighbors could not talk to each other without fear of spies. But your father, who was born in Shambala, brought me back here to spare me further suffering. I lived here happily for a few years, before the wars grew so terrible that they reached even this last refuge of peace and sanity. A bomb dropped, whether by accident or design no one knows, close enough to cause an avalanche on Karakal. The beautiful city was destroyed, all of the ancient wise people who lived there were killed, the sacred lake was buried in the debris, as was the city, and our mountain gave up its dome for the horns it wears today.*

The Terton, our beloved Ama-La, devised a plan to allow the few of us who survived to rebuild our land. She was a brilliant linguist, an actress, a physician, and a hypnotist, skilled in all of the ancient psychic sciences. At the time, four powers conducted the war on Tibetan soil, and she convinced each of them that she worked for them as an officer in a top security prison camp. In that way she was able to rescue prisoners who seemed to her to be people who belonged here. Most of these were soldiers, but a few, such as Tatiana Enokin and Keith Marsh, were civilians who blundered into the war zone. For the sake of security, we continued the deception even when the prisoners were brought here, in this way not only protecting ourselves but learning what these people were like under harsh circumstances. Their labor helped us exhume our city and our lake. Unfortunately, one does not always learn the best side of people while holding them prisoner, and the person we chose to play commandant, the former Chinese freedom fighter, Nyima Wu, was all too adept as an autocrat.

The American Colonel Merridew, the same man who coaches you children in sports, fought us even while he was a prisoner, as did the heroic Sergeant Du P. Danielson.

You have all heard the story of how Colonel Merridew rescued from the jaws of a snow lion the child Pema, who grew up to be his wife and the mother of Chime Cincinnati. He was grievously injured, but after that, relations between the guards and the prisoners grew friendlier.

Unfortunately, as people grew closer in Shambala, they grew increasingly more hostile in the outside world. We heard reports from the outside world of a cache of nuclear weapons still remaining in a small, fanatical country. Our supply helicopters became more erratic. I myself trekked into the mountains to meet the choppers, but they didn't come as often, or dropped our supplies in the snow. On my last trip some of our younger people risked leaving Shambala to try to find out what had become of our chopper. Then one night we saw the sky blaze with flashes like a fireworks show. Nobody said anything to anyone else, but I knew in my heart that the worst had happened in the outside world. That same night, Sergeant Danielson disappeared. He had escaped while the rest of us watched the world die.

Oh, yes, children, Sergeant Danielson knew very well what was happening. He knew that the end of the world he had known had come. But you see, he also had a family, and although he had decided long ago he could not live with them, he wished to die protecting them as best he could. He never made it, of course. The very next pack train, meeting refugees from the outside world, brought him back. I was with them. I saw for myself that he had turned into an ancient man, reverting, when no longer protected by Shambala, to his true age. He had dwelled a long time among us.

Colonel Merridew also wished to leave, but when he tried to go, Ama-La, knowing the same fate would befall him and the others if they stepped beyond Shambala, voluntarily walked across the border and died. Nyima Wu, trying to prevent Ama-La's death, died herself. But the rest of us lived and have continued to live under the sacred shell of protection provided to us in this magic place. Our lake miraculously resurfaced, and you, my children, have been miraculously born to the survivors of the disaster, and now we celebrate your childhood birthdays, for you are the world's future.

That was the part of the story everyone knew. Auntie Dolma told it to all of the children on their birthdays. Mike did not find it as entertaining as the fairy tales in his hand-copied books where each event happened to specific people, with details. But it *was* a true story, much of it about people he actually knew. He thought it would be much better once he had heard the rest of it, the part the adults would tell him tonight, including what the elders thought his own role would be. He sort of hoped it had something to do with marrying the princess and living happily ever after. Fortunately, all the disastrous stuff seemed to have happened in the last generation. He said aloud to Chime, "I can't imagine all that killing and dying, can you? I mean, have you ever even known anybody who was seriously sick?"

"Your mother said she used to be sick a lot."

"Not since I've know her," Mike said, shaking his head. "About the only time anyone ever seems to be hurting or sick is when somebody has a baby. It seems to me that there are getting to be a few too many now. If we're all going to live such a long time, what's the hurry? I don't see why we have to have enough babies for the whole world right here. Nobody really knows what's out there."

"Not exactly, maybe, although some of the adults did witness the end, remember. Billions of people would have been killed by the missiles alone, not to mention the aftermath, the unnatural winters, the firestorms, the radiation."

"Well, I don't see how it can have killed everybody. Surely some people hid."

"Yes, but what are they eating and drinking? How are they fighting off dangers? Even if there are still people left out there, and even if they are still having babies, most of their babies probably would not survive starvation, all of the disease that's surely running rampant after so much death, and radiation sickness."

"Sure, I know all of that. But it just doesn't seem real somehow. It's got nothing to do with us. Have you ever seen the place where they used to land the helicopter to bring in supplies? Do you know of anyone who has ever made that trip in our whole lives? And they used to make it all the time! They don't even want to check. Our parents are so cautious they make the rabbits look brave. It's not that I don't want a family, Chime, because I do. But I'd like to spend some time with my wives when they weren't having to feed babies. There should be more time to teach the older children without always having to *tend* to babies. What if we get so many people here, there won't be any place for them to live? By the time all these babies grow up and have babies, what if—" He stopped and brushed the rhododendron petals from her springy curls. "What if there are no more trees for them, no more room to play, nothing but the snow? I mean, I *like* the snow, but what if there's not enough food?"

She patted his arm and said, "Dear Meekay, how earnest and full of foresight you are. But I don't think you should spoil your birthday with too much worry. The soil here is so rich, the lake so nurturing, that more trees will grow, and the land will always provide us with food. We have more animals among us now than were found in all of Tibet during the last war."

He hated it when she talked like that, as if she really was old enough to be his grandmother instead of being the same age as Isme. Isme never acted as if she knew more than he did.

Beyond the grove, houses built on stilts were crouched above the beds of reeds at the stream's marshy end. More houses crowded the lower slopes of the mountains beyond the carved stone mound of Danielson's grave. Nyima and her first four children lived there, in a pretty stone house with a reed-thatched roof built specially for them by Henri Thibideaux, Nyima Dolma's father.

Nyima Dolma, Nyima's third child, was Mike's only niece. With men having several wives and women having several husbands, you couldn't tell who you were related to without looking at the records. Auntie Dolma collected those from the women once a month. Keith Marsh thought maybe Shambala should adopt a totem system, similar to what his Amerind ancestors had used, to keep clan and family lines straight. The elders were considering it. Mike knew for sure he was not related to either Isme or Chime Cincinnati, but he wasn't clear about anybody any younger than they were except for his own sister and her children.

They followed the path around the pool, brushing against the stilts of houses, past the flower-strewn grave of Sergeant Danielson, and up the path toward Nyima's stone house. Mike's eldest nephew squatted outside the door, his little sister between his knees.

"How is your mother?" Mike asked. "Has she had—"

Just then a scream rent the air, thin and angry, followed by another and another.

Isme rushed outside with her hands covering her ears.

"What happened? What's the matter?" Mike asked her, because his feet absolutely would not approach the door from which he heard his sister sobbing now.

"The baby. There's something wrong with it."

"How can that be?" Mike said.

Chime frowned thoughtfully and pushed aside the curtain across the door, making the bamboo beads clack against each other as they parted.

Mike put his arm around Isme, who continued to cover her ears with her hands, and the two of them followed Chime inside. The house had only one room, and unlike the communal housing on the hill, this one had no running water or heat. Earthen pots of water and wet rags sat around the bloody mess that was Nyima's sleeping mat, and the hot, sharp scent of blood mingled with the fumes of the oil lamps. Auntie Dolma knelt beside the mat, trying to give the baby to Nyima, who was trying to hold him, but the red, wrinkled infant kept twisting away from her as if in pain, his little eyes squeezed shut as he screeched furiously.

"I've never seen a baby like this," Auntie Dolma said, pushing her thick glasses back up onto her sweaty nose. "All Kalapa babies are peaceful and happy . What can be wrong with this one?"

"Hmm," Chime Cincinnati said. She too knelt and looked at the baby from every angle she could manage. Every time she tried to look into his face he squirmed away, though he never turned back to his mother. "Hmm," Chime said again, and reached for a little arm and held it, which made the baby flail and cry even louder. "No soul. Very curious."

"Chime Cincinnati, what a cruel thing to say!" Isme cried. "Of course he has a soul. You're frightening Nyima. He's just fussier than ordinary."

Chime shrugged and patted Nyima on the shoulder. Nyima flinched miserably away from her. Chime shrugged again and swept the curtain aside as she left the house.

Mike, who couldn't bear the scene, followed her. "How could you say that?" he demanded. "I thought you were Nyima's friend!"

Chime shook her head, puzzled. "I thought at first the baby was a demon, but no, not even that. Do you remember when I was small and you used to read me from your fairy-tale books? Remember the stories about fairies stealing human children and leaving enchanted blocks of wood in their place?"

"Sure. I remember. But there are no fairies around here."

"No," she said sadly. "And yet, here is a baby's body with nothing inside. I do not believe, in all of my lives, that I have ever seen such a thing."

"Me neither." He began walking with her back toward the lake, then thought of his sister and the ugly baby born on his birthday and felt vaguely ashamed, as if because it was his birthday, he was somehow to blame. Hadn't he just been saying how there were too many babies and almost complaining about how healthy everyone was? Now look what had happened to his nephew. "Look, you'll tell my mom and dad about this? I don't want to leave right now and—I think maybe we should cancel the party too. I don't feel much like celebrating."

"Sure, Meekay," she said, and was gone.

He stayed with Nyima all day, trying to help with the uncooperative baby in any way he could. His parents arrived a short time after Chime left. His mother helped Nyima clean herself and the baby. His father, who found that the baby did not want to be held and rocked, made little flat jokes to cover up for his sorrow. Nobody said very much until supper.

Over a cold rice bowl and a vegetable momo, his mother gave Mike the notebooks containing her prison diaries. "Most of what we were going to tell you about us is in here," she told him. "Please read it, and then your father and I will be glad to answer your questions."

His father gave him a pocketknife with many blades, a corkscrew, and a small flashlight. Isme did not return, and he didn't see Chime Cincinnati again until the next changeling was born.

In the next few weeks six more babies were born in the same condition as Mike's nephew. Though each was an individual tragedy, each was also a cause for fear and worry among the people of the valley. The less well-educated, especially among the refugees who had come shortly after the night of the missiles, believed the state of the babies to be an inauspicious omen, signaling the end of the magical protection of Shambala, although Mike's father assured them that according to scriptures the protection was supposed to last many generations. Others, more scientifically, figured that the magic of Shambala did not protect them from radiation after all and that somehow or other the state of the newborns was radiation-poisoning induced.

At first no one paid much attention to Chime Cincinnati, although she was there at or just after each birth. As she had with Mike's nephew, she would look the child over, shake her head and mutter to herself, "Hmm. No soul." After a while people did talk of her odd behavior and began to think of her as unlucky. Eventually everyone left her strictly alone, especially pregnant women.

Mike took his copied fairy tales to his sister's house and read them to her children while she tried to cope with the new baby. She would not name it, nor would the father, a nomad guerrilla refugee. Mike's mother called the baby "Fred," just for something to call it.

When Isme's eighteenth birthday came a few months later, Mike had still not decided to trade his books for a bride gift, nor did he have any other fine thing to give to Isme to tell her that he wanted to become her husband. It hardly mattered.

Girls were not in the mood for courtship by that time. Every baby born since Nyima had Mike's nephew was in much the same condition. There was talk among the more hard-bitten former refugees of putting the children to death so that they did not command valuable camp supplies.

By then birthdays had ceased to be occasions for kites and dragon dancers, lavish gifts and one of Henri Thibideaux's witty ice sculptures. Boys turned twenty-one quietly, and girls at eighteen were choosing to pass up their option of beginning their families at that age.

Mike watched as, at dinner, Chime Cincinnati gave Isme a small packet tied up in a piece of old cloth.

"Thanks, Chime," Isme said, her tone a ghost of the excitement a girl ought to feel on such an occasion. "What is it?"

"An herb to keep you from conceiving, my friend," Chime said bluntly. Some people hissed in their breath, others gasped. You'd have thought she was the thirteenth fairy at the christening of the Sleeping Beauty, but the gift made sense to Mike.

"I have a little something for you too, Isme," said Tsering Li, Chime's mother's half brother. He was tall and good-looking and extremely good at games, and he smiled possessively at Isme, though Mike did not recall ever seeing them together before. "My father brought it with him when he came across to Shambala. It belonged to his mother. I want you to have it, for luck." He gave her a silver ring with a dragon set in it.

From the sweet sad smile with which Isme accepted the ring and the gravity with which she placed it on her finger, Mike knew that he had lost out, this time around anyway. Perhaps Tsering Li and Isme would not marry just yet, but that ring was a promise between them all the same. Just as well. The world was no longer safe for babies and it was no longer safe for romance.

Mike vowed silently that he would spend the rest of his life digging in the tunnels beneath the city. If he could not have life, he would learn the secrets of the dead.

CHAPTER II

Chime Cincinnati peered over Mike's shoulder, casting a shadow across the beam of the miner's lamp strapped to his forehead. "What have you in there, Meekay?"

Mike had been spending as much time as possible in the last few months digging in the bowels of Kalapa, away from Isme, away from the nasal keening of the unnatural newborns. He wasn't used to company anymore, except for the companionable remarks of his father and fellow workmen. He could certainly do without Chime Cincinnati intruding on him, bringing up matters he was trying to forget in the thrusts of his shovel, the excitement of each small new find. "You shouldn't really be here, you know," he told her. "This area isn't properly shored up yet."

"Oh, it's all right. Today is my eighteenth birthday, and tonight at my party your father will officially tell everyone that I am the reincarnation of the Terton, and as such I'm allowed everywhere."

"Happy birthday," he said. "I regret that I have no material gift to give you at this time, however, I will give you instead a very good piece of advice. You should stop speaking of yourself as if you are different from everybody else. People would like you much better."

He hadn't intended to say that, but now that he had, it felt good. He'd been getting very fed up with her air of detachment, even amusement, when his sister, the girl he loved, his father and mother, his nieces and nephews, and the entire city were in an uproar.

Chime Cincinnati merely gazed up at him with large sad eyes and said in a small, low voice, "But I *am* different. I am the Terton."

Exasperated, Mike flung aside the handpick he'd been using to gradually enlarge the size of the opening to the new tunnel. It clattered against the rubble piled ceiling-high next to the support beams. "You keep saying that, when everybody knows the Terton died with Nyima Wu to show our parents the dangers of the outside world. Your mother saved your father that day and she tells the story far too often, so you have decided to call yourself the Terton to get her attention and make yourself seem important. It works just the opposite when you do that. You act like you're better than anybody else. I'll bet the *real* Terton, who was a bodhisattva, has found Nirvana now, having delivered everybody safely here. She would find you comical if she could hear how you carry on."

Chime sighed and slumped against the wall. "I wish you were right. Although I'm sure you're correct when you say it's comical. I don't talk about being the Terton to make myself important, as you say, Meekay. I say it because it is true. You yourself were present when my true nature was first recognized. There have been other tests too, that your father and the elders have done, and I have passed them all. Your parents know and all of the other elders—and I have always known. They only waited until my eighteenth birthday to announce it because they felt a child shouldn't have to bear such responsibility. Publicly, anyway. Although it seems to me that it matters little whether people know who I am or if they think I'm just crazy. But please understand, Meekay, that when I talk about myself differently, it's because I contain more than one self and it's very hard to sort out who is in charge of what without getting confused. Mostly, I'm just me, Chime, boiling rice on kitchen duty when it's my turn, studying, meditating, gardening, eating, drinking, or sleeping. Other times I know things that Chime cannot know. Is this so difficult for you to believe? Have you not read of the Dalai Lama? He too recalled all of his previous incarnations."

"You are not the Dalai Lama, Chime Cincinnati, and whether or not you are the Terton remains to be seen. I do know that you are a girl who has made cruel and thoughtless remarks about sick babies, and you embarrassed Isme in front of everyone with that joke you played on her, giving her such a crude gift."

"Ah, Isme!" Chime Cincinnati smiled now, the flash of her teeth lighting her whole face. "Now I see why you are angry with me. But, Meekay, my gift to Isme was in earnest and not a joke. I would have given the same to Nyima if I'd known what would happen to her. Also, though I can't explain to you how I know, what I said about the babies is true. Still, what you say is also true." She patted him on the arm in her grandmotherly way. "And I thank you for the birthday gift of your wisdom, Meekay. I am honored that you chose to bestow it on me. I am simply so comfortable here among my own people that I forget to guard my speech as I had to in past lives to conceal my identity."

"Chime Cincinnati!" he cried, exasperated with her. "That's just the kind of thing I'm talking about. Look, whether or not you're the Terton, Father says it will be generations before it's safe to go into the outer world. The Terton's duty was to guide the people here. It's over for now. And even if the Terton has not reached Nirvana and will reincarnate again, as long as there's nothing special for her to do with her next life, I think she's entitled to sit one out."

"When your mother gave you her journals, didn't you read them?"

"Of course I did. And even if I hadn't, I remember the time when you claimed the Terton's book when we were children, but really, I don't think that was knowledge, Chime. I think you wanted to chew on the pages. You were only a baby."

"You are a very practical person, Meekay," she told him. "Very rooted in this world."

"You mean unlike someone with your advanced spiritual attainment?" he asked scornfully.

"No, I'm serious. Being spiritual is all very well, but a person can hardly earn good karma if they don't take care of their tasks in their present life. You know how to pay attention to the moment. That's very good. Everyone says you are a very useful person, a great help to the older men, especially your father."

Mike felt his face warm with shame for having been so nasty to her, and with pleasure as well. One nice thing about Chime Cincinnati. She was pretty hard to offend, and she was quick to point out a person's merit. He'd always disliked that as part of her "more enlightened than thou" persona, but now it seemed to him that it was just part of her personality. He felt more kindly toward her than he had since his new nephew was born. "Well, I just want to learn how to take care of this place since it's the only home we have. I like helping father with this. It's interesting, learning what Kalapa was like in the old days."

"What is this hole you're making here?" she asked, peering into it.

"Father says it leads to a new tunnel. As you can see, we've worked quite far down the mountain on the old superstructure and have already excavated many of the upper levels. This part here was storage cellars, and we've found many implements, seeds, and other useful things still intact. Soon we'll find out if there really were all those tunnels leading here the stories tell of. Father says he never knew of them in his time, nor did he ever hear that they had been used, even when he was a boy. So they may have just been metaphorical. Mom says religious language is like that sometimes. My guess is that the original builders dug so low because the valley is relatively small and they wished to make optimum use of the space available."

"Very sensible," she said. "I'm surprised you found the opening, with this wall covering it."

"Not uncommon in a structure of this age," Mike told her, happy to be in his element, enlightening someone else about the things he knew best. "The ancients were always adding things onto their buildings as new rooms became necessary, knocking out walls to make larger rooms or blocking off old passageways with rooms too badly deteriorated to be useful anymore. Even before the avalanche, there'd be earthquakes that would ruin one of these lower corridors, so they just closed it off. Or sometimes someone would just come up with a more efficient design for how to run the compound and they'd redesign the passages, like I said, closing off old ones, creating new ones. This is probably one of those."

A utility lamp swung overhead from one of the long orange extension cords that snaked throughout the lower corridors. The bulb dimmed, then brightened again, and far off in the bowels of the complex the generator hesitated, coughed, then resumed its rumbling.

"What's in there, I wonder?" Chime said, nudging him aside to peek into the hole. "It's dark in there. And listen—what's that sound?"

Mike listened. With his ear to the hole he could hear a steady roar, as if an avalanche boomed on and on. A shiver ran up his spine.

"What could it be?" he asked. "Echoes from the avalanches?"

"Maybe," she said. "You know, you should read some of the sacred texts I've been studying. They say that Shambala was once connected to the outside world—all over the world, actually—by a maze of tunnels. At the entrance to some of those tunnels, little pockets of Shambala were still there. That's why people were always talking of hidden magical valleys all over Tibet."

"All over Tibet? That's an awful lot of tunnels, Chime Cincinnati," he told her. But just the same, the elders who had come to Kalapa as refugees from the war-torn world beyond had mentioned such stories. Silly stories, surely, but when a person lived in a land preserved by magical and spiritual means, it seemed a little foolhardy to go around condemning other people as merely superstitious. The refugees also claimed that as they crossed the border, fleeing into Shambala just ahead of the missiles, feeling the heat and seeing the green glow of the sky behind them, they had heard the screams of the dying from all over the world. They said they continued to hear the screams for three days afterward.

Mike pulled his army knife from his pocket and shined the little flashlight into the hole. The beam played over rubble and dust and a spiderweb or two. "I imagine the noise is an echo from the source of the lake. We're down below the water level now."

Chime nodded, and put her hand over his to guide the flashlight to play over every available surface, then sighed and backed away again. "When will this hole be larger?"

"Oh, probably tomorrow we'll start opening up the passage. Father wants to make sure it's properly supported first, of course."

"Of course," she said, sighing again and giving the hole a last longing look before she returned to the surface.

(HAPTER III

All the next day Mike and his father, Lobsang Taring, worked on en-
larging the hole, first ascertaining that they weren't disturbing any important existing structures on the other side. Often Taring worked with
a crew of other people, but during the initial excavation he preferred
to work alone or with only Mike or Mike's mother to help him.

Outside, the weather was as beautiful as it always was, the air soft
with the fragance of the flowers, grass, and fresh-turned earth warmed
by the sun, the dazzling white of the mountains soaring above, the lake
sparkling below. Mike had stopped taking his morning walks, and told

himself that he no longer missed all of that. These days, at any hour of the day or night, you could hear the mewling cries of the new babies throughout the valley. Nowadays he preferred the close smelly darkness of the tunnels with the swaying light of the hanging lamp, the incense, sweat, and musty odor of the underground passages, his father's voice giving instructions, joking or singing.

When the hole was large enough to fit Lobsang's chest and shoulders—though not Mike's, since he was much larger than his father—the roaring noise was loud enough that the men had to raise their voices to hear each other.

"What's causing that, Dad? Wind? Water?" Mike asked, shining his flashlight around the interior of the hole again. The beam caught a faint glitter of something, and Mike wedged his utility knife in the debris just inside the hole so that the flashlight beam stayed fixed on the glitter while he chipped the hole wider all around it. The dust of rock and mortar assaulted his eyes and nostrils, which were already full of the stuff.

"Don't you know, son, that's the cries of the spirits of the outer world, clamoring to enter Shambala?" his father asked, his brown eyes twinkling in his pitted face like sunlit pools in porous stone.

"Not you too. Everybody is talking so much about spirits and things these days."

"People are upset about the babies. I have known Shambala longer than anyone here now, except perhaps for one person, and I have never known such a thing to happen. Shambala has always been a healing place, able to mend wounds and cure illnesses of soul and body. Something is very wrong here. Which reminds me, it's time to knock off now and wash up for dinner. There's to be a meeting right afterward."

Mike groaned. He hated the meetings. "Father, if you are the most senior elder, can't you just say what should be done and have the others listen?"

His father pretended to quake all over, shaking his knees in a comical fashion so that dirt and soot sprinkled off his skin and clothing. "Never say such a thing. Every person here has suffered as the result of others wanting power. No one wishes to have anything to do with a structure that sets one person above another, for any reason."

• • •

Nyima's family was already adrift inside the dining hall. She looked diminished, harried and desperate, as did the other adults who these days seemed to be wading through a sea of weeping children. Her next-to-youngest was the only quiet child in the room, nuzzled under the wad of her jacket, suckling. The new baby screamed, red-faced and wild-eyed, while one of the older girls bounced it vigorously up and down. Two out of three people in the room were under the age of five, and all of them were sniffling, whining, crying or out and out shrieking. The red-faced baby was thin, its skin flaccid. Nyima looked almost as bad. She had lost weight, and under her eyes were huge dark circles, as if she had been dead two days already.

Mike picked up his niece Porbu, the second-oldest child, and rocked her automatically. It was like this every night in the dining hall, until the mothers were able to take the children away again. There was talk of excluding them from communal dining and having someone deliver their food instead, but many of the women opposed such a move. The problem was a community problem, they insisted, and if the consequences were shared community-wide, then the entire community would work on finding the solution. Every night when he came to the dining hall, Mike thought that he would hear that Nyima's youngest child, still unnamed, would die. It seldom ate or drank, and did so on no predictable schedule. It seemed to exist only to vent its mindless rage on its family and disrupt the peace of others.

The other damaged children were just the same. Now even the kids who had been happy and healthy before began to feel the influence of the sick ones. They cried more, were more aggressive.

Even Porbu, who had always been a smiling, loving child, wriggled restlessly against him and whimpered. There was a cut over her left eye, black and blue around the redness. Nyima saw Mike examining it. "One of the older boys hit her yesterday, said her brother was a demon and that it was our fault, what's been happening. They say we have bad karma because Mother is American and they ended the world and spread the radiation."

"No one believed that," Mike said with more force than he felt.

Nyima lifted the baby to her shoulder and patted it until it bubbled milk. She didn't argue with him but her face bore a pitying expression. It was all Mike could do to choke down his momos, stew and butter tea.

The damaged children, their mothers and siblings, had to clear the hall before the meeting could begin, so that the voices of the rest of the community could be heard.

Mike sat alone now on the hard earthen floor of the stone-walled hall, thinking that it was all very well that nobody wanted to be a leader, but that didn't keep everybody from having and voicing opinions on every aspect of community life at great length, so that the meetings dragged on throughout the night and sometimes into the next day. Each time one of the damaged babies was born, extra meetings were held and the same people said the same things over and over again.

The difference between this one and the last was that Chime Cincinnati had just turned eighteen and this was the first meeting she had attended as a responsible adult.

"These babies are simply unfortunate individuals with an excess of karmic debt," began one woman who, like Auntie Dolma, had been sterilized by the Chinese. She was one of the animal tenders. Her voice contained a certain smugness.

Many people agreed with her, accepted that rationale as the proper one under the circumstances and let it pass; but Chime, being Chime, didn't. She shook her head, "I tell you, these children have no karmic debt. They have no karma at all right now. They are without souls."

"Then their parents have accrued bad karma—" someone began.

"This is not a religious problem, it's a medical one," said Henri Thibideaux, an American, like Mike's mother, formerly one of her cellmates and the closest thing the compound had to a doctor. Having just read in his mother's journals about Thibideaux's youth as a Cajun itinerant bird-cleaner and the errands of mercy that had led to his capture, Mike listened to him with more interest than usual. "These kids obviously have some kind of a nervous disorder."

"Possibly brought on by radiation poisoning," added Keith Marsh.

Someone nearby, someone Mike couldn't see, muttered, "He *would* say that. It's convenient to ignore religion when you don't share it. Shambala was intended for Tibetans."

Marsh lifted his head and flared his nostrils. He had heard. "I can understand why you wouldn't want to repeat your remark aloud, whoever you are. I think you should bear in mind that it was not just one race of people who ended the world, but people of many races who thought, 'This place should be ours and ours alone.' And now look. There's only one place left, and you would start the same attitude here over birth defects in unfortunate children."

Mike grinned. Good response. Marsh, Isme's father—another person discussed at length in his mother's journals—was an interesting fellow. Unlike the other Americans, Marsh was not a soldier but a civilian peace activist and demolitions expert. Isme sat in a lotus position beside her father, her head lowered, face curtained by wings of pale hair until she looked up sharply as her father finished, and brushed her hair behind her shoulders with one slim brown hand, one full breast rounding softly against the fabric of her tunic.

Mike was still contemplating this vision when Chime spoke again, though her words only partially made sense because he was preoccupied.

". . . another expedition to the outside," she was saying.

"Unwise," said Dorji the yak herder, who had been a member of the Tibetan guerrilla forces before the world ended.

"Those of us who know the way are too old to make the journey," Auntie Dolma said.

Isme said, "That's silly, Auntie Dolma. You're still young."

"I am not. *You* are young. I appear young, as does your father, as does Lobsang Taring. The stories I tell you are not merely for your amusement, my child. Many among us who appear little older than yourselves are very old indeed, and our true age would catch up with us if we tried to guide any of you youngsters across the border."

"Besides," Mike's father said, "whether the problem is radiation sickness or karma or even, as Chime Cincinnati seems to think, lack of a soul, what good will that long and perilous journey do?" He was not arguing with Isme as much as asking Chime Cincinnati a sincere question, Mike saw. He wished his father would not encourage Chime.

"Last night you all learned that I am the Terton, although I have been told it is annoying for me to say so," Chime Cincinnati said with a hint of a smile at Mike. She was completely serious, however, as she continued, "As such, I tell you now that I see this problem of soulless babies as a sign to me that it is time for me to go again into the outside world."

"Impossible. You would die out there," three people said at once.

"Too much radioactivity," one of the refugees said.

"Many years have passed," Chime pointed out. "And even if I got radiation sickness, once I returned home, I am sure the healing nature of Shambala would cure me."

"I read books which said that bands of evil people who survived would exploit the weak," Chime's grandmother, the former prison camp guard Tsering, told her. "Brutal people might torture you and force you to lead them back to us."

Chime started to object again but her father, George Merridew, the former colonel, interrupted harshly. "There are no more people out there," he declared. "Baby girl, you don't know anything about the world. I saw a nice old lady and a young one die just from going into the *air* after the bomb dropped. Nobody could have survived that."

"With respect, Papa," Chime said with a little bow to him, "I am a baby no longer. I *was* that nice old lady, and a part of me knows more about the world than even you could guess. That is why I want to go out there. I believe there are still people out there, and it is my task as Terton to guide them safely here."

Merridew ran a dark brown hand through his nappy black hair. "Honey, you're takin' all this reincarnation jazz way too literally. Even if you were—and I'm not sayin' I believe it—but even if you were Ama-La in your last life, that doesn't mean you have to go runnin' outside now. And I'll tell you somethin' I'll bet you *don't* know. America's global strike capability was sufficient, when I was captured, to wipe out every life on the face of the earth, and it had to be even more powerful than that by the time they unleashed the nukes. You want to do something with your life, Chime honey, you do it here, among the living, 'cause there isn't anybody out there anymore."

Keith Marsh, Isme's father, cleared his throat and said softly, "I think you're probably right, George, in assuming that the missiles pretty well wiped everyone out, but you must remember that after you were captured, the North American Continental Allied Forces devoted quite a bit of energy to ferreting out and disarming nuclear devices wherever they found them. Part of my duty with the World Peace Organization was to disarm devices in places where the military could not go. Later on, instead of building up their offensive capability, NACAF devoted more of their own arsenal to deterrent devices. It's possible some people survived the initial attacks but it's hard to imagine them surviving this long."

Chime had been nodding enthusiastic agreement until Marsh got to the last sentence. She searched the faces around her impatiently, looking for one person to agree with her.

Mike's mother, Viveka, had always had a soft spot for Chime Cincinnati. She saw, as Mike did, the dismay, almost desperation, in the lines of Chime's body, and said softly, "I personally don't see any problem with some of us who know the way, Tania maybe, and Tea and myself, leading Chime and some of the youngsters back to the helicopter landing point. Then if the radiation looked like it had cleared up, the kids could cross over and have a look-see for survivors."

"Even if you can't see radiation, it's still there, Viv," Thibideaux said.

"Maybe the effects have worn off now," Mike's mother argued. "They were working on a way to make cleaner bombs when I joined the service—you know, give the radiation a shorter half-life and like that? To make the bombed countries safer to conquer afterward." She turned to Mike's father, who she always called Tea, for support, but he seemed to be lost in gazing at Chime Cincinnati. His expression was one of resignation and sadness, but he shrugged and nodded, concurring with his wife's idea and yet knowing that even his support would not conquer the collective fear the survivors had for what remained of the outside world.

The others proved him right, for Mike's mom's suggestion was at once countered by loud rehashings of all of the old objections.

Chime had been standing beside Isme, who now reached up and took her hand, squeezing it sympathetically. Chime smiled down at her, her lip trembling a little, her eyes very bright and her jaw set as hard as her father's. She knelt and murmured something back to Isme, her murmur accompanied by fierce little clenchings of her hand, and Isme gave her a pitying look and nodded soothingly.

Mike, who had been wishing someone would give Chime her comeuppance, found that he was saddened to see it happen. The elders weren't even willing to try to understand what she was saying. Isme seemed to be feeling the same thing. He watched the two girls, Isme's bright head with its sheaf of yellow hair touching Chime's dark curls. Chime looked as if someone had tied her up and made her watch while they killed a favorite pet. But all the sad expressions or pleading arguments in the world wouldn't do her any good now. She wasn't going to get her way. The elders were arguing away, loudly and repetitively, as if to drown out the very idea that an outside world existed. They weren't saying anything new or intelligent now, just talking to hear themselves talk. Mike leaned back against the wall as the voices swelled and surged around him.

He closed his eyes for a moment, remembering long ago seeing a similar look to the one Chime wore now.

He had been on his sleeping mat in the old children's compound where he and the other kids had slept when they were little.

He remembered the sleeping hall well. In bad weather the big central room had also been the school, though often the children spent their days with one class at a time filing into the underground library in study groups. In good weather the children studied outdoors. Of course, the littlest children slept with their parents, but as soon as they were big enough, they moved inside to sleep beside the other children. The mats were filled every week with fresh, sweet grass, and when the rhododendrons and wildflowers bloomed, they collected blossoms and petals for their mats. The mats were spread side by side, in order of the owner's age. Mike's was spread on the big-kid side with the other boys.

When he was a kid, for some reason Mike would often wake in the middle of the night and lie thinking or reading under his blanket. He tented the cloth over his butter lamp, enjoying the pungency of the smoke as the scent of privacy. He loved reading of high adventure and faraway places while knowing he was safe here, in a place countless heroes would endure horrible perils to reach if they could.

He was ten and was trying to understand the Tantra, but he felt torn between reading about that stuff and rereading his favorite one of the Hardy Boys books. He decided to read the Hardy Boys. He suspected that once he did begin to understand the Tantra, he would not be able to read it and still get back to sleep. He was three pages into the Hardy Boys story when he heard the whimper, half howl, half whine. It reminded him of the cry of the snow lion cub when it was lost on the mountain last spring before Thibideaux coaxed it down. Mike sat up, pulling his lamp out from beneath the covers and shielding it with his hand. In the darkness of the rows of five- to seven-year-olds, a small figure flared like a candle flame.

He could not see the hair in the darkness, the dark skin was in shadow too, but the pale pajamas and the whites of the eyes were plain enough in the moonlight pouring in through the ceiling skylight.

Mike recognized six-year-old Chime clear across the room by the way she moved. She padded on bare feet between the sleeping mats in a straight line to the lakeward entrance to the compound.

The children were forbidden to leave the sleeping compound at night, unsupervised. Mike was one of the oldest in the compound, however, and he thought that he would easily be forgiven for leaving long enough to guide Chime back to safety.

Throwing aside his blanket, Mike followed her outside. Shambala at night could be dangerous. The sons and daughters of the snow lions prowled the mountains, and wolves roamed the valley, along with the yaks, the kiang or wild asses, and other animals. Also, there was the lake to fall into, cliffs to fall off of, and all sorts of other dangers.

Like yetis. Those big hairy monsters with the white fur and the ape faces. Missing links, abominable snowmen. Lots of his books mentioned them. All the older people said there used to be yetis in Tibet. They were supposed to be really dangerous, and he had read about them carrying off people—like little kids, for instance.

Chime was well ahead of him, walking very fast down the terraced path through the garden, toward the lake. Fortunately, although the path was too steep to run down, he too could walk very fast, and his legs were much longer than a six-year-old's.

He caught up with her as she reached the shores of the lake, her feet padding through the grass and onto the moonlit gemstones that ringed the banks. The wavelets dampened her toes. The lake was very deep in the middle—so deep, no one knew how far a person would sink before they reached the bottom.

Mike tried to call to her but his voice wouldn't come, as voices sometimes would not in dreams. But he ran after her and caught her by the shoulders and pulled her back until he could lift her up so that her face was even with his. Her entire behind fit between his wrist and elbow with room left over. Her wide brown eyes were open and staring at first, her mouth quiet as a stone, as if it had never emitted a sound. Her baby's face wore an expression that was an incredible mixture of helplessness, pain, and longing, before her lower lip began to quake, her face fell apart, and she wailed.

"It's okay, Chime Cincinnati, it's me, Meekay," he told her. Even though his mother always called him Mike, for a time his father had called him Mickey, after an old friend in Montana. The other children, most of them at least part Tibetan, like him, always said his name as "Meekay." He asked, "What are you doing out here?"

Chime instantly ceased wailing and squirmed in his arms to look around her. Her face softened with relief and her little arms clutched his neck for a moment as she rubbed her face dry on his pajama jacket. "I was sleeping," she told him matter-of-factly. "And then I heard— listen, Meekay!"

He listened, his hair pricking at the urgency in her childish voice. He heard the sucking and hissing of the lake waters, the whisper of little showers of snow sweeping down on them with the breeze from the crests of the mountains. He heard the wild night birds singing in the rhododendron forests. Under his feet he could almost hear the grass growing, and it seemed as if he could hear the crops on the hillside ripening. Deeper still, water surged through the great ceramic pipes his father had repaired to provide water and hot-water heat to the compound.

But these were not what Chime referred to when she asked, "Don't you hear them, Meekay?" Her little hand gripped his cheek so hard she almost pulled off his ear. "Hear them calling?"

He shrugged impatiently, and then—yes, there was something more. Another kind of rumble, maybe a groan or voices, muttering something. Something sad and lost, angry and frustrated, needy. It seemed as though there were a lot of voices, but they were very far away and only the intensity of their pain carried them to his ears.

Then, the next moment, he thought he had imagined hearing

anything, and the groan or murmur or whatever was gone, drowned in the howl of a wolf. Up in the yak pens the animals stirred nervously. When the mournful howl died away, Mike listened again but heard nothing more.

Chime, seemingly satisfied, rubbed her eyes and said, "I'm sleepy," and he set her down and they walked back up the hill and crept back out of the moonlight and into the darkness of the sleeping compound.

Mike jerked awake to find himself in the dining hall with the meeting still in progress. Chime Cincinnati was no longer in sight, which somehow alarmed him. He couldn't believe she had given up so easily.

He wanted to ask Isme what Chime had said to her, but Isme was deep in whispered conversation with Tsering Li.

Mike watched Isme and Tsering Li exchange confidences until he could shake some life back into his feet, which had gone to sleep with the rest of him, then he made his way—with great dignity, he hoped— from the dining hall, looking around for Chime.

The night outside was brisk, with a little wind and brilliant stars. He sometimes wondered if the stars all crowded into the skies over Shambala because the rest of the sky was dead too. That was not very scientific, but he wondered, fleetingly, anyway, as he often had before.

He wondered too why he had dreamed of Chime instead of dreaming of Isme. He knew Chime better, of course, and the dream had been more memory than dream, something he had completely forgotten about until now, when her current even-odder-than-usual behavior made him think of it. She had never walked in her sleep again after that time, but now he also recalled many subsequent nights in the children's compound when she would awake weeping and he would start from his sleep at the touch of a small hand on his shoulder and look up into wet brown eyes and would have to rock her while she whispered that "they" were waiting for her. "They" were lost and alone and needed her to come and find them.

He imagined then that she might be crying because she was afraid of what she thought waited for her in the outer world. He suddenly realized she had been crying instead because, as a child, she was unable to go beyond Shambala to meet it.

CHAPTER
IV

That's what the meeting had been all about. That's what she was trying to do. She wanted to go investigate those voices. She *knew* they were out there, and she had been trying to convince the elders to help her launch an expedition to go find them. Mike suddenly felt extremely ill at ease that she had disappeared from the meeting like that. He didn't suppose for a minute she was lying on her bed crying. In fact, he was very relieved not to spot her in her winter clothing heading for the mountain pass.

His relief faded when he recalled her interest in the new passage under excavation, the passage with the mysterious noises. Then he remembered her interest in the stories of tunnels connecting the outside world to Shambala.

Mike wondered what he was so worried about. She couldn't just take off. Any journey, by any route, would need a little practical preparation. She'd need food, winter clothing, blankets, a flashlight. A flashlight? He clearly remembered leaving his, its solar-battery-powered beam gleaming off some object inside the hole. Like a beacon. A beacon for determined but very impractical girls. She could be badly hurt in those passages, alone, with no one to hear her in the dark, and Mike was suddenly convinced that's where she was, winding her way down to the new hole.

He had to catch up with her. He sprinted to the entrance of the old underground compound, grabbed and lit one of the oil lamps kept by the entrance for those who had to go below after the generator was shut down for the day.

He half ran, half walked through the twisting corridors, protecting the lamp flame with his cupped hand, past the storerooms and through hallways that were barely navigable paths through piles of junk, down toward the new hole.

He knew the passages well, mazelike as they were, the doors to the library, the old dining room, formerly the reception room for the high lama, the room that was once headquarters for Nyima Wu during the time when Kalapa Compound had been disguised by Wu and the Terton as a prison camp.

His parents had personally uncovered, reinforced, and reclaimed most of the rooms on the lower level, and he felt in some ways as if he now moved like a blood corpuscle through the veins and arteries of some larger sibling of his.

He had only been down here once or twice at night, after the chug of the generator stilled for the day. He thought of his mother's journals, how it must have been for her, kept alone in a cell here during the first part of her stay, not knowing she was pregnant and losing a baby, seeing the walls breathe, hearing voices in the generator during the day, voices from the walls at night, chanting.

He listened closely but all he could hear was the fall of his own sandals on the stone-tiled floor, the settling of the earth, the scurry of a rat, his own breathing, very loud.

And then his breathing was offset half a beat by other, deeper breathing that emerged in a half pant, half groan—And his own hurried footsteps were counterpointed, as he turned the corner, by the rapid slap of other sandals on the tiles up ahead of him. He knew it was Chime Cincinnati. He knew it was.

She was coming back to the hole because somehow she thought it had something to do with the voices she heard, the babies she said had no souls, and the sudden compulsion she had to leave Shambala.

He quickened his steps, trotting through the long twisting corridors leading downward and ever more downward. How could she so unerringly be heading for the place he and his father had just discovered?

His lamp illuminated only a small circle of light, within which his shadow jigged, grew and shrank, but in less time than he would have believed possible, he saw another light ahead of him.

Chime, her back to him, poked her front half through the ragged hole which was now two feet wide by three feet long.

"Chime Cincinnati!" he shouted to her. "Stop! Don't go in there. It's very dangerous."

His shout delayed her while she twisted and smiled at him, her smile unearthly in the combined glow of her lamp and the beam of his flashlight. He closed the distance between them. He had never seen her this way before. She practically vibrated with excitement, the veins pulsing in her small dark throat beneath the wild black ringlets.

"It's not dangerous," she argued, not bothering to offer any logical support for her words, turning away from him to hitch herself up into the opening. He grabbed for her, but before he could get a grip on her, she had hoisted her hips through the hole, slipped her legs in after, and walked over to the glittering object the flashlight illuminated. She had left her own oil lamp behind on the outside of the hole when she climbed in, and now he retrieved his flashlight from the place where it was wedged and switched it off.

"Meekay, please turn it back on," she said.

"Come out of there, Chime. I have an idea what you're up to, and you're crazy. It's very dangerous in there and I won't be a party to it. Come out. You'll hurt yourself there in the dark."

"Meekay, stop being difficult and trying to sound like my father," she said, then wheedled, "Please, let me have the flashlight for a moment. Oh! Look there! I think I've found a golden prayer wheel. It's a guide of some kind. I remember this now."

She was just trying to tempt him with something she knew he would love to find and show to his father. He knew that, but he shined the light inside the hole anyway. Maybe she'd come out once she had a chance to look. Anyway, he'd have to carry her back up to the top if she fell and hurt herself in the dark.

He waited a few moments while she poked and prodded, investigating everything within the range of the oil lamp he extended into the hole. His breathing had quieted now, and the roar he had heard from the hole before was louder than it had been during the day. It came from far off inside the hole. This was no single room or short abandoned passageway, judging from the roar and its echoes.

He couldn't see much, but she seemed delighted with what she saw inside the hole. "Chime, it's time to go now," he said after a while.

She turned around, grinning affectionately at him, but he saw that she was trembling with some strong emotion and her black eyes were wet, the tears leaving shining tracks on her dark cheeks.

"I'm sorry but I can't come back with you, Meekay," she said. "I always knew you would be the key somehow, and you were. You found this place, this portal, and it's time to go now."

And with that, she left the hole and disappeared into the darkness.

What could he do? No one would hear him if he yelled, and if he ran for help, she would go farther forward. She had no supplies with her, no protective gear, not even a coat, and whatever powers she thought she had, she was just one girl. She wasn't even very good at martial arts, to the disappointment of her father. Too spiritual, too cerebral, too inwardly focused, her mother said. Her father said she had her head up her ass a lot.

Mike could have kicked himself. He should have turned on the generator, he should have gone for help, but he had only suspected, he hadn't really known. And now she was retreating deeper into the hole.

She was going to do it. She was going to defy everybody and leave Shambala. Maybe she was right about this hole because her former selves told her, as she claimed they could, or maybe she'd just found old blueprints or something. But she was nuts enough to try it. Damn her. What a dumb idea. Shambala was safe and warm, even in the winter, with friends and family and food and shelter. He definitely didn't want to leave all that. He wasn't afraid of what was in the hole, not really. Fear wasn't what he was feeling at all. He was just angry at her for forcing him to leave when he didn't want to.

But he knew he had to follow her. Without even a flashlight, she'd be lost down here. His father said these lower tunnels had so many twists and turns, you could stay down here for months and never cross the same path twice. If he left her now, no matter what she *intended* to do, she'd be hopelessly lost. He pocketed his flashlight and set his oil lamp down. There was no time to go back for food or even a sweater, but maybe he could catch up with her, maybe he could bring her back and get her to at least wait until she was better prepared.

"Chime! Chime Cincinnati, you stop right there and wait for me!" he cried, climbing through the hole. "Wait, Chime, I'm bringing the light! Wait for me!"

CHAPTER V

Chime Cincinnati plunged ahead of Mike, half groping in darkness as absolute as if a bag had been thrust over her head, her hands stretching out in front of her so she wouldn't accidentally walk into anything. Her faith that this was the right course of action was justified not by her head, but by her feet, which walked resolutely forward as if they were possessed of knowledge the rest of her was not privy to. That was the trouble with having so many former incarnations. The former selves tended to get overzealous at times and start directing parts of her body to do things without consulting with her current personality first.

The part of her that was a girl just turned eighteen leaving behind everything and everyone she knew had many trepidations about this path she now followed, but the bodhisattva she had been for several past generations exalted.

To that part, the portion of her being that had been and was becoming again the Terton, her current life to date had been rather like a tedious extended holiday where she was always tolerated as a guest but had no useful work to do. Her work was just beginning again, and she knew that however frightening it was, however hazardous, it would be absolutely necessary for the sake of the world.

Lobsang Taring knew what she must do, but he had not been able to help her this time. No, that was wrong. He and his son had found this portal for her, so once more Taring had enabled her in her role as the Terton, as he had when she was Ama-La and several incarnations prior to that one.

Meanwhile she had worked and studied, even though no one but Taring, who had forgotten much of his early training, had ever been learned enough to instruct her in even the most elementary skills necessary to the fulfillment of her own dharma. She could only use the books of her past incarnation and hope that she was learning the things she needed to know.

Sometimes, when she slept or her mind drifted, she became aware that she was visualizing herself performing tasks and rituals with which she was totally unfamiliar. She knew at those times that such dreams were manifestations of her former selves trying to instruct her present body, but as soon as she tried to pay attention, the lesson dissolved. Meditation had always been difficult for this present restless young body, which would have preferred to be admired by young men, to dance, to plan the names and faces of children she doubted she would ever find time to bear. Lobsang Taring said she was no less learned or earnest than she had been in former lives, and he ought to know.

But only sometimes did she gain access to a piece of the secret that was her inner self. Like now, when her feet carried her as surely as if they knew what she was doing, though all of her other senses were useless.

The old soul within her told her young mind to stop dwelling on its past concerns, which were behind her, to be quiet now and follow where her feet led her. Her shoulders straightened and fell somewhat, letting her hands dangle by her sides and her neck relax as her knees, ankles, and feet carried her down the maze of corridors. A sense of calm, even of happiness, flowed like honey over the knives of her fears.

Mike, larger than Chime, stumbled over objects in his path, almost sprawling headlong as he tried to race after her, hollering to her, listening for replies, clutching his flashlight in one hand. He scrambled, climbed up and over and down obstacles until he totally lost track of how long he had been away or how far he had come. Once, he had looked behind him briefly and felt a jolt of panic when he found he could no longer see the light of his oil lamp shining through the entrance hole.

Maybe he should start unraveling his clothes and leaving a trail for himself of the threads; except that he'd never be able to see well enough to pick out the thread. Even if he did, thread was so fine it would break and he would never find it with only his flashlight beam.

He called to Chime over and over, cringing a little at the sound of his voice being swallowed by the roaring darkness, thinking of the stories of the great mining disasters his father liked to tell. But if the tunnels hadn't already collapsed from the noise pounding through them, they certainly wouldn't succumb to his puny little human raised voice, and maybe if he was close enough, Chime would hear him and wait.

At first the footing was made difficult by fallen debris, collapsed timbers, articles of furniture strewn across the passage, but after a while he entered corridors that were less damaged and the walking was easier. He could see by his flashlight that these passages were merely the continuation of all of the other long, downward-sloping hallways he and his parents had already excavated. Those passages were honeycombed with rooms, many of them storage rooms for useful things, so perhaps these were too. Sure enough, as he shone the thin pale beam to one side and then the other, he saw the darkened holes on either side of the hallway, and, telling himself Chime could be hiding in one of them, allowed himself a few seconds to explore each one. He found another room like the one on the upper levels that bulged with seed packets, but the other rooms were empty.

He imagined starving to death, though so far he wasn't even hungry. Had it really been such a short time ago that he sat in the warm and well-lit dining hall digesting his dinner while listening to the elders argue?

The farther down the corridor he traveled, the more pervasive grew the roaring, until it became a barrier against which he must push, its sound overpowering every other sensation, so that he almost did not feel his feet hit the floor or his hand hold the flashlight. His voice had stopped crying Chime's name of its own volition, and only his eyes kept staring at the darkness unwinding before him, until suddenly he found that the darkness was a solid wall in front of him and he had reached the end of the corridor.

For just a moment he felt trapped, and then it was the roaring that saved him. He had yet to reach its source, so he knew he could not have reached the end of his journey. Besides, Chime had to be ahead of him somewhere. He moved his light a little to the left and saw that he had been standing to one side of a pair of huge doors. He leaned against them and they swung open with surprising ease, responding to his first touch.

On the other side of the doors his eyes and nose discovered the source of the roaring noise. His nose filled with the heavy smell of wetness that suddenly dewed his skin and dampened the tip of his tongue with a sweet familiar mineral taste. His flashlight beam struck sparks of purple, ruby, green, and another iridescence to which he could put no name. It came from geode-inlaid tile and crystalline walls along which flowed a surging underground river. Just as the river reached the wall with the double doors, it bent into sheer rock and vanished. This, he realized, must be the source of "the jewel in the eye of the lotus" that was the sacred lake of Shambala.

The cavern was so immense that Mike's flashlight beam could not find the ceiling. He was inspecting the walls, gazing around him, and did not see the piece of golden statuary until he banged into it with his shins and let out a yelp, the noise instantly swallowed by the river's voice. He bent to examine the object, his flashlight picking up the valleys and brazen highlights of the design. It bore no dust, no doubt thanks to the humidity from the river water, but more amazingly, neither was it tarnished or moldy. The design was of a circle on a pedestal, and in the center of the pedestal was the *Rin-chen gDugs,* the Precious Parasol— his father had dug up several other examples of this first of the Eight Auspicious Symbols once used as altar bronzes throughout Shambala. This one was knee high, the parasol in the middle looking something like a chafing dish with ornamental carving and a knob on the top of the lid, with ribbons twirling around the base. Mike forgot about Chime for a moment, thinking how pleased his father would be at this discovery. His father had taught him the meaning of the symbols too. The parasol was supposed to give protection from evil.

He gave it a pat and walked on more carefully, watching the path ahead of him, and thus avoided more bruises when he came upon *gSer-gyi Nya,* the Two Golden Fish, in outer design similar to the parasol, but within the circle two fish bumped noses. The fish were supposed to be symbolic of beings saved from the ocean of earthly suffering, his father said. That sounded good too, which Mike supposed was why these were called the *auspicious* symbols.

They were Buddhist symbols, as his father had at one time been a Buddhist lama or teacher, though Buddhism was practiced by very few of the residents of Kalapa. Too many people had lived too long under the materialism of the PRC.

Why had the ancients placed these symbols along the river, so far from the main part of the city? He shone his light across the water and noticed for the first time that the wall on the other side of the river was lined with alcoves. Holding his arm straight in front of him, he probed an alcove with the flashlight beam. He almost dropped his light into the water when he saw the form of someone seated in lotus position just above the water level. He decided that's what the auspicious symbols were for, to mark the area containing these statues.

On the other side of this alcove was another statue, but this one slumped a little, the head tilted forward and slightly away from the direction he had come. Mike banged into the third altar bronze, the *gTer-chen-phoi Bum-pa* or Vase of Golden Treasures, said to contain spiritual jewels, as he walked upstream to view the third alcove and the third statue.

This statue slumped too, and Mike's flashlight beam picked up the gleam of an eye. He realized that the figures in the alcoves weren't statues at all, but life-sized human bodies wrapped with gilded bandages. Mummies, then, such as the Egyptians once made. His father had told him that sometimes the great lamas were mummified too. Why were they kept in here, where it was so damp? Maybe the mummies were too holy to rot.

Mike's eyes began playing tricks on him, the flashlight beam bouncing off the tumbling waters, sending shadows dancing across the face of the mummy, so that the bandages seemed to part in a grin.

Mike walked on so quickly that he barely dodged the *Padma bZang-po,* the Excellent Lotus Flower, emblem of original purity.

He crossed the corridor away from the statuary. He had to find Chime, and although the auspicious symbols and the statues were interesting, the wet from the river was soaking through his clothing, the statues gave him the creeps, and it wouldn't be the least bit auspicious if he fell over one of the symbols and broke his leg or his neck.

"Chime!" he hollered with more force than before, and played the light all along the wall and floor ahead of him. That was when he saw the wall sconce holding the torch. Well, sure, they'd have to light this place with something, and he didn't think they had electricity back in the old days—at least, not all through Kalapa. He pulled the torch down from its sconce and lit it with one of the wooden matches he carried in a little plastic case in his pocket. The light was much brighter, though smokier, than that of the flashlight, and it would help him save the flashlight's power.

The torch allowed him to see a greater distance, for which he was grateful. He had begun to worry that perhaps Chime had taken a side tunnel or fallen into the water, but felt reassured that his torchlight showed him no sign of her. He trotted onward through the main tunnel, panting slightly, not realizing at first that the corridor had started to tilt upward. Then he came to the first stairs and saw that the water was

roaring and tumbling with more agitation than before and that it bil-
lowed into white spray. As he climbed farther, the corridor definitely
sloped steeply up along the side of a great waterfall pouring down a
natural wall. No body lay amid the churning froth, however, or clung
to rocks, and he thought he would have seen her by now if she had
been drowned.

CHAPTER
VI

The soles of Chime's feet seemed to have eyes and emotions all their own, renewing an acquaintance with the floor beneath them, remembering each rise and fall of the pavement, each impediment to be skirted, sending impressions and memories to her brain of the waiting mummies of dead rimpoches on the far banks of the river, the auspicious symbols marking the way, the ceremonies conducted when the mortal remains of the rimpoches were ferried across the water to their cloisters and left there as if in meditation on the affairs of Shambala. Theirs had been such powerful spirits that their shrunken remains were consulted for years afterward by the high lamas on matters of policy pertaining to Shambala. She remembered their names and faces, men of compassion, intelligence, and strength, men whose souls were so strong that even the faintest whiff of herb-embalmed flesh filtering through the tropical mist of the river's cavern filled her with joy and resolution.

Yes. She was on the right path. Relief flooded through her. She felt her senses open up. More than her third eye opened—she was eyes all over, ears all over, noses all over, and the air, the precious atmosphere of Shambala, rare and sacred even here on these lower levels, was as tangible to her as if she were swimming submerged in smooth beads of sandalwood and jade.

How odd that while Shambala was the goal, staying there had kept her half deadened to herself, to the world. *This* was the right thing to do. The babies *were* a sign. The babies were as dead inside as she had begun to feel.

Not seeing her people again would be a small price to pay, a price she had often paid in her former lives. It was part of the risk, and she was willing, eager, to take it, but at the same time the eighteen-year-old girl she was in this life bid a wistful good-bye to those she was leaving behind.

Though the Terton in her grew stronger with every step, the girl who housed the Terton worried over the dangers of which her elders had warned—perhaps she *would* die of radiation or be killed outside in some other way. It would have been better if the others had been willing to come too.

No, the Terton in her argued, anyone else would have held her back, hampered her, anyone except perhaps Lobsang Taring, who had been her guide and her grandfather in former lives but was, in this life, an older adult unfailingly tender to her and understanding of her. But Taring was an old man now. Only the Terton, now young enough to cross the boundaries of Shambala, yet armed with the memories of former lives, had been destined for this journey.

In her last incarnation the Terton had been Ama-La, the old lady doctor, and before that a young Chinese guard, and before that a man brutally mistreated in a Chinese prison camp. Was the guard that she had been kinder because she recalled the prisoner she had also been, or had she remembered any of her life as a prisoner when she was a guard? Perhaps she only recalled the logistics of leading the appropriate people to Shambala. When she was Taring's granddaughter, the girl who was to become Ama-La, had he warned her then against going outside as now those who cherished her did? No, probably not. That was before the end of the world.

Despite her joy, despite knowing that she was on the right path, Chime felt mosquitoes of fear nipping at her and drawing blood from time to time. She smiled a jittery inward smile. As a much-reincarnated Buddhist, she probably shouldn't allow herself even so much as a mental flyswatter with which to battle them.

She walked on and on, listening to the slap and tinkle within the greater roar of the water, in essence only one droplet merging with another as one life merged with another, with only the brief hiccough of bodily death in between. That being true, there was nothing to be afraid of. She concentrated on the river-muffled slap of her footsteps, on the water sounds. Memories returned to her of silent well-wishers, the shells of herself and former friends and teachers watching from the far side of the water.

For a time she climbed and concentrated on her footsteps and her breath and the water. And then for a long time the pathway was level and smooth beneath her feet and the calmer, sweeter sounds of the water were closer to her ear than the great roaring. The coolness and damp of the water sparkled on her skin, the smell in her nostrils not dank or moldy, but rich with the aroma of the life and decay of many small plant and animal beings.

The eyes in her feet told her that these small life-forms were unusually vital and vigorous, and their emanations fairly vibrated within the cavern, echoing like the dying peal of bells.

The long smooth walk at the top of the climb, followed by the initially gentle slope downward which made breathing easier and her feet tread faster, soothed and centered her, calming both fear and elation.

The calmness allowed her more access than she had ever previously enjoyed to the sensory memories of her former lives, so that she was not surprised so much as she otherwise would have been when the water sounds beside her changed direction and were very much before her, lukewarm liquid gurgling around her toes and tickling them, then sliding beneath the balls of her feet to lick beneath her arches, envelop her heels, eddy around her calves and shins. Finally the water firmly grabbed at her knees and dragged her in up to her chest into a strong current.

The water's surface remained smooth only a very short time before plunging her into another raging cascade.

Mike breasted the crest of the fall and thought surely he could catch up with Chime now if they were on the same path. At least this part of the cavern did not seem to have many side passages or rooms for her to stray into, and he knew he was stronger and his legs were longer and he could outrun her. He just had to find her again first.

As soon as he caught his breath from the climb, he jogged down the long smooth corridor, noting that here the water bubbled to the surface, as if once more fed from below, and also that the walls ran with rivulets that channeled across the floor under smooth, wide-tiled bridges and joined the river there. He noticed these things only peripherally, however, as his eyes searched beyond the flame of his torch for the paleness of Chime's clothing.

He felt a mild physical relief and pleasure as the downward slope helped his progress, lending wings to his feet and extra breath to his lungs.

Then suddenly, up ahead of him, there she was, and he cheered inwardly at the sight of her short, pajama-suit-clad body padding along in front of him. He cried out to her, but the roar of falling water was still too loud for him to make his voice heard to her, even at this distance. He sprinted forward, bounding after her, the torch carried dangerously before him like a lance with the flame licking back toward him. Its heat seared his hand when he grasped for Chime as she disappeared into the current. He leapt forward, only to find his feet meeting not pavement, but the deep gleaming water abandoning its banks to swirl in front of him.

The torch was smothered and torn from his grip as the current caught his still-running legs and buckled his knees so that he fell into the river, struggling to breathe air instead of water as he tumbled toward the roaring waterfall.

CHAPTER VII

Chime plunged into the water and bobbed back up like one of the bubbles, her ears full of water and the roar of water. The current bore her up and turned her around and around, tumbling her like jet-driven dice down the falls. She struggled to keep her head above the surface until she realized that even when the water boiled into her mouth, parts of her remained in contact with the river bottom. And those parts reminded her that the downward slant of the falls was not perpendicular, but merely sharply tilted. Furthermore, the river, though fast, was not deep. Taking a deep breath, she dived forward into a sledding position, and her head stayed easily above the surface, eyes staring ahead of her into the wet rushing darkness.

It was even fun. The water was everywhere now, and the roar increased as centrifugal force swept her down and around bends and twists in the bed, throwing her up against cavern walls which skinned her shins, shoulders, arms, and back as she pushed away, back into the stream and downward again. At these bends the roaring was the loudest, the water the deepest, and tricky eddies and whirlpools appeared. Had one of them caught her, she was too small and had too little strength to have pulled herself clear.

However, the older part of her was well-prepared for these perils, piloting her slender body in such a way that she avoided the worst of the dangers.

She was panting with the effort to keep control of her emotions and release control of her body to the part of her that could take care of it better than the conscious part—she knew very well that she should not be afraid, even as she saw, rounding the next bend, that the roof of the cavern was becoming lower and lower, closer and closer to the stream, the passage ever more narrow. First she turned her cheek against the surface of the water to breathe the air trapped between the ceiling and the water, but as the flow carried her on, she had time for only one deep breath before the water closed over her head as she was pulled farther and farther in.

Mike too discovered that he could navigate the gradual pitch of the falls without serious problems—being larger and stronger than Chime, he avoided the cavern walls more successfully, though he too took scrapes and bruises as he pushed against them. He could see nothing but was carried along by the current for what seemed to him like days. The water, at least, was not chillingly cold, though he could avoid whirlpools by the feel of the flow and the temperature against him. The mingling of the hot springs that fed the hot water system of Kalapa with the mountain runoff kept the springs at a bearable temperature.

Mike didn't think too much, except to hope Chime hadn't drowned—so he could have the pleasure of killing her himself. He found it impossible to remember what it was like to be dry. Thibideaux had told him once of vast amusement parks back in the land where Thibideaux and Mike's mother had been born, parks full of nothing but rides and safe adventures for children and their parents—one of these Thibideaux remembered was called a water slide. This waterfall must be a little like that entertaining ride, only much longer. Surely it would soon end and dry land would be at hand and he would try to find Chime and they would work their way back. Or forward. Whatever. Just so he could reach dry land and walk upright again.

He did not see the ceiling lower, but he felt its pressure against his head and, like Chime, eventually had to turn his face to take the last breath before the water closed chillingly over his scalp and swallowed him whole.

Gagging as he sucked water into his lungs, he couldn't even scream as the whirling waters dragged him, not farther down, but up into a luminous blue vortex.

CHAPTER VIII

Chime's inner self knew better than to let the body do anything so foolish as breathe water, and she popped up from the whirlpool expelling her last breath and sucking in raw new air. The sky above her was blue, the water around her was blue, and she was a small brown dot floating in the middle of a vast lake capped by a cloudless sky. Despite the clarity of the sky, puffs of fog rolled across the surface of the lake and a thin gray strip separated one edge of blue water from the rim of the sky.

Before she could decide whether to swim toward the grayness or not, something rammed into her legs and she backpaddled away from the whirlpool. Mike's body bobbed to the surface. She should have known he would follow her. It had not escaped her notice that ever since she was a little girl, he had been there trying to keep her out of trouble. Perhaps now that Lobsang Taring was too old to be guardian of the Terton, Mike had unwittingly donned the role as a hereditary one? Nevertheless, now was the time to guard her guardian or he'd drown.

She plunged her arm back into the whirlpool, struggling to grab him and draw him out without pulling herself back in.

She hadn't even noticed him following, absorbed as she was in her protective meditation and the onslaught of her recognition of those higher pieces of her personality. But she felt a lightness in her mind, a bubble of relief—similar to what she'd felt at leaving Kalapa—to see that he had come, that she would have a companion after all. She fished for him more deeply and finally grabbed him by the hair and tugged.

Ordinarily, even his comparatively heavy body would be buoyed up by the water and she would have been able to tow him, but he was still in the whirlpool. Its force held his feet although it seemed to be content to spit him to the surface and spin him there. He lay within it, facedown, hair floating, clothing stuck to him like scum. His limp, outstretched hands were bluish.

She reached for his shoulder, but fog much thicker than Chime had ever seen before bloomed between her face and Mike's body, and her thrusting hand slid over him and missed its grip. She grabbed again, touching his sleeked hair and running her hand down his head and neck until she was able to take him under the shoulder with her other hand, and this time she pulled him toward her, toward the sapphire brilliance of the sky and the lake.

But as the whirlpool released its prey and Mike's body bumped against hers like a floating log, the fog attached spiderweblike tendrils to him and began to wrap him in its folds.

The day after Mike had saved her, as he supposed, from sleep-walking into the lake when she was little more than a baby, he gave her a swimming lesson and showed her how even someone as small as she was could tow a body as large as his to the shore of the lake and resuscitate it.

Now his karma had come full circle as she used the lesson he had given her to try to save him, towing him and his private cloud with her toward the gray strip between sky and lake that she hoped was land and not a storm. Despite the blueness of the sky, she could not see the mountains.

The underground river had been flowing downward before they popped up into the lake, and since they had come down from the mountains, they should now be able to look up into them, unless they had traveled much farther than she believed possible.

But then, she reflected, the world would be very changed now. Who knew if the mountains beyond her home even stood as mountains any longer?

Mike's body suddenly heaved in her arms and his hands flew to her neck and pushed her under the water.

"Don't ruin anything," a voice from within the fog said. "I don't want to wake up crippled."

Mike vaguely remembered trying to breathe and choking on water, being sucked up into the bottom of the blue vortex. The next thing he knew, he was up above, looking down at his body floating in the whirlpool. Could he be *dead*? Was that possible? He hadn't breathed *that* much water.

Then he saw Chime Cincinnati grabbing for him, wrestling his inert body onto its back and hooking her elbow under his chin in the position he had taught her, then flipping over onto her back.

Good! Now she had only to haul him to shore and pump the water from his lungs so he could use them again, and he'd be able to climb back into his body. He wasn't sure how he had come to leave it to begin with, but now, looking down on himself, he could somehow see *inside* himself, and it didn't seem to him that his lungs were all that full. Watching Chime's struggle to hold onto him, he decided that he could probably re-merge with his physical self right now without too much harm and maybe rouse his body enough to help her.

He huffed himself up and dove toward his body, but he bounced right off again as the body heaved upward and its hands grasped Chime around the throat and pushed her under.

The sight of his own hands choking Chime when *he* wanted to save her made him feel dizzy with disorientation.

"Don't ruin anything. I don't want my new body to be mute or crippled," a woman's voice said.

A piece of fog steamed toward the flailing forms of his body and Chime. The fog coalesced into the agitated shape of a pale young woman wearing white shorts and a sleeveless top.

She was speaking to Mike's body as it drowned Chime, and she hovered just over Chime's gasping mouth, bloodless hands steepled in a diving position, as if she was about to plunge down Chime's throat. Mike had read about astral beings, and figured that this woman was one and that for the time being so was he. And if she could maneuver her astral self, so could he.

He steepled his hands, as she had, and dived toward the flailing bodies, wrapping protectively around Chime. At least now that he no longer had a body, he didn't have to worry about drowning, he thought, when his body pulled Chime's under the water, and with it pulled his own . . . astral form, he supposed it was, for want of a better term.

All around him shadowy fish-shaped forms swam in and out of the shadowy leafy forms swaying up from the bottom of the lake with the movement of the water. Something as large as the dining hall in Kalapa darkened the water behind him, cutting his body, Chime, himself, and the cloud-woman off from the whirlpool.

"Let go of her. You're killing her!" Mike said to the person staring out of his own eyes. His eyes looked back at him, startled.

The cloud-woman said, "Don't listen to him, Richie. He's just the spook who used to have your body. I want one too. There's not enough to go around, and it's about time these two shared."

Mike released Chime and grabbed his body's hands with his astral hands. "Hands, release Chime," he commanded, unable to think of any other way to handle the situation. The first time, his astral hands went right through the physical ones as well as through Chime's throat, but the second time, he simply tried to keep his astral hands over the physical ones and concentrate on easing their grip.

The eyes in Mike's body looked even more startled and wary, and finally the hands flew up in a gesture of surrender, letting Chime sink toward the bottom. "I can't do it, Toni-Marie. It's murder," Mike's body said in a voice very similar to his own but also more different than could be accounted for merely by having its vocal cords waterlogged.

"Dammitall," the woman ghost said, diving for Chime's inert body. Mike dived too, and wrapped himself around Chime again, swatting at the female ghost.

"Let go of her, you!" the woman ghost demanded in a voice as shrill as a bird cry. "She's mine! I'm sick of being dead, and you're not going to cheat me out of the first living body I've found in twenty years!"

"Wake up, Chime Cincinnati," Mike screamed into Chime's slack face. "Wake up! I can't make you swim."

The woman ghost flowed around them like a shark, looking for a way past Mike to Chime's body. She wheedled, "I can save her. I'm a good swimmer."

"Go away!" he yelled at her again.

Chime Cincinnati's eyes popped open just then and, blowing bubbles, she began struggling back toward the surface, Mike's and the woman's astral forms streaking behind her.

"Chime!" he cried with relief when he saw her feet pedaling below the surface. Above the water, her mouth took in great gulps of air.

She grinned at his body's face and said, "I'm fine now, Meekay." Mike's face grinned back at her. It didn't even look like himself to Mike now.

"Good," he said.

"Richie, dammit, get her! You can't just leave me out here after all we've been through together!"

The man in Mike's body looked up and swirled in the water to look behind him, his expression mingling annoyance and bewilderment. Mike thought that perhaps although Richie could still hear the woman, now that he inhabited Mike's body in the physical world, their bond might be weakening.

Before his own bond with Chime weakened, Mike had to warn her. "That's not me, Chime Cincinnati. The guy who looks like me just tried to drown you. Swim away, fast!"

Chime stared straight at him—the astral him, not the physical him—and plunged away from his body, toward the gray line that possibly marked the shore.

Mike followed close behind her. After a perplexed look upward and all around him, so did the person inhabiting Mike's body.

Chime's swimming had never been more than perfunctory. Although she liked the water, she was too preoccupied with her studies to become proficient at any physical activity other than yoga exercises. Mike's body was inhabited by a good swimmer who knew how to use muscles already conditioned by long swims in the sacred lake of Kalapa.

"You can still get her, Richie! Atta boy!" the woman ghost was urging.

"Leave them alone, evil spirit!" Mike commanded her, floating in front of her until she drifted right through him. "He's not listening to you anymore."

Chime's stroke was flagging, and Richie caught up with her easily. He grabbed her but she slipped away from him and wearily splashed on.

The gray line between the blue halves of the world looked as far away and indistinct to Mike as it had when he first saw it.

"That's a hell of a long swim," the woman ghost said, stopping in midair. "I think we may all lose out here—Richie got a body and all of a sudden doesn't believe in ghosts anymore, and your girlfriend is too pooped to make it. With my luck they'll both drown and then nobody'll have a body. We just got greedy, I guess. Saw you guys and thought, oh boy, fresh meat. . . ."

But Mike was watching a black ripple in the blue water, a ripple that left a wake of its own.

Using his astral eyes to look beneath the waves, he saw the cause of the ripple—it looked like a cross between a whale, an eel, and a giant sea horse. In size it was larger than he had ever imagined a lake creature could be, its coils spreading clear across the lake as far as he could see. Its head was horselike, with spines resembling a mane along the crest of its neck and head. It surfaced frequently for air.

"What is that?" he asked, cutting her off.

The female ghost craned forward a little but otherwise didn't approach the monster. "I don't know, but you better hope it's not hungry."

The monster undulated closer to the swimmers, and Mike's astral body closed the distance between him and Chime. The water foamed like the bottom of a waterfall, swamping the swimmers in its turbulence. Richie gasped and choked, causing Mike a few pangs of worry about his lungs. Chime tried to swim doggedly on but her arms were poor oars in such turbulence.

The monster's great coils pumped in and out of the water, creating a massive wake behind and to the sides of its immense body. Mike had the sudden notion that since in his astral form he could address ghosts, perhaps he could also communicate with monsters and somehow convince this one to undulate elsewhere.

He hovered near the great head, peering into the nearest well-deep eye, and saw there a maelstrom that was nothing natural or animal but full of some sort of preternatural force. "Monster?" he ventured tentatively, and that was all, before he was blasted backward by a torrent of tremendously intense emotion—grief, anger, pain, joy, lust, and more grief.

The monster creature moved up and down with greater speed and velocity, and Mike realized that in addition to swamping the swimmers, it was driving them closer to the smoky line dividing the blue of the lake from the blue of the sky. Now, in fact, the smokiness was resolving into thin gray light illuminating gray beach and gray trees beyond, and the fogbound feet of the mountains.

The monster turned back on itself, its head leading the rest of it somewhat closer to the swimmers, and the waves it created swept the two people up onto the beach where they lay prostrate. The female ghost flew to their side, hovering over Chime. Mike joined them as the monster abruptly stopped its undulations and dove back into the lake.

Even as he joined Chime and his own body, he couldn't help wondering what the monster's purpose had been. Chime was gasping for breath, to the disappointment of the female ghost, and Mike's body, with Richie's spirit clinging to it, once more looked drowned.

"Meekay?" Chime coughed, looking over at his body.

"That's not me, Chime Cincinnati. This is one of two ghosts. The female ghost tried to make the male ghost drown you so she could have your body, but he relented." He knew it sounded confusing, but she not only seemed to hear him, but also seemed to understand him. "Chime?"

"Yes, Meekay?"

"Could you please resuscitate him—me, I mean? I hate to watch myself die, even if I'm no longer in my body."

"One thing must be done first." She turned to the female ghost just as if she was any other person and said in the formal, sort of stilted old-fashioned way she sometimes talked, "I will address the spirit in Meekay's body, but you should heed my words also to be released from the death and rebirth cycle and attain Nirvana."

"Oh, no you don't," the female ghost said, and promptly disappeared.

Chime sighed and hauled herself up on her skinny arms. She bent close to the right ear of Mike's body's, coughed three times and said in a much deeper intonation than Mike would have believed could come from her, "*Homage to the gurus, the three kayas,*" the first lines of the Tibetan Book of the Dead, or the Great Liberation Through Hearing, as it was known to Buddhists.

Apparently it was known to Richie also. Chime had spoken only a few lines when Mike's body deflated as a thin mist smoked from his mouth and instantly dissipated. The atmosphere felt charged as it might after a thunderstorm, with excitement and something like joy.

"Meekay, quickly," Chime said, and Mike forgot about everything but becoming whole, merging again with his body as Chime pumped the water from his lungs and breathed air into them.

He opened the eyes of his body and found them blurred with weariness. Chime Cincinnati looked down at him as if he was some sort of metaphysical puzzle. Water dripped from her nappy curls onto his chest.

He twisted under her in time to throw up a bolus of water and to cough, feeling with gratitude the weight of the bone and flesh containing him as his ribs ached with the effort, his sternum heaved, and his neck convulsed.

"Thanks, Chime," he said. "I came along to protect you but I guess we saved each other."

Chime smiled a tight little smile and nodded, then coughed and hugged herself to control her shivering. All of their clothing was soaked, and their sandals had disappeared in the water. Mike unfastened his pocket flap, and to his relief felt the utility knife and the canister of matches, which had not also been lost.

The sky no longer shone so blue, and the water had darkened to a deep pewter color. The shapes he had seen from the water seemed lost in haze now, so that the landscape spread flat and featureless all around them. There was no sign of the lake monster.

"I was afraid that c-c-creature was g-going to g-g-get you," he told her between chattering teeth. "But I think m-maybe it was t-trying to p-p-push you to shore instead."

Chime coughed into her crossed arms and smiled thinly. "I don't think the serpent of Samsara cared whether it swept us ashore or drowned us. It's not like it's a real person, you know, just the embodiment of the turbulence of material existence." This phrase should have sounded as ridiculously pretentious as he had always thought Chime's utterances sounded, delivered in a wispy girlish voice by a young female person, but it didn't. In fact, somehow the earnest, sleepy way Chime said this made it seem more important.

"But it saved our lives," Mike said.

She looked up at him, her eyelids quivering over eyes so tired they seemed glazed. "Is that how you see it? I thought it was pushing us away from the whirlpool which brought us here, cutting us off from home."

"But—Chime?"

Exhausted from the swim and her efforts to resuscitate his body, she lay down on the lakeshore, curled onto her side and fell into a deep sleep. Mike lay down beside her, hunched himself into a tight ball and slept too. He supposed he really ought to stay awake and remain on guard, but since he'd already been dead twice that day and possessed once, he felt that precautions were a little after the fact.

CHAPTER IX

When Mike awoke, he felt well-rested, and sore enough to reassure himself that he was still in his corporeal body. He was also extremely hungry. Chime was still sleeping, her hand curled under her cheek, a slight smile on her face. The sky was once more brilliant blue, and the lake just as blue, with no sign of either the ghosts or the monster.

Mike decided he would try to catch for breakfast some of the lake fish whose cousins he had glimpsed near the whirlpool. He had neither string nor hook, but that was the lazy way to fish anyway.

He would fish in the challenging way Henri Thibideaux had once taught him, lie very still beside the water until a fish came along and then catch it in his hands.

Shivering, he found a high place a little ways from where Chime lay and flopped down on his belly, hands poised above the surface. He seemed to be in luck, for he saw the shapes of several good-sized fish darting through the water beneath him.

The sun had not risen as yet, so he couldn't see the gleam of the scales, but a fish shadow flickered directly beneath his hands. He scooped into the water where the fish was supposed to be, and grabbed. Where scales and fins should have at least brushed his hand, his fingers sliced through nothing but water.

He swore to himself, but saw to his surprise that the shadow of the fish was still hovering unconcernedly beneath the surface, and the other fish shadows wove through the water with as little fear. In the lake at home, they would have all swam away.

He dipped again, plunging his arms into the cool water up to his armpits, with no different results except that momentarily the shadow of the fish dissipated, only to coalesce when he withdrew his hands from the water. Triangular head shape, oval body, and split tail reconnected and the fish shadow kept swimming.

Chills writhed down Mike's back as if his pajama suit was suddenly full of minnows. The ghost of people were bad enough, but *fish* ghosts?

He didn't like the idea. He didn't much like this place either. The fog behaved in a very suspicious manner here—no puffs played on the surface of the lake today, nor around the edge, where fog logically and scientifically ought to be; instead it hovered on the shore, looming up to cover the forest beyond.

Anyway, he was still hungry and still cold, and even if he found no food in the forest, moving around would warm him and he could find some wood for a fire. He pulled his match canister from his jacket pocket and opened it. The matches looked dry, but there weren't many of them. He hoped they'd find some people soon.

He glanced over at Chime. She had burrowed her face deep into her arms and had drawn her legs up under her chin, trying to keep warm.

He thought about waking her but then decided he'd stay in sight of her. There were the ghosts, after all, and the monster.

He wondered, walking toward the hazy gray trees looming just beyond, if they really ought to eat any food they found here. Of course, they *might* still be within Shambala, but he doubted it. He had never heard of a place like this within the borders, with the mountains so far away. So, if he took it as a given that this *was* outside the borders, wouldn't everything be tainted with radiation? It would make them sick. Maybe if they just ate a little, not too much, it would be all right. If they didn't eat anything until they found their way back home, they'd die for sure.

He set out for the trees, looking back over his shoulder often to see Chime huddled against the morning cold. He expected to walk right into the tall forest at once, but though he waded through weeds and thorn bushes and swampy patches where reeds grew up through ground that looked solid but was in fact mud or water, the tall trees he saw through the fog were always just a little farther away.

Penetrating the fog, he walked through trees about as tall as he was, the branches twisted and misshapen, the conformation more bushy than treelike. This looked much like the area where people had chopped down the trees to obtain the wood for the buildings Thibideaux was constructing. Or rather, it looked like that area had looked for about a year after the trees had been chopped down. Trees grew very quickly in Shambala, as did everything. But these were baby trees, he knew, and he passed one after another without ever walking among the tall timber outlined in the haze.

Searching the ground for deadfall, he found a few green twigs, but nothing of any size. He tore up handfuls of grasses from beneath the trees, where the ground was less damp. Clumps of black, foul-smelling earth came away on the roots. He shook this off as best he could and turned to take what he had found back to the shore. Perhaps he would find driftwood if he walked down the beach. Or he would wake Chime and they would go back into the tall trees.

He knew there was a mountain pass leading back home somewhere right outside the borders of Shambala. He was certain he had glimpsed the shadowy feet of the mountains through the fogbound forest.

In stooping to gather fuel, he wandered farther than he'd intended. It took him two or three minutes to trot back to the edge of the lake.

The lake was now obscured by billows of fog—the same sort of fog he had seen yesterday. Sticking out from the fog as if from beneath the hem of a filmy gown was Chime's bare brown foot. Hugging his nest of grass and twigs close to his chest, he ran into that ominous fog, shouting, "Get away from her, you ghosts! Scat! Vamoose!" as if he was shooing geese away from seeds waiting to go in the ground, or a snow lion cub from the yak pen.

Two paces from Chime's foot he dropped his ignitables and began flailing at the fog with both arms. "Go away! Leave her alone!"

"Okay, okay," the voice of the female ghost answered him petulantly. "I was just *checking*, for pity's sake. It's a little lonesome here without Richie. I knew he'd studied Buddhism once when he was in college, but I had no idea he was the type to actually go floating off to Nirvana the first time somebody suggested it. Not me, man. I just want another hot little body to call my own, and your girlfriend was just lying here, so I thought—"

"Just go away and leave us alone," Mike growled at her.

In the rent he had made in the ghostly fog, Chime sat up rubbing her eyes. "Meekay, don't frighten the spirit away. We need her help."

Mike snorted. Leave it to Chime to side with the ghosts! Next thing he knew, she'd probably be taking credit for them.

She continued, speaking to the fog, "Ghost, I am very sorry that I cannot offer this body to you at present. I still need it, you see. But if you will help us, we will try to help you too."

"Like you helped Richie? I was just telling your friend here that that's not for me. Look honey, if you're not going to fall into a coma right now so I can crawl into your epidermis, the only way you can help me is for you and him to get together and get it on." Here the ghost made a graphic gesture that did not at all fit in with Mike's idea of ethereal. "And I," the ghost's voice rose theatrically as she placed her pale hand over the location of her heart, "can be the spirit of your little newborn chee-ild. What do you say?"

Chime didn't answer her at once, but sat there with her legs crossed, her dark eyes staring into the ghost's, which were the blue of the sky and water, so that it seemed you literally looked into the world *through* her eyes.

Chime's voice was soft and kind as she said, "I did not think to let you bid your friend good-bye. But he was ready for enlightenment, he longed for it, far more than he longed for Mike's body or to take mine for you. Did you not know?"

"He wasn't much of a talker," the ghost said. "And look, I don't want to insult your religion or anything, especially since it looks like you guys were right, at least about the reincarnation thing, but I don't *want* to go to Nirvana, Heaven, Paradise, Valhalla, or the other place either. I just want a nice body with lungs and a heart and arms and legs that move and a mouth that tastes something besides twenty-two different flavors of air pollution. I'd like my feet to touch the goddamn ground again."

"Is that all you wish for?" Chime asked. "To continue the death and rebirth cycle?"

"Well, no. But it's good for starters. I just want to *live* again."

"Then why haven't you been reborn? Surely some life-form has survived to reproduce?"

"Well, yeah, there are a few living people scattered around Asia, okay, and when we were first blown to kingdom come, Richie and I checked it out. But we couldn't stand the competition. For every living human out there there's about a jillion other ghosts all wanting the same thing we—well, I—did, to have another go-round at life."

"What of plants or animals? They reproduce more quickly than humans."

"Even if I wanted to be a plant or an animal, it's the same thing. Almost all of them were killed—the high winds up here scoured what little vegetation there was right off the mountains, the firestorms and nuclear winter finished what the missiles started. And all of them, all the animals and plants, left ghosts too, so there's still competition here. Much as I want to stay human, every time something new is born, I'm drawn to it in spite of myself—the way some girls are—well, used to be—about men? I mean, I know it's not what I want, I know there's not much future in it, but I just can't help myself, it looks so good. I just think about it and all of a sudden I'm in there mingling with several thousand other ghosts to get in on the birth, hatching, blooming, sprouting, whatever. But there's tree ghosts and fish ghosts and grass ghosts too—"

"I saw them this morning," Mike put in. "I've never heard of such things before."

"I cannot recall such things either," Chime said, her eyes half closed, as if she was trying to look inside herself for such a memory. Abruptly, she stopped and looked back up at them. "But then, I have never before to my knowledge been abroad in the world when it was so totally destroyed."

"You don't know the half of it," the ghost said. "Up here there never was a lot, I guess, being so high. That's why we came up here, finally, me and Richie. Every time some new thing would be born down below, which was not all that often, we were off like we'd heard a fire alarm. And every single time, there'd be ghosts so thick you couldn't tell who was who, they just all looked like a big thick cloud. We never even got close.

"You know, I think there's some kind of natural discriminatory process that's going on down there—like, since we're foreigners, we got *last* pick, meaning none. I guess that's just fair since we pretty much have been able to roam around while most of the other spooks are more or less stuck in the general vicinity where they died. Anyway, we never stood a chance, and eventually we drifted up here where there was even less chance, sort of out of range of any budding life, because it's bad enough being dead without being driven crazy all the time too. So, well, when we saw you bob up on the lake like that, when nothing ever had before, one of you conveniently drowned but not quite dead and the other one not likely to make it, I just naturally figured you were meant for us. Guess I was a little premature. I always was the impetuous type."

Mike shook his head, "Oh no, you can't pass it off so lightly. Your friend possessed my body before I was dead, and you tried to get him to kill Chime."

"Well, ex-cooose me, but when you've been dead as long as I have, where there's nothing but ghosts, you get a different perspective on that kind of thing. From here it looks to me like you're pretty privileged characters to be alive and—say, you *are* young. Were you guys actually born *after* the missiles? You look healthy too, standard number of fingers and toes and so on, reasonably well-fed. Now, how the hell did you pull that off?"

"We were born in Shambala," Chime said. "The trouble of the world reached us only remotely there."

"Shambala? Is that anything like Shangri-La? I thought the Chinese took that over back in the twentieth century."

"That was Tibet," Mike told her. "Shambala was kept a secret, and one lady—Chime's supposed to be—" He cast a sidelong glance at Chime.

"I *am* the reincarnation of the Terton, is what my friend is trying to say," Chime said firmly, but with a little laughing smile at Mike. "It is my task throughout all of my lifetimes to guide worthy beings to Shambala."

"Well, if there's still healthy specimens like you guys being born there, I'm surprised you aren't being deluged by spooks."

"We have powerful shields—spiritual shields," Chime said. "Those who might have known of us have probably already joined us or have long ago reached enlightenment and have no need of us."

"It was a secret even from the *dead*?" the ghost asked. "Wow, that's some secret."

"*You* didn't know about it," Mike reminded her.

"Guess not. So, well then, are you offering to take me back there with you?"

"Yes, certainly," Chime said. "But first we need your help."

"Besides," Mike said sternly, "only *worthy* spirits may enter Shambala, and you have a little matter of some very bad karma to clean up after trying to kill us."

"I told you that was a misunderstanding. Besides, I didn't think you had karma after you were dead. But I'm game. What can I do for you?"

"Lead us into the world to find the living, so that we may bring them back to the safety of Shambala," Chime Cincinnati told her.

"That's a snap," the ghost said. "I can smell the living from miles away like I used to be able to smell coffee brewing in the morning. It's like I've got some kind of homing device."

"Wonderful," Chime said. "Lead us to the nearest living beings then, please."

"Wait a minute," Mike said. "Chime Cincinnati, we have to go home now. She can wait out here for us, but we have to go back and get help and clothes and food and stuff. Our parents, the others, will be worried. I only came to find you because I thought you'd get lost underground. We can't stay *now*. I've got responsibilities, even if you don't."

"Oh, Meekay, you know that I did not leave home to come to this place simply because I was lost. I have responsibilities too, and this is the only place I can fulfill them."

"Chime, be reasonable," he said. "Everyone in Kalapa will be worried about us, and they were already so worried."

He had visions of his parents climbing the mountain passes, looking into all the holes and tunnels, calling for them until they were hoarse. His father and mother would cling together and cry, reproach themselves for not giving him that one last birthday, and Chime's mother would cry with Chime's grandfather while Chime's father and grandmother looked stony-faced and grim.

Chime answered him, saying, "Everyone in Kalapa will realize that I meant it when I told them that the time has come at last for me to do that which it is my destiny, life after life, to fulfill. They will probably, however, be very worried about *you*, and I hope we will find a way to get word to them or to send you back soon."

Then Mike thought of Isme. Now that he had left, she would see how much he had meant to her. She would cry and cry and send Tsering Li away while she grieved for Mike. Or maybe she wouldn't. Maybe she wouldn't notice. Actually, Chime was right. By now his father was probably reassuring everyone that Chime was fulfilling her karmic journey and that Mike had no doubt gone to help her. As if he *wanted* to be here, Mike thought. He *wanted* to be home—home with his family and friends, where he knew what to expect and had work he enjoyed. It wasn't that he was afraid to be out here—he hadn't seen anything much to be afraid of except the ghost, who was now harmless enough, and that lake monster, who had turned out not to be too dangerous either. He had only come this far to try to protect Chime. And now she was acting as if he was a big baby crying to go home.

The very idea made him angry. "Send *me* back? Chime Cincinnati, we must both go back or neither of us will go back. You can't survive out here alone. I don't care how saintly you were in your last life, you can't live where there's no food, no shelter, no warm clothing. You are small and not very strong and have never been away from home before and, Chime, there is nothing *out* here! Nothing but monsters and—and—"

"Ghosts?" asked the ghost plaintively. "Say, Chime, I'm with him. Let's just go back to Shambala now and you can get living help instead of just an old haunt like me. I can crawl into the next available baby—"

She drew the last word out so that Mike felt that if she had had a physical mouth, it would have been watering with longing.

"I'm sorry, Meekay, and you too, ghost, but it's not as if I know the way home already," Chime told them. "I can't see the mountains any more than you can, and even if I could, as you keep pointing out, Meekay, we have nothing to help us survive the trip through the mountains and back home. If we try to go back into the lake, I think the whirlpool will spit us up again, if the lake monster lets us get that far. That is a very special kind of lake monster, I think. So if we need help, it only makes sense to go find more people who can at least give us provisions for the trip, don't you think? Since we are going to help them too, they should be glad to. Come on now, we need to move while there is enough light."

"But Chime Cincinnati," Mike said, "how will we lead them to Shambala if we don't know the way either?"

"Oh, I expect when the proper time comes, I'll be able to find the way. But meanwhile . . . " She kept walking.

The ghost shrugged at Mike as if to say, "What can you do with someone like that?" and wafted after her.

(HAPTER
X

Chime led them down the beach and up a path worn deep in rock. She thought this might have been a hermitage once, or the site of pilgrimages. No beings living or dead save themselves polished these stones now, however. Once, a squirrel-shaped patch of fog crossed their path; once, a deer that even had a bit of color to it. Then abruptly the path ended in a pile of rock through which leaked a stream feeding into the lake.

"Perhaps it is time for you to guide us now, ghost," Chime said.

"Sure, but I haven't exactly made this trip by paths before, you know. These days I'm more of an as-the-crow-flies kind of girl."

"Chime Cincinnati, I don't think it's a good idea for us to follow her," Mike cautioned. "After all, she did try to kill us—"

"Sheesh! You really hold a grudge, don't you, bub?" the ghost asked.

"And we don't know anything about her," Mike concluded. "Including where she's from, who her family are, how she got here, or *anything*."

"Of course, Meekay, you are right," Chime said. He could hardly believe his ears. Was she actually going to *listen* to him? "Ghost, I apologize. I am Chime Cincinnati, born of the union of Pema born of the union of the guardians Tsering and Samdup. My father is the former Colonel George Washington Merridew—his father was an astronaut, I think, or maybe it was his grandfather. He doesn't talk about it much. Or his mother. This is my friend and, er, protector—Meekay."

"Mike," Mike corrected. "I'm Mike, son of Viveka Vanachek, who was the daughter of Peace Vanachek and the granddaughter of Viveka and Ananda, all of them from America. My father is Lobsang Taring, who was born long ago in Shambala."

The ghost hovered in front of them, sitting cross-legged three feet above the ground with her chin resting on the heel of her hand. "Uh-huh. Great. Why does she," she pointed to Chime, "always talk like her words ought to be written in calligraphy or decorated with Celtic knots or something?"

"Because she's the Terton and she's a bodhisattva and she's lived a lot of other lives and in the last one she was an old lady, what's it to you?" Mike said, glaring into the rock through the bottomless blue eyes.

"Also," Chime said mildly, "perhaps because I read and study a great deal, I have adopted the diction of my books rather than that of my current peers. But that is of no consequence. Please tell us about yourself."

"I'm Antoinette Marie Adair of the Dallas Adairs, but folks call me Toni-Marie. My great-great-great-grandfather was one of the leading figures in the environmental revolution, and his daughter, my great-great-maiden aunt, was the inventor of the reactor recycler—you know, the process that recycles nuclear waste? Sure could use him around here now, I guess. My daddy carried on the family business, fighting fires."

"We are pleased to meet you, Toni-Marie," Chime told her. "How did you come to be here?"

"Beats me. Like I was telling your buddy Mike here, one minute my boyfriend Richie and I were cruising the South China Sea enjoying the fireworks from the war on the land, and the next minute, *blooey!* I guess maybe we were literally blown to kingdom come."

"So you couldn't just watch the war from a distance after all, could you?" Mike chided.

"Hey, it wasn't like that. Richie wanted me to see this part of the world because he was into the religion and had traveled over here in the places where it wasn't so dangerous. We were going to get married and it was a big part of his life he wanted me to know about. I'm really going to miss him. And my family. You guys didn't hear anything about what happened in North America, did you?"

"No," Chime said, "but maybe when you lead us to other living beings they will have heard something."

"That's right. I keep forgetting they'll talk to you. Most of them just get freaked out about us ghosts."

"I wonder why," Mike said, resorting to sarcasm as his only chance to get a word of sanity in between these two bizarre females.

Toni-Marie led them around the rock slide and a little to the east of it. They walked silently for some time, Chime lost in thought and Mike trying to keep alert for any possible danger. He no longer seriously mistrusted Toni-Marie, but she *had* said there were many other ghosts.

In time they came to a place where at least a few bushes, weeds, reeds, and young trees had begun to grow. Mike was troubled, however, that he had not yet been able to see the sun.

When they got to where the ghost was leading them, he understood why. The sun had not climbed as high as they were yet. The ghost drifted along before them, her shape becoming more and more real all the time, a young blond woman with a graceful step even if she hadn't been gliding. He could see the knitted stitches in the cable-knit sweater she wore like a cape around her shoulders.

Toni-Marie saw him staring at her clothing and laughed, "Not exactly a traditional winding sheet or grave shroud, but much less corny

than those long filmy negligees you always see girl ghosts decked out
in on the holovids. And it's a hell of a lot better than being consigned
to eternity in my wet suit, flippers, and goggles, which is what I had
on just before I changed."

With that she glided out before them, looked down, then said,
"Okay, here we are. You guys stop right there. Now look down."

They did, and Mike momentarily felt a little sick with vertigo.
Spread out below them was not just a valley, but other mountains, their
tops covered with snow and cloud. The sun was below them too, not
yet high enough in the sky to reach the peak that cupped the lake from
which they had emerged. The mountains that cupped Kalapa must then
be in the other direction, higher even than this great peak.

Mike gulped.

"Pretty impressive, eh?" Toni-Marie asked. "That flat part way off
in the distance is the central plateau of Tibet. Over that way somewhere
is Pakistan and India, and over there someplace is China. There's a pair
of beings on our way down out of these mountains, but they're not all
that interesting to ghosts and not that hospitable, though they might
be to you. They're what you might call a real odd couple." She grinned.
"You'll see what I mean. There's a few odd people hidden underground,
most of them guys in bunkers. One older ghost we talked to said the
women mostly didn't survive—there was some sex initially, and childbirth, but the babies were abnormal and the mothers died having them.
There's one valley pretty close by that we all know must have lots of
people, but no ghost who goes there—and a lot of them do—is ever
seen again. You'd think if they all got bodies, some of them would
come out again—but nope. One or two places Richie and I checked
out did have people of both sexes, but they weren't having babies
anymore. I know it's dangerous, but all this time with nothin' to do—
you'd think in spite of everything, people would be breeding like rabbits.
Sometimes ghosts would go down to those people and like, get them
excited, to try to stir something up, but they've gotten real cautious."

"Did you ever do that?" Mike asked, fascinated.

"Well, I could never get at most of the living people still around
here, but yeah, I tried it once."

Mike was impressed. Toni-Marie might be dead and might be a

little casual about the lines between life and death, but she had been a real person too, had traveled the world, had been in love, and had even tried to seduce her way out of her predicament. She was pretty too. The ghost was turning out to be more interesting than most of the living girls he knew. "So when you did you were being like what they call a succubus in the mythology books?"

"I was being what they called anxious for those icebergs to get it on and make babies for me to come back as so I could have a life again," she said. "But I imagine the people we, uh, tried to persuade would have thought of it as kind of like that old incubus and succubus legend. And it made Richie jealous, so I didn't do it again. That was about the time we figured it was too crazy down there and headed for high ground."

CHAPTER XI

They walked for several hours down the narrow, winding path leading to the lower slopes and flood plains. Chime felt a few misgivings about how the journey had begun so far. Toni-Marie was not a bad sort of ghost, once you got to know her, but it just seemed to her that a Tibetan ghost—preferably some ancient hermit or lama—would have been more fitting. Of course, Toni-Marie might actually be a disguised Dakini, a Buddhist angel, but somehow Chime doubted it. Chime's true self had not fully informed her present body what to expect, but she had hoped for something a little more traditional, a bit more like someone out of the books of wisdom and the tapestries Lobsang Taring dug up. Something she could recognize.

But if the company wasn't particularly awe-inspiring, the scenery was. Peaks rising like stalagmites from the land below, ribbons of shining black, blue, and opal-colored water, some red-tinged or orange, gems of alpine lakes spilling waterfalls down the jagged teeth of the mountains. Flood plains vast and sluggish as a huge snake, pocked with craters, were still blackened in patches miles wide after more than two decades. In other places pieces of mountains had been blown away, passes closed, new passes fractured in the rock, and gouges scored both flatlands and mountains where rivers had been torn from their channels, lakes evaporated in beds, towns obliterated from the face of the earth.

Of course, not all of this could be blamed on the ultimate nuclear disaster. A lot of it had been happening since the mid-twentieth century. Rather than heeding the suggestion of the fourteenth Dalai Lama that Tibet be used as a peace zone and a great international wildlife refuge and park, China had continued her depredations in the country until the early twenty-first century, when several countries began using Tibet not as a peace zone but as a battleground. Here the People's Republic of China, the Soviet Republics, and India had launched strikes at each other in an attempt to gain hegemony, maintain their borders, or affect the balance of power, while the North American–Canadian Allied Forces sent troops and weapons to all sides in order to be sure that no one side ever gained enough of a tactical edge to actually win, and thereby stop, the war.

Some of this she intuited with the help of her former self, some of it was part of her reading, some of it came from the stories of the older people in Kalapa. Because time was necessarily blurred in Kalapa, it was hard to put those stories told by the elders into proper sequence here.

As she tried to place her bare feet in the most worn and least rocky places in the path, it occurred to Chime that there was no snow on this peak, so much higher than others below it. Could it be that the hot springs within the peak kept the ground too warm to hold snow? Or was it simply magic? She wished her former self would explain more of the mysteries.

Mike diligently followed Toni-Marie, watching for slide areas, rocks along the trail, and sinking spots the ghost merely floated over. Chime was content to follow behind him, thinking her own thoughts and trying to absorb and analyze little flashes of memory that came back to her when she viewed different aspects of the scene below. She looked off to the side and down often, and the rest of the time was staring either at the trail or at a spot in the small of Mike's back, just above his rear. So she was not prepared when she turned her eyes back from the view below to fasten them again on Mike's back only to find that it had disappeared behind a thick, churning fog that had not been there a moment before.

Tendrils of the fog reached for her, scooping her with beckoning dankness into an atmosphere so thick that she couldn't see her hands in front of her face.

This fog was extremely suspect. "Toni-Marie?" she called into it, at the same time trying to sense the ghost and discern if she was once more playing deadly tricks.

Toni-Marie didn't answer; however, Chime was able to see that within the fog and creating it was a mob of ghosts, milling about on the mountainside, pushing and shoving, some carrying things on their backs, others armed with the ghosts of weapons. One spirit shinnied up her pant leg and another probed her sleeve and still another dove down her collar. She stood perfectly still. Ahead of her she heard Mike swearing and yelling for her and for Toni-Marie.

"O spirits wandering the bardo," she said, addressing the ghosts, which seemed like the thing to do. "I know how you hunger to be housed once more in flesh, and we are here to help you, but we cannot do it if you won't allow us to pass."

These ghosts, however, were not reasonable. The day that had been warm as she moved down the sunlit path was now windy and bitter cold. "Please," she said, elbowing her way through a large soldier-ghost. "You must excuse us now. Please drift aside. This trail is quite narrow, and our bodies broken to bits will be of no use to you. Excuse me, please. Coming through."

"Toni-Marie!" Mike cried, swinging his arms and batting at the ghosts so hard Chime feared he would overbalance and fall off the mountain. "Toni-Marie, tell them to leave us alone."

A voice called back faintly from the babble that might have been the wind blowing through the rocks but wasn't. "Me and whose army?"

There was a burnt smell about these ghosts, as if all the swirling clouds were ash. Chime wondered if perhaps their bodies *were* ash, volcanic ash, radioactive ash. At any rate, they tickled through her clothes and pressed close to her eyes and tried to get into her nostrils and ears. She wanted to bat at them as Mike was doing, but the older part of herself restrained her and she found herself on the verge of tears instead. She thought of how sad and frightened they must have been to be taken from the earth so suddenly. In their day there was no spiritual preparation, no teachings to help them find their way.

She tried to shuffle her way toward Mike's voice. "Dammit! Get out of my—ptui—" He spat and coughed ash.

Their voices were such a babble. "Spirits, let us pass. We clearly are not vehicles for you, as our bodies are still inhabited," Chime said.

"Not by you, not for long," the voice of a minor rock slide snickered.

"You think you're so superior, walking around in bodies," gabbled the pebbles underfoot.

"We'll show you," hissed the wind. "We'll drive your fancy bodies off the mountain."

"Ghosts own the earth! Only ghosts!" Another cold gust roared as it tugged Chime sideways, away from the mountain.

She shuffled farther forward, one hand stretched out to touch the mountainside, one forward searching for Mike. Her whole body was bent forward to counter the onslaught of the ashen ghosts, and she had begun coughing as they invaded her respiratory passages.

"Meekay!" she shouted, choked on his name and at the same time stubbed her foot on a stone and fell forward, cracking a shin. "Meekay!" she screamed again, and wanted to cry to him for help, but her mouth was filled with ash, and stones rained down on her head. She rolled to her side to avoid them and found the top part of her body leaning out over nothing. The ash swirled above her and around her face, but her eyes could see through the thin layer of ghost and ash to the valley yawning below.

Mike called back to her—her name, she thought, but his voice too was thickened and distorted by a mouthful of ashy spirit. And then, abruptly, it choked off as if he had had the breath knocked out of him.

"Meekay!" she cried once more, miserably. Now she was weeping both from physical irritation and from a realization of what the condition of the world meant personally to her. If she died here, the Terton for the first time would be competing with more ghosts than the world had ever before held. How could she reincarnate and complete her task? Naturally, she could eschew rebirth and be transmitted straight to Nirvana if she wanted, but what about her mission, what about Shambala, what about poor Meekay? Her precipitous actions had gotten him into this.

Why oh why had the Terton chosen such a frail and unworthy vessel as herself to carry out such critical work? And from within her, her own voice answered, "Any vessel is strong and worthy when filled with calmness, purpose, and—oh yes, the correct terminology."

Chime's mouth opened, and from it issued a word she hadn't remembered until just then.

"Kalagiya!" she yelled at the top of her lungs, the magic word that she had encountered once in her reading. Use of this word was supposedly one of the advantages accruing to those born in Shambala. It was supposed to guarantee them help.

Mike screamed as if in answer and then grunted again, a surprised exclamation of a grunt. From the corner of her eye Chime saw a brilliant white flash of light, then heard running steps followed by a clear, startled shriek.

For that moment she had hung with her upper half suspended over the gorge, but as she twisted to try to see Mike, she threw herself off balance, her arms flailing the air, and she began to topple forward.

Abruptly, another flash of light dazzled her eyes and a large, warm, fur-clad arm caught her around the middle, while something was passed before her face.

She was hoisted into the air and carried into a place from which she perceived, as the ghost ash blew away from her nostrils, an extremely gamy odor.

Her face, numb from the cold, began to warm with icy prickles as it rested against her rescuer's warm coat. She twisted it away to speak to him. "Meekay, my friend, is he safe?"

A huge mouth with an upper lip split under the nose parted to grin with bright, sharp teeth. Lips, nose, cheeks and ears, jowls, scalp, everything on the head and face was covered by short white fur. Perhaps the term "safe" was not exactly applicable in this case.

CHAPTER XII

"Yetis are not, of course, vegetarians, no matter how much the Buddhists of old liked to think so. How could they be? The snow-covered mountains they were said to frequent are bare of any vegetation most of the year."

The yeti sat across the fire from them, cross-legged. Mike thought its face was less apelike, as he'd been led to believe by his books, and more like that of a large cat. The white fur around the face was definitely a ruff, though the ears were small and close to the head, and the nose was closer to the face than that of many of the big cats. The face was definitely a face, not a muzzle and eyes, but still there was a catty look about the creature. Even its big hands and feet were pawlike at the palms, and the yeti could retract its claws, as it did now, and presumably as it had done when its human-looking footprints were sited so many times in the past. It also would have had to retract its claws when it clicked the flash on the camera still dangling around its neck. But the claws would be very useful for climbing—or fighting anything but ghosts. Its tail appeared to be more useful for balance than gripping, and on hearing itself discussed, the yeti waved the tail gently back and forth against its knee.

"And yetis are quite large, as you can see. Thank goodness we found so much canned Spam."

Mike turned his attention back to the speaker, a short, wiry woman with white hair that looked as if it had been cut with an army knife, which it undoubtedly had. He'd been deposited with her in this cavern when the yeti went back to get Chime away from the ghosts.

"Ma'am?" Mike asked, looking at her closely.

"Yes, young man?"

"Are you alive? I mean, really alive?"

"I suppose that depends upon your definition of alive, but my vital signs have not yet ceased to function, if that's what you mean." She thought for a moment. "I believe I am, however, quite blind. Fortunately, although I haven't had much need for that camera for its original purpose in many years, Vajra has discovered that it does an admirable job of dissolving the physical emanations of the dead who insist in loitering around our entranceway. Fortunately, those long-lasting batteries were quite as good as their advertisements claim, and kept well frozen. Vajra had seen me work the camera many times before the world's unfortunate mishap with the missiles."

The yeti darkened the doorway, depositing Chime beside Mike. Chime looked back up at the creature as if she couldn't believe her eyes. Mike understood the sentiment.

The old lady said, "Welcome, child. Thank you, Vajra."

The yeti rumbled deep in its throat in response. It narrowed its eyes slowly into a blink and opened them again twice, the light bouncing off them as if they were diamonds, and settled down beside her.

"Where did the Spam come from?" Chime asked.

"Oh, that. Military stockpile. The soldiers were always squirreling things away all over the country."

While she spoke, a rattling and moaning arose from the entrance of the cave. Mike shivered, knowing what the wind carried. "The ghosts are trying to get into your cave," he said.

"So I hear. Vajra, dear, will you please be so kind as to shake out the spirit trap?" She clucked disapprovingly. "I'm afraid that after that mob scene today it may have become clogged. They're more of an inconvenience than anything, always trying to get at you while you sleep. They usually don't venture up here in such numbers anymore. We're well-defended by our spirit traps, and I suppose we're both too old to interest them now, though no one really knows how long yetis live. We haven't encountered other *living* human beings up this high, although Vajra has met them all across Tibet, India, and China when he goes out foraging. Still, very few of the living have ventured above-ground. Afraid of radiation, you know. You young people are quite a novelty for the resident spirit world."

Vajra hefted a framework of Spam cans stacked and strung together with pieces of colored yarn and towed it past the fire and to the entrance of the cave. After an interlude of more rattling and howling from that direction, Vajra reappeared, carrying another device, this one colored strings on a framework of plastic rings strung together with metal wire.

"Kindly allow the young man to inspect our defenses, Vajra," the woman said. To Mike and Chime she added, "These are our spirit traps. Our predecessor also had the foresight to provide us with the prototype. They were once favored by ethnic Tibetans for filtering out moribund influences."

"You must have been here a very long time, Auntie," Chime said, calling the woman by the Kalapan honorific for senior females. It was polite to call all older women Auntie, older men Uncle, unless there was some more appropriate specific bond of kinship. Even if you didn't think the person was related to you, what with reincarnation and the plural unions formed to keep the gene pool healthy, you never knew. If you weren't related now, wait a year or two.

"Oh my, yes. I hate to think how long ago. I came to this place to study the yeti for my graduate degree at the University of Lhasa. Vajra has showed me a great deal about this region. I am Dr. Locana Hoa Chung, by the way. What are your names?"

"I am Mike and this is Chime Cincinnati," Mike answered, bracing himself for all the questions about how they came to be wandering around in the mountains.

The questions never came. Dr. Chung merely nodded politely and said, "We are pleased that you have come." Mike thought for some reason that she might add "at last," but she didn't.

"I understand now how, by employing the wisdom of others, you have defended yourself from ghosts," Chime said slowly. "But how have you avoided radiation sickness?"

"That's rather an odd story actually. This cave seems to be part of an underground network. I have no idea how far it goes, though Vajra uses it freely. I'm sure that had I been a paleologist I'd have been thrilled. But actually, I've always been a wee bit claustrophobic. Vajra had been living here since the rest of his family was slain by the Chinese trying to build a road through the mountains. Vajra's family had been living in another cave, and the road-building crew dynamited the mountain, collapsing the cave on his family. He took me to the site and showed me before—well, before I was blinded."

"How did that happen?" Mike asked, a little absently. He was watching Vajra's tail, wondering how he kept it from freezing off during very cold weather, and thinking that its graceful waving looked almost as if Vajra had a third arm, a conservative version of those statues of deities in the books Chime was always studying.

"Oh, child, you know." She waved her hand to encompass everything in the cave and out. "When the world ended. I watched the missiles cross the sky and the fireballs go up—the ones in the directions of Lhasa and Katmandu were very remote, and I didn't understand at first what I was watching. But the fireballs across the Indian-Pakistani border were much closer and I shouldn't have been watching them directly. My fault. I should have realized. I should have paid better attention. Vajra slept through the whole thing. Fortunately for me, he found me sitting in the mouth of the cave and pulled me in before the aftershocks and radiation storms hit. We already had ample supplies Vajra took from the soldiers' stockpiles. I suppose if any of the soldiers found us they would have wanted to shoot me as a spy, although whose spy it would be difficult to say, given the complexion of international politics as it was then. Vajra rolled stones in front of the entrance as his people have always done to escape detection, and we stayed below for quite some time. There's an underground spring here too. So all in all we avoided the radiation by staying isolated belowground until the last few years. It's all the same to me, of course, now that I'm blind, but Vajra seemed to feel it was safe for us to be closer to the surface now. He has very good instincts about most things."

"Maybe you could come home with—" Mike began, but Chime kicked his knee with her bare toe. "That is," he added, "if we had a home to go to and weren't lost from it anyway. And besides," he cast a sidelong glance at Chime, "we have to find the other people left alive in the world, though I don't see how we're supposed to find anyone on foot with no shoes or food, especially if we keep having to fight off ghosts all the time."

"I'm sure we can find some boots for you, and coats, before Vajra leads you below. And I am so sorry. I forget my manners. I hope you are fond of Spam?"

They slept that night in a pile of old sleeping bags redolent of yeti, but that was not such a bad smell. The whole cave smelled like that, a ripe, warm smell, with the sharp scent of the fire an integral part of it. Or was it that the ashes of the ghosts had not been fully cleaned from their nostrils?

Mike thought that he would fall asleep in a moment, but he lay awake after the fire had gone out and Vajra crawled away to a ledge he liked to sleep on while the old lady disappeared into a corner.

"Chime?"

"Hmm?"

"Doesn't this all seem too convenient to you? I mean, if Vajra hadn't really picked me up and hauled me in here, and if I wasn't this very minute full of Spam, I'd think I was dreaming. But I never heard of anyone dreaming about Spam before. I also was thinking maybe Vajra and Dr. Chung might be ghosts themselves, but I don't think so, do you?"

"No, Meekay. I think they are real. And they weren't convenient. They were really necessary. I am a little surprised at the form they took, however."

"Huh?"

"I never expected her to be a professor or him to appear as a yeti. It just never occurred to me."

"What do you mean?"

"Didn't you notice their names? Oh, Meekay, if only you had studied the great teachings instead of colored fairy tales, Robert Louis Stevenson, and the Hardy Boys."

"There's nothing wrong with the Hardy Boys," he protested, but she didn't answer except to give a little snort. So he lay there wondering what names she'd meant. Vajra was as good a name for a yeti as any, he supposed. A vajra was one of the old Tibetan symbols, he knew that much. It was supposed to be made from a lightning bolt or something. He had wanted to ask more questions, but although the old lady and the yeti had been very nice, something about them, about the things Dr. Chung had not talked about—like where she was from and who her family were—made him feel that it would have been impolite and perhaps unwise to pry. The yeti and the old woman had saved their lives. That was all he had to know about them for now.

CHAPTER XIII

Mike clumped along behind Vajra in a pair of previously owned army boots that smelled so strongly of their former occupant, after all these years, that they might as well have contained that soldier's ghost. The coat was nice, though, a parka of indestructible machine-made material rather than fabric hand-spun and woven or knitted, as was most of the fabric in Kalapa. The best items were socks, a hat, and mittens spun and knitted from Vajra's fur.

"Well, he does *shed* a great deal in the springtime," Dr. Chung had told them, "And one has to do something or we'd be smothered by a ceiling-high accumulation of the stuff. It spins very nicely. And I find knitting soothing, now that reading and writing are no longer possible for me and I have no other source of entertainment. Of course, I'm afraid these things come only in my size and that I sometimes make errors, but they should keep you warm enough."

Right now the socks were on Mike's feet, padding out the army boots. The yeti scent vied for dominance with the stench from the boots.

He and Chime each carried a smaller version of the spirit trap. Instead of the brightly colored yarns like those strung across the old traps, these were primarily Vajra-white, olive drab, blue, and sometimes dark red or brown. Vajra also wore the camera around his neck.

"I'm afraid we've pretty well relocated most of the military stores close by," Dr. Chung had told them that morning. "But Vajra will show you how to spot them and will also show you where the bunkers are. Some of them, especially the ones where native Tibetans and Chinese hid, put out food for him once the worst of the blast was over, and he tried to contact them to see if there was anything we could do for them. You can see from the fact that they are willing to share something so precious as food the position the yeti holds in their mythology and belief systems, despite the years under the thumb of the Red government and all the wars."

Chime had nodded wisely. "In difficult times, people fall back on old beliefs," she said, and this made Mike feel uneasy again. Now he could hear the older self inside her, the old woman she would become, should they survive this. No, that was wrong, the older self was a past self, not a future self. Although knowing one of them would *have* a future self was reassuring, if somewhat confusing. Although he had lived in Shambala all his life, Mike had never had the intricacies of incarnations brought to his attention in such a personal manner. His father talked of such things, so Mike knew they were true, but young people were by and large encouraged to follow their own courses of study. Many of the ethnic Tibetans who had originally taken shelter in Kalapa resented the fact that children were not automatically schooled in Buddhism. Mike's father, who was more learned than anyone else in the city, having once been a lama himself, offered to tutor the children of interested parties in the fundamentals of Buddhism and to help them locate the proper books from the library. However, he pointed out that no great teachers were left in Kalapa, all of them having died in the avalanche, and the great lamas of Tibet had all been banished or killed by the Chinese conquerors long ago.

Chime was one who read all of those books. Mike began to wish he had paid more attention to that sort of reading, but like many others, he found the old books in the ancient Tibetan language difficult to interpret and time-consuming to translate from the Tibetan spoken in camp. From the time she was an infant, Chime had gravitated toward those books and could be found among them part of every day. She was always trying to talk about her readings, and spoke of compassion a lot, which was one reason he was so angry with her over what she said about Nyima's baby. She still hadn't explained all that business. Why did she think the names of Dr. Chung and the yeti were significant? What was the word she had cried while he was being pushed off the mountain by the smoky ghosts?

They were in this together now, and it was only fair that if she knew more than he did, she could at least fill him in on it. On the other hand, there were times when he felt he would just as soon not know.

They reached the foot of the mountain by mid-morning, and by mid-afternoon were walking along another ridge overlooking a valley. Vajra pointed with his chin to a spot beside a small brown stream. A small group of people stood there around a kneeling woman. Her hands seemed to be bound. One man, Chinese from the look of him, pointed down at the woman, and a second man raised a knife above her head. The knife came down twice, wielded with great force by the second man, and the woman's head separated from her body. Her executioner held it aloft by its hair. Another man reached for it, then suddenly both men turned and stared—eyelids stretched to their fullest, and eyes protruding as if to touch something that their visual function could not make their brains believe—in the direction of Mike, Chime, and Vajra. Others were staring, just as intently, in other directions. The head of the murdered woman had been turned in their direction, its eyes clenched in expectation of death, its bloody lips clamped grimly together. Suddenly the head's eyes flew open too, still full of the memory of pain, to stare with horror at something that transcended their own death, and the mouth opened in a silent scream.

Mike stared back at the head for a moment, then at Chime—who had begun murmuring rhythmically to herself—and at Vajra, who shrugged. When he turned around again, both the executed woman and her killers were gone.

Chime stopped murmuring and Mike saw that her face was wet. She wiped her nose on her jacket sleeve and asked Vajra, "Was that how it was for you too at the end of the world?"

Vajra grunted once and ran ahead of them. Mike, his skin feeling like the surface of the sacred lake on a windy day, fell behind long enough to foul his teeth with the remains of his undigested breakfast.

They continued walking down that valley and into the ridge between two mountains. Oddly enough, the ridge was paved with stone, almost as smooth as a road, except that the stones showed signs of having been carved in the familiar graceful swoops and lines that spelled out the five sacred syllables—*om mani padme hum*—along their flat sides.

"Mani stones," he said to Chime, to hear the sound of his own voice above the wind as much as anything. The wind was raw this morning, its edge sharp and unfriendly. "I suppose they were part of a mountain shrine, and when the fires burned, they were fused into the mountain like this." She nodded, knelt and touched the stones, splaying her fingers across the carving. "I guess the prayer flags probably burned up," he said.

She said nothing. He supposed she was meditating, but he wished she'd wait until they got somewhere where he had something else to occupy him. He did not much care for this outside world. Below them stretched another valley, bleak and lonely, and he walked and walked. The mountains hid the wan sun very early in the day, and they made it as far as the next ridge before the darkness overtook them.

The yeti stepped out from behind a boulder just in front of them and grinned a fang-filled grin that made Mike hope he still had plenty of Spam to share.

Vajra did not stay for supper, however. He gestured, drawing them around the corner, and nodded downward. A metal cup and a piece of foil paper lay in the middle of this wilderness. Vajra motioned the two of them to be quiet and stand aside. In a moment a chunk of rock slid aside and a small pale hand appeared, like that of the lady in the lake if she had had fingers like little white worms. Instead of bringing a sword, this hand held another mug. Mike looked back to Vajra to see what to do, but the yeti had disappeared.

The hand reached up and snatched away the first mug, leaving another one full of some milky-looking substance, then disappeared and returned again with a flat cake which it placed on the plate before withdrawing.

"Wait," Chime said, standing beside the hole. "We want to talk to you."

"Go away, spooks," a crackly voice whispered from below. "Take this and go."

"We're alive," Chime said. "And we've come to help you."

"Help me out of my food, you mean. Help me get the sore-sickness. Help me out of body and soul. Pa told me what spooks'll do if you let 'em come close."

"Please," Chime said. "We haven't come to take anything away. We've come to help you."

"Right," the voice wheezed. Mike was inclined to agree with the voice. While Chime had apparently embarked on this mission of hers to help others, she didn't have a lot of resources to offer. Her plan to save others and take them back to Shambala depended on being able to return there themselves, which was not going to be all that simple. On the whole, he thought the voice had a point.

"We won't eat your food," Chime promised. "We have plenty of food."

"I'll bet you do. Everyone knows if you eat food from up there, you get the sore-sickness, grow eight arms and die."

"No," Chime promised. "This is *good* food. Really. And we aren't mutants and we're not dead."

Not yet anyway, Mike thought.

The voice didn't answer this time. The hole closed shut and they were left standing outside in the dark with the empty dishes.

The entire valley was barren of animals or plants—nothing but fused rock, actually, although tiny lichens did cling to the stones near the entrance to the underground home of the crackly voice.

"Chime, I think maybe we should find someone who wants our help. If we don't go away, these people might kill us," Mike said.

"I think that's a strong possibility no matter what we do," Chime said. "I would like more Spam. How about you?"

Mike agreed, and they sat there for some time, chewing thoughtfully. It seemed to Mike that this might be a good time to broach his questions. "What was that word you used back on the mountain when the ghosts were after us?" he asked her.

Her dark face blended in with the night except for highlights that sheened it along her cheeks, chin, and forehead, the dance of her eyes and the flash of her teeth. "That word was our birthright, Meekay. Something no one else can claim right now. I am sure I have read it in my studies, but honestly, it just came to me. My former self enlightened me in our moment of need. It is the word that summons aid from Shambala for true pilgrims. Of course," she said, considering, "most pilgrimages have been carried out to *find* Shambala, not to leave it, but as you and I are from there, it worked just as well. I suppose my former selves have used it occasionally in the past."

"Well, I'm glad they let you in on it before it was too late. I don't suppose they've told you where we are exactly or how we can get back home, have they?"

"Not exactly," she admitted. "But I have some clues that the world has altered on more than one plane."

No moon shone overhead, but streaks of starlight striped the sky, stars falling in a meteor shower. Mike wondered what the sky had been like before the end, when airplanes and satellites crowded the skies.

"More than one plane, yes," he said, his eyes still turned upward.

"What was metaphysical is manifesting itself physically."

"For instance?" Mike asked.

"Well, the lake serpent. In the literature, samsara, the cycle of death and rebirth, is personified as a great serpent. Perhaps the serpent was merely a mutated eel, but it was guarding the entrance to an underworld. There was bright blue light in the sky, and smoky white light—these things are mentioned in the literature as being things one encounters going through the bardo, the Isles of the Dead. You and I are not dead, and yet we are seeing many things that dead people see. I think that perhaps since so much of the world is now dead, many features of the bardo are manifesting themselves here in the deadness of the physical world. Do you see?"

"I think so. You mean that because there's been so much death, the afterworld has sort of settled down over the real world now?"

"Both worlds are real, Meekay."

"I guess so. But how about the yeti and Dr. Chung?" he asked. "What did you mean when you said something about their names?"

"Vajrasattva-Aksobhya, the thunderbolt jewel who destroys all other weapons and jewels, is also one of the helpful beings one meets going through the bardo, one of the ones who tries to direct you toward enlightenment. His consort is Buddha-Locana, the Buddha-Eye. Dr. Chung's first name is Locana."

"Yes, but she can't be any kind of an eye. She's blind."

"Mike, if you had only read a little in the teachings, you'd know that there are five kinds of eyes, the physical or bodily eye, the Buddha eye, the dharma eye, the wisdom eye, and the heavenly eye. The Buddha eye is a female principle. Through it can be discerned the ultimate nature of reality—that is, what is real, what is illusion. For instance," her eyes held his meaningfully, "if what had been considered abstract images and metaphors suddenly came into physical form, then the nature of reality would be shifting, fluid."

"Oh," he said, thinking it over and still finding it a little tough to grasp that symbols might come to life or spiritual entities seen only by the dead would suddenly appear to living people as mutant lake monsters, elderly Ph.D.'s, and yetis. "Maybe. Don't you think maybe you might be reading a lot into things, though? If these, like, gods are walking the earth now, where were they when the earth needed them?"

Chime sighed. "You are very much of this world, Mike. A very practical and grounded person. But I sometimes think it will take you many more lives to reach enlightenment."

"Fine," he said. "But I'm not ready to start other lives right now. I've just gotten started with this one, and it seems to me that if we go around treating normal—well, you know, maybe not normal, but real people—as if they were holy symbols or something, we could be not dealing with what's right here, might miss something and end up another one of these damn ghosts. They seem to think being alive has a lot of value, and I'd say they were in a position to know."

Chime shook her head slowly and smiled her grandmotherly, indulgent smile.

Mike ignored it and said, "Furthermore, I think we'd better post guard tonight to keep the ghosts from trying to take us over while we sleep, or probably more to the point, to keep whoever lives down there from coming up and finishing us off for our food."

"A worthy, if cynical idea," she said. "I will be happy to take the first watch. I have some thinking to do."

She didn't prove to be much of a guard. Mike's mind leaped from a confused dream of sea serpents and winged fairy creatures to complete alertness as the sound of the fairy hill opening to swallow the sea creature jerked him awake. Chime was sitting in her lotus position, eyes closed, hands resting on knees with thumbs and forefingers touching, meditating.

A space in the earth opened, and the rock that concealed the opening was a full two feet from where it had been. Mike shifted only slightly, still pretending to be asleep. The voice had been shy before. He wanted to see what its owner was up to before scaring it away, although it was very nearly scaring him into grabbing Chime and running. His heart thudded against the ground so loudly, he thought that if there were other people inside the underground dwelling, they must think he was beating a drum on top of them.

The small pale hand with its wormlike fingers reached up out of the hole and was soon joined by another such hand, then the top of a dirty, thatch-haired head and a pair of dark eyes.

Mike's own hand was lying near the hole, and he inched it forward. The slightly popped dark eyes stared at Chime and at Mike's face and paid no attention to Mike's apparently sleeping hand.

The worm-fingered hands braced on the side of the hole and more of the face showed, a face of the same racial mixture as his own, Caucasian-Amerasian one. The American influence on this set of features gave it slack cheeks and a lumpy nose.

Chime, without changing position or opening her eyes said, "Come close. We are no danger to you."

The person—through his slitted eyes Mike still couldn't see if it was male or female—retreated down the hole for a moment or two then peeked back up.

"Come. Really, it's all right. We've come to help you."

"Pa's sleeping. Give me the food now," the voice said. Now that it was aboveground, it still sounded raspy and dry, but not as if it belonged to an old person.

"Yes, certainly. There's some left. Come. Tell me who you are, how long you have been here."

"Always," the scruffy person said. The head raised to show a rounded chin and then an extremely thin sweater covering skinny shoulders, sagging breasts, and a bony rib cage. Female, then.

"My name is Chime—"

"Chim-mee." A leg which did not seem capable of supporting even the insignificant weight of its owner swung up out of the hole like a spider leg, soon followed by another one. The woman squatted beside the hole and stared at them. An awful stench came from her body. She smelled much deader than the ghosts.

"And you are?"

"I am."

"No, I mean, what's your name?"

"Eve," she said. " 'Cause Pa says I'm first woman." Having divulged so much information, she subsided to rocking on her heels and carefully watching the packs of food and supplies.

"There are other women left alive, Eve, and other men too."

"Him?" Eve asked, pointing a white-worm finger at Mike.

"You can wake up now, Meekay," Chime said without looking his way.

Mike drew himself up, trying to look fierce. Chime remained relaxed, but he felt as if he was strung with vibrating springs. Eve kept glancing at him, her pop eyes slightly rolling, even more skittish of him than he was of her.

Chime slowly unfolded from her lotus position and held out her hand to Eve. "We are friends. We have come to help you, Eve. You and your pa. Does he live with you?"

Eve looked fearfully at the hole and nodded several times.

"Would he come out and talk to us?"

"No. Out here you die. You're dead."

"No. No, we're not. Maybe there's some radiation left, but it kills you over a period of years. We're all right for now. Our home is safe. We want to take you there."

"I have to go now," Eve said, looking back into the hole. "Little'un will wake soon. Pa will come."

"He didn't come before," Chime said.

"He don't like feedin' spooks, but you bet he'd like to get his hands on big ol' live'uns like you. If he knows you're live'uns, he'll kill you."

"Why?" Chime asked. "We mean you no harm."

Eve grinned through sharp, broken yellow teeth. Her breath stank. "Naw. Not harm. You mean food." She smacked her lips. Mike was a little surprised at this show of humor, which was what he guessed it was.

"He's welcome to our food. We can take you where there's plenty of food," Chime said.

Mike was not entirely too sure that Eve had meant the father would kill them for the Spam. Her grin and lip smacking had sounded to him as if she thought her father might eat *them*.

She was now staring into the darkness surrounding them. "You can stay up here and not die?" she asked.

"That remains to be seen," Mike said.

"We can where we come from," Chime said. "It's very beautiful there. Grass, trees, flowers, fish, animals—"

Eve waved her hand dismissively. "Oh, yeah. That stuff. I've seen pictures in Pa's books."

"How did you come to be here? How did your pa come to be here?" Chime asked gently. The starlight touched her face with fingers of soft, mysterious light. Mike could not recall ever hearing her speak so gently, not even to the children.

"He came in the war," Eve said. "He is an AmeriCan, you know. And an officer. Intelligence. He worked with my ma's people, for China. When the Indians caught Ma's people, Pa and her got away and came here to live in our grave. She had me. All her people were killed by the Indians."

"Is your mother down there too, then?" Chime asked.

The starlight that stroked Chime's face with such tenderness only deepened the grime and ugliness of Eve's sickly pale skin.

"Have you never seen the sun?" Mike interrupted.

She shrugged. "Sorta. I used to see it when I was little, but I don't remember it very well. Pa says it will burn me."

"What does your mother say?" Chime asked.

"She said she would just be a minute. But she didn't come back for a long time and then there was the loud noises and the grave shook."

"Grave?"

She smiled again through her sharp broken teeth. "Grave-cave, home-sweet-home. There." She nodded at the ground.

Mike told himself that this woman was a victim of ignorance and great tragedy, that she couldn't help the way she looked—probably had no idea that she looked any different from them—that the sinister cast to her eye was the result of being cramped away in what he presumed was a small hole in the ground for most of her life. At least she was willing to talk to them. He told himself he was only cold as they talked because he'd been still so long, sleeping, and he needed to get his circulation going. Still, looking at her ragged teeth and popped rolling eyes, eyes with too much white around them—sanpaku eyes, Auntie Dolma called them, sign of the evil eye in old times, certainly a sign of instability even in modern Shambala—he wished dawn would come and she'd bolt for her hole so they could continue their journey without her.

"Could you convince your father to come out and talk to us too?" Chime asked.

"You said you had food. Food to share?"

"Only if you share yours with us," Mike answered for Chime, feeling that traveling with a compassionate saint had more than its share of liabilities. "We have a long journey and many people to try to save. You can come with us if you want to, but we need to conserve food."

"Pa's sleeping, but when he wakes up I'll ask him," she said.

"Couldn't you wake him?" Chime asked.

The woman's eyes popped wider in alarm. "Oh, no. Don't wake Pa. Not if you don't want a chunk bit out of you. I'll ask later," she said, and popped down the hole.

Mike took Chime by the elbow, raised her to her feet and shone his light on the path again. "Let's get out of here," he said.

"Meekay, this is what we came to this place to do."

"Chime Cincinnati, she as much as said her father looks upon other people as food and punishes her by biting chunks out of her. I may be wrong but I think that such people are part of the reason the elders didn't want us to come outside."

"This is possible. Still, we must try to help as many survivors as we can."

"We'll be able to help more if we don't get killed by the first ones we meet. Come *on*."

He pulled at her, and finally she said, "Oh, very well. But only because I think we can travel faster by ourselves. We can return to help Eve later."

"Much later," he said.

With only the starlight to show them the way, they started up the mountain pass that led to the next valley. The path was not too steep, and they were about a quarter of the way up when they heard the scrape of rock below. They stood in darkness on the side of the mountain while the wind whipped around them, tearing at the spirit catchers each of them still carried, and penetrating their coats.

A torch sprouted from the ground below them, its flickering a fitful jig of shadows and light that lit the cul-de-sac between rock and mountain with dancing demons.

The emergence of Eve's pa was not as slow as hers—he popped out of the cave with a single boost, like a jack-in-the-box—reached into his belt and pulled forth something that gleamed dully in the torchlight.

"Okay, now," he said. "Don't be shy. I can hear you out there. I reckoned when you come by earlier, Eve was talkin' to the ghosts again, but she said you're alive and healthy and invited her for dinner. We haven't seen enough live folks for Eve to learn manners and know to invite y'all down to our place for dinner, but I want you to come on back now and do that little thing. Us survivors should be friendly. Y'all come on back down here an' tell ol' Buzz what's goin' on out there these days."

He picked up the torch and it lit his face with hellish lickings of flame. His eyes were as popped as his daughter's and his mouth gleamed in the torchlight with wetness or possibly grease.

"Th-Thanks, but we need to be going," Mike called down. "We'll return for you on our way back."

"Don't be so hasty, son. It's nighttime now—the monsters will be out." He grinned when he said this, and his teeth looked funny—as if he had a mouthful of little yellow needles. They're filed, Mike thought. Like Queequeg the cannibal's in *Moby Dick*. "They come around here 'cause Evie leaves out food for stuff, no matter what I tell her. You stay out here roamin' around by yourselves, though, you're advertisin' yourselves as a entrée. You come on down to the cave with Eve and me and we'll make you comfy."

The firelight flickered off his eyes, shining and predatory.

"We'll return for you, we promise," Chime called down, and then added slowly and quietly to Mike, "I've known this man before, in another life." Her eyes held Mike's for a long time, there in the darkness. He could feel the presence of the man grinning up at them from below, hear the excited thump of his heart, smell the fetid breath blowing from his mouth, read the terrible thoughts rolling through that head. Mike felt recognition wash over him like cold rain, turning his skin to goose-flesh.

"Chime, Buzz is the name of the man in Mom's diaries, the one who raped her before she came to the camps. He was an AmCan agent for the Chinese." When Mike said it aloud, it didn't sound like enough to provoke such a strong reaction in him, but the recognition of this man as the one who had harmed his mother shook him profoundly. "Isn't it strange for us to meet this particular man here? Like he messed up Mom's life and has waited through the end of the world, and all these years, to get us too?"

"Not so strange when you consider that one meets the same people life after life—though usually they've undergone rebirth in the meantime too. My karma seems to be bound up with this fellow. . . ." She peered down at him, seeming to look as much within herself as outside. "Yes, of course, you're right. He was the one who interrogated your mother. I was there too, as Ama-La. What he told me about her made me interested in her, what he did to her made me want to help her. He was always a very brutal man, but now—" She shuddered and started climbing again.

The man below raised the dull metal object into the torchlight and pointed it in their direction. Mike lifted Chime off the ground, swung her to the other side of him and fell on top of her as a dull thud exploded and something burned past them to strike sparks from the piece of mountainside where they had been standing.

"You ain't goin' nowhere without you come and sample my hospitality," the man said, and fired again. "In fact, I'm real peeved at Eve for not bringin' y'all down while she had you here. We ain't had much company around here, and the girl don't know how to act. Have to beat some manners into her, I reckon."

He started loping up the path toward them, and Mike rolled off Chime and, half dragging her with him, began backing up the hill, his eyes never leaving the man.

In the darkness Mike stumbled finding his footing, but he scrambled backward, keeping hold of Chime.

Another shot thumped into the mountain path which now rose to a steep incline. Mike boosted Chime up and ahead of him, sweat rolling down his face despite the cold.

He knew when the next shot hit him that he had been anticipating it ever since he saw the gun, and realized who Buzz was. At first all he felt was the impact, as if something had run into him hard and knocked him down, and then he felt the breeze at his side, as if half of his torso had been blown away, the warm sticky rush of blood running down his leg, soaking his coat, covering his hands. He sagged against the mountain for the moment, only grunting to himself.

When the hot jaws of burning pain clamped down on him a half a second later, he bit his arm, trying not to scream, not to give away his position. Chime was scampering away now, high ahead of him. A scream would bring her back down. He gathered himself up and drove through the pain as if it was dirt and stone he must dig through, and climbed, feeling blood leave his body every time he lifted his hand for another handhold.

They didn't stop climbing until dawn, when they reached the top of the ridge. Below, a lifeless landscape spread in all directions.

The sun warmed to its metallic, slightly spicy essence the smears of blood staining the rock where Mike had dragged himself along, the bloody fingerprints gripping grainy stone upon which he had braced himself.

He hurt terribly, the ache extending to every pore and every hair on his body. But from somewhere within himself he remembered how to keep functioning through the pain, to remember the mission, and not to betray his companion, though everything else spun dizzily through the lightness in his head. He was incredibly thirsty, as if water could replace the blood he'd lost.

But the part of him that was not focused on his own pain and thirst heard no pursuing sounds, no feet chinking into mountainside, no other scrabble of loose gravel as hands quested for holds.

Mike hauled himself up to lie beside Chime, and he stretched out upon the bare earth panting, his heart drumming against the rock. His eyes swam and the blood frozen on his coat made him very cold.

"Chime?" he asked, his voice sounding hollow and distant to him.

A scrabbling sound, and she said impatiently, "What?" between panting breaths of her own. Then her face was in front of his and she said, sadly, "Oh, Meekay, you should have let me know. I would have returned."

"No need us—both being—killed. Chime?"

"Yes, Meekay?"

Her hands and breath were warm as she lifted his feet and propped a rock under them, then wrapped him in something else warm—her own coat. Her hands were at his wound, wiping and applying pressure that hurt worse in some ways, though it made the blood stop coming so fast.

"Who . . . was I? You know—reincarnation? I didn't find out on my birthday. Nyima's baby . . ."

One hand stayed on his wound, continuing to apply pressure as she wormed her way under him so that his upper body rested on her knees, his head against the warmth of her body. Good. This way he could keep her warm too. His thirst was assuaged a little as something wet and salty fell against his lips and he licked.

"Sergeant Danielson, Meekay. Your parents, Thibideaux, and Keith

Marsh were all almost sure of it. And now—what you just did—I'm also sure of it. I did not know you were so brave. . . ."

The hand she had placed against the pulse in his neck left a draft for a moment, and presently the lip of a canteen pressed his chin and barley beer poured into his mouth.

He swallowed and grinned up at her. "Me neither," he said, and felt the tears again.

He licked his lips again, the world swimming around him, her face dissolving with it. "Chime Cincinnati," he said to her, quite clearly, "I don't think we should go any farther. This outside world is too treacherous and unfriendly, and I need to go home now. I'm sorry, but I don't think I can do it alone, and I want to tell Isme—tell her—tell father to tell her—take me home, Chime. I'm tired and I don't feel very well. Please. Let's go home now."

"You are bleeding very badly, Meekay," she said, and her voice sounded the way his body felt. More warm wetness fell against his face. "I don't think I can take you home right now, and we have to be quiet so that man doesn't find us. But I will get you home. I will."

The canteen shook at his chin and then went away, and her hand stroked his hair and forehead again. "But you must listen to me now, in case we are separated. O son of noble family, now the time has come for you to seek a path. As soon as your breath stops . . ."

Her words continued for hours, but he was soon distracted by darkness and the cessation of his heartbeat.

". . . This is the dharmata," Chime's voice continued, though it trembled and faded at times, "open and empty like space, luminous void, pure, naked mind without center or circumference. Recognize, then, and rest in that state, and I too will show you at the same time."

Mike's open eyes stared up at her, unseeing. She was a bodhisattva and the end product of many past lives. She was a saint and she knew all about the cycle of life and death. But the boy in her arms had been like her brother, who comforted her in her nightmares and followed her into her destiny. Now he was to be stranded out here with so many other ghosts.

She ceased for a moment reciting the Great Liberation Through

Hearing, the counseling of the dying and dead as they embarked on the journey through the bardo, and threw back her head and howled, "Kalagiya! Kalagiya!" But no magical help came, and she covered Mike's body with the unfused mani stones that had once marked this place as one of prayer.

CHAPTER XIV

Section Two
THE LIVING DEAD

Chime Cincinnati recited the Book of the Dead and called on the power of the magic of Shambala until she was hoarse, and after that watched by Mike's grave for his ghost to emerge. She was exhausted, however, and slipped from meditation into a dreaming state and back again, and did not see the ghost. She didn't think Mike was headed for Nirvana yet, unless he had listened to those last words she had spoken over him with more heed than he usually paid her.

She would miss him. More than his kindness and protectiveness, which were more necessary for him to demonstrate than for her to receive, she would miss his self-assured superiority and his scornful demands that she explain herself. Sometimes all of the ideas she was acquiring, along with those she remembered, seemed to soar and dart around in the top of her head like hummingbirds. She knew very well what they were and what they meant, but Mike made her stop them and bring them down to earth and show them to him so that he could see the wings and feathers and that which made them work. Showing him added to her own appreciation of them.

His life had been very short this time, but he had traveled farther than he knew from the place where he started. Sergeant Danielson had been a man born in a test tube and raised by the military, who thought they could program him like a computer to be a killing machine, never taking into account that even a man with no flesh and blood parents is a human who may long for his family. Danielson had married, but the warrior instilled in him drove him to treat his family like enemies. He'd died, still a stranger to those in Shambala, seeking his wife's forgiveness. Mike had been born in Shambala with the war far away and his immediate family and a large extended family all around him. He had been a good son, a good brother, a good friend, and would have made a good husband. He had wanted nothing more than to remain in Shambala, but had followed Chime to keep her from harm, which he had done, in the end, with the courage of a pain-hardened warrior.

Yes, Mike's life had been brutally short, but it had been a definite improvement on Danielson's.

"You had better make progress too," the wind whispered with his voice. She looked up, searching for him, but the breeze brushed her ear, cautioning, "Listen."

She listened. Was that the wind in the trees? Ah, no, she was thinking of home now. Of this place in the past. Here there were no trees, only melted stone. But below, the stones were looser—she remembered the feel of gravel against her palms, scratching her knees and shins. The sound was not the rustle of leaves but the muffled clicking of stone against stone, followed by the "chuck" of a foot jabbing into the cracks in larger stones.

She worried that she could not see Mike's ghost, but perhaps it was not yet strong enough to make itself visible to her. She felt reassured that she could hear him, that he had contacted her. Everything had changed here—even death, even the bardo. Mike's body had died but she did not want to lose touch with his spirit. She must help him find his way back to Shambala or to Nirvana. No matter who else she saved, she would not abandon him to wander the desolate earth so far from the home he loved. Her determination on his behalf was not purely sentimental—those born in Shambala, according to the texts, must reincarnate in Shambala. None of the other ghosts were finding their way into Shambala. Apparently they would all need help, but if Mike's spirit was not to remain forever in the bardo, it urgently needed to return to Shambala. Chime did not think his spirit would be able to penetrate the magic barrier protecting his native land any better than the other ghosts. They would all need her help.

The light filtering through the heavy cloud cover was a furtive, blotchy thing now, deepening the valley and spreading cancers of darkness across the faces of neighboring peaks. She must leave this place and find her way down the other side of the mountain. Perhaps her pursuer would not be able to follow in the darkness.

Having grown up in the mountains, not to mention having spent many lifetimes growing up in mountains, she was nimble, with small, strong hands and feet, and made it down the folds and crevices of rock without too much problem. Her former selves were no more familiar with the bomb-altered terrain than her present self, and offered no advice while she climbed, slid, crawled, groped, and fell down to the floor of the valley below.

She paused at the bottom, listening, picking out the wind from any other noise. She heard neither ghostly whisperings nor human pursuit. Either her pursuer had given up or perhaps had decided to rest at the top for the night.

Before her stretched a long broad valley crisscrossed with streams and the scars of deserted streambeds, already blackening with shadow. The water glistened faintly against a landscape so barren as to appear sterile—scrubbed rock, that was all.

She looked back up at the face of the cliff. Out there in the valley she would be an easy target. Here there was some cover, but on the other hand, she might fall asleep and not wake up before Buzz overtook her.

If she kept moving in the darkness, by morning she would surely reach the cover of the distant mountains.

Flickers of movement teased the corner of her eye and she looked back out across the plains.

Bouncing shapes of white light bobbed across the plains, heading away from her. As she stared, she saw that the white was only the most visible part in the darkness, but that it represented the undersides and legs of a herd of wild asses, their black tails flicking against their buttocks, their beige sides blending with the rock. They looked very real, and she felt her heart lighten at the sight of them.

She trotted after them, her pack bouncing against her back as she hopped narrow streamlets and splashed through wider ones, sometimes slipping on the rock, once falling, but never losing sight of the galloping wild asses—*kiang;* her memory provided the archaic Tibetan word. The wild asses had been extinct for decades, even before the missiles struck. Overhunting for sport and food had killed off the breed.

These must be the ghosts of *kiang* then, she thought, though she continued following them with no less enthusiasm. Her present eyes had never seen these animals before. In Shambala there was insufficient room for the animals that lived there to roam so freely across the plains. The bounding of their bodies was like music to her.

She ran behind them until she was winded, and when they plunged on ahead of her, she watched them grow smaller with a sadness that blossomed quickly into grief, the grief and regret she still felt for Mike's passing, the loneliness of being out here in this desolate and hostile world alone.

We are always alone at the core, her former incarnations informed her sternly. *In the end there is nothing but the kernel of self. All places are new and strange when seen for the first time. And all people who pass are merely journeying momentarily on another plane.*

"Pretty permanently, I'd say," Chime's current self responded. "These souls are stuck. Where is Meekay? Let's send out a call for him—"

Meekay is in the ghost realm with the others, and both he and they will

all remain there until I do that which I came to do. I must follow the kiang.
*I must find and aid the others who still live. I will best serve Meekay by
serving my purpose.*

"But I can't go much farther—"

*Practice correct breathing. This body knows the rhythms. Send the mind
ahead and follow the* kiang, *swiftly, swiftly. I sense this is important.*

Chime's body was indeed trained in the breathing, though she had
never in this life practiced the walking trance used by ancient adepts.
Once within this trance, called the *lung-gom,* a human being could
tirelessly walk great distances with inhuman swiftness. Ama-La, Chime's
former self, had been an accomplished *lung-gom-pas,* and both Chime's
own father and Mike's mother, as well as others, reported having been
hypnotized by Ama-La so that they could make the long and hazardous
journey to Tibet in a *lung-gom* state.

Chime spent several minutes adjusting her breathing, and visualized
herself flying over the valley. When she began walking again, her gait
was no longer bouncing or wearied. She moved in a swift flow after
the *kiang,* her feet barely brushing the streams and barren rocky earth.

She smelled the char in the air, she saw the moon rise and set, she
saw the stars blinking and falling above the valley, their reflections
mirrored in the ripples of the streams, she felt the silken scarves of wind
brush her face and heard it singing around her with the voices of a
thousand ghosts, she tasted—nothing, dryness, a hint of ashes. The
kiang kicked and leapt ahead of her, leaving no odor, no scat, not so
much as a hair floating on the breeze.

Then, as if no time had passed, she found herself about to walk
into the face of the mountain on the far side of the valley, where the
last of the *kiang* had disappeared half a heartbeat before.

She sat down abruptly, staring back where she had come. She could
not make out Mike's grave on top of the distant peak. She could not
see another being following her. That was good.

"Stretch," her former self commanded, and she rolled over to find
that she was laying in a bed of wildflowers, the first vegetation she had
seen in the valley. She stretched her back, legs, arms, and shoulders,
while her eyes drank in the color of the blossoms.

She never before had seen this brilliant color in a blossom. The flowers were the color of the sacred lake, blue-green, teal, turquoise, but with an iridescence that made them appear to be many other colors at the same time. Each blossom was at least as large as her hand, many larger than her head.

The flower patch was triangular in shape, and the point of the triangle ended at the cliff wall before her, a foot or two from where she sat. The base of the triangle spread out about ten yards beyond her. From a distance, she thought, these flowers might be mistaken for a pond or a streamlet.

They seemed to be growing directly from the rock in a most un-natural manner. She lay down again, staring through the stems and leaves toward the mountain, and beheld—more stems and leaves. Brush-ing the flowers aside, she saw that they concealed an opening beneath their foliage, an opening that would require crawling, certainly, but one that must certainly not be ignored, if for no other reason, as the moun-tain climbers used to say, than because it was *there*.

She crawled with her elbows and her knees, her belly flat on the ground, and her head passed through the flowers and beneath rock that bumped her skull as she crawled.

For a time the passage narrowed. Beneath her she felt small rocks, their sharp edges pressing through the mounds of flower petals and through her torn pants and gloves into her already abraded flesh. The ground seemed to tilt downward, then more sharply down until her blood rushed into her head and hands. The coat tangled around her and she thought she should have removed it before trying this.

She began to worry lest she crawl into a place so narrow that she would be stuck in it head first. But she still felt flower petals between her and the rocks, and that encouraged her. The flowers would not be here without light or air. She pulled herself one more wriggle forward.

Abruptly, she smelt a breath of air—not especially fragrant, as she would have expected from the flowers, but more of a stench tainted with excrement. But her nose told her that nevertheless it was relatively *fresh* stench signifying *more* air, which she had smelled previously. When she raised her head to sniff further, her head no longer bumped the top of the aperture.

Experimentally, she rose onto her elbows and still didn't touch the top. Ahead of her the darkness gave way to light, the shadowed flowers, flowing far in front of her, bursting into teal brilliance just ahead. Greatly heartened, she crawled forward more rapidly, then found she was able to stoop, then stand, and she walked quite confidently out of the cave into the bowl of a deep crater open to the sky. From a massive snow mountain opposite her an ice field flowed down toward her, culminating in a deep blue pool.

The crater was a vast open space nearly as wide as the valley, and the carpet of the blue-green blossoms extended into it to form a crescent from the cave's opening.

The lesser peaks surrounding her were like enormous arrowheads sticking out of the ground. Beyond them she could see the tips of other snow peaks, though none so great as the one directly in front of her.

But the strangest thing about this place was that the inner walls of the enclosure, the sides of the mountains, were striated and striped like the pictures of tigers Thibideaux had once showed her.

Chime trotted forward so that she could touch the inner wall and investigate. The flowers grew quite tall here and tangled her feet so that she had to step very high to free them of the blossoms, not an easy thing to do encumbered with a coat, boots and a pack.

Ah, she saw now—the rock was folded in fanlike layers, and the ridges stuck out in plates with deep spaces between them. Her cave, she realized, was what remained of a mountain pass. Only the flowers could locate what was left of the opening—well, the flowers and herself, with their help.

The sun would take a long time to fully reach this place, but now it struck the side of the snow peak and stroked the glacier, striking diamonds from its snow and sapphires from its clefts, dazzling her.

At the pool the ghosts of the *kiang* drank silently, their forms wavering, shifting, fading.

Overhead the cries of swooping birds called down to her but no visible wings supported the cries.

She trotted farther forward—what was that in the distance, against the cliff? It was not striated the way the walls were but seemed squarish and—could it be a building? How could it have remained so untouched? She ran forward now, and abruptly her foot splashed into something black and malodorous oozing around the roots of the flowers, soaking quickly into the leather of her boots.

"I see you've found the cesspool," a voice said, and a bald head peered out from among the flowers.

"I beg your pardon," Chime Cincinnati said politely, "but are you a *living* being?"

"You are standing in the proof of it," the head answered.

CHAPTER XV

"Pay no attention to that man digging up your body. That kind of thing doesn't concern you anymore," Toni-Marie said.

Mike thought he must be in shock. He remembered Chime Cincinnati's voice chanting at him and him telling her something about Isme, but he couldn't remember what. Now he seemed to be looking down on the mountaintop at the cairn of stones he had watched Chime build over—over him.

At the moment, a man in rags was removing the stones, throwing them aside until Mike could see his own face.

Mike had seen the man, who he was pretty sure was his murderer, coming up the mountain. He had tried to tell Chime Cincinnati to leave the mountain, and for the first time since he'd known her, had been glad she was so receptive to weird stuff like messages from the dead.

He'd stayed behind, thinking to somehow delay his killer, but that hadn't been necessary. Buzz had paused on his own to disassemble Mike's funeral cairn.

Mike had been absorbed in watching the gruesome process when Toni-Marie had appeared beside him.

"What—What's he doing that for?" Mike asked.

"Your guess is as good as mine. You weren't an organ donor by any chance, were you? No? Then he's probably going to eat you."

That snapped him alert again, though he still felt numb and drifty. He was vaguely comforted by Toni-Marie's presence. She sat cross-legged in midair a little to his right. "Don't worry, kid," she told him. "This sudden death business takes a little getting used to. You should have heard the rest of us right after. *Heavy* denial, man."

"*Eat* me? You mean he's a cannibal, like in Robert Louis Stevenson's books?"

"Gross, huh? But food's scarce, and think of it this way, he's actually just kind of recycling you. Of course, the worst part about it is that he shot you so that he could, but hey, it's a rough world out there—man eat man, know what I mean?"

"No," Mike admitted. He watched the man pull the stones from his former body's chest and hands. "We must stop him."

"Stop him? Why? Like I said, buddy, he's none of your business anymore, unless, of course, his kid has another bambino. Then maybe one of us could get reborn." She paused a moment. "Nah. Trust me. Richie and I spent a little time hanging around this guy's hole. You don't want to be reborn into *his* family. Shooting people isn't the only way he manufactures his own food."

"What do you mean?"

"I'll give you a little hint. Little Evie is almost always knocked up, Daddy is the only man around, there's never more than one baby crawling around the hole, and about every nine months or so there's little piles of baby bones littering the ground. The spooks that try to get reborn into the living world via Evie's womb are back out here in the spirit world so fast they get whiplash."

Mike stared at her uncomprehending for a moment, then what she meant sunk in and he was suddenly aware of the benefit of lacking a corporeal digestive system. "That's horrible. We can't let him get Chime Cincinnati."

"Whoa, cowboy. She's not your problem either. She is living and looking out for the living, and you, son, are D-E-A-D, and that spells dead. Savvy?"

"You talk like my dad," he told her.

"What?"

"My dad. You talk like him—cowboy talk, except you don't have a Tibetan accent."

"You gonna go back there?"

"Back where?"

"You know, where you came from? Take your mom a ghostly message, 'Don't wait up, Mom. I'm gonna be late.' Something like that?"

"Is that what I'm supposed to do?" he asked, aware that she was half making fun of him, but still feeling too dazed to know how to respond.

"Well, you're one of the few I've met since my own demise who's in any position to do something like that—I mean, most of us, if our parents weren't already dead, they died when we did—all at once, you know, whoom!"

"I hadn't thought of it that way."

"Yeah, so I don't really know what's customary over here, but I used to watch ghost stories sometimes, and I know the living seemed to get quite a kick out of messages from the dead. You think your mom would?"

He shrugged. "She wouldn't be all that surprised to see a ghost— she's seen a lot. But she'd be sad to see that I'm dead. I suppose I could go back long enough to tell her to give my fairy-tale books to Auntie Dolma to read to the kids."

"What a guy," Toni-Marie said. "Always thinking of others. So, hey, can I go with you when you go?"

"I don't see why not. But I don't want to go now. I need to help Chime Cincinnati. She's all alone out here and doesn't know anyone." He nodded down at the man who was now dragging his body over to the edge of the mountain path and propping it up on its side, preparing to roll it down the hill. "I can't just desert her while that cannibal is after her."

"Honey, it's not like it's all that *unusual* to be a cannibal in this day and age. A lot of the survivors have resorted to it. Especially when they can find somebody who isn't half eaten up with radiation sickness. You're pheasant under glass to that guy."

"Are there no helpful, kind people left at all?" he asked.

"Does the phrase 'Charity begins at home' ring any bells?" she answered.

"I suppose it does," he said. "Which is why we have to warn Chime Cincinnati."

"You don't think maybe she *knows*?"

"Yes, but she is alone and I vowed to help her find survivors and return with them to Shambala. I mean to do so."

"Okay, buddy, whatever you say, but to tell you the truth, I think the expiration date is up on vows you took while you were alive. Time to start a whole new existence now—"

"Perhaps for you. But Chime Cincinnati is a bodhisattva—she has a higher spiritual purpose. She always used to say so, and I thought she was just trying to make herself important, but I've seen now that her mission is to transcend the death of the world, so it seems to me that the least I can do is to transcend my own death to help her."

"Transcend death?" Toni-Marie thought it over for a moment, then said skeptically, "It'd be refreshing if something did—something besides ghosthood, I mean, or just disappearing off into Nirvana like Richie did." She looked sad and kind of far-off for a moment, then slapped her knee, which didn't make any noise since both the hand and the knee were incorporeal, and said, "Okay, if you're so worried about her, let's go, then."

"Right now?"

"Sure."

"How? She's way ahead of us."

Toni Marie launched herself off the side of the mountain with little more than a wiggle and swooped down toward the plains, calling back, "You're a ghost now. Waft, dammit."

Just about anything was better than hanging around there watching what was about to become of his earthly remains, so Mike, who felt a little silly wiggling, took what would have been a deep breath if he still needed to do that sort of thing, veed his hands in front of him, closed his eyes and dived off the mountain. Since he was thinking of ending up where Toni-Marie was, that's where he was when he opened his eyes again, leveled out over the valley. With a certain degree of embarrassment he abandoned the diving pose and let his arms relax at his sides while he swooped along with her.

"Where is she?" he asked.

"She was here just a minute ago—I felt her."

"You did?"

"Oh, yeah. Like I told you, we've got like built-in life detectors. Can tell a live one from miles away. But we have to watch out for those whatchacallems, the yarn thingies—"

"Spirit traps?" Mike asked.

"Yeah. Oh, hey, there she is, over there."

They swooped across the valley in less time than it used to take Mike to hop a drainage ditch.

"That's funny," Toni-Marie said. "She's vanished."

"If anything happened to her—" Mike said.

"No, she's around here someplace. Let's circle. Hey, doesn't this make you feel like a sea gull?"

"What's a sea gull?"

She altered her ectoplasmic manifestation to resemble a large white and gray bird and mewed at him through a grinning beak.

"I will be a *gho,*" he said, and changed into one of the gold and white birds that flew around the mountaintops at home. He was able to change himself just by thinking of the bird. He hoped he had it right. He made an alteration in his wingspan just by thinking about it. "This is great. Can we change into anything?"

"Well, sort of. Mostly we just look real to each other—I mean, really real. Sometimes I don't think the live-o's can see us at all, other times they're apt to think we're one of them. But it's not like you can really fool anybody—I mean, most of us can do it, at least the ones from the—you know, the last day. Some of them haven't figured it out, of course, and keep going back over their death or getting stuck. But Richie and I used to amuse ourselves this way all the time."

"Maybe the others can't do it," he suggested.

"Could be. There are some who hadn't reincarnated yet when the missiles started—some pretty old ones around here, actually. Like I told you before, a lot of them are stuck where they died. I'm glad I'm not, and it looks like you're not either."

"That mass of ghosts that tried to throw us off the cliff—did you know any of them?"

"Not really. Most of them were Chinese soldiers. They don't want much to do with foreigners, even after death. I'm glad you're here. With Richie gone, it's going to be lonesome around here."

"I won't be here long," he said. "Once we've helped Chime accomplish her mission, I'm going back home to reincarnate."

"I'll come with you," she said, as if expecting him to say she couldn't.

"Sure," he said. "But we have to find Chime first."

They circled several more times before he finally saw her—this time he spotted her before Toni-Marie did.

But meanwhile he got used to swooping and gliding over the valley floor and the high pointed ridges.

He thought himself back and forth across the valley to the glaciated peak beyond several times. Ghost flight was a funny thing, for although he traveled very fast, he still was aware of every detail of the landscape below him, as if it was imprinted on his memory and he passed through time rather than space. The valley they'd descended to from the first mountain peak was white and barren as chalk, netted with murky blue streams in which swam more ghost fish. The turquoise flowers with their huge blossoms glowed with something more energetic than mere life—and when he spotted Chime, he realized that the energy of the flowers had overpowered her. The flowers were iridescent and waving, whereas Chime's life shone with a jade translucence much bigger than her actual self had been.

He swooped lower to see her more clearly, and saw her small dark form addressing another presence—this one golden-looking from the air.

"Stop!" Toni-Marie cried.

Chime looked up just then, and Mike called her.

"They've set wards against us spirits," Toni warned him in her sea-gull voice, but he wasn't sure what she was talking about. He wanted to reach Chime, to reassure her that he was okay.

He drifted a little lower and suddenly found his wingtip snared, and the more he struggled, the more of his form followed it, until something sucked him into a small, dense space, smaller than a grave, close and bad-smelling.

Overhead, Toni-Marie circled and flapped, mewing, "I told you so," and then he heard no more.

"Hello there," Chime called out to the head as she waded through the cesspool. "My name is Chime Cincinnati and I am the present incarnation of the Terton of Shambala. I'm here to lead you and other living beings to the safety of Kalapa."

"Ten thousand welcomes," the bald head said. It rose above the flowers to reveal that beneath it was a tall, elegant old man dressed in a woolen robe trimmed with fur and brilliant embroidery. Fur boots covered his feet and were bound with braided ropes of black and, surprisingly, silver shoelaces. "Ten thousand times ten thousand welcomes. From far away, for many days, I have felt your emanations, holy one. But I scarcely dared to think you would honor us with your presence so soon. Come, rest in our valley, teach us, learn from us and enjoy the company of our remarkable community."

"Thank you," she said. "How far does your cesspool extend? Can you direct me to the shortest and least messy route out of it?"

"Perhaps you could levitate from it, Rimpoche?" he suggested, calling her by the honorific "precious one" accorded to great lamas. "Unless perhaps you do not wish to squander your psychic powers to solve such an earthly problem."

"I don't know," she said. "I have not yet tried levitation—not in my present body at least. But you're right, of course. I'm sure it must be more difficult with such earthly stuff binding one's feet to the material world."

"In that case, kindly accept my humble assistance," he said, extending a staff to her. She pulled herself along it until she stood once more on solid ground.

"Come to the lake to wipe away the worst of the muck," he suggested. "But it is much too cold to bathe in. For that you must come to the hermitage with me and we will see that you have a proper hot shower."

"That's very kind," she said. "I expect the lake water must also be tainted with radioactivity."

"Perhaps it would have been any other place, or someplace not under my protection," he said, striding gracefully beside her. "But I have developed through my own practice a few skills which enable me to purify that which we need and make it wholesome."

When they reached the shores of the lake, the man sat down on the bank and Chime sat down beside him, stripped off her boots and opened her pack, pulling out the cap, the mittens, the spirit trap, and six cans of Spam in her search for something to clean her boots with.

"You won't need that here," he said, indicating the spirit trap. "We have excellent wards against the dead."

"I understand the need for it," she said, "But I find it very sad. They are so lost. I am worried for Meekay—my companion who came with me from Shambala. He was killed a day ago. I have not yet found his spirit, and I think it still wanders the bardo. If this place is warded against him, then I mustn't stay long. He will be frightened and alone."

"The spirits of the dead roam outside our valley in great numbers. Surely your friend will have companionship," the man said. He turned and she felt compelled to stop rummaging and look into his eyes. They were very beautiful eyes, not dark brown, like the eyes of most people with such an Asian cast to their features, but warm amber, like honey or golden coins. For their light color, they had surprising depth. The eyes held her gaze for a very long time, searching her face. "We need you here, among the living," he said, pressing his hands over the cleaner of hers.

She smiled at him, a little uncertainly. He was an imposing man, much taller than most Asians, slender, his features so finely molded that his baldness served only to accent the height and angle of his cheekbones, the strength of his jaw, the tilt of his eyes and the flare of his nostrils. His lips were well drawn but deeply cushioned and sensual-looking. All of this belied the impression that this man had lived many years—his skin was so tightly molded to his features and bones that there were few wrinkles, little sign of looseness. Only the silver brows and lashes crowning his golden eyes, and the porcelain translucence of his skin, betrayed his years.

He continued gazing at her as if he wanted to know and understand everything she could possibly tell him about herself. But she didn't want to talk about herself at the moment, she wanted him to enlist his sympathy for Meekay and the ghosts. This man had an aura of power about him that could be very helpful to her mission.

"Meekay is a Shambala being and can only reincarnate in Shambala, and to return there he must accompany me, since I am the Terton. The other ghosts are searching for any living form to occupy, and they are mostly very angry and very lost. Like Meekay, they were deprived of their lives suddenly and violently, but he died defending me, while their deaths were needless and senseless, as is their anger." She shuddered, remembering the ghosts on the mountain before Vajra had come to help them.

"Such all-encompassing compassion and sensitivity!" he said admiringly. "You are indeed the very incarnation of Tara the merciful goddess. But we have the living to think of here. My dear, from your youthful appearance, I'd say you haven't been in this incarnation long, am I right?"

She nodded.

"Please accept then this word of advice. Even for a saint, there are limits to what can be done for people. You'll lose your serenity trying to take care of everyone."

"Where *is* everyone?" Chime asked.

"Why, they're waiting in the palace. Can you not see them?"

"Is that the palace over there?" she asked, pointing to the building.

"Yes, do you see them?"

"Not really."

"You're not supposed to see them 'really.' Come now, you're only looking with your water eye. You must look for them with your flesh eye, with which the enlightened may see things eighteen days' walk distant."

"Oh," Chime said. He had been testing her and she seemed to have failed. He had called her Tara, as if she had claimed to be the patron goddess of Tibet. Evidently, he knew she was someone of metaphysical import but was not willing to take her own word for who she was. But then, they hadn't known each other very long. She shrugged. "Well, as you noticed, I have only been in this incarnation a short time so I haven't yet practiced many skills. I haven't had the benefit of a teacher either, so perhaps you can instruct me in relearning some of the techniques."

"Really? But surely you must be—let's see, the thirty-second king—pardon me, queen—of Shambala." He was testing again, trying to see if she would claim to be more than she was.

"Oh, no. I'm not a queen. Just the guide. And it is true I have much to learn. I read about the five kinds of eyes, and it's true I do *sense* distant things, but they are not clear enough usually for me to claim to actually see them."

"But what of the monks and lamas of Shambala? Have they taught you nothing? There must be many great teachers there."

"There used to be but they died before I was born. Our country underwent a great catastrophe due to the war—Kalapa and most of the holy people were destroyed. In recent years the city has been more of a refugee camp—and of course all of the outer areas of Shambala were depopulated long ago by one thing or another. Now there's only one community of us, and mostly we do practical things."

"I see. The last enclave of pure Tibetan ethnicity, eh? Perhaps not devoted to the spiritual aspects of the old kingdom but maintaining the racial lines?"

"Oh, no. I myself am half American. As is Meekay. Many are of mixed heritage—Chinese, Indian, American, Russian, and of course Tibetan. It was my policy in former lives to ensure that Shambala would be a haven for as many different types of the best of the people of the earth as came within my sphere of influence."

"Fascinating," he said. "Such a wise policy, diversity. My own enclave is also multinational—handpicked people, in my case. Naturally, using my wisdom eye, I saw how things were in the world and gathered about me those who should be saved. A fine group—"

"What is your name?" Chime asked him.

"During the old times I was known as Cao Li and was a civilian administrator for the Chinese. When my official duties ended and I was free to pursue my calling of providing this haven against the last days of earth, I became known as the Guru Meru, having named myself for the great mountain at the center of Buddhism."

"Meru Rimpoche," she said politely, bowing over her hands.

"Not so formal, my dear. You are a colleague and may call me simply Meru if you desire or Master Meru if it pleases you because of the difference in our years. Everyone here simply calls me Master."

"Very well. I will too then, Master," Chime said meekly. She noticed with amusement that already she had gone from being possibly an honored queen to a colleague, and now it seemed might come to be regarded as a pupil. Not that it mattered. This man's vision of the world beyond perhaps was clouded with some illusions, but no doubt he still knew much that she needed to learn. After a moment, as they walked toward the building, she spoke again. "Master?"

"Yes, my child?"

"How is it that you have set wards for the ghosts, which deter them from entering this place, and yet I was led here by the ghosts of a herd of *kiang*?"

"Why, my dear, that is very simple. The ghosts of animals are not intelligent enough to respond to magic as do the ghosts of humans. Besides, animal ghosts present no threat. I formulated my wards to work exclusively on higher beings for that reason."

"I see," she said, though she didn't, not even with her wisdom eye. It seemed to her that if wards kept off ghosts, they ought to work on the ghostiness of the ghost, not the species, but on the other hand, it was fortunate that such was not the case or she would not have found this place.

Steep flights of steps wound up the mountainside to the square stone building. The glacier dripped down one side, hugging one wall of the structure, as the ice field flowed down toward the pool like a frozen waterfall.

"I think you're going to find this quite surprising," the self-appointed Master said. And she did.

Once inside the building, her eyes swam with spots as she grew used to a dim interior lit by hundreds of candles and lamps, assuredly not yak-butter lamps, for they smoked with a fragile fragrance as sweet as that of the flowers that grew beside the sacred lake at home.

The light gleamed off shining metal wrought into beautiful shapes and rich velvety tapestries that softened the stone walls. The candlelight brought extra depth to the colors, so that the blues seemed bottomless, the rose warm enough to thaw frozen limbs, the green as dense as a forest, the saffron bright as the sun. Moving through the entrance hall to the rooms, she saw jewel-tiled mosaics and honey-grained woods, opulent and costly.

Meru said, "Please excuse this hovel. I'm sure your home in Shambala is much grander."

"I've been told that it used to be magnificent but I don't recall such details—I think that perhaps it once looked as nice as this."

He let out his breath. "What a great tragedy that must have been when it was all ruined." She thought she detected relief and a little smugness in his voice. "Of course, Tibet was rumored to be riddled with secret valleys, but this one and Shambala are the only ones I know about. How I would have loved to have seen it before—"

"Oh, it's getting quite nice again," she assured him. "Artisan-doctor Thibideaux has made us some very interesting new buildings, and the children are painting murals. Meekay's parents have begun to make an underground museum for all of the relics of our former glory. And most of the library was preserved. All in all, after a great deal of work, Kalapa is comfortable and everyone is fairly happy. Well, they were before—"

"Before what?"

But they had now come into a large room where a dozen or so people were grazing listlessly at a buffet table and carrying champagne flutes in their hands.

They were of both sexes, and all were adults between the ages of about twenty and sixty. There were no children. Chime had no time to notice anything further before a tall man wearing a shirt of the same wool as the Master's robe looked up and said, "My God, it's a new face!"

"It is! It is!" cried one of the younger women. "I've never seen her before. Master, where did you get her?"

"Are you sure she's not—contaminated?" another woman asked.

"She doesn't look as if she is—not any more than the rest of us," another man said.

"But she *does* stink."

"I crawled through the flowers," Chime explained. But the Master cut into the clamor, raising his hand for silence.

"My friends, this is Chime and she has come to join us, to teach us and to learn from us. I have been so fascinated hearing her talk of her travels that I had grown used to the stink," he said. "Chime, I'm sure you would like a bath before dining."

"Oh, no, that's all right," Chime said, eyeing a table laden with all sorts of delicacies—eggs, fruits and vegetables, as well as cheeses, and, of course, the champagne, which had an orange tinge to it in the glasses. "I've been living on Spam," she explained when she saw them stare at her staring.

"Inez, my dear, if you would be so kind as to fix her a plate and take her to the showers, find her some clothing," the Master said. "I'm sure we will have plenty of time to speak with Chime after she has eaten and refreshed herself."

Chime decided to save Inez the trouble and was already loading herself a plate with fresh bread, a salad of fresh vegetables, and another of fresh fruits and nuts, scrambled eggs, as well as a number of other dishes she didn't immediately identify. Inez, a beautiful middle-aged woman with hair the color of moon on snow, waited until Chime was done and led her deeper into the structure. Chime happily followed, wolfing down food.

CHAPTER XVI

Mike knew he was finally truly dead. He heard nothing, saw nothing, tasted nothing, felt nothing except—cramped. If he hadn't known he was dead because Chime Cincinnati had recited the Great Liberation Through Hearing from the Book of the Dead over his body, if he hadn't seen that man unbury his lifeless corpse and drag it across the mountaintop, he would have thought he'd been buried alive. He didn't mind the cramped quarters so much—he had spent much of his time since childhood below ground working in narrow underground passages, but it was boring being compressed into this small place with nothing much to think about.

If Chime and the Great Liberation Through Hearing were right, shouldn't he be seeing projections from his own mind, figures from the bardo to lead him back to a womb or lead him to Nirvana? Where was Toni-Marie? Oh yes, he'd forgotten. There were no longer any wombs willing to give birth, and so he was stuck with the rest of the ghosts. It would have to be Nirvana for him, then. The thought saddened him. He didn't feel ready for Nirvana. He hadn't been ready for death either, but at least up until now he had enjoyed the dubious comfort of knowing he had lots of company. He still felt the presence of other ghosts, but he could not contact them.

"Toni-Marie?" he called, his own thought ringing through him. "Chime?"

"Ah!" an answering thought responded, and suddenly he did see something—two bright golden lights with a long black door in the center of each.

"Now we're getting someplace," he said. "I can't remember what golden lights are supposed to mean in terms of the bardo—Chime only went through the ritual once."

The bright lights shuttered themselves once, then opened again and seemed to move closer, "It means that I finally have a toy worthy of my play, prey," another voice whispered silkily through the darkness.

"Nyah nyah, you can't hurt me," Mike said with weary bravado to this new threat. "Too late. I'm dead already."

"So? It's all the same to me. I like dead things."

A sharp blow to the side of Mike's casket shook him up, but not as much as the consequent fall and bounce and spin that gave even his ghost self vertigo, whirling and rolling end over end.

"I never realized the journey of the dead was quite so energetic," he gasped.

Abruptly the spinning stopped, then another blow caused the casket to fly upward and twirl around, come to a soft landing, spin around three more times, then roll over and over until once again Mike was glad he had been separated from the parts of him that were capable of getting sick.

Another toss in the air and Mike caught a glimpse of golden lights on the way back down again, just before the casket smashed with a tinkling of glassy shards. He was free!

"That was fun," the voice was saying. "Do you know any other games?"

Being a ghost, Mike now saw, had advantages. Freed from his prison, he could see in the darkness. The golden lights had disappeared but he didn't need them. He was hovering at the roof of a cave, and below him shelves and shelves of dark bottles lined the wall for what seemed like miles, leading back into the cave and around the next bend. To his right, some sort of tubing led to the roof of the cave and into the mouths of several more bottles. A complex apparatus sat humming on a table, and Mike wondered that he had not heard it—but perhaps he only heard the projections of the living.

The cave seemed to be made of some white flowing stone—marble perhaps. On the floor the shards of another bottle lay beside the over-sized paws of a smallish snow-lion-like creature which unconcernedly licked its shoulder blade.

"You might say thank you," the creature said. "And, according to certain barbarian beliefs, you're now supposed to grant me three wishes."

"What?"

"I let you out of your bottle. When someone lets a genie out of a bottle, according to certain pre-Islamic texts, the genie grants that some-one three wishes."

"I'm not a genie. I'm a ghost."

"I knew that." The creature finished preening and turned the golden lamps back around to face him—of course, they were gleaming animal eyes, only they now appeared much smaller, more the size of some of the old golden coins Mike and his father had unearthed from the ruins of Shambala. "But you can't blame a cat for trying."

"Is that your name? Cat?"

"No, my name is Mu Mao, and I was many lives ago a master of the Tao, in several more lives a Zen master, but more recently I was regional director of public relations for the Autonomous Region of Tibet under the auspices of the People's Republic of China. As you see, I acquired much merit and have now evolved into a higher life-form."

"What is your life-form exactly?" Mike asked.

"I'm a cat—sort of. My mother was a cat. My mother's mother was a cat. But my father, according to family mythology, was a somewhat larger form, just passing through. My litter mates were not so fortunate as I, though siblings of my mother's gave me something of my history before they too died. That's the physical history of this body, of course, not my spiritual history, much of which I learned through an astrologer who was also a high member in the party. I always was a curious being. Nothing ultimately matters, of course, but I've always wanted to know what it was that didn't matter, if for no other reason than to disdain it."

"You said your litter mates were not so fortunate . . ."

"Ah, yes. Well, my mother escaped long enough to mate with a snow lion, and died giving birth to myself and my litter mates, who did not survive. I was raised by one of my aunties, who died some years ago." Mu Mao lay on his belly and stretched out his paws—and stretched them and stretched them. They were as big as rice bowls, these paws, with hairy tufts in between the toe pads. The cat's body had stripes of orange and spots of dark gray stippled all over its dense thick coat. The tail was short and clubbed, the ears tufted with fur, the face deceptively round and sweet.

"How did your mother survive the end of the world?" Mike asked.

"Her companion was among those chosen by Meru the Magician, the being who presides over this valley, to be brought here from other parts of the world to survive the end. Whether Meru knew because he read the newspapers or from his divinations, I couldn't say, but he's been the guardian of this valley for many years and claims to have lived many lifetimes."

"Everybody seems to be doing that," Mike said. "I think that's pretty peculiar since I have only had this life and possibly one other that I know about, while you and Chime Cincinnati reel off whole genealogies of who you used to be before. It gives you unfair advantages, if you ask me."

"Not so peculiar," the cat said, resting its head on its paws. "You have to consider that a person only comes to have knowledge of past lives and reaches higher evolution through accumulated wisdom and good karma—or by cheating, in the case of certain magicians. Therefore, after a disaster, who is more likely to survive in disproportionate numbers than those who are in full possession of all of their wisdoms?"

"I suppose so," Mike said absently. He was now engrossed in studying the bottles completely covering the cave walls. "Are these ghosts too?"

"Umm," the cat said. "Meru's been collecting them."

"*Why?*" Mike asked.

"Well, for one thing, to keep them away from here. Before people here die, he encases them in ice farther along in the cave. You know what ghosts are like. . . ."

"No," Mike said belligerently, "what are *we* ghosts like?"

"You're always wanting to inhabit the nearest body, for one thing. I thought you people were Buddhist. Don't any of you believe in Nirvana? Oh well, I suppose that's expecting too much worthiness of mere mortals. Anyhow, Meru has promised his followers that if they let him ice them when they first become ill of radiation sickness or any other sign of deterioration, he'll keep their bodies whole until whatever afflicts them can be cured. Meanwhile, of course, it would be an awful mess if other spirits possessed the bodies—not only would it displace the spirits that are still clinging to those bodies, it would also make the body live again, trapped in the ice with a raging spirit inside. So he's bottling the spirits—as he tells others—to save them for when there are more bodies. He tells the others he's benefiting everybody this way."

"I can tell you from personal experience he's wrong," Mike said. "It's awful being bottled. At least out here you can float around and look for opportunities, so to speak. In there you can't do anything. You might as well be—"

"Yes, I see your point," the cat said. "Oh, look, here comes another one. . . ."

A milky mist filled the tubes, and Mike heard an eerie scream as the vapor was sucked into the tubes. "Oh, shit!" the screamer said, as the machine corked the bottle and set it in line for shelving.

"Toni-Marie, is that you?" Mike asked, knowing, of course, that it was.

"Mikey, where are you, where am I? What *is* this shit? Get me out of here."

"I don't think I can. Cat . . ." The cat remained in a posture that indicated it was sleeping. "Mu Mao, could you break this bottle too?"

"Undoubtedly."

"Well?"

"If I choose to. I can break all these bottles if I choose to. As it is, I'm afraid harsh words will be spoken about broken glass."

"But it's wrong to confine people's spirits this way," Mike protested.

"Don't complain to me. I didn't invent this apparatus and I did tell you Meru is a more or less *evil* magician."

"But then why won't you help us?"

"Us? Us? I let you out, didn't I?"

"Yes, but it was an accident."

"Oh, no, I meant to do that."

"Well, then? Can't you let her out too, or are you in league with this magician? Maybe you're his familiar? I read about those."

"I'm nothing of the sort. I spend a great deal of effort to avoid any familiarity at all with that person. But as for this, well . . . " The lamping eyes surveyed the broken glass. "Does the term 'to shit in one's nest' ring any bells for you? I would be blamed, and Meru has only tolerated me because of my mother's former companion, who is not at all well, though she hides it from Meru because she dreads being frozen. He is not in the least fond of me and will not be sentimental about disposing of me once the companion is on ice, so to speak. I'm sure he senses that I have been what he claims to be, and knows that I have surpassed him to reach my present advanced state. The man has not learned to conquer his own passions—especially jealousy. That's almost a required flaw for an evil magician."

"Mikey? Mikey!" Toni-Marie's voice sounded muffled now.

The cat rose, its tail switching, and stood with its forepaws on the tabletop, holding the bottle. Mu Mao sniffed the bottle and gave it a delicate tap with a paw.

"Mikeee!" Toni-Marie cried.

"I must remember to get here more often when the spirits are fresh," Mu Mao said. "So much more interesting that way."

"Don't toy with her," Mike growled.

"I thought that's what you wanted me to do." The cat blinked gold eyes at him.

"Look, you could come with us—"

"With spirits?"

"Well, with us and Chime Cincinnati. We're going to find survivors and take them back to Shambala."

"But I'm quite comfortable here." The stubby tail jerked back and forth, belying the silky tone of the response.

"If you come with us to Shambala, you'll stay young and healthy for many lifetimes."

"Hmm. I have already enjoyed many lifetimes. Why, the grandfather of my last self was—"

"And how about the father of your present self?" Mike asked. He was finally getting the hang of the terminology, after listening to first Chime, now Mu Mao. "The noble snow lions, symbols of Tibet, roam the hills of Shambala. Presumably some of them will be as interested in genealogy as you are."

Without a word the cat pounced, slapping Toni-Marie's bottle to the floor, where it broke.

She flowed up out of the glass shards and shook herself back into shape, smoothing down her ectoplasmic shorts and tank top. "Oh, a kitty!" she said. "I thought it was something terrible had hold of me in there, and here it was a little ol' pussycat."

Mu Mao sat down and washed beneath his tail.

CHAPTER XVII

"How did you come to be here, Inez?" Chime asked as she pulled on a woolen robe similar to the Master's—this one embroidered with flowers and birds. Chime popped another slice of brandied peach into her mouth and licked in the syrup.

"The same way everybody else did. I was one of the chosen. Good karma, I guess. Either that or my brilliance as an actress, or maybe it was just because I was married to Art and he thought Meru was the wisest thing since Einstein. Then again," she shrugged, "maybe it's what it usually was—the way I filled out a bikini."

Her voice was light, brittle and ironic, though she wore a quirky little smile as she spoke. Chime did not feel as if she knew enough about Meru and his enclave to be able to read the nuances in what people said yet, so she did not question Inez's tone but instead said, "I can't help wondering, when so many people all over Tibet were lost, why Master Meru brought a few people *into* the country specifically to save them."

"Simple, sweetie. Our Master is just a teensy bit of a snob. He likes company, but it had to be the *right* company. Not just any Tom, Dick, or Taring would do. And he's a collector—did you happen to take note of the ambience of this place? Nothing but the best, some of it loot from the destroyed monasteries and the rich Tibetans who, ah, donated their goodies to the Chinese 'cause' in the 1900s. Partly it was bought, of course, with the money *we* donated to this cause, which I have to admit has not been a total scam. We did survive the end of the world in high style, just like he promised. My point is, he likes collecting people the same way he likes collecting stuff."

Chime thought that collecting was a very strange pastime for a Buddhist adept, who was supposed to practice nonmaterialism and understand the changeable nature of life, but she wasn't there to criticize. "Who has he collected exactly?" she asked.

"You seem to be the most recent acquisition," Inez said, with a wry cock of her eyebrow that took in Chime from head to toe. "And anybody else who amused him or who he thought might be real useful. There's Andreanna Sokolski, the opera singer, her daughter Melody, who was born after the end, and her husband Harry Greenberg, who was the AmCan representative for the West Coast corridor. He's on hold now, though."

"On hold?"

"On ice. Back in the cavern. You know, deep-freeze sleep. Cryowhasis, like in the old sci-fi movies. Harry got a radiation lesion on his neck, and Meru froze him till there's a cure—supposedly."

"That's very good," Chime said. "I think if we can carry him in ice back to Shambala, he will be made well again. It will be very difficult though, very hazardous."

"Shambala? What's that?"

"It is a sacred place magically protected from the bombs where some people live peacefully in the last refuge of humankind."

"No kidding? That sounds a lot like Shangri-La, which is where we're supposed to be now. That's what Meru claimed anyway."

"Did he?" Chime asked eagerly, feeling a flutter of excitement at the prospect. "Perhaps it is. Perhaps this is one of the lost valleys of Shambala—there were supposed to be nine originally, but so far as I know, all were uninhabited in my previous incarnation's time save only Kalapa. At any rate, you are fortunate he collected you people in this place to save you from the missiles and the radiation."

Inez tilted her splayed hand back and forth on slender wrist bones. "More or less," she said. "A lot of the people on hold had the beginnings of radiation sickness. But some of them were a little cocky about staying out here instead of back in the caverns when the fireworks started."

"That must have been very frightening," Chime said.

"Exciting, though," Inez admitted. "One of the things Meru collected was information networks for his computer systems, so we've got some great holovids of it all. I'm sure he'd be tickled to show you."

"I . . . would find that . . . fascinating," Chime said. "But who else is here in this community? Tell me what you know of them. I'm curious why Master Meru chose whom he chose."

"As to why, there were probably three main criteria—they had to be useful, rich, and a little on the weird side, so that they'd listen to Meru. Also, they couldn't be too old or really indispensable where they were, since, of course, we all had to drop out without telling anyone on the outside where we were going. Karl and Inga Meissen are engineers, used to be corporation officers in West Germany. Their daughter Gretel looks a lot like Melody Greenberg, Harry and Madame Andreanna's daughter. Both of those girls were born about five years after the big one went up. *Do not ask* why Gretel, who is of ze pure Aryan stock, has Asian eyes. Especially *do not ask* Master Meru. Then there's Ito Kurasawa and his girlfriend Kyoko, a doctor who headed the radioactive medicine department at the Hiroshima University Hospital in Japan. Kurasawa-san held the patents on a lot of the recycling inventions used in AmCan.

"The Valasquez-Stroms are botanists who helped Meru set up the garden grotto. Sven Strom is on hold now. Then there's Mrs. Bertinelli, a chef who made a fortune off her gourmet cookbooks, and her husband, an Italian architect and interior designer who had to be put on hold almost as soon as he had designed the inside of this place. Monsieur Cointreaux is a computer specialist who set up the networks for Meru, and madame was a famous fashion designer and model. We did have good old Prince Tommy, who was something like thirty-sixth in line for the throne of England when there was an England. But Tommy got iced two months ago. Oh yeah, and Full Moon Akesh, who was a big music star in AmCan—he got put on hold last week, after the sores broke out."

"Is that all?"

"Well, that's all the families, except for my beloved Arthur and me—we're actors, or at least Art was. I retired to do the hausfrau number. Otherwise, there was the pilot, Grady Stone. Poor Stoney"—Her voice broke for a moment, then she continued, with forced brightness—"He was seriously *not* pleased about the idea of getting put on hold. And there's the servants, of course. But a lot of them have died. Oh, yeah, and Mrs. Li, Meru's wife, is back there too, but he had stored her here before he brought any of us. Cancer, I think he said."

"The servants died? They were not put on hold?"

"No. They weren't really part of the colony. Meru only put Stoney"—Inez's still-lovely blue eyes brimmed when she said the man's name again—"put Stoney on hold because he figures we'll need him to fly us out of here. Otherwise, Meru says he has an obligation to sort out only the genes of 'the most successful and productive people for future generations.' Can you believe the guy?"

"Oh, yes, I can," Chime said, trying to control her tone and her facial expression but ending up on the wry side.

Inez gave her another cocked eyebrow and a knowing look.

"What kind of birds are these?" Chime asked, fingering the embroidery on her jumper. "I've never seen such flowers."

"Oh, these are the work of Madame Cointreaux—she designed them, anyway. Some of the others help with the embroidery. Madame has offered to teach me, but she's very picky and I am not yet *that* bored."

Chime was bending down to lace on her new boots when she felt something soft bump against the backs of her calves.

"It's that damned cat again. Scram, you begging beast," Inez said without rancor and with a touch of affection. "There's nothing here for you."

But Chime was on her haunches, her hands cupped around the cat's ears, scratching, her nose even with its nose. "Ah," she said. "Is that so?"

Inez Murdock left the new girl with the cat. Inez was afraid she'd said too much already—too much in case the girl was already under Meru's spell. Not enough if anything she'd said had the power to prevent the girl from succumbing to Meru. He could be so charming at first and seem so wise, so sexy and charismatic. Every person there had felt that charm at one time. Some of them, even after all these years, still hung on to every word the "Master" said, hoping to win a little more of his approval. For others, once the charm wore off, there were other means of control, other pressures. What do you do when you join a cult on a lark, and by the time you outgrow it, the world has ended and there's nobody but you and the other, still-convinced cultists? Inez didn't know. Mostly she played along. She was more than a little afraid of Meru.

When she came into the dining room, he was posturing the way he did, playing to a circle of his favorites.

"There she was, a perfect little black orchid, wandering in the cesspool, dazed and utterly disoriented," Meru was saying with an elegant lift of his hand. "She had no idea where *she* was, no idea who *I* was, but she claims to be from Shambala, where she's some sort of holy woman. She's much too young to be any such thing, of course. Such enlightenment requires years of study—and yet, her aura is *very* unusual, and her vibrations are extraordinary."

"I also find it extraordinary," Kyoko Taminaga said, "that she is apparently healthy, with no ill effects from traveling out there."

"Yes, a bouncing healthy girl, all right. And rather attractive, that black Indo-Asian combination, don't you think?" Art Murdock asked Karl Meissen, who grinned wolfishly. Karl would. Other than Art and

Meru, Karl was the most implacable lech in the valley, and the biggest pervert. Except maybe for his wife.

"And *young,*" Inga Meissen said. "Too young to have been affected by the bombs, I think. Her chromosomes could be pristine."

"I don't see why it matters," Inez put in casually. "After all, if the *men* all have radiation poisoning, all any woman is going to be able to produce is another little mutant anyway."

"I don't know how you'd know that, sweetheart," Art said. "God knows you haven't been interested in experimenting."

"You do enough for both of us, precious," she snapped.

"Children, children," the Master said.

Inez wanted to scream at him to keep out of it. He had promised them a utopia here, and all he'd done was drag the whole damned bunch of them out thousands of miles from home to watch everyone else die while they survived, cooped up in these goddamn caves with the goddamn mountains looming over them. He had calmed one of her fears—that of being wiped out—given her just the reassurance she wanted, and now she was stuck with it. And with the rest of these people, who were getting crazier by the day.

But she held her tongue and her temper. She had popped off 157occasionally while she was drinking, but Meru and the others put a stop to that, depriving her of her only escape. Well, to be honest, she had kind of decided to stop on her own anyway. When she was drunk, she heard a lot of voices that did not belong to anybody here—ghosts, Meru had told her, but without elaborating. She hated it. This was like living in a dungeon. When she tried getting drunk it was more like living in a nightmare—but she was getting too scared to be out of control around these people, who were all too willing to control her if she didn't want to do it herself. Meru had nasty ways of getting back at you, and even nastier threats of what he *could* do to you, if he chose.

Those who followed him faithfully never heard the threats or saw that side of him. But Stoney had crossed him. Inez didn't know how or why but hoped it wasn't over her, because she would have rather had the pilot to hold on to than have him win some fight with Meru in her honor. Whatever had happened between them, all of a sudden Kyoko discovered that Stoney was infected with radiation disease, and Stoney was in deep freeze back in the hold cave now.

The hold cave gave her the horrors. Meru's idea of pillow talk, during the last few gasps of their affair, had been telling her what he could do to her when she was back there still alive but unable to move, encased naked in the ice. She'd wisecracked that that was the first time she'd ever had a lover who *wanted* her to be frigid, but the joke was to cover up her repulsion.

If his creepiness bothered anybody else, they were smart enough not to let on, and lately she'd been following their example, saying "Yes, Master" and "No, Master," and "Please and thank you, Master." He responded by treating her like a maid, asking her to do all of the little jobs he didn't like doing himself. She smiled and bloody well did them. She had become a better actress here than she had ever been in front of a camera.

She could still hear Stoney hollering his lungs out before Kyoko gave him the shot and Art and Karl helped Meru put poor Stoney in ice. She heard and felt other things too, things he did in *back* of the hold cave, in the section where they had all stayed during the first terrifying years after the missiles went up.

He and Bertinelli had spent a lot of time unpacking crates and crates of glass bottles and installing shelves—another collection, she supposed. He told them all the room had something to do with protecting them while they were on hold, but she got this awful feeling from back there everytime she went into the garden. The feeling was an echo and a deepening of what she already felt—despair and bitter disappointment that this was all life was ever going to be.

At times she wished that she and Art had had children—maybe she could have been one of those devoted mamas who got all her kicks through her kids—but then, she knew that didn't really work, and besides, why subject a kid to this? With her luck she'd have had a daughter, and it was creepy already the way all the old bulls were trying to get next to Melody and Gretel, trying to make deals with the girls' parents.

The low birth rate, once *he* said it was probably safe to have babies, displeased Meru. He had been hoping to found a dynasty or something. But except for Melody and Gretel, the only children born after that time were either born dead or so badly messed up they had to be buried. No ice for them. Meru, of course, had been very comforting to the parents, especially Inga Meissen. The more the other men were around him, the more they grew to be like him.

Meru was all smiles and charm again as the new girl appeared in the hall.

"Speaking of our new guest, here she is."

When Chime entered the room, dressed in a red silk blouse with the woolen jumper embroidered with birds and flowers of many colors, it was like someone opened a door and let in fresh ozone. Inez's depression set a little more lightly on her shoulders and she had the dumb feeling that somehow or other this kid might change things. Immediately Inez's more cynical side added, *If* Meru didn't eat her alive first. Chime carried her dirty plate to the sink and washed and dried it before returning to the others. The big mottled cat had followed her into the room, and it gave Meru a disdainful look as it twined through Chime's ankles to stand beside her.

"Thank you for your hospitality," Chime said to the group at large. "I feel much better now, having bathed and eaten. A little sleep and I shall be better yet—"

"Inez, please show our guest—"

"No, no, I didn't mean that I want to sleep *now*." Chime laughed. "I have much of this excellent place to see yet. And Inez tells me you have holovids of the end of the world. I would like to see them very much. I was born afterward, you know."

"Yes, so were Melody and Gretel and the other young folk of our compound," Meru told her, smoothly taking her arm and leading her away from the others. That would make her feel special, confided in, favored. Anyhow, that was the effect this little ploy of Meru's had had on Inez when she'd first met him. Meru said, "We, of course, discouraged childbirth in the first few years in order not to expose fetuses to any possible radiation. Girls your age and Melody's, however, as long as you show no symptoms, should be able to conceive with relatively low risk."

"I'll bear that in mind when I decide to have a child," Chime answered, her head bowed earnestly to catch his every word. "Although I must tell you that in my home we are having some difficulty with new babies that I think is unrelated to radiation. Others do not agree with me, however."

"If you've broken your fast sufficiently," Meru said, paying little attention to what she said and steering her toward the back of the house and the entrance to the garden cave, "I'll show you the rest of our little world. I think you'll find our gardens quite astonishing."

"So animals survived here too?" Chime asked, reaching down to pet the cat, who purred possessively up at her.

"Domestic ones," Meru said. "Some of the faithful had the foresight to make provisions for beloved pets as well as members of their families. Of course, most of the original animals are long since deceased. One woman brought several cats. The large mongrel cat salivating on your hand is a descendant of one of those beasts. The litter mates had to be destroyed—terrible mutations, two heads, internal organs wrong side out, furless, skinless—but that one seemed to escape any effects except for its size and adaptive characteristics. When I get the time, I plan to examine its internal organs and cells closely to try to identify why its adaptation was so successful, strictly in the interest of seeing if I can discover anything that may help human offspring, you understand—"

"And of course it's still a very healthy cat and you need to wait until it dies," Chime said.

"Naturally," he said smoothly. "Although medical research has never stinted at sacrificing specimens for the greater good. However, with so few things alive these days, the vitality of even a rather worthless, parasitic beast should be held precious."

"And besides," Chime said shrewdly, "if it gets sick from radiation or other ill effects before it dies naturally, those facts would naturally influence your findings."

Meru gave her a speculative look, an arch of silver eyebrows over golden eyes. "I knew that you were a spiritual leader but I had no idea you also had a scientific bent. You sound quite professional for such a young thing."

Chime shrugged. "In my last life I was a doctor and spent the early part of my career in research. If you and your people choose to come to Kalapa, I will share my journals with you. You may find them of interest."

"How kind," he said, but asked her nothing more about it. Rather, now he picked up a magnesium candle and led her through a darkened passage that smelled of damp. The air grew gradually warmer as they walked, and the floor wetter. And as they rounded a bend, the singing of water trinkling down the cavern wall grew louder—never roaring, but merely adding harmonies and countermelodies, like the gamelan orchestras of Bali, a thousand chimes, a thousand gongs, a thousand bells, but very soft, very sweet.

The light increased too, and in another turn Chime stood with Meru at the entrance of a huge underground room. Down the walls rivulets of water danced and sparkled until they met in the center of the room in a sequined pool bordered with lilies and fruit trees. High overhead a great natural crystal lens reflected, refracted, and stored the light, warming and lighting the oversized grotto, coaxing to brilliant life the greenery, the rainbow spectrum bursting from the blossoms, fruits and berries shimmering among the fresh leaves. The delicious fragrance of life filled Chime's nostrils and she smiled.

"This place *is* part of Shambala," she acknowledged.

The Master beamed. "Did I not say so? How could you doubt it? Of course, I've added improvements here and there—reflectors in places where more light is needed, deflectors in places where less humidity is needed, and one of our number was a botanical engineer who altered existing species to fit this environment. And of course it was necessary to add some topsoil from the valley—"

"But didn't that contaminate—"

"Before the missiles were fired. I had this place ready long before then, of course, and my colony in place, as well as all the sources of information that let us know what was happening in the outside world."

"It sounds as if you knew when the missiles would be fired," she said.

"I had my sources. It took a great deal of money to finance this project, and I learned much in the course of my business transactions. Officially, I held a position with the Chinese government, but in reality my role was broader. I was in my own modest way a power broker. Not a major one—certainly the things I sold have made no difference in the ultimate outcome, but they did put me in a position to be alerted to critical political and military events."

"An odd avocation for a holy man," Chime remarked. She was seeing several levels in Meru's conversation—one was that he was confiding in her things many people would have kept secret, the sources of his income, his research. On another level he was confiding in her what he wanted her to know in order to impress her with the fact that he was confiding in her. And on yet a deeper level, he really did want to confide his accomplishments to someone he thought might appreciate them. She found it startling that a man of his age would continue to manipulate not only in the interests of gaining and keeping power, but also in order to have people approve of what he did, no matter what it was.

"I suppose it would seem to be," Meru said. "However, like yourself, I believe it has been my fate to lead others to safety. I knew that it would be difficult and at times might seem to go against what I had been taught, but it was my calling, and in answering, I've taken appropriate measures and whatever precautions seem necessary."

The last was added, Chime thought, as a warning. "I see. Well, this is very beautiful. You must have been extremely successful at your other business."

"Of course, the colonists knew who they were ahead of time and also became investors," Meru said.

"Ah, that was not the way in Shambala. Ours was also a desperate situation, and my former self also did what she thought necessary to secure the safety of Shambala and its people. Those she chose were brought to Shambala—sometimes against their will, I am sorry to say, although their alternatives were always far worse." She said this to reassure him that she was not competing with him, that in former lives she too had had difficult ethical choices to make.

He smiled gently at her and pressed her hand. The cat growled low in its throat. "You have been a remarkable woman. I felt from the first moment I knew of your presence that you were someone in whom I would finally find a friend."

"But you have so many friends—"

He waved his free hand dismissively. "My followers. My children. They depend on me, and although all of them have been accomplished people in their own endeavors, none of them have shared, as you have, this awesome responsibility for maintaining not just life, but civilization, on the ravaged face of the earth. It has been very lonely here for me," he said with another press of her hand and a tear welling up in his eye that Chime thought was a genuine and deep expression of the sorrow he felt for himself. "Until you."

"Why did you not choose people who could help you more? Who would be better company to you?" she asked, though she thought the answer was that such people would not permit him to exercise the power he held over this community.

"For many reasons, the chief of which is that people of our particular caliber are not common. But I was constrained from selecting even those who would have been my next-best companions, those I knew to be highly sensitive to and aware of otherworldly and psychic influences. Those people would be having a difficult time if they were alive today, amidst the ghosts and memories of the dead world. I knew we would have to deal with such things, of course, so in my selection of my 'colonists' I chose those who would be least receptive. In most instances I think my choices have been wise—these are, after all, people gifted in their own fields. But they could not, alas, be gifted on all of the levels that you and I are. Otherwise, they would have been overwhelmed by the emanations from the ghosts before I was able to get my defenses in working order."

"Your defenses?" Chime asked.

He turned to her with a penetrating look, taking both of her hands in his. "Yes, would you like to see them? The hold room contains my defense for the living against death. The Hall of Souls contains my defense for the living against the dead. I have a slight warding charm on it to discourage the curiosity of any of my children who might disturb my experiments. I fear the nature of the work might alarm them. My little spell won't even be noticed by someone of your power."

"You honor me," Chime said, making a little bow.

He returned the bow, gazing at her deeply over his steepled hands. "No, my dear lady, it is I who am honored to at last have someone with whom to share these accomplishments."

As they walked through the foliage and flowers, Chime was more sure than ever that this place could only be an outlet from Shambala, and that this man was indeed its guardian. She could see that in many ways he had done exactly as she had, found people and things worth preserving and brought them back to the relative safety of this valley. Because it was so distant from the center of Shambala, and its powers not so great as those of her home, it could not keep its inhabitants quite so safe, and therefore, perhaps, its guardian could not be quite so scrupulous in what he did to protect his charge. Chime tried not to judge Meru, or to be influenced by what Inez Murdock had told her about him. He had indeed had a difficult task, and he had accomplished it thus far, keeping this handful of people alive. She wondered, though, how willing he would be when the time came to relinquish his control and his colonists to the greater protection of Shambala. He had not yet shown any curiosity about Shambala itself, only about her personally.

They stepped across a streamlet feeding into the pool at the far end of the cavern and through an arch of greenery into another cool cave, and once more Chime felt the walls press closely around them, then open out. This time the air grew colder and drier as they walked, the stream disappearing down a side passage. Chime wished she had kept her coat with her. The woolen jumper was warm enough but her silk blouse was far too light for the cold in this place.

Meru paused to pick up another magnesium candle. He lit it, and pulled at a rope apparatus that lowered something tinkly toward him. Shards of colored light broke across his face as he set the magnesium candle carefully in a slot and thereby lit a spectacular lamp, a kaleido-scope of prismatic surfaces that reflected and magnified the candle's flame to spectral brilliance that lit the cavern's folded marble walls with darts of bouncing, twirling color.

"How beautiful!" Chime said, spinning around with the light, watching it play on the walls.

"Your delight in it delights me my dear, and I'm sure it would also please the designer of the lamp, Signor Bertinelli." He swept his hand to one section of the wall, where a man's form was sculpted in ice.

"How clever," Chime said. "The lamp creates patterns like people's faces in the walls—"

"Those *are* people's faces, my dear. This is the holding cavern, where I keep the bodies of the sick and injured in cryogenic stasis within the walls until such time as I can revive them to health. That's Marco Bertinelli, who designed the lamp not only to provide light for this room, but to imbue it with a properly awesome atmosphere. Next to him is Sven Strom, the botanist who, with his wife, Lupe Valasquez, helped me design the gardens. I put him nearest the entrance to the outer cave, so he could watch over his plants. Over there is my beloved wife, Mu."

Chime raised her eyebrows questioningly, encouraging him to say more.

He smiled down at her. "I said I was a holy man. I never said I was a monk, my dear. Yes, I was married. It was through Mu that I first discovered this place."

"Oh, yes?"

"She lived here with her father. A holy man and, except for his daughter, a hermit, a man who had no idea how to speak to other human beings and no notion of how to carry out the task for which this valley was destined. He knew what needed to be done, you see, but he was not the proper agent. When I first met him, while I was working with the Chinese, I felt the power of the valley and persuaded him to tell me what he knew. I also fell in love with his daughter, Mu. As you can see, she suffered greatly from the ravages of the disease, and even before that she had put on weight and did not age very well, but in her youth she was very beautiful—her father's treasure. He died shortly after we were married."

"That was when you began to assemble your colony?" Chime asked.

"Yes. Of course, it was all very secret and I could not allow my Chinese masters to know of it. At first I used my influence as an official to make the trips and gather the supplies I needed, but that ended when the Chinese pulled back into Lhasa during the air wars. I remained here. It was isolated, and I was able to acquire quite a good pilot who served me in exchange for refuge here. That's Stoney over there."

Chime peered into the corner to get a better look at the pilot whose name had brought tears to Inez's eyes.

But Meru was saying, "You can see, looking at these helpless bodies of our sleeping friends, how disastrous it would be to allow ghosts to enter this compound."

"Naturally. But I'm curious. If you have stayed in this valley the whole time, when did you first learn about the ghosts?"

"We were plagued with them quite heavily for the first year or two after the end of the wars. You've been out there. You know what the ghosts are like, invading us, lurking by the heads of the sleeping, that sort of thing. Of course I anticipated it, and I did put up my wards over the valley. I was able to include the body of my wife in such protection as well, but one drains one's powers and concentration maintaining so many wholly magical defenses against such a continual onslaught. So as soon as we could, I used the special glass bottles I had asked Bertinelli to have made for me using my own formula, and Karl and Inga Meissen helped me design the apparatus in the next room, although I believe they think it will eventually have something to do with alcoholic spirits rather than the other sort." He gave her a small smile with a bit of a twinkle in the edges, sharing his little joke.

"I see," she said. But what she saw, what she was looking at, was the condition of the presumably still-living bodies encased in ice, their features as still and cold as carved stone. Most looked peaceful—Meru's wife's torso was broad, but her cheeks and eye sockets were sunken to an extent that made Chime wonder if the poor woman was merely frozen or had died.

By contrast, the pilot, whose features were chiseled, rather than sunken, whose hair remained intact, and who showed no signs of disease, looked instead to be in the prime of life. He also did not look happy about being frozen. His mouth was clenched in a grimace, his fists clenched on either side of his body, his chest seemed to heave outward, and one knee was slightly raised, as if he were about to kick.

"This process of freezing people, is it painful?" Chime asked, nodding to the pilot.

"Oh, no. But Stoney was difficult. When Kyoko discovered his disease, which appeared as a small lesion beneath his hairline, he underwent a period of extreme depression, concurrent with one of hostility and then denial. Actually, we put him on hold not only because of the disease process, which as you can see was not very far advanced, but because in a community this size he presented a real danger to the security and sanity of the others as his own sanity began to slip. It was the kindest thing to do for everyone's sake."

Chime said nothing. But she was receiving a feeling of oppression and fearfulness that was overwhelming in its intensity. All of Meru's eloquent arguments, explanations, and protestations of good intentions were drastically outweighed by the expression of anguish in every line of the pilot's frozen body. She realized she was looking at Meru's chief method of controlling any colonist who did not submit to his control. If the pressure from the other, still-faithful followers was not enough to still the doubts of anyone who wished to make their own decisions, this power Meru exercised over life and death, seemingly with the most benign of motives, would control the strays.

Something warm and soft bumped against her legs again. The cat's upturned face looked at her quizzically, the citrine eyes narrowed, the tufted ears twitching. She reached down and stroked the stripes between the ears, not for the sake of pleasing the cat but to comfort herself.

"You may carry me," the cat spoke to her mind. "It will be safer for both of us."

Chime reached down and scooped the animal up, burying her fingers deep in its plush coat, glad of its warmth in this freezing compartment. The cat struggled from its scooped position to put its paws on her shoulder, then mangled the embroidery of her wool jumper as it climbed up her chest and onto her shoulders, where it dangled paws down both forearms and rested its cheek against hers. It was as warm as a coat.

"That beast seems to like you," Meru said, his lip lifted fastidiously, with distaste. "It doesn't normally like anyone."

"I like this cat too," Chime said. "Perhaps if it is a burden on your resources, I might take it with me when I continue my journey? It will be company, now that Meekay is no longer living."

Meru turned around, his blue eyes wide and enveloping, the prism lamp casting rainbows onto his skin that made his expression at once elusive of emotion and grotesque. "But, my dear, you're here safe with us now. You mustn't think of leaving. We have need of your wisdom, your youth, your—"

They had been walking through the door into the next passage, and Chime rose on tiptoe to peer over his shoulder. "Is that the apparatus you were telling me about over there?" she asked, pointing to the gleam bouncing back from a variety of tubes and containers. As they entered, the cat jumped down from her shoulders and settled itself back in the shadows, stretched out in the middle of the floor.

"Ah yes, that is my spirit reservoir, what you might call a personality detention facility."

"Really?" Chime asked, and she could hear the alteration in her own voice, which grew as cold as the walls of the hold room.

Meru began an enthusiastic explanation. He did not, as she feared he might, notice the way she inched away from him. He must have gotten used to ignoring small signs of displeasure from his colonists, which would interfere with his vision of himself as their savior. Only when the small signs became open rebellion would he take notice . . . and action?

But his whole attention was centered on his explanation of the endless rows of shelves containing bottles and the mysterious device spread out on the tables in front of her.

"I call this the Hall of Souls, because it is. The device you see before you acts somewhat as a mechanized spirit trap. The wards and charms funnel the spirits to this spot, where, sensing an opening potentially leading to habitable bodies, the spirits squeeze themselves into this opening, where they are caught by other magical means in the collection tubes, from which they are further channeled into these bottles."

"*Why?*" Chime asked. "Why not simply make your ward close off the valley entirely? Wouldn't that protect your people as well?"

"Yes, but bear in mind that our colony will grow—we will have a need for spirits to inhabit the bodies of our children. It would be useful to have many to choose from, to which end I test, study, and examine these spirits to see which will be suitable and useful for the future."

Chime said softly, as gently as possible, "But while you detain those spirits here, they are unable to search for either enlightenment or for rebirth in some other place. You are depriving them of their journey through the bardo."

"Yes, my dear, I considered that. But the bardo is timeless and life finite. Surely it does no harm to detain these spirits a bit longer here, where they might find a rebirth under optimum circumstances, rather than letting them drift around out there? If they were going to find enlightenment, they would not have come looking for bodies here, and as for finding other places to be reborn, that is more difficult than you might imagine. You will be able to see this in the little program I will treat you to when we return to the palace. I think once you see it you will agree that we now live in an age and place where natural life of any kind has been rendered impossible. We must take destiny into our own hands if we are to survive, if there is to be any sort of reality.

"Initially, I did not undertake this enterprise for the purpose of collecting these seeking souls—I merely wanted to preserve the spirits of those among my people who had to be put on hold. You see, these bottles here," he pointed to half a dozen or so on the table, "separate from the others, are those of the people in the next room. Here's the prototype, the one containing the soul of Mu, this is Sven Strom's, this one belongs to Grady Stone, and here is Marco Bertinelli's."

CHAPTER XVIII

Meru showed Chime back to the garden, and she returned to the living quarters, walking straight through the building and out the front door. She could not leave the building fast enough to suit her, but hurried down the path to the pool, the cat running after her heels. She sat down cross-legged by the water, taking deep gulps of fresh air, exhaling the stagnant and decaying atmosphere of the compound.

When she had calmed her breathing, she said, "Cat—"

"Mu Mao," the cat corrected, but gently, wrapping a clawed paw reassuringly around her arm, digging in only a little. She stroked the paw. "And now that you are no longer in the company of the odious evil magician, I have a surprise for you."

"A surprise?"

"Boo!" a voice said in her ear. The ghost in white shorts, Toni-Marie, darted in front of Chime, making a face and waggling her fingers in her ears.

"Chime Cincinnati, what have you gotten yourself into now?" Meekay's voice asked her, then he too popped into sight.

Chime had never been so glad to see anyone in her life. If they had had bodies, she would have embraced them. "Meekay! Toni-Marie! You're here. How did you escape Meru's wardings?"

"We didn't," Mike admitted.

"But the bottles—you would have been caught in the bottles."

"Oh, yeah, we did that too," Toni-Marie said.

"But how did you get out?"

"I released them," the cat said, licking a paw and running it over his ears.

"You have to get out of this place now, Chime," Mike said.

"Yes, I suppose I do," she replied. "It's just that it's beginning to seem like every time I meet living beings, I have to run away from them, when my mission is to help them."

"We were listening to what that Meru guy was telling you in the caves," Toni-Marie said.

"You were? But I didn't sense your presence and I don't think he did."

"Just because the ghosts you've seen so far have been blatantly visible doesn't mean we can't be subtle when we want to. The cat here told us Meru was the one who set the ghost traps, and we weren't anxious to be noticed."

"*I* knew they were there," Mu Mao said. "I stretched out in front of the broken glass to disguise it so Meru wouldn't see."

"Take it from me, Chime," Toni-Marie continued, "that guy is definitely *not* worth saving, even if he'd let you."

"But he's not the only one here. There are others."

"That is so," Mu Mao said with a thoughtful twitch of his whiskers. "Of course, it's all the same to me since I am quite happy simply to be.

However, you, Chime, as the Terton, are an interventionist by definition. I suppose therefore you must start intervening. And you are quite correct in your assertion that Meru, whom we all agree is not worth saving, is not the only one to consider. *Some* of these people have pleasant aspects to their personalities if you approach them singly. They have been known to share tidbits of food, to produce warm places on the furniture, and they sometimes use their hands for the benefit of others who have no thumbs. Collectively they are by and large hysterical, unhappy, and forever engaged in establishing order of dominance, but that is to be expected."

Mike interposed his translucent presence between her and the cat's smiling face. "Chime Cincinnati, you must leave here at once. This is a terrible place for the dead, much less the living."

"Oh, Meekay," she said. "I feared the world would be a frightening place for the living, but I had no idea it would be fearsome even for the dead. We'll flee soon, my friend, but first I must see what can be done for the people in the thrall of Meru and for the poor souls trapped in the cave. Now, I suppose I should go back in there and *meet* some of those people. Meru has promised to show me vids of the end of the world."

"Now that," Toni-Marie said, "I'd like to see. For a little longer than the last time."

Chime shook her head. "Meru has too much power over ghosts, it seems to me. I wouldn't like for him to know you were here."

"We'll sneak in after the vids start," Mike promised. "I want to see too."

The cat crouched low, inching forward on the grass as if he were hunting. "We will all use the greatest stealth," he said.

Dinner was served at a beautiful table as long as three of the ones in the dining hall at Shambala. The armchair at the head of the table was empty.

Chime looked uncertainly at it and the table, where others were already seated. "Come sit by me, young lady," a small man with a large head of thinning curly gray hair said.

Chime accepted the chair, but immediately Inez Murdock sat down on her other side, giving the man a challenging look. "Chime, I'd like you to meet my husband, Arthur. Art, this is Chime—what city was that, honey?"

"Cincinnati," Chime said. "The birthplace of my father."

"Chime Cincinnati."

A young blond woman with strong features and a sturdy build set a vegetable casserole on the table in front of Chime.

Inez said, "And this is Gretel Meissen. Gretel, meet Chime."

"Ah, the swimmer in the sewer," Gretel said, wiping her hands on the apron she wore over her tunic and taking a chair herself.

Chime laughed. "Not before this meal, thank goodness. That dish smells wonderful, Gretel. Did you prepare it yourself?"

"Frau Bertinelli is the chef," Gretel answered shortly.

A buxom woman with rich dark hair bearing just a few gray streaks smoothed her skirt and her hair as she entered the room from the kitchen. "We may begin. The Master will be detained for a while. I took him a plate already."

As the woman seated herself, Inez said, "Allegra, have you met Chime?"

"No," she said, her smile a little wan in a face with much potential for vibrancy. "It's nice to see someone new, Chime. Please, help yourself. There is a great deal of everything. Except meat. I can't get used to fixing pasta and bean curd, even after all these years."

"Thank you," Chime said. "Is this a vegetarian community, then?"

"Not really," answered a trim, athletic woman at the other end of the table. Her gray hair was cut short and bore vestiges of red. Her skin had a weathered look, and her eyes seemed unusually dark and large behind round tortoiseshell-framed spectacles. "Not by doctrine or anything like that. But we felt the growing area was best used for the garden than for grazing, and were not sure how the animals would withstand radiation. All in all, it seemed wisest not to bring them here. Do you have animals where you came from? Where did you say it was?"

"Shambala," Chime answered. "We butcher animals occasionally, although it is not our usual way to kill. Still, we have a large community to feed, with many children. Mostly we use eggs and fish and chickens, which are easy to breed, but occasionally we sacrifice a yak or a sheep, if the herd is sufficiently large. Excuse me, madame, but you are . . . ?"

"Lupe Valasquez. I am pleased to meet you. Tell me more about this place you are from. Do the crops and animals not suffer from the radiation?"

"It never reached us," Chime replied. "We have protection."

"*Fas*cinating," said a woman whose heavy fair features matched Gretel's. "And what would that be? Protection against bombs!"

"Excuse me, Inga," a sweet-faced Asian woman said softly, "but I think perhaps Chime's community is not so closely monitored as I monitor ours, so perhaps she is mistaken about that protection."

"Kyoko Taminaga, the doc," Inez whispered.

"Kyo, don't be a pompous ass," a woman with a beautiful contralto voice said. Chime looked around Art to see the source—another woman. This one was quite elderly. She did not wear a tunic like the others, but instead wore a black crepe dress of some shining fabric, the bosom bedecked with glittering jewels and pearls. "We have only your word for it that Harry or any of the others were contaminated. *Who,* my dear, is going to say when *you* are to be iced? Do you perform self-examinations as rigorously as you subject us to them?"

"Our diva, the grande dame Sokolski," Art said, squeezing Chime's knee. "She's still pissed about her hubby getting iced."

"Madame Andreanna, if you do not appreciate our protections, whatever possessed you to favor us with your presence?" asked the balding, florid man seated next to Inga Meissen.

The Japanese man sitting next to Dr. Taminaga, Chime noticed, was busy scribbling away on a notepad, seemingly oblivious to the conversation. Every once in a while he'd look at it and grunt, and finally he handed it down to Chime, who saw that it was covered with mathematical equations.

"There!" he said triumphantly, "*That* is how much protection it would take to deflect the radiation we have been able to measure since coming here."

Chime looked at the incomprehensible scrawl then nodded and smiled. "Thank you," she said politely. "I have often wondered about that. Perhaps later you will explain this to me?"

The man, who Chime figured must be Ito Kurasawa, nodded in what was almost a bow. Chime bowed back.

Next to Inez a cadaverously thin man with straight graying hair and a large nose leaned over the table, elbows together over one side of his plate, and asked, "What I would like to know, Chimmee, is what brings you here if where you come from is so much more wonderful than thees place?"

"That's Emile Cointreaux, the painter," Inez whispered.

Chime nodded and said, "That is very easy, sir. I've come to find people like you and guide you back to Shambala. But I am also curious, what brings you here?"

He shrugged. "Fear? The terror of the annihilation perhaps? The force of an interesting personality?"

Beside him, a woman's voice, also with a French accent, said, "Admit it, Emile, you just wanted true seclusion to paint for a while."

He laughed, a short laugh that wished to contain humor but ended up as an admission of despair. "Oui, ma chère, and I have it now. Chimmee, tell me, shall I paint your portrait? I have now gone through all of the great schools—impressioniste, cubiste, expressioniste—and I have arrived back at realiste, so it will not be too bad. What do you say?"

Chime smiled, but before she could answer, Madame Cointreaux said, "Do you know, Chimmee, I think we come here perhaps because we do not at first believe Meru. For myself, I wished to be under the first bomb—cat-a-bloom! Ça! Voilà! Fini. So I think, yes, Tibet, they fight over Tibet always—Tibet will *not* be safe, as Meru tells Emile. Therefore I go, and when the time comes, I die. *Tout suite.* But it was not as I expected—the Master was quite correct in everything he said, and here we are." She sighed. "Still alive." She sounded very disappointed.

"Madame, I hope you will feel differently if you come with me to Shambala. We would love to have someone with your skill teach us to make garments like these and embroider as you do."

"Well, I for one love it here!" said a buxom young blonde. "I think it's divine!"

"That, Melody, is because you've never known anything else," Gretel Meissen said.

"Neither have you!" Melody said.

"No, but I would like to see what is beyond the mountains."

Before Chime could learn any more, Meru appeared at the head of the table. Chime knew he had to have come from the hallway while she wasn't looking, but she couldn't help feeling as if he'd just materialized.

"Our Gretel would like to see what lies beyond the mountains, would she?" Meru said, with an indulgent smile in Gretel's direction. "Your memory is very short, liebchen, but we were going to show the vids again for the benefit of our new friend anyway. So if you are all quite finished now, perhaps Art would be so kind as to boot up the vid sequence? I think it would be a good idea for us all to see once more what we escaped. I will join you afterward. I have some work to conclude in my study."

"I'd be honored," Art said, smiling at Chime, taking her arm as if they were starting a dance, the others following behind them as he steered her into a room she had not yet seen, a place where richly upholstered chairs were arranged around a wall screen.

She sat in the front, with Inez on one side of her, the others scattered throughout the room. After a few moments Art returned, holding a small black box full of buttons in his hand, and sat on her other side.

His free hand was about to drop to her knee when Mu Mao slipped into the room, jumped up on her lap and sprawled his spotted plush length across her thighs, covering her from waist to knees.

"Good kitty, Mu," Mike's voice whispered beside her ear. "If the dirty old man tries anything, take off his arm."

"Now then," Art said, "if we could have complete silence."

"Ooo, ooo, here it comes, the news commentator act," Inez said to Chime, then, more boisterously, "Quiet on the set, everyone."

Art's thumb jabbed downward and the lamp flicked out as a vision of the Potala, the former palace of the Dalai Lama in Lhasa, filled one side of the room. Half of the squared-off structure was in ruins, crumbling to the city below.

"As some of us remember, even before that fateful day, much of Tibet, India, the People's Republic of China, Mongolia, and the Soviet Federation already lay in ruins from the protracted conflicts for hegemony over the majority of Asia and Eurasia as represented by the Soviet

Middle East. Into this equation the North American Continental Alliance, NACA, added balance by providing troops and weapons to even out all odds. The interference of NACAF troops also prolonged all of the conflicts between other nations, so that NACAF essentially had no vested interest in any particular outcome but had people fighting on all sides. The only interest NACAF troops had in common with each other was that they prolonged conventional warfare while eliminating nuclear weapons in all of the countries where they fought. Unfortunately, this operation was carried out with that great oxymoron, military intelligence, and there were quite a few oversights, particularly when fronts were switched from country to country, or, as we say in show business, venue to venue. When the theater of operations—and I do mean theater—switched from the Middle East to Asia, Iraniaq was still left with a bad attitude and a considerable secret arsenal."

He clicked the button again, and this time the Potala blew up.

"Art, sweetie, *we've* all heard it a million times," Inez yawned.

"I'm showing this for Chime's benefit."

"I am aware of the background," Chime said. "From my previous lives and also from the stories of my elders in Shambala."

"Right, so enough with the history lesson already," Inez said. "The long and the short of it, honey, is that Iraniaq—at least they *think* it started there—got pissed off and popped its cork at Israel, which then popped its cork, and when Uzbekistan joined in on behalf of brother Arabs, that involved the other Soviet states, then Mongolia wanted to play, and pretty soon there were razors flying through the air, as the saying goes. There—see."

The hologram filled the air before them with a sky streaking with ribbons of light. The Potala disintegrated and turned into a dust cloud with fire at its roots. Three people, a man, a woman, and a child in a basket, died at Chime's feet.

"My dear, you're throbbing with emotion," Art said, kneading her shoulder. Mu Mao lazily reached a paw into Art's lap and did some kneading too. Art pulled back. "Surely you've seen that shot. We just use it for the intro."

Chime shook her head, feeling dizzy. It was coming back to her now, that night, watching the streaks destroying the world outside in the night sky of Shambala.

"Next vid, *s'il vous plaît*." Emile Cointreaux sounded tense now.

"Sure. Now then, this is what Lhasa looked like after the first strike, click, Beijing, click, Calcutta—the reports said the Ganges was actually sterile for a while after this, till the bodies clogging it began decomposing, anyway, after the cooling."

"What reports?" Chime asked. "Where did you get these pictures?"

"We're on satellite hookup, of course, though the receptors are on the mountaintop rather than the basin. The Master had it all rigged beforehand. Of course, many of our sources blinked out afterward, but meanwhile we got pretty much a blow-by-blow description until the tracking stations were taken out or the human operators died. Now then, as you can see, here's what happened to Pakistan."

"Where?"

"That black smudge in front of us. I'm glad these vids don't include smell."

The black smudge was succeeded by a quick series of others, which Art claimed to be Iraniaq, Kathmandu, Delhi, Vladivostok, Moscow, St. Petersburg, and so on.

Finally, an anthill appeared on the screen, swarming with insects, and Chime thought it must be one of Meru's experiments that had gotten in with the other holovids by mistake.

"That's Saigon. With their natural enemies gone, the insects took over a lot of Southeast Asia." Suddenly an arm flung up and Chime realized that the sort of twisting black object she had seen in one corner of the vid was actually a person covered in insects.

"Here you have the Russian countryside at noon."

A skeletal man sifted through soil to pull forth a rotting leaf, which he tried to eat.

"The Chinese countryside . . ." Art's voice continued, and now the vid was full of skeletons and half-rotting corpses. One or two people who were still living looked as if they were about to drop through the bodies. One bent over a corpse with a knife and started sawing. "They boil the flesh for food," Art said. "The animals all died first, of course, especially the cats and dogs." He gave Mu Mao a smug glare.

"Surely there are still some living elsewhere, as there are here," Chime said.

"Well, there *were*. Here's the makeshift hospital in Ethiopia a few days afterward—but of course the cities that didn't take major hits were overrun by refugees, and cut off from supplies from the countryside. Looting and riots did almost as much damage as the bombs. The radiation sickness, all of the new viruses and bacteria the insects and rotting carcasses have introduced, lack of hygiene—people have gotten pretty spoiled. Oh, here you can see London, Paris."

"Merde!" Cointreaux said softly.

"Ah, Chimmee, if only you could have seen Paris at night before—" Madame Cointreaux began.

"I'd have loved to see the Eiffel Tower and the Seine, like those pictures you showed me, madame," Melody said softly.

"What about AmCan?" Chime asked, her voice coming out slow and a little slurred from having to force words past the horrible pictures, not only in front of her, but forming in her mind via extrapolation.

Art shook his head. "Hard to tell. We've got shots of the park, but the smoke from the burning forest obscured North America. Nothing recorded."

"He refers," Lupe Valasquez said, her voice thrumming with emotion, "to what used to be South and Central America, before the norteamericanos wiped out all of the people and turned my mother's homeland into a huge park. Now even the trees are gone."

Art clicked again and a piece of something—rock? Chime couldn't tell—poked up from turbulent waters. "Here's all that's left of Japan."

Kurasawa's silhouette doubled up as if in pain and a low hiss escaped his lips. Dr. Taminaga said coldly, "That, Chime, is why *I* accepted Master Meru's offer to come here. Between the earthquakes and the tidal waves, the meltdowns of the nuclear reactors and the volcanic eruptions, combined with the raised sea level created by the melting of the poles, Japan was obliterated from the face of the earth. This was not unexpected. Scientists had been predicting such an event in the case of nuclear holocaust for generations."

Art clicked off the button. "That's all, folks. Curtain. Final bow. You've just seen the last transmissions of all of our cameras. Nobody left but us chickens, as my Kansan grandma used to say."

"He doesn't have to sound so smug," Mike said to Chime.

"I think they're all smug." Toni-Marie, to Chime's surprise, sounded as if she was crying. "Watching us all die like that from their little hidey-hole here."

"Well, my dear, what did you think?" This was Meru's voice, and with it the light blinked on again and the holograms ceased.

Chime twisted in her chair to look at him. She wiped her chin and realized for the first time that her own face was wet. "I think," she said judiciously, "that the world has undergone terrible pain. I see why, with all of that destruction and death, you wanted to preserve beautiful things and talented people here with you, even as we have done in Shambala. But even having witnessed the horrible things you've shown me, I believe that there are still living people out there who need refuge. If you or any of your people would like to come with me to Shambala, I welcome you. If several of your people would like to come, perhaps we could find a way to take with us those persons now on hold? In Shambala they can be cured."

"Oh, I very much doubt that," Kyo Taminaga protested.

"God, Chime, you sure are sneaky," Toni-Marie groaned in one ear. "Why didn't you send him an engraved invitation to stop you instead of beating around the bush like that?"

"I owe him that honesty," Chime thought back at her. "He has achieved a good thing here, in the preservation of these people, along with any misguided or evil acts he may be committing. He is a curious man who loves beauty and science—perhaps he will come with us if only to satisfy his curiosity and to find more stimulation?"

"And perhaps *not*," Mike thought. Chime could feel his nervousness, and felt her own at having the ghosts so near while Meru was in the room with his attention focused on her. *Would* he spot them?

"Maybe she's right, Meru," Inez Murdock said. "Time's running out for all of us, you know, just like it is for them out there. Are we just going to sit here on our butts while the world takes its course, or at some point are we going to jump back in and *do* something? Aren't you getting tired of this little empire, *Master*, really? I know I'm about as sick of looking at everybody here as I ever hope to be of anything in my life." She glanced at Chime for support, her eyes apprehensive but reflecting a glimmer of the hope Chime felt for them all.

"Quite the little activist all of a sudden, aren't you, darling?" Art asked. "Lovey, are you nuts? We just reviewed End of the World 101. Weren't you paying attention? There's *nothing*, repeat *nothing*, to go back to. Or on to. Or anything."

Inez turned on her husband. "That's just why you never were a very good actor, Art baby. No fucking imagination. If there's no place to go to, then where did *she* come from?" she demanded, pointing at Chime.

Meru clucked his tongue and shook his head in a fatherly manner. "Come come, Inez, you are as overstimulated as a child showing off for company. There is almost a feverish quality to you. Really, I think our Dr. Kyo should examine both of you. You have raised a very good point in asking where Chime comes from. She is a lovely, intelligent, and spiritual person, and we would all like to believe with her that she comes from some magical place that will embrace us all. However, I'm sure logic and common sense will tell any of you that this is not probable. More likely she has somehow survived in apparently good shape through events so terrible they have induced a dementia. In my eagerness to gather her into the fold, I neglected the safety and health of the rest of you. I wonder now if she *is* free of contamination or if she is possessed of some disease which has also infected our own Inez? Both of you consider what you have just seen, consider the outside world plagued with ghosts and spirits, and consider your realistic options. Tomorrow Kyo will conduct a thorough examination. It may be best for both of you to go on hold until this problem is identified and a cure found."

"Oh, come *on*, Master. You can't keep putting everyone who disagrees with you on hold or you're going to get real lonesome before long," Inez said, searching his face for something—perhaps for a man she had once believed in enough to follow to the ends of the earth. "What if it's real, Meru? You've been scaring us and yourself with these vids for thirty-five years now. Isn't it possible they don't tell everything? You *know* there's nothing wrong with Chime or with me. Don't *you* want to see this place she's talking about? What are we doing here? We have a colony of people past fifty, and only two young girls for a lot of old goats. That just isn't healthy. The people in the meat locker aren't the only ones on hold, Meru, We're all in suspended animation. I can't imagine having even less to do than I've been doing all these years. God, just to go shopping again!"

"That's the spirit," Toni-Marie cheered.

Inez looked as if she'd been doused in cold water. She sprang from her chair and batted at her ears, "Oh, shit, I'm being haunted."

"There now, you see?" Meru said. "What did I tell you?" He gave Chime a very severe look. "You are, as I feared, infested, are you not?"

"Oh no. It's only Toni-Marie and Meekay," Chime Cincinnati told him. "They wanted to see the end of the world too."

"Knowing how I have planned to keep this place wholesome and free of marauding spirits, you've brought ghosts among us," Meru said with a sad shake of his head.

"No," Chime protested. "They came by themselves, or rather, they came to see that no harm came to me, and were caught in your traps. Please do not be concerned. These are not just any ghosts. Meekay is the spirit of my companion from Shambala, of whom I spoke to you when first I arrived. Toni-Marie is a highborn young woman of good family from AmCan. She has forsaken the standard hungry-ghost behavior to assist other spirits."

Meru reached into the sleeve of his robe and pulled out a pinch of something that he flung toward Chime. Toni-Marie and Mike appeared on either side of her, Toni-Marie looking shame-faced and Mike defiant.

"Jesus Christ, Meru, those are *ghosts!*" Art Murdock screamed. "You said we'd never have to put up with ghosts here!" He whirled on Inez. "You see, you dumb bitch? See what you've let in here?"

Inez nodded, her face buried in her hands, soblike sounds coming from her as her body trembled and heaved.

"Well, pardon me, but I didn't ask to be dead," Toni-Marie said to the room at large. "Honestly, this is so prejudiced."

But Chime was watching Meru, who took something from his pocket and began waving it around, declaiming all sorts of odd-sounding words. They weren't Tibetan, or Sanskrit, or any of the languages she knew, though they sounded like them. Then she realized, as he finished, that he *was* speaking in Sanskrit, except he was talking backward.

She tried to follow what he was saying but couldn't mentally transpose the words fast enough. Mike and Toni-Marie, who had been very clear, began to waver, segment, and fade as Meru's voice rose and fell.

"Chime, Chime, you're breaking up here," Mike cried, as his image turned into blurred stripes until she could no longer see him. "Where are you?"

"Spirits who would haunt this sacred valley and who refused to be ruled by me," for dramatic effect Meru was repeating his last sentences in English, the common language of the compound, "I command you to go forth and wander the ends of the earth."

"Oh, hell!" Toni-Marie's voice cried, and then they were gone.

CHAPTER XIX

Meru, Chime, the people, the room, the hermitage, the valley, spun out of sight as Meru intoned his spell and the phrase "ends of the earth" echoed from the mountaintops.

Mike twirled end over end, tangling with Toni-Marie, spinning high in the air and rocketing forward with terrifying speed, as if he'd been shot from a cannon. Finally he saw nothing but Toni-Marie, whose expression mirrored the dismay and bewilderment he felt.

"Oh, this is great," Mike moaned. "Why did you have to open your big mouth? Look where it got us."

"Sorry," Toni-Marie said, "I just got a little carried away. . . . Well," she said, after considering the void around her, "I guess we both got a *lot* carried away, actually. Where the hell *are* we?"

"I don't know," Mike admitted. "But Meru said we had to wander the ends of the earth. Since all there is left of the earth is ends, maybe we get to pick."

"Just so it's not here," Toni-Marie said. "Where do you want to go?"

"Home, of course. Kalapa. Shambala."

"No desire to travel abroad at all, eh?"

"Let's just go home," Mike said impatiently. "You're the one with the experience at getting around. Help me."

"Pardon me," Toni-Marie sniffed. "I lost my ruby slippers someplace, and anyhow, right now I'm incorporeal and haven't got any heels to click together." She looked all around her at absolutely nothing and grew, if anything, paler.

Mike decided that maybe trying to take command was the wrong tactic, and switched to wheedling. "Toni-Marie, did I tell you about all the babies being born there?"

"You may have mentioned something."

"And there are no ghosts there," he added. "Nobody competing for the chance to be reborn into those cute little babies at all."

"Really? Well then, take us home to Aunt Om. Take us home to Aunt Om."

"Quit kidding around. You'll confuse whatever it is that lets us move around."

"Look, Mike, all I can do is show you technique. I've never been to your place before so I don't know, except for the name, what it's like. If I can't visualize it, I can't get there."

"Okay," he said, concentrating, "Then think of a horned mountain and a beautiful lake, lots of people—"

"I'm thinking, I'm thinking."

Mike's visualization started as if he was seeing something through a tiny thawed place in a frosted window—the horned peak of Karakal, with the tip of the chorten Thibideaux had built rearing from the top of the hill on which Kalapa compound scrawled. Then he thought of the compound itself, the buildings one by one, the lake, the rhodo-dendron forest, his sister's house, the moon over Karakal . . .

"There, I see the mountain!" Toni-Marie cried. "Is that it down there?"

It was. Mike swooped down toward the compound, then found himself spinning back up above the topmost peaks of Karakal again. Toni-Marie was spinning too.

"Huh?" she said. "Something repulsed us."

"Maybe the protective barrier is reacting to us as if we were alive."

He could see the barrier, a thinly scattered sparkling with a faint greenish tinge to it. Beyond it lay home, the dining hall, his parents' sleeping quarters, Isme. He thought with longing of his old bed, his parents sleeping nearby. They seemed so close, so much *his*, that it seemed impossible that he could not reach them. "Father, Mother, it's me, Mike," he said. "We're trying to come home but we can't get in. Please help us."

"What do you expect them to do?" Toni-Marie said. "Climb a ladder? Send a big dog with a flask of bourbon?"

He whirled angrily on her. "I expect them to do what they can if they can sense me, hear me. Chime Cincinnati heard you and all of the other ghosts out here. My mother used to hear the ghosts of the monks of the monastery, and my father is a very wise man. They don't know where we are. They don't know that I'm dead and that Chime needs help. They don't know we can't get back in."

"You think it's going to help, sending out psychic messages through that force field around your homestead?" Toni-Marie asked skeptically.

Mike gave her a defiant look. "I think I won't know unless I try," he said. "Mother, Father, it's me, Mike. I've been killed but Chime is alive. Only we need help. Please send someone for us, break the barrier, guide us home. Mother, Father, please help me."

After he repeated his message many times, weeping with frustration, Toni tapped him on the shoulder and said, "Look, sport, if they haven't received your transmission yet they're not going to. Let's try getting in another way, the way you and Chime came."

He nodded and joined her in concentrating on that place, back at the wide blue lake, just above the whirlpool, and there they were, poised above it. For one moment Mike thought, It's going to work—all we have to do is dive. But just as they were poised to leap into the mael-strom, the lake monster undulated between them and the hole. Toni-Marie ducked around him but to no avail, and Mike tried to go through him, but was repulsed in the same way he had been by the shield of Shambala.

"It's not going to let us in, Mike."

"We need Chime's help," he said. "She said that anyone who wanted back in probably would. She's the guide to Shambala. I'm sure she could get us back in."

"I don't know, Mikey, but I don't think it's such a good idea to face that magician again."

"We have to try," he said stubbornly.

But this time too they were unable to get close to their goal. They found the flat plain again, crisscrossed by streams. But when they tried to enter the valley, the wards repulsed them as effectively as Shambala's shield.

"Well, that's out. The only way back in there is through that hole, and we don't want to get trapped in the collector thingy again," Toni-Marie said with a shudder. "The nice kitty might not be around to help us out this time."

"Maybe Chime will come out."

"Yeah, well, and maybe she won't." She was silent a moment and then said, "Mike, I think we maybe ought to explore other options."

"*What* other options?"

"Well, go someplace else. Since you guys showed up I've seen three magic places and met two major magicians, counting your girlfriend."

"She's not my girlfriend and she's not a magician—not really. She's just a kid—well, a kid who's lived lots of previous lives as this very learned and saintly person. She doesn't really do magic—it's just that because she's still remembering all of these previous lives, she senses stuff and knows how to do stuff that nobody our age should be able to do."

"Uh-huh. I bet that's what she says to all the boys. But look, maybe there's some magicians in other places too, and some other people—from the looks of those vids, the missiles didn't wipe out nearly as many people as I thought. There might be pockets of people still alive everyplace, or at least be other kinds of magical places here on earth. Maybe we could get help there. Maybe there are all kinds of babies being born other places and we could get new bodies and come back and—"

"Chime says I can only be reborn in Shambala, because I was born there."

"Maybe we can find someone to take the spell off so you can get back there, then."

"Well, we could just wait for her to come out."

"But what if she doesn't? What if he keeps her?"

"I don't think he could, do you? I mean, that's not supposed to happen to a Terton. And anyway, if it did, she would just continue there until—until she died too and then—"

"And then, maybe as a ghost, she wouldn't be able to get back into Shambala either and there'd be nobody to guide anybody in or out and we'd all just be stuck out here in limbo. Mike, there have to be other magicians somewhere who can help us."

"I don't know why you're so sure of that."

"Because as my great-aunt Gaia-Jean the water witch used to say, magic is nothing but science flying by the seat of its pants. A lot of the technology, all those mechanisms and electronic doodads that science produced, have been blown sky high now, so it's back to square one. Anybody who can figure out how to survive and help other people survive is apt to be pretty powerful, don't you think? Like Meru, or Chime. Maybe the old-time magicians knew how to draw on us—not just the living, but the ghost spirits too, to make things work. The magicians are the ones who know about both worlds, and some of them are supposed to have been able to go between worlds. Seems to me that since I've already met two—well, three if you count the cat—they have had a better survival rate than most people too. So it stands to reason that if we scrounge around we ought to be able to find one piddly little magician left alive on this planet who will be able to get us into Shambala without Chime."

"Well, maybe. But you sure are coming up with a lot of unsupported theories."

"Yeah, well, I didn't make up most of it—I read it somewhere or saw it on the vid or something. And before I met you, there wasn't a whole lot else to do than, you know, ponder the nature of mortality and that kind of thing. Richie and I used to talk about it a lot. So, anyway, tell me, if you were going to look for magical power, where would you look?"

"Other than Shambala, you mean?"

"Yeah."

Mike thought back to his fairy-tale books, to the stories he'd heard his mother tell, to the stories Auntie Dolma told, and remembered his favorites. "Ireland," he said finally. "I guess it's no more magical than China or Germany or Russia or other places around England maybe, but it's an island. If we go to Ireland, at least we'll know where we are when we start looking."

Lobsang Taring sat up suddenly in the middle of the night, his senses alert, his ears attuned to the sound that had awakened him from a deep sleep.

He heard sobs and was momentarily confused, until he realized that Viv was crying in her sleep. He touched her and she opened her eyes. "Mike," she said. "He's . . ."

The dream came back to him then of his son's voice, calling to them. "I know," he said. "I know."

CHAPTER XX

Inez knew she had screwed up big as soon as Meru banished Chime's ghost friends. Just went to show how much this place was getting on her nerves. The ghosts hadn't been at all scary or threatening—some blond girl in a pair of shorts, and a good-looking young boy in a pair of padded pajamas similar to the ones Chime had worn through the cesspool.

Inez was also alarmed. She had begun to think that most of Meru's tricks were just that—tricks, or mumbo-jumbo-enhanced technological developments like the hold caves. When the ghosts first appeared, she thought Meru was siccing them on her as a punishment for her moment of rebellion.

He loomed over Chime like he wanted to make her disapppear too, and poor Chime looked as lost as a wild raccoon that had found its way onto an L.A. freeway. With the most paternal and loving expression on his face, Meru was reminding them all that their existence depended on his beneficence. Inez wanted to gag, but instead she threw herself at his feet and clutched his knees, crying, "Oh, Master, how could I ever have doubted you? I'm just so silly sometimes—it's just that I get bored and—oh, but those horrible ghosts!" She gave a realistic shudder then looked at him with the tears she could always call up at will, making her eyes bright and shiny.

Meru wasn't stupid, but he was susceptible to her, and since he believed that he knew what was best for everybody else, it didn't take much convincing to persuade him she agreed with him. Her main problem was not overdoing it.

He knelt and took her face in his hands, raising her. "My poor Inez, of course a woman, an artist, of your sensitivity would be strongly affected by all this. Everything is under control now, the ghosts are gone, and my safeguards will protect us."

He turned to Chime, shaking his head in a kindly way. "Poor girl, I don't know how far you have come, to be so lonely that you accepted ghosts for companions. It's very unwholesome for the living to keep close company with the dead. I hope that our fellowship may help you recover your sense of balance. Run along now, my dear, and show Chime to her room."

"Yes, Master," Inez said meekly but with a lingering look that was full of the promise of her newly recovered devotion.

She extricated Chime from Art, who was enjoying comforting her with croons and pats. Inez jabbed him on the arm with a forefinger.

Art drew his hand back and made a grand gesture of presenting Chime to Inez, an expression of wounded innocence on his face. Inez plucked at Chime's sleeve, shooed the cat down from her lap as if it did not weigh close to thirty pounds and have claws like scythes, and led Chime back through the house.

As soon as they were out of earshot from the others, Inez apologized. "Chime, I'm so sorry. I didn't realize the spooks were with you. But Meru's right, you know, sweetie. Ghosts are so creepy—"

"They remind us of our own mortality," Chime said, "And I think that is a good thing, although sometimes, of course, it is better to bear in mind only this life."

"What did you mean when you said that girl wasn't acting like a 'hungry ghost'? Is that the kind that eats people?"

"Oh, no. Although I recently met a living man who *does*. No, a hungry ghost is one that no amount of nourishment or riches can satisfy. This ghost is always looking to be reborn over and over, trying to satisfy its greed. When Meekay and I first met Toni-Marie, she seemed to be a hungry ghost, but I think she may be at last starting to grow toward another phase. You see, a hungry ghost can have everything and still be hungry, because this sort of being is not satisfying the need for what he truly must have—and that is enlightenment."

"Sounds familiar," Inez said. "I guess all of us, if we were dead, might be that kind of ghost."

"Perhaps," Chime said, and after a moment she asked urgently, "Inez, did you mean it when you apologized to Meru? Have you been, could you be, happy here?"

"Happy? Well, now, that depends. I'm living—surviving, at least, and that means I've won, doesn't it?"

"But won what? In the end you will die too."

"Honey, I am not exactly the cerebral type. All this philosophy is lost on me. I go nuts in here. I *want* to leave and I wish we could go *home*, but you saw the film. Lord only knows what's out there, and here at least we're safe."

"Yes, safe from the outside." Chime sank down on the bed, looking small and very worried. "It is sad for me to be without Meekay. Usually when someone dies, you should not feel sorrow for them, because they will either continue to work through their karma or be headed for Nirvana, unless of course they become so lost they end up in Hell—I wish I hadn't thought of that. Of course, many would say that the earth as it is now is a Hell shared by the living and dead. Oh, dear. I wonder where he is. I hope he can find his way back."

"I wouldn't count on it," Inez said. "You knew this ghost like from a long time back, huh?"

"Oh, yes. He has been like my brother to me in Shambala, though I think I've only known him in one previous life."

"Funny, back before I'd met any personally, I used to think that ghosts were kind of a kick. Once I even paid a woman to help me contact the dead to find out what my future was—poor bitch didn't have nearly enough imagination to come up with anything near the truth. Of course, back then ghosts didn't seem so scary. You read about them for years in books—oh, yeah, I used to read when I was a girl. My family couldn't afford a computer until my folks joined NACAF and Mama caught a general's eye and we got a cushy post in New Zealand. It was a staging area for supervising trouble in Asia back then. From way back. This general was a lover, not a fighter, know what I mean?"

Chime was easy to talk to. She stopped looking anxious and perked up while Inez talked. Inez sat down beside her on the bed. The bedroom, which had originally belonged to one of the servants, was small, with no other place to sit, just the bed, some pegs for clothing, a shelf by the cot for a candle, no window, and no lock on the door.

Chime scooted to the head of the bed and sat cross-legged, rocking a little and nodding while Inez continued telling how a nice girl like herself ended up in a place like this. The cat jumped up beside her and rested its chin on her foot. Inez had the oddest sensation that it understood every word she said.

"The general saw my talent, encouraged me to go to all the films they showed for the soldiers, bought me a holovid player so I could study all the greats, and got a buddy of his in L.A. to sponsor me so I could return to the NAC and begin my career. I was younger than you even, I'll bet, when that happened. I got a couple of small parts, just to test my appeal, and then this producer and I began to develop a more personal relationship, something not based on *his* relationship with the general. I got better parts then, thought I was on a rising tide, till I met Art. He was a hot property back then, my leading man in *Miss Scarlett Rises Again,* which was a reclamation film about how the descendant of Scarlett O'Hara saves the South from pollution while finding true love with a major polluter, who she reforms, of course. It would have been my breakthrough, except that the producer lost interest when he saw what was happening between Art and me.

"From then on I mostly just did small parts in Art's pictures. He met Meru while doing a war flick on location here in Tibet—it wasn't quite so hot in this zone then. War flicks were very popular in the NAC. Everyone was so patriotic there back then. The economic thing was still sifting out the unrich, so somebody we knew was always sort of dropping out and joining up with the military. We'd have parties for them and promise to write, and then nobody'd ever hear from them again, of course. I was very popular on the recruiting circuit, being a successful NACAF brat myself and still in touch with Mom. Dad got killed, I think, sometime shortly after Mama took up with the general. But enough about me, sweetie, tell me about yourself."

"Like what?" Chime asked.

Inez leaned forward and whispered, "Like what *is* this place you come from that you talking about it makes Meru break out in a cold sweat? How have you managed to wander around out there all by your lonely without going stark-raving mad, and how did your buddy get turned into a ghost?"

"Oh, that," Chime said, laughing. "To begin with, as I think I mentioned, I am the reincarnation of the Terton of Shambala. Mike and I are from the community of Kalapa, a place rebuilt on the ruins of the mighty city that was once Shambala's capital. My father in this life was a soldier like your father, a heroic man from a long line of military leaders. He cared for his soldiers, and for the civilians under his command. More than once he risked his own life to save them, until he was captured. It's all rather complicated, but in a former life I managed to save him so he would be in Shambala when the missiles came. He in turn saved my mother from the attack of a hunger-crazed snow lion," she said, stroking the chin of the snow cat lying beside her belly-up on the bed. "My last incarnation died demonstrating to him and the others the folly of leaving the protection of Shambala while the after-effects of the missiles were still so thick in the air. The combination of radiation and the protective barrier of Shambala killed me very quickly, though as you see, not permanently. I was reborn to them some

years later, and when I reached my majority of eighteen years, my friend
Mike found a way for me to leave Shambala, and here I am."

"Oh," Inez said, so stunned by the oddity of Chime's background
that all she could think to say was, "Well, your parents must be worried
sick about you." Not that her own folks had ever worried a whole lot
about her.

"Perhaps," Chime said. "But they should have been prepared. I
told everyone that the time had come for me to leave Shambala, and
only those of us my age are really able to do so. To go overland is a
very difficult journey, and my father, like so many of the others, is nearly
110 years old now. Even Meekay's mother is in her seventies now."

"Well, obviously *they* wouldn't be in any shape to climb mountains,
but—"

"Oh, but they are, as long as the mountains are within Shambala.
They and the others all seem to be very little older than they were when
first they entered the protection of Kalapa, and can climb mountains
to their heart's content within the protected realm. Once they leave,
however, they revert to their true age, and my father, at least, would
not survive the experience, nor would others in the community who
are much older than he is. So it is up to the young to come to the aid
of the outside world, and it is my ancient duty to lead others—"

Inez couldn't believe what she was hearing. "Wait a minute, wait
a minute. Slow down. You're honestly saying you don't get *old* in this
place you come from?"

Chime nodded. "As a matter of fact, if you are becoming old out
here from too much worry or illness or other bad conditions, in Shambala you heal and begin to look younger. It is a healing place too. Food
grows quickly and is very healthful."

"That's what you meant when you told Meru if you took the people
on hold with you, this place would *cure* radiation sickness?" Inez hadn't
taken any of that too seriously before. She'd known Chime was someone
special, had felt that she had some knowledge, something that would
offer hope none of the rest of them had had, but she had no idea until
now that the truth would be so spectacular, or that she herself would
be so ready to believe—after falling for Meru—that what Chime was
telling her really was true.

But Chime was nodding. "Yes, most certainly."

"I'll be damned," Inez said.

"Oh no, not if you can come with me." Chime dimpled a little, making her little joke.

Inez grinned back at her and said, "No, I mean, Meru promised that this was Shangri-La, that it was a safe place where we would be free from any of the after-effects of the war and the—you know, the missiles. *His* idea of not aging is being put on ice, like the poor suckers in the hold room. And I'll bet you could tell from the way he was threatening us with it earlier tonight that he doesn't always use it to save the lives of sick people. I noticed that right after certain people had little disagreements with him, Kyo found some kind of sickness in them and they had to go on hold whether they liked it or not. That's what happened to Stoney." Inez stopped, remembering for a moment the smell and the *warmth* of his skin, trying to remember how he smelled. Poor baby.

"The pilot?" Chime asked.

Inez inhaled deeply and waggled her shoulders to try to release the tension she felt building as she talked about him. "That's right. The guy who flew us in here. Big good-lookin' guy, honest like nobody else, the only one here who was perfectly happy wherever he was, really. There was nothing wrong with him the night before Meru had him put away. You may have already figured it out, but Stoney and I had a thing, an affair. Art and I had gone our separate ways by then, and Stoney and I—maybe Meru was jealous. I was involved with him for a while too, before we came here, though God knows he's gotten it on with enough of the other women. In case you hadn't noticed, it's mostly men in the hold room—men and *his* wife.

"But I expect the real reason he put Stoney away was because he knew too much. Stoney knew I was restless, and he put it to Meru that maybe he should start flying little forays out across the country to see if any survivors were around. He kept the plane in good condition, and he actually just wanted any excuse to fly again. It was a mistake to bring it up to Meru, though, because a very short time after Stoney confronted Meru, voilà, what did Kyo find but a radiation sickness lesion! Surprise, surprise, surprise—" Inez stopped, choking on anger and bitterness.

"It took about four other guys to convince Stoney that being put on hold was a good idea."

"Yes," Chime said. "He does not look at all pleased to be frozen in the ice cave. Meru showed him to me."

A shudder ran delicately down Inez's back. "You mean you went *in* that place."

"Oh, yes. Meru showed it to me this morning. Have you never been there?"

"Not since the early days, when we hid back in the caves to escape the impact of the first blasts. He set it up after that and told none of us to go back there unless he asked us to. As if anybody would. The whole place is gruesome. Lupe Valasquez gardens back in the caves sometimes, but I can't stand it."

She was seeing Stoney again, when they took him away. "Chime, I think Meru is really nuts, and I think he's scared of you because you're what he claims to be and isn't. We've got to get you out of here, and you have to take me with you while I'm still able to go." She looked down at her hands, still fine-skinned, but the flesh was looser on the bone now, webbed with lines like old leather. She didn't want to get older and older here in this godforsaken little valley, never seeing anyone new or doing anything different again. She missed the routines of her life in the NAC, choosing clothes, going to hairdressers, creaming her face, making up, playing in the jewelry, even dieting. But it wasn't like that was all there was to life. It was just a pleasurable buildup to whatever you were preparing yourself *for;* work on a play or a film, a gala where you'd meet interesting people, travel, the premiere of some wonderful event, a new man. Here there were no more possibilities, and if she was hungry for anything at all, she was starving for those. "I was lying when I said I was okay here, Chime. I'd do anything to get out."

"Including go back into the caves?" Chime asked.

Inez took a deep breath and said, "Well, okay, even that, though maybe you'd just kind of need somebody to stand guard, you know, *outside?*"

"It's natural you would feel that way, Inez, but I think you might be interested to know that Meru has put a little magic spell on the caves to *make* you not want to go in there. The caves may be one of the entrances to Shambala. I don't think Meru was lying when he told you that this was Shangri-La, which is how westerners know my country, but this place is so far from the center, its powers are much weaker. Probably the network of caves has become blocked by the avalanches and earthquakes that occurred when the missiles dropped. Nevertheless, before I leave this place, I must free the people trapped in the hold room. Are there others here who would come with us?"

Inez shook her head slowly. "No. Not right now anyway. Meru has them all pretty well buffaloed. Maybe—if we had time to convince them—at least some of them would come, but I think if we try, Meru will have both of us made over into ice sculptures."

"Very well. Then we will start with the souls he has trapped," she said. "When does Meru sleep?"

Inez smiled a long, slow smile, thinking of Meru's face and how glad he was when she rejoined him. He might be weird, but he'd rather have her warm and alive than iced over, despite his threats. In lieu of an award-winning film role, convincing him of her devotion long enough to make sure he had an unusually good night's sleep that night would have to do. "Whenever we need him to. You just leave it to me," she told Chime.

CHAPTER XXI

Thinking of Ireland, they spun through the void until they found themselves overlooking a small body of land in the middle of a surging sea.
Every mud-brown debris-laden wave cast pieces of the shattered past
upon the blackened, broken shores. The bodies of birds and animals,
some malformed, some skeletal remains, mingled with timbers and the
wrecks of boats, broken bottles, an enormous Guinness sign, torn and
mud-soaked lengths of cloth, plastic sheeting, bandages, the roofs of
houses. The shores were lacking in shelter, lacking in life-forms except
for a few carrion-eating birds that might have mutated from sea gulls.

No cities stood, no towns, and the filth of the sea bled into a river that attempted to pour relative purity back into the mess. A heavy brown mist that could have been smoke obscured much of the island, but the shoreline was etched in filthy blackness bleeding into the sea like kohl liner weeping from a dead eye.

Looking down at it, Mike felt like weeping himself. "The edges of Ireland," he said, running his spectral finger along the coastline, "they're—"

"Gone." Toni-Marie finished the sentence for him. "Dublin, Belfast, Limerick, Cork, all the ports and castles, all the pubs and shops. Kaput."

"But this was a place of much power," Mike said. "In my fairy books it talked of ancient civilizations and wizards and leprechauns—"

Toni-Marie shook her head. "That was a long time ago, pal. If ever. Those were folk tales. Made-up stuff."

"Next thing, you'll be telling me you don't believe in ghosts either," Mike said.

"But that's different," she began, then grinned slowly and said, "Well, anyway, nobody talked seriously about fairies when Richie and I came over for the Harping of the Harbor. The talk was all about normal stuff, music and boats and good ports, except that Ireland was a little like the southern states in the NAC—when they talked of war, the war was old—here it was *really* old. All one war, actually. Kind of like one of those tundra fires Dad used to fight in Alaska, never really burn out, just burn low, underground for a while."

"Underground!" Mike said. "Of course, that's where the people will be. In the faerie mounds. They're like the tunnels of Tibet, I think. All of those stories of people going in, and when they came out an hour or so later, they were seven years older."

"Underground isn't a bad idea," Toni-Marie agreed. "Let's follow the river inland. I *think* this may be the Shannon. If we didn't run out of Ireland about here, a little ways out to sea is where Limerick would have been."

Inland the forests had begun to claim the banks, and where the river spread itself into lakes, the waters were calm and silver. Where cultivated farmlands had been, there were rows and rows of markers;

stone, wood, rock-filled plastic bleach bottles were standing guard over the graves of those lucky enough to have had someone around to bury them.

As they crossed one lake, fleets of small patched boats rowed determinedly toward an island containing something that made Mike grin triumphantly at Toni-Marie—a castle. Or at least the ruins of one, stonework blending with the silver of the lake and the smudge of mist blurring the foliage surrounding it.

About this time they saw that other ghosts were also drifting toward the castle and from it, chatting with each other or with the living rowing the boats or smoking along the shores. A few ruined buildings clung close to the castle, and piercing the mist, Mike made out what looked like a stone space rocket, which he pointed out to Toni-Marie.

"It's just a silo," she said. "Come on. Let's see what's going on in there."

Outside the castle a sign like the one they had seen on the beach was propped up against the stonework. GUINNESS, it said. From inside came the sound of music and laughter.

Mike smiled with wonder at the sound. "There must be a magician here," he told Toni-Marie.

Inside people were drinking, eating, arguing, and singing—not all that many *living* people, but some, though the merriest and most genuine laughter came from the mouths of the dead.

The living were hollow-eyed and gaunt and their conversations were querulous, their faces sickly. One child playing at its mother's feet had the start of a second head on its shoulder, and what looked like two men turned out to be one joined at the torso, Siamese twins.

But there was an attempt at normalcy, even some flirting going on between odd-looking people who seemed to find attraction simply in the fact of the other one's living flesh.

As they had noticed before, the dead mixed freely with the living, and the living didn't seem to notice or care. Ghosts snuck sips of the beverage that was being drunk by most of the people—a brew clearer than water and seeming to emanate from a collection of tubes and tubs behind the bar.

Mike approached one of the ghosts who had been sneaking sips from the mug of a skeletally thin woman who was preoccupied, whispering something that seemed to be funny to a dark-haired man. "Excuse me—"

The ghost, that of a youngish man in a T-shirt that said READ THE DEAD—JOYCE, and sporting a wispy blond mustache, looked vaguely startled. "And what would you be, then?"

"My name's Mike. I'm here—we're here—looking for a great magician." Toni-Marie made a face when Mike said this, but he still thought she was being entirely too skeptical and squeamish of supernatural matters for someone who was herself a wraith. He hoped the Irish ghost would be more reasonable.

"Just like that, eh?" the ghost in the T-shirt asked. " 'Here I am, where's your great magicians?' Why don't you get your own great bloody magicians? Or don't they have any where you come from, wherever that might be?"

"Yes," Mike said. "There are at least two great magicians in Tibet, and one of them has banished us from the side of the other one, so we are hoping that one of yours could reunite us with her."

"Is that all?" the ghost said, laughing at him. "Don't want much, do you, lad? Tibetan, is it? And the lass? Is she Tibetan too?" he asked with a wink through Mike at Toni-Marie, who winked back.

"No, she's Texan."

"Ah."

"Yes, and she wants to find a magician too, so could you tell us where we might find one?"

"Not living. None have been alive here for hundreds of years, but dead, now . . ."

Mike turned to Toni-Marie. "What do you think? Is dead okay? He says there aren't any still alive."

She shrugged, and smiling, moved forward to speak to the Irish ghost. "This is amazing the way you guys can mingle so freely with the living here." She began to move in time to a song being sung in one corner, the living singer stopping occasionally when he forgot the lyrics, until one of the ghosts nearby whispered the words in his ear. "I mean, look at that. We got sent away because I said something *agreeable* to a living woman. The living are scared to death of us."

"Ah, well, you see, being dead has always been respectable in Ireland. The best party you ever get happens after you die."

"That's terrific," Toni-Marie said. "But doesn't it make people nervous to know that you're sitting around, waiting for a body so you can reincarnate?"

"Oh, no no no, not a bit of it. They believe in dyin' but they don't believe in reincarnatin', so they really don't care. Before we died, we didn't believe in it either, so nobody's in any particular hurry to go back to livin', which, as you can see from the shape of some of these folk, has its drawbacks. We get great respect this way, you see, bein' the dear departed without actually havin' to *depart*. Since them as knows better than us decides when's a good time for us each to reenter life, it's no good us gettin' impatient even if we were inclined. These poor souls still hangin' on to their lives mostly don't even notice us, them stayin' too full of poteen, that bein' about the only safe thing to drink *or* eat around here these days. They only worry about us in specific cases—at births, of course, and when they're alerted that their own end is drawin' nigh."

"You said somebody decides who gets to live next," Mike said. "Who would that be?"

The ghost smiled, teasing. "And who would that be but the great magician you're after searchin' for?"

Just then another ghost stood in the doorway and cried to the room aloud, "O'Brien says to send out the call, Mary McGinty's laborin' hard and 'tis time to soul her baby. Anyone interested in applyin' for the position come right along."

"Bloody great fool, bellowing out like that," their informant said.

"Yes indeed," Toni-Marie said. "Doesn't he realize that the fewer ghosts who know, the better chance he'll have of being reborn?"

"Ah, it's not that I was referrin' to. O'Brien regulates that very well, which it's his job to do, him bein' clergy. No, but the bellowin' out of it like that is sure to attract the attention of the less desirable element."

"Who are they?" Mike asked. "I thought you said everything was pretty well decided and everybody was happy with it."

"Not quite everybody. There's always someone to start a row.

There's a few as so hate any form of rule or governance that they won't even follow the lead of the clergy. Even after a soul is properly chosen, they try to mess up the process, kidnap the baby and try to drive the new soul from it, while meantime one of their own bedevils the parents by pretending to be the real baby. Sick is what it is, I say. Just plain sick."

"Changelings," Mike told Toni-Marie with an I-told-you-so nod of his head. "He's talking about changelings."

The cottage where Mary McGinty lay was raw and cold, built of sod and driftwood, and various trash of a useful size. It was a shack, a lean-to, where Mary McGinty lay on a mattress of messy rags. Mike felt a sharp sense of déjà vu, thinking of his sister and the ill-fated birth of her child.

Beside the midwife stood another man, one who looked like one of the giants in the illustrations in Mike's fairy-tale books. The man was red-haired, red-bearded, red-nosed, and rotund, dressed in a soiled white shirt and a shabby black suit too small for him.

It took Mike a moment to realize that the man was a ghost, he seemed so robust and so completely in command as he held at bay the queue of spirits crowding the room. Some seemed to have definite designs on the child, others were merely curious.

"You two!" the red man called. "What do ye think ye're doin' over there? The queue's clear around the square by now."

"We're just watching," Toni-Marie said.

"Are you Mr. O'Brien, sir?" Mike asked.

"That I am, lad, and the scourge of them as tries to get above themselves, thinkin' just because they're dead there's no order in the universe. There are several hundred souls before you to claim the right to be reborn in this child."

"Actually, sir, we just came to find you," Mike said.

"Then you can wait until my business here is done," he said. "Now then, the rest of you can go home. The spirit of Fiona O'Grady has first claim here. Fiona love, go to Mary now." A woman's ghost from the front of the line stepped forward and knelt beside the mother, then looked up at O'Brien for approval.

"That's right, love, just think yourself in there just like you was goin' any other place. You'll bond with the little one there. Go quickly, Fiona-that-was, we've need of your kind back on earth again."

Mike opened his mouth, closed it, opened it again, and finally asked aloud, "How do you know who to pick?"

"Silence!" O'Brien thundered. "Have you no respect for the livin'? In with ye, Fiona."

Fiona's ghost, that of a plain-faced but graceful woman, gave a last jubilant smile to O'Brien and the ghosts gathered around, tenderly laid her hands on Mary McGinty's heaving abdomen, then flowed into her own wrists until she disappeared. A moment later a squalling baby crowned between Mary's thighs.

Toni-Marie whispered to Mike, "Fiona O'Grady? Of course, she was the leader of the Irish peace movement! She's the one who got the orange and green factions to cooperate with each other, send the English and NACAF armies packing, and clean up crime in Ireland. The country was reunified just before Richie and I sailed off for the China Sea. Must have had about six months worth of peace before the world blew up."

Twenty minutes later the midwife proclaimed, "A boy!"

"I can't look," Mary said wearily when the midwife tried to hand her the squalling child. "Is he—normal, my babe?"

"Glory be and he is," the midwife assured her. "Well, there is a little extra finger on one hand, but other than that he's perfect. What's his name to be?"

The other ghosts were fading away as all of this occurred, but in spite of O'Brien's forbidding mien, Toni-Marie and Mike pressed closer.

Mary inspected the baby herself and said, "I guess I'll name him after his father."

"And what name would that be?"

"Well, I'm sure I don't know *yet*. It'll have to wait a bit until I see who he resembles."

O'Brien's ghost watched the three living people, the two women and the new infant boy with the soul of Fiona O'Grady, and mused, "Ah, that Mary! And to think, when I was a priest, I might have condemned such a wonderful woman." Then he saw Toni-Marie and Mike still there and said, "What's the matter with you two? Do I look as if I'm in need of haunting? You were askin' earlier, boy, how I pick, and there's good examples right there before you."

"Yes, sir," Toni-Marie said. "And I can see how ordinary folks like us wouldn't stand a chance when there's people like Fiona O'Grady who have to be reborn into the world."

O'Brien rose to his feet, patted spectral dirt from his spectral pants and said, "Well, now there you'd be mistaken. For one thing, there aren't that many souls as good as Fiona's choosin' to be reborn into this world—"

"Do the Irish have bodhisattvas too?" Mike asked.

"Everyone has them, lad, thanks be to God. People who are good enough to go on to a higher reward but instead come back to show the light to their fellow human beings. Ah yes, we need the Fiona O'Gradys to brave the future, to have principles and vision and the intelligence to lead people forward out of brutish lives of sickness and want. But there aren't that many of them, and even if there were, I wouldn't be choosin' to send too many back in the same generation. They're strong-minded people, visionaries, and each has a different agenda for how mankind is supposed to work. It would be awful confusin' to have too many of them at once. No, for every one of them I'd send a hundred or two hundred of the practical, clever souls like the midwife, people who have been in this world a few times and learned a few things, who take life as it is without much fuss and who can make themselves useful and implement the grand ideas of the Fionas of the world. But for every two hundred of them, I'll send a thousand simple, lusty souls like Mary McGinty."

"Who were those people in *their* last lives?" Toni-Marie asked. Mike thought that if she could have taken notes, she would have. He was certain that if O'Brien would accommodate her, Toni-Marie would be reborn right here and forget about him and Chime and all of the people in Tibet. And why not? Mike knew he'd miss her company, though.

"Horses, deer, rabbits maybe, in some cases," O'Brien said with an indulgent smile at the new mother, who was now leaning back nursing the baby while the midwife cleaned her bed. Meanwhile, a trio of men holding hats in their hands stood outside the doorway, looking anxiously in. "Your higher animals, experiencing their first lives as humans. Like Mary here they're wantin' nothin' so much as to cram all of the eating, drinking, sleeping, and loving they can cram into this life, and are even more occupied with omittin' not a single wondrous function of the body—be it birthin' or burpin'—than they are fearful of the myriad terrible fates that may befall them, up to and includin' bringin' monsters onto the face of the earth."

Toni-Marie was nodding enthusiastically with everything O'Brien said, but Mike asked, "Ah, then it is a new spirit to rejoice so much in the flesh."

O'Brien shrugged. "Not necessarily. The fairie were very old spirits who could choose to be reborn as trees or animals or people, as they liked. The point is, these spirits are vital enough to withstand the earth as it is now. Maybe in the future, when they've lived more lives, they'll recall when they were deer or rabbits and decide this was a totem, like the Native American folk." He said, "Or venerate trees, not so much because they think they're God but because they remember being trees.

"And who," O'Brien asked in a friendlier tone, now that he was not so busy, "might *you* be, and what is it that you're wantin'?"

"I'm Mike Taring-Vanachek, of Shambala, and this is Toni-Marie Adair of Texas. We were told you're a great magician," Mike said. "And might be able to help us return to Shambala. You see—"

"There's no such person in Ireland."

"Well, we realize he or she might be dead," Toni-Marie said. "That really doesn't matter to us, as long as we get back to Shambala. Mike's from there, you see, and he can only reincarnate there, and Chime Cincinnati, she's like this holy woman and—"

"Young woman, I think there's a few things about the magicians of Ireland, of whom you might say I'm the last, that you don't under-stand," O'Brien told her.

"Such as?"

"Well, for one thing, most of the old Celtic magicians—the Druids, you know—existed a long time before this."

"I know that, but they reincarnated, right?"

"Yes, but Ireland has been a very religious country for a long time. The magicians were reborn into times that didn't appreciate such things as sorcery, so some of them emigrated, some converted—"

"Like you?" Mike asked. "You must be a very great holy man, but you wear no special robes."

"Yeah," Toni-Marie said. "What are you, a priest?"

"Isn't that a good question, now? I've been a little bit of everything, to tell you the truth. In the beginning I may have been one of the Tuatha de Daman, then one of the sidhe, the fairy folk, and later on I was a Druid. Oh yes, quite a few lifetimes at it till along come the Christians. Well, I didn't jump back into the religious side at once but was a harper and a harper's son, and a shanachie, carrying the old tales down, till in one life I switched over to Christianity and became a priest. I was a bit of a rabble rouser in that life, so in the very next one I was a Protestant minister. In this last life I was an unaffiliated theologian and a fiddler on the weekends. After all these lives, I've found bein' affiliated with one church or the other rather limitin', and no matter what you call yourself, those with supernatural connections have supernatural responsibilities. It's that way whether you wear a collar or worship God through His countenance as revealed in the trees."

"Then you're sort of an Irish bodhisattva who hasn't yet been reborn?" Mike asked.

"That's one way of puttin' it, I suppose. When you've been through ghosthood a certain number of times, the afterworld begins to linger with you even after you're reborn, and you see things from a bit broader viewpoint. Now, as to the other Druids and magicians and so forth, I don't know. I'd always assumed they'd gotten tired of human life and gone to the Summer Country, Heaven, Paradise, Nirvana, Valhalla, whatever. I always assumed I'd go there too, which just goes to show you even magicians don't know everything about the afterlife, now do they? Anyway, it doesn't seem to be my role to know all about it this time around. I'm just the traffic cop, and only Irish need apply. Shambala and Texas are quite outside my territory, though as you can see, there is a very great deal that is inside it. Which reminds me, Morris O'Leary is mortally sick and about to join us. I must assign him a banshee. Good day to you, then."

Chime awoke to find herself adrift on a sea of mist—she could see no walls, no floor, and could only feel the bed beneath her.

"Psst, the fatal hour is upon us," a disembodied voice said. "You should pardon the expression."

"Inez? What is this?" Chime asked. "I can't see you."

"Oh, you mean the fog from the pool and streams and stuff in the garden? It's especially bad in these back rooms of the house. That's why I never come back here." There was a shudder in her voice followed by, "Meru's out like a light. Come on."

Chime decided she didn't want to know how Meru came to be unconscious. She fumbled until she found her candle and then fumbled for her matches. With the candle held low, the light pierced the fog so she could see where she was stepping. She had gone to bed with her clothes on, so she was ready to meet Inez at the door. With the one candle between them, the two women padded through the house, onto the stone path leading through the garden cave.

The cave was an eerie sight. Its flowers were closed and shrouded by darkness, except for the white blossoms that shone with night-blooming radiance through the fog to seek the wavering moonlight drizzling through the huge crystal lens overhead. Moonlight and fog swirled together with the milky fire of an opal.

The dampness penetrated Chime's clothing and chilled her as the colder, drier air and snow outside had not done. Inez was bundled in a large coat and hat of some sort of animal furs, and wore white flat-heeled shoes and heavy woolen socks that looked odd with the coat, though much more sensible than her usual high-heeled shoes.

Their footsteps were light and stealthy, though twice they splashed into the streams crossing the path instead of stepping over them. At one point Chime thought she heard Inez bump into a bush, but then Inez stopped and said, "Did you stumble or something?"

"No. Didn't you?"

"No. Then what was that noise?"

They both listened and heard nothing but when they resumed walking, it seemed to Chime that she heard a third, maybe a fourth, set of feet padding lightly behind them, stopping when they stopped to listen. She didn't think it was Meru. She couldn't tell who it was—the individual was not sending thoughts to her. Inez was broadcasting her own fear so loudly, Chime doubted she would have been able to read the mind of the intruder anyway.

As they drew nearer to the hold cave, Inez's steps grew more and more hesitant, and despite the cold, perspiration broke out on her brow and upper lip and her breath came in fast, shallow gulps. Finally Inez stopped dead still in a particularly heavy patch of mist and said, "I'm sorry, Chime, I can't do it. I can't go through with this—not even to get away from Meru, not even to be young again. I'm too scared."

"But there is nothing to be frightened of, Inez," Chime soothed, and was trying to think of something philosophical and wise to say that didn't have to do with the impermanence of life. She didn't get the chance.

She had turned to face the footsteps and was about to walk back toward them to show Inez that she was not afraid. Suddenly a large flying projectile hit her squarely in the chest and knocked her sprawling on her back, half on the path, half in the plants, the back of her head submerged in a stream. Cold and wetness pierced her scalp.

The projectile began pumping at her chest and a low rumbling noise emitted from it.

Inez whispered in a half-strangled voice, "Oh, my God, they've got you! Oh, Chime, I—"

"It's okay, Inez," Chime laughed. "It's just the cat."

The guilty party regarded her through ecstatically slitted golden eyes. "Fooled you," Mu Mao said.

Chime scooped the animal into her arms and dumped him off in the path, then stood up, laughing. "You played a good trick on us, didn't you? Foolish cat, what if we had been armed?"

Mu Mao arranged the fur tuft between the toes of his right forepaw with a flick of his tongue. "If you had been armed, I would never have charged. Foolish girl, I knew it was you."

"You frightened poor Inez, cat. That is going to give you a certain amount of karmic debt to work through."

"I like stalking. I'm a cat in this life. It's my dharma to stalk. What can I say? As for Inez, she had it coming. Ask her about that coat, if she wants to play the offended party when furred creatures frighten her."

"Mu Mao says to ask you about your coat, Inez," Chime whispered dutifully.

"It's a very good fake, and besides, they would have died anyway." Inez sniffed. "Stop fiddling around with that damn animal and help me find the candle. You dropped it when you fell."

Chime got down on her hands and knees and felt around for the candle but found nothing. Then she heard a splash, and a very wet candle dropped onto the back of her hand. The cat's golden eyes glinted at her with amusement. It washed the wet paw it had used to bat the candle out of the water to her.

"Oh dear," she said, "I don't think it will light that way."

"It doesn't matter," the cat said. "I see perfectly well in darkness and I will lead you, and thus ensure that you will not be without the benefit of my counsel."

He stayed close in front of Chime so that his tail brushed the hem of her skirt, and they followed him through the garden without further incident, until they felt the encroaching chill of the chamber beyond creeping through the narrow passage between the garden and the room where the dead were encased in ice.

Inez pulled big fur mittens out of the pocket of her coat and slipped them on, and Chime tucked her hands into her armpits and thought that she surely must manage to reclaim her coat before they escaped.

She felt an openness before her, more air against her face, cold air, and the cat said, "This is the entrance to the 'holding' place."

Chime stuck out her left hand and groped along the side for the magnesium candle she had seen Meru use, then groped to the center and tried to find the prismatic lamp.

"What are you doing?" Inez asked. "Chime, we can't be in here."

"I'm turning on the light," Chime said. "Inez, there is a small magic spell on this place that makes you afraid of it. Knowing this, you must let the spell have no power over you."

"Okay, okay. You're right. The only thing that's scary about this place is Meru, and I've taken care of him. Everybody else just makes me afraid that what's happened to them could happen to me, which it could, if I don't help you. Come on, Inez, baby, you can do it. One baby step, two baby steps. I'm in." She looked at Chime, who was holding her candle up to examine the frozen, desperate face of the pilot. "Holy Jesus, Mary, and Joseph," she breathed, then added with a look at Chime. "And Buddha, of course."

"Yes," Chime said. "We will need all the help we can get."

CHAPTER XXII

O'Brien did not change his mind and offer to allow Toni-Marie to be reborn in Ireland, so the ghosts once more found themselves adrift in the ether.

"Hmm," Toni-Marie said, "seems like the Irish have a system worked out for them."

"I thought it was very efficient," Mike said. "Perhaps in Shambala, Chime will be much like Mr. O'Brien."

"Well, yes, except that she's not a ghost. Yet. Or wasn't when we left."

"I would have liked to have tried being a banshee—maybe we could start banshees in Shambala. They sounded like fun in my books, wearing long faces and moaning and groaning."

"Speak for yourself," Toni-Marie said. "I'm not into that—I remember something about them always washing out grave garments at wells and riverbanks. I'm not really the domestic type, myself. So where next?"

"You pick this time. My information seems to be outdated, and I've never lived away from Shambala. Where do *you* think we could find a great magician?"

"I think maybe we need another kind of magician—someone more, I don't know, *eastern*. Let's go back and try the Middle East."

"Like the Arabian Nights?"

"Something like that, updated about three thousand years. Think of munitions factories, synthetic fabric plants, solar-powered palaces and cars and capped-off oil wells. Think of women in veils, men wearing headcloths and robes, sand, palm trees, camels . . ."

Mike drifted on her words, his own imagination filling in the details, adding belly dancing houris, peaceful oases, genies popping out of lamps, and bustling bazaars.

He drifted through impressions of silk gently billowing from satiny flesh, of dark eyes flashing above jeweled gauze, the clink of coins as hips undulated, the softness of a richly flowered carpet underfoot, the tap of drums and the ringing of silver bells, the sweet juices of rare fruits dribbling onto his tongue, tangy perfumes spicing the air.

Instead he found himself hovering above the smoking ruins of a burned-out street, little glowing coals still winking from the ruins of buildings, bones and decomposing bodies everywhere.

"Where *are* we?" he asked Toni-Marie, whose expression was one of dismay.

"I don't know," she said dryly. "One burned-out husk of a city looks pretty much like another one."

Just then a white horse reared above the smoky pall, bearing on its tassel-and-bell-bedecked back a rider in white robes carrying a flaming sword. The rider's eyes were fiery red, and as he reined in next to them, causing the horse to rear threateningly above them, he demanded, "What are you infidel spirits doing in Allah's air space?"

• • •

"How are you planning to thaw him out?" Inez asked, rubbing her forearms with her mittened hands.

"Tantric magic," Chime said, and thought silently, *if* I can remember how it works or *if* my former self informs me. So that Inez, who was already frightened, would not hamper her efforts by lack of confidence in her, Chime commanded in a firm voice, "You watch the entrance."

"As if I could help it," Inez said.

Chime lit the prismatic lantern with the magnesium candle, the cold colored light bouncing off the ice-sepulchered bodies embedded in the sides of the cave. The pilot seemed to be running toward her, the fingers of his hands outstretched. She stretched her own and pressed them to his. The cold of the ice burned her skin, sending chills up her fingertips to her shoulders, her back, and neck.

And yet, you need not be cold, a voice from within her said. *Breathe the tumo fire breath, create the fire within you, and you too can sit naked on a snowbank and have ice water poured over you and still be warm. Now, first remove your clothing and turn out the light.*

Chime sighed, and argued with herself in a low muttering tone that caused Inez to turn and see who she was talking to. "With all respect, while I am sure that I am correct in this matter, I think it is better if you-who-I-have-been help me-who-I-am to rediscover the rhythm of the fire breathing and to build the fire within ourself, and then, if appropriate, when I am quite warm, I will remove my clothing and melt the ice with the warmth generated by this meditation."

Have you studied nothing in this life? Do you not know that comfort cannot be a consideration in the higher meditations?

"I was thinking more of health and good sense."

Those have nothing to do with metaphysics. You must sit nude in the cold and dark as far from humanity as possible.

"Very well. If I must, then I must," Chime said, and began peeling layers.

"What the hell are you doing?" Inez demanded.

"Magic. My former self informs me I must be nude to do this magic so that I may thaw the pilot's body."

"With Stoney, that might do it okay. But if this is really just his body, what are you going to do with it if the soul is still, you know, back there with the spook trap?"

"Inez, you are a far more perspicacious woman than anyone would guess at first meeting."

"Thanks—I think. Nobody ever called me that before."

"We'll go get the bottles," Chime said, and without bothering to replace her clothing, stepped out of the ice chamber, carrying the magnesium candle into the cave filled with lost souls that had been neatly bottled and shelved according to vintage. Except for those separate ones on the table. She filled Inez's arms and her own just as they heard an enormous crash, followed by the thump of paws hitting the cave floor.

"Hmmm," Mu Mao said, dabbing at the broken glass with a paw. "These seem to have stayed dead."

"I don't suppose, venerable master, that you noticed if the bottles were open or not before you broke them," Chime said.

"Well no. In leaping to the top shelf to obtain the best vantage point for my experiment, I, er, began it with more precipitousness than figured in my original calculations when the shelf did not bear my weight."

"The cat?" Inez said from Chime's elbow. "We could get caught any time and you're talking to the cat?"

"Your experiment has merit, venerable Mu Mao," Chime said, ignoring Inez for the moment. "However, I ask that in the interests of preventing great confusion, you delay further actual pouncing activity. When I have completed my own experiment in the next room, please feel free to resume with my blessings."

"A reasonable request," the cat said.

Chime and Inez returned to the ice chamber, and Chime handed Inez the bottle Meru had identified as being that of the pilot. "When the body is free of the ice, break the seal of the bottle," Chime told her.

"Okay," Inez said. "I'll decant *this* Stoney when I see *that* Stoney start to thaw."

Chime, facing toward the pilot's frozen body, reached up and doused the prism lamp and afterward the magnesium candle.

"Hey, how am I going to see him thaw if I can't see my hand in front of my face?" Inez demanded.

"Quiet, please," Chime told her in a voice that sounded somehow older, deeper, and not quite like hers at all. "When the time is right, I think you will have no problem seeing. Meanwhile, be still as a stone."

"Or still as Stoney," Inez twittered, but her joke fell into silence, and so did she.

Compose yourself, Chime's inner self commanded.

"It is very hard when I am so cold and there is much danger. I am filled with dread that that awful man may find us and imprison us in this ice and our souls in bottles also. Then what would we all do?"

Such thoughts must be put from you.

"I know, but he is a cunning man, very misguided, but very powerful and quite ruthless when it comes to enforcing his will."

Put away pride. Put away anger. Reject hatred. Reject fear, sloth, stupidity, the desire for the things belonging to other beings, to other times. Breathe these feelings out as you inhale blessings, the five wisdoms, the spirit of the Buddha, all that is good, all that is worthy, all that is noble in the world, such as it is. Take these things into yourself. That's it.

Chime did as directed and felt less cold as she concentrated on divesting herself of her less worthy emotions.

Now, dismiss your cares—dismiss your thoughts. Dismiss all from your mind, all from your being, save the golden lotus—the one growing from your navel.

Through her closed eyes Chime saw her bellybutton, saw the flower growing from it, and within the core of the flower, shining like the sun, a word, a sound that somehow had a life of its own, and above it another such word, a note of music, a beam of light, a breathing organism. The vibrations of the second sound quivered tangibly in the air, so strong that they formed a shape of light and color. From within that shape a woman stepped.

Dorjee Naljorma, her inner self said.

"But how can that be?" Chime said. "That's me!"

As in a dream, Chime knew the woman before her was herself, though she didn't look anything like Chime. *You are to identify with her, but let's not get carried away. There's work to do,* her inner self informed her. *Now, do you see a fiery letter A sitting in your navel and the Tibetan letter Ha at the top of your head?*

She did. A fiery letter A burned in the center of her belly, although it spread only a little warmth and did not burn. Looking at this, she began to breathe more slowly, more deeply, and imagined the air from her lungs fueling the little flame, causing it to grow. Her breathing deepened even more, and she held each breath a little longer than the last.

The fire climbed her body, and her spirit coaxed it as if it was a wild cub coming to nurse, up and up an invisible artery running along the nerves in the center of her body.

The little fire that had begun in her belly formed a thin flaming line up the middle of her body, up her throat, over her chin, lips, and nose to the top of her head. She breathed deeply, encouraging it to continue growing, nursing it until it grew in diameter to the size of her finger, then the size of her arm, her breath fanning it to ever greater expansion until her whole body was consumed by the glorious blaze.

When Chime burst into flames, Inez stuffed her fist in her mouth and lurched forward, only to trip over a furry body.

The cat hissed warningly at her, which was enough to give Inez time to think her way out of her panic. She had confidence in Chime. She felt that Chime knew what she was doing. Chime was magic. She just had no idea Chime had intended to ignite.

Where the girl had been was only a huge blazing tube of fire, its flames beating with a hot wind that made Inez want to shed her fur coat. Inez couldn't see Chime through the flames. It took every ounce of self-control she possessed not to run from the room or to throw herself at the flames and try to beat them out with her hands. She had to tell herself again and again that this was mystic stuff, the flames weren't made with fuel and a match, that Chime wasn't screaming and she wasn't being hurt.

Inez realized she was kneeling in a pool of warm water, her hands, her knees, and the hem of her coat covered with it. Looking up, she saw by the light of the fire that the walls were beginning to melt and run. The hot wind billowing from the fire column was evaporating the water to steam.

Then, as quickly as it had begun, the wind grew still, the fiery waves sinking lower, until the blazing ocean of flame in front of her sank and was absorbed—into the pores of Chime's skin. The girl was sitting exactly where she had been before, a fiery streak the size of a pencil running up the front of her body. As Inez watched, the stream grew thinner, until it was no bigger around than a hair. The whole floor of the cavern was gleaming wet except for the steamy area surrounding the girl's bottom, and the wall in front of her, which now clearly held a man-sized form. Stoney?

Oh, yeah, right, Stoney! Remembering her duty, Inez smashed the bottle against the floor as if she was christening a ship. Chime's body, still glowing faintly and fuzzily with heat and steam, was obscured for a split second as something flew past her.

The man in the wall moved, fell forward, across Chime's shimmering body.

Chime jerked from her trance, and Stoney—for now Inez could tell by the way he moved, something she remembered achingly well—dusted at her shoulders and head with his hands. "Sorry, sweetheart. Whew, you're warm. And, uh, bare."

"Stoney!" Inez ran to the two naked people, Stoney examining himself as if getting reacquainted with his body while Chime sat calmly, staring at him. "That was some trick, kiddo," Inez said to Chime. "You sure you're okay—not singed or anything?"

Chime blinked twice and smiled a blinding smile full of white teeth. "No. I am quite well. And very pleased with myself. I've always known I was the Terton but I am pleased to find that despite my ignorance I can still perform certain magicks."

"Much obliged, ma'am," Stoney said.

Just then the sound of breaking glass followed by a great deal of hissing, spitting, and an angry yowling, emanated from the chamber with all the bottles in it.

Without bothering to put on her shoes to protect her feet from the broken glass, Chime sprinted away. Inez scooped up her clothing, then seeing Stoney standing there as if stunned, took off her mink and tenderly wrapped it around him. "There, flyboy," she said with a kiss on his cheek, which was very warm though it smelled like the cave. "Make sure you don't get it dirty. There's not a single dry cleaner left alive on the face of the planet, for all I know."

CHAPTER XXIII

"What happened?" Chime asked. Well she might. The glass tubing and bottles on the ghost-collecting table were shattered and Mu Mao crouched beneath the table, expressing his displeasure in no uncertain terms.

"A demon, lady," the cat spat. "A demon entered through the spirit hole and broke the glass. See, there it is. Stay back. It's nasty."

"And that," the demon said, "looks tasty. What is it?"

Chime stared hard at this new ghostish form. It was more sub-stantial than many and looked familiar. And Mu Mao was right. It *was* nasty. "You're the girl who lives in that hole. Your father killed Meekay."

"So? It was nothing personal. He kills everything. Got to eat. That's what he says. I never thought he meant me."

"He *ate* you?"

"Um-hm. To teach me a lesson. Hope he busted what's left of his teeth. That's what saved me before—that and the babies. He thought the babies were more tenderer."

"Mu Mao, uncrouch yourself. As you can see, this is no demon, though she was related to one. How did you escape the ghost catcher?" Chime asked the ghost of Buzz's daughter.

"That furry thing broke it. I guess I scared it, coming through the tubing."

"I was *not* scared," Mu Mao said, rising from his crouch to try to look impassive. The effect was spoiled by the fluff of fur along the ridge of his back. "Merely raising the alarm at an unexpected intrusion."

"That won't be the last one either," the ghost said to Chime. "Pa's decided the surface's safe since he met you. You bein' loose, he knows there's at least one more good meal to be had."

"Chime!" Inez called from the next room. "Chime, we've got a few more sleeping beauties on our hands than we reckoned for! You thawed them *all* out when you thawed out Stoney, and now they're all over the floor."

Chime turned to answer, and the ghost of Buzz's daughter flashed past her, toward the room with the soulless thawed-out bodies. "Break the other bottles, quickly!" Chime called to Inez.

"A worthy pursuit," the cat said approvingly, and launched himself at the top shelf of ghost receptacles.

"Not those, Mu Mao! Not yet. It's only fair to let the souls departed from those bodies resume their original shapes first."

She didn't stick around to see if the cat heeded her, but ran back into the ice chamber, splashing through the corridor and tripping over someone as she sought Inez. She couldn't see her at first for the steam rising from the warm water still flooding the slightly sunken floor of the room, as the walls melted into waterfalls, depositing on the floor the people who had been encased in ice.

"Don't come in here in your bare feet!" Inez cried, to the sound of breaking glass. "Hand me the candle and I'll light the lamp."

The prisms danced across a nightmare. Arms, legs, heads, and hands writhed up from the water on the floor, casting wild shadows to jig among the prisms on the wet walls.

Stoney stumbled from one to another, trying to help the living, sometimes sloshing back down into the soup with them, to the detriment of Inez's fur coat.

Meanwhile the ghosts mingled with the steam and water, concealing living and dead body parts. Eventually they sorted themselves out and found the right bodies, though a few of the souls apparently had not survived being bottled, and a few of the bodies had not survived the cryogenic process. The body of Li, Meru's wife, lay sloshing back and forth in the water while the woman's spirit knelt over the body, weeping. The plump body of a nude man was jammed against one wall by another body jackknifed against it. Neither of those bodies was claimed by a ghost.

"Poor Sven," Inez said. "Never even got to eat one of his own carrots."

"Who are they, Inez?" Chime asked.

"Sven Strom, the botanist who designed the garden, and Prince Tommy. Poor bastards. Where are their ghosts? Do you think they got out?"

"I hope so," Chime said grimly. She was bending over the ghost of Mu Meru. "Mrs. Meru, can you understand me?"

The ghost didn't look up, so Chime was not sure whether she did or not.

"Who *is* this chick?" Stoney asked Inez.

"Oh, this is Chime Cincinnati. She's kind of like a, uh, a . . . say, do you remember those old old vids of Superman?"

"Yeah, sure. That's what made me want to fly originally."

"She's kind of like that only she's not from another planet. She's just from a place where you get to be always young. It's the *real* Shangri-La except it's actually called Shambala. We're going with her. You can fly us there if she shows you the way, can't you?"

"Sure, no problem. Only I can't promise to find it by the seat of my pants." He grinned, with a glance down the front of the sopping fur coat.

Mu Mao appeared at the doorway. "Can I break the other bottles *now*, Chime?"

But Chime Cincinnati was reciting the Great Liberation Through Hearing over the body and ghost of Mu Li Meru and did not seem to hear the cat.

Buzz Horn was an old man now, and he knew that, though he could still sire himself a good meal. Now, however, if he played his cards right, he wouldn't need to eat kinfolk anymore. If two people had been able to survive up here on the surface, then there must be something to live on, and he meant to have himself some of it.

His eyes weren't as good as they used to be, but the black girl's trail wasn't even cold by the time he packed the gook boy's body back to his hole. He'd boiled up some meat for the trail and had planned to leave the rest for Eve. That hadn't been good enough for her, though, nosiree. She hadn't even believed him when he told her he'd be back for her. She'd started crying, grown woman like that, crying for her daddy like she didn't have better sense. So he'd shot her, but hadn't had time to do much else before he left. He'd wanted to find that trail again before nightfall, and he had been in luck.

He'd found tracks and other signs of the girl in the valley, headed toward the mountains, which was how he'd figured she'd go. He'd camped halfway across the valley, out in the open, sleeping with one eye and both ears open. Nothing had come near him, not even the wind. The next day he'd walked all day, and toward sundown spotted the blue-green flowers from the corner of his eye and set his course back toward them. He could see that she'd lain down in them, and he'd followed the mashed-down blossoms, low-crawling over them until he'd smelled the sewage, a sweet scent to him, since it meant he'd find the girl at the end of it and maybe a whole nest of survivors. He'd hidden in the flowers until way after dark, speculating on who would be there and how he could best make use of them in the way he used to dream about what he would do with a trillion dollars or a harem full of female NACAF senior officers.

• • •

"You don't have to act that way," Mike said, edging in front of Toni-Marie as if she could be hurt by the white-robed rider's flaming sword. "We're just looking for a magician."

"There are no magicians in this place," the rider intoned, "only the dead."

The wild-eyed apparition plunged his fiery sword toward the smoke, and suddenly they could see that the smoke was composed of thousands upon thousands of milling, ashen-faced, desperate-looking ghosts—men, women, and children, all swirling together over the ruins of their homes.

"Can we just go talk to them?" Mike asked. "As long as we're here . . ." It seemed unlikely that any of the hopeless looking beings swirling around them could know of a magician. Still, there were so many of them; perhaps someone would know something.

"This is no time for such things," the being said. "These people are awaiting entry to Paradise. They died in battle and they expected immediate entry." The wildness in his eyes now became the expression of someone who was harassed beyond the patience of even a saint. "The only problem is, we never anticipated we would have to handle many applicants at once. There's no room. Normally there aren't so many women and children awaiting entry either, but the cursed infidel missiles slaughtered our people wholesale."

"That's not how I heard it, buddy," Toni-Marie said with an anger Mike had not heard in her voice before. "I heard you guys fired the first volley."

"A preemptive strike, that was all. A small dispute among old enemies, which the defenders of this place thought they would settle for good, to the benefit of all. There was no need for foreigners to become involved. No need for all of this."

"Looks like it killed everyone, Toni-Marie," Mike said. "I don't guess we'd find any magic here anyway."

"There is magic here," the swordsman said, "but it is needed by our own people. All of our magical energies are now directed at en-larging Paradise and easing the way of the fallen. The living, instead of praying toward this end, are concentrating their magic on finding food and water each day, surviving each night. Some of the dead have become restless and have begun to trouble the living, so the living are also praying to be delivered from the wrath of the dead."

"Then there *are* survivors."

"Of course."

"Pardon our ignorance. We didn't see any."

"Most of them are underground, of course, in the specially built bunkers, waiting for the smoke to clear. Already many of the ghosts are haunting their dreams, demanding to know why they had to die when the people in the bunkers made the decisions. Leave them alone, I tell the applicants for Paradise. Nobody lives forever, and when their time comes, you can be sure that I will remember to enter in their record the suffering they have caused."

"And you wouldn't happen to know if any magicians of fairly high magnitude are among the survivors down there, would you?" Mike asked the angel.

"Yes, I would say it was highly likely that *most* of the survivors living underground are mighty and terrible magicians of the highest magnitude, but I'm afraid you will have much competition if you wish to haunt them. There are a few others before you." He waved the sword at the smoke again and again, individual faces and placating hands turned toward the angel expectantly, yearning for deliverance.

Then, as if they were pieces in a clock instead of the souls of living individuals, they all turned away as from below a voice boomed out over a loudspeaker. "The crowd of unclean dead will disperse, taking their poisons with them, so that the righteous may once more rise aboveground. I repeat. You will now disperse and find another place to haunt. The living need to live in the area contaminated by your presence. Do not delude yourselves into thinking you still live. You are quite dead. The only people in this city to survive were those of us below the surface. Do not delude yourselves into thinking that there will be a place in Paradise for you any time in the future. Obviously you are unworthy or you would have been there already along with all of the other souls who died for our holy cause. Go from this place. Go haunt the desert. But we repeat, you must leave the surface of this city to us."

The ghosts grew even more bewildered, however, and looked back to the angel.

"Poor things," Toni-Marie said. "*Can* they leave? Do they have to stay all cooped up here in the city? Can't they sort of float around and see the scenery, keep an eye out for new babies to be reborn into?"

"That is *not* our way," the angel said. "The people in the bunkers below are mistaken. These spirits will remain here until space can be found for them in Paradise. You need to excuse me now. I must bespeak whomever is issuing that announcement. These spirits are still merely unhappy, but if the living continue to gloat and degrade them in such a fashion, I fear they will become quite righteously angry and there will be even more dead to deal with. Meanwhile, if you seek the magic that is peculiar to my people, I suggest you try places farther from the cities."

They left reluctantly, and drifted over the ghost smoke of the desert until they felt themselves drawn to one small patch of greenery, a pool set in its center, and a ring of about ten women, each whirling around and around so that their long black hair and full skirts scythed the air, the whole spinning ring revolving around the pool. The dancers were chanting and whooping as they whirled. Off to the side, three other women pounded double-sided drums made of large cans covered with some sort of skin. Three others played reed pipes. The noise level was about on a par with one of those crowded bazaars Mike had been hoping for.

As the group whirled, the dance drew Mike and Toni-Marie into its vortex. Toni-Marie tried a little pirouette. "Yeah," she said, "this is more like it!"

The music abruptly changed pace, the dancers slowed, then stopped. Mike saw the one standing immediately in front of them blink. Her eyes, which had been turned up so that only the underside of the eyeball showed as a mere crescent hanging above the whites, now returned to normal, except that one of them was half covered with a milky film.

They were all wild-looking women, with long tangled black or graying hair and fierce black brows over hawklike noses. Many had the lesions of radiation sickness, and one woman looked as if she was about to faint, but pushed away her weakness to say, "Oh, dear. Look what the lord has sent us. Is this Aisha the temptress herself and a consort?"

"No," an older woman with graying hair falling out in patches replied. "See you, the woman has fair hair and her immodest dress is of foreign manufacture. These are the ghosts of strangers. Greetings, ghosts. What brings you here? Do you wish us to make union with God on your behalf?"

"Well, you *could* say that. Are you women magicians?" Toni-Marie asked.

"We are the New Sufias of St. Sophia."

"You're living, aren't you?" Mike said, realizing that he couldn't see through any of them.

"That's right," the woman said cautiously. "And you're not, are you?"

"No. We're looking for magicians. Are you by any chance?"

"I am," the woman said. "I am the Lalla Laylah. I am a healer primarily, but I cannot heal death."

"Oh, no, that's not what we need. We have someone who can help us reincarnate, but we've been cursed by an evil magician to wander the ends of the earth and we were just hoping you could remove the curse so we could get back together with our friend and return to Shambala."

"Is that all?" She laughed ruefully. "I thought you were going to ask for something difficult, like praying that sanity and health would return to the earth. That's what we've been doing. I'm sorry. I can't help you. I don't know where this Shambala is. You're welcome to join in the dance, however, and seek oneness with God. Of course, you'd need to adhere to all of our other doctrines too."

"Could that get us back to Tibet?"

"Perhaps. We are hoping for bodily union with God to enable us to better the lot of our fellow survivors. But you didn't survive, did you?"

"No, not physically anyway, though our spirits are in good shape. We just need to get back to my friend Chime. See, I came from a place where peace and sanity still exist, and Chime and I left to come and help other survivors. We'd be glad to help you if you could just help me rejoin her."

"What about this woman?" the gray-haired one demanded. "Did your other woman cast you out because of her?"

"Oh, no, no, nothing like that. We had a run-in with an evil magician is all. That's why we're looking for a good magician to break the spell and send us back."

"I'm very sorry," the woman said, "but we can't help you—we are using every bit of magic we have to try to help ourselves and what remains of our people. You're welcome to try it if you like."

"What does it involve?" Toni-Marie asked.

"It's easy enough. You just spin around and around as we did, putting yourself into a trance so that you become one with God." As she spoke, the woman began spinning again, and all the others joined her.

Toni-Marie turned a few pirouettes, but Mike just looked confused, so the next time she passed him, she hooked elbows with him and spun him around in "swing your partner" square-dance style. The women's hair whipped through them as they all whirled around the pool until the women's hair and skirts were blurred again and Toni-Marie and Mike blended, if not with God, then with each other.

But when at last they stopped, they were no longer by the pool with the women, but back out over the vast empty desert.

"Well, so much for the Middle East," Toni-Marie said. "Let's try Africa. Really, I'll bet there's power there if anywhere."

"We're not having much luck, are we?" Mike sighed.

"No, but I have a feeling Africa will be different. The people had a very strong folk religion up until the end, despite centuries of oppression and a whole lot of interference from NACAF. The shamans were supposed to have amazing powers. Besides, a witch doctor's the next best thing to a ghost doctor, huh? It's been a little on the monotheistic side around here for really *potent* magic."

But all they found, though they searched the entire continent, was ruined city after ruined city, burned vegetation, dried riverbeds and lakes. They wondered where all the ghosts were until they heard a humming below them and saw the waves of hungry insects swarming over everything. At least here everyone had already found another life to be born into. The insects blanketed all that had come before them and all that was left of a once lush continent ripped apart by racial conflict and greed. Besides the insects, only bones, ashes, and bloodstains on the ruins remained. And all the bones were white, all the ashes were black, and all of the bloodstains were a uniform brown.

CHAPTER XXIV

Mrs. Meru apparently had been a very good woman. No sooner did Chime start reciting the Great Liberation than the ghost dropped her hands, smiled up at Chime, and dissolved. "Another soul attains enlightenment," Chime murmured prayerfully.

"*Now* I will break the other bottles," Mu Mao said. "After which we will all go elsewhere."

"I'll go ready the aircraft," Stoney said.

"Wait, what about them?" Inez asked, indicating the naked, dazed, and wet people shivering in the cooling cavern.

"Yes, we must see to them at once. And they will be among the first to return to Shambala," Chime said. "Can the plane take high altitudes, Stoney?"

He shrugged in the fur coat, the prismatic lamp fragmenting his face into triangles of blue, green, pink, and gold. "It got us this far, didn't it? Just give me coordinates and I'll find it."

"That I cannot do. But I will take you there as soon as a few other matters are attended to."

Mu Mao jerked his tail impatiently and turned to go.

"Mu Mao, you who were once a master of the Tao and of the dharma, will you forego the momentary pleasure of breaking the bottles and help me instead with another matter?"

"Perhaps. If it interests me."

"I had originally planned to span much more territory before returning to Shambala, however, the condition of these people compels me to wish to take them to safety as quickly as possible. Perhaps there are others who also need help. If so, I must learn of them out here, away from Shambala's protective shield. Also, something must be done about these ghosts. Meekay could help me but I don't know where he is. Even walking *lung-gom* style, aboveground, would be too slow when I don't know where to look. So I must go another way—it takes a ghost to find a ghost, I suppose."

"You would leave your body?" the cat asked incredulously. "With all those hungry ghosts dying for flesh to inhabit?"

"I think that would be the fastest and best way for everyone, yes. But you see the difficulty. I would very much like to have a body to return to, and I could not guide anyone to Shambala if I myself have no physical form. Therefore, I wish you to delay breaking any more bottles so that there won't be so many ghosts ready to possess my body once I leave it. I will need to make a few spirit catchers, and then you must show me a good place outside the wards Meru has set upon the valley. I will not be able to find Meekay from within this place. Lastly, I will need a guard to protect me. Have you any interest in such a task?"

"How do you think that I can protect you from ghosts, lady?"

"I would not presume to tell you how to perform the many wonders of which you are capable, cat. I merely ask if you are willing to employ your skills to the purpose I propose."

"Chime, are you going to stand around all night staring at the cat? We're all freezing," Inez said, making extravagant gestures that involved not only her hands and face but her whole upper torso.

"Yes, of course," Chime said. "We must get food and clothing for these people before doing anything else."

"You could do with a little clothing yourself," Inez said.

Chime looked down at her own nudity. Though her skin no longer glowed with the tumo fires, she still felt warm and the water evaporated under her footsteps.

"I guess I could. I don't suppose the clothing storage is back here anywhere."

"I think I found something here," Stoney said from the cave connecting the food cave to the holding chamber. "Yeah, here's my pants and my favorite leather jacket, and this looks like Bertinelli's workout suit."

Chime, Stoney, and Inez helped the others sort out their clothing. Chime spoke with first one and then another of the people who had been on hold, starting with Stoney. "I was told you displayed much courage against Meru. We'll need your courage and skill to get us to safety again."

"That's a definite affirmative," the pilot said.

When she introduced herself to Full Moon Akesh, he grinned at her from his full height of five feet, flashing damaged and broken white teeth in his black face when she told him how in Shambala her father cherished tapes of Akesh's music.

"I'm okay," the architect Marco Bertinelli said in answer to her inquiry. "But I'm starving."

"No problem there. Plenty of food. At least Meru sees to that," Inez said.

"Yeah, great," Stoney said. "I'll just waltz in for dinner and he'll kill the fatted calf and welcome me with open arms, I'm sure."

"Maybe not, but we can always graze," Inez said with a sweeping gesture toward the garden cavern. "There's lots of food there."

"I'll go gather some food," Chime said. "If Meru comes I'll tell him I always need a late snack."

"Is that going to delay us getting back to Shambala?" Inez asked. Her gestures were increasingly larger and more dramatic as she got more and more nervous. If she smoked, she'd be waving her cigarette holder, burning a swath around her with the tip of her cigarette.

"Maybe a little. I was just telling Mu Mao that I must enter into a trance state before we go, to try to locate other survivors in this area and warn them of Buzz's presence, also to try to find and assist Meekay and other ghosts back to Shambala, where they may rest before being reborn. Actually, I should probably do a little screening first so that we get the more highly evolved spirits, but there is no time."

"Then I shall help you gather food and minister to these people," Inez said with a grand gesture. "I once played Mother Teresa in a military school play, you know."

"Ah, it's good to have someone with experience at saintliness available for consultation," Chime teased. "Good. Come help me gather food, and then perhaps you could speed things up somewhat by taking these people farther back into the cave to feed them, where Meru is unlikely to look, while Stoney prepares the airplane and I do a bit of astral reconnaissance?"

"B-Back in the cave? *Farther* back, you mean? By myself?"

"With the survivors of the hold room. Can you do it, Inez?" Chime gave her a long and searching look.

Inez took a deep breath and nodded. They stepped into the outer cave. There was no longer any need for special illumination, as the sky beyond the crystal lens was already fading from black to gray.

They gathered foods that could easily be eaten raw, though Chime feared the food would be hard on digestive systems so long unused. "As soon as they're settled and seem a little more together," Inez said, "I'll stroll back into the building as if nothing had happened and pick up some other things."

"An excellent plan," Chime said. "You're a courageous and resourceful person, Inez."

Inez looked uncomfortable though pleased with the compliment, and said, "As long as Meru isn't back here fiddling around, I should be able to come and go without anyone noticing too much. Maybe I can get one of the others to create a diversion."

Buzz couldn't believe how easy it was. No ghosts to wade through, no security precautions, no trip wires or booby traps. He just waltzed right into the building in time for breakfast. His first idea, when he saw the place, was that he would wait for nightfall again and then kill everyone in their beds except maybe for any younger women. But then he smelled food cooking and decided that it might be a good idea to scope out the lay of the land before he decided who or what was disposable.

The group of rich people eating steaming meats and breads off china plates with silverware looked at him as if they'd seen something a hell of a lot more uncommon than a ghost.

"Who . . . are . . . *you*?" an old man asked in French-accented English.

Buzz grinned at them through his sewage-soaked beard and grabbed a handful of bacon, grinning even wider as he saw the disgust pass their faces when his filthy hands touched their food. "I sure am glad I found you folks," he said between mouthfuls. "I've been walkin' for days and days and I began to think I was the last man in the world, y'know? Terrible thing, wasn't it?"

"Melody," the Frenchman said, "perhaps you'd fix Monsieur—"

"Horn, Buzz Horn," Buzz said. "Sergeant Horn, actually, for years, but that's all over now, isn't it? Let bygones be bygones I say." He stuck out his hand to shake the Frenchman's, and when the man declined to shake, clapped him hard on the shoulder instead, leaving a filthy handprint on the man's clean tunic. His hands were as hard as petrified wood from years of digging, strangling, and breaking bones for marrow. He also trailed a path of filth across a plate of scrambled eggs and a tray of melon slices.

He enjoyed the expressions of horror and disgust on their prissy faces, but later, when he had eaten, showered, trimmed his beard and hair, and dressed in one of the wool tunics they favored, he regretted the first impression he must have made. There had been a time when he could charm and cajole what he wanted from people. Back in the old days, when he commanded the guerrilla band and collected intelligence for the Chinese allies, he had had a little finesse. He was disturbed to think that twenty years in a hole with nothing to occupy him but incest, murder, and cannibalism could erase all of his other talents.

So when the luscious little Melody came to collect him and take him to her leader, he didn't leap on her, cut her, or tear off her arm and start eating it.

He smiled uncertainly and ran his hand over his newly shorn hair, felt his rough beard, shaped into a gray distinguished U. She smiled up at him, her big blue eyes pitying.

"Honey, would you mind lettin' a feeble old man lean on your arm?" he asked. "I've been starving in a hole for twenty years, and I can't tell you how good it is to see civilized folks again. Do you know, I—I used to have a little girl of my own, about your age too, she would have been, if she'd lived. Poor little Evie. Sure was hard on her after her mama died."

"It's been a terrible time for everyone, sir," Melody said. "But you're safe now."

"Oh, yes, honey, I'm just sure I am. But I tell you, it's been a long haul. It's like heaven seein' your clean and well-fed faces after all these years. A man has to do some terrible things to stay alive."

"That's all behind you now, sir. The Master says the time is drawing nigh for us to start rebuilding civilization again, and it must be true. You're the second new visitor we've had. The other one was—"

Buzz groaned and leaned heavily against her, so that she sagged against the wall from his weight. "Oh, no. Don't tell me. It wasn't that black she-devil, was it? Oh, honey, you didn't let her in here, did you? Why, that girl is plain crazy. She and her boyfriend found my hole, and after I gave them hospitality, they tried to kill me and stole all my other food. That's when I figured it must be safe to be up here topside. I managed to kill the boyfriend, but that girl is slippery." He sighed, as if with regret, and pretended to wipe a tear with the heel of his hand. "I swear I never thought it would come to this. A slip of a girl no older than you tryin' to kill me for a bite of food, and me havin' to kill a man over no more than that. I don't know how I managed to survive so long but sometimes I wish I'd just been right under them missiles, you know what I mean?"

"You mustn't feel that way, sir. The Master will take care of everything now. I find it hard to believe Chime would harm you, but the Master will protect you here. Maybe Chime was just hungry too. She hasn't caused any trouble since she's been here except for bringing in a couple of ghosts. Here we are. Now you can meet the Master and tell him all about it." She opened the door to a very plush library and study with enough books to warm the whole house for a long winter. "Master, here is the newcomer, Buzz Horn. Mr. Horn, this is—"

"Buzz?" The so-called Master turned around. Buzz recognized him at once—the man Melody called the Master looked little different than he had twenty-five years ago, a little grayer, maybe, a little plumper.

"Well, for Christ's sakes, Cao Li, if I'd known you was such a close neighbor, I'd have come over to borrow a cup of sugar a long time ago."

CHAPTER
XXV

Chime helped Inez guide the hold room survivors back into the caves beyond the shelves full of bottled souls. The shelves did not continue forever, and beyond that area were other, warmer rooms where Meru's colony had sheltered during the first years after the nuclear holocaust. In one of these rooms was stored the spirit traps, presumably consigned to oblivion after Meru invented his more sophisticated version. Chime and Inez set up several of these in front of the entrance, and Chime tucked four into the front of her wet dress.

When everyone seemed settled, Chime, the cat, and Stoney left as

Inez, true to her remembered role as Lady Bountiful, began distributing food and helping those who were too weak to feed themselves.

"The plane isn't inside the compound," Stoney said. "It's out in the valley."

"I suppose we'll just have to brave the cesspool again," Chime said. "Is there any way out of here without going through the main building?"

"There is for the agile and clever," Mu Mao said. "The striations on the outer wall form folds beneath these waterfalls. There is an opening a little bigger than a cat between the lens in the cave and the rock it rests on."

"Lead us then, O agile and clever one," Chime told him. The cat smoked ahead of them, occasionally staring back at them with impassive golden eyes. Once more they passed through the Hall of Souls and through the cave room that had held the iced bodies, the floor still wet with several inches of water. They did not light another candle as they passed through. All of the living bodies had been rescued from this place already—or so they believed.

In the garden cave, the cat entered a waterfall and leapt from ledge to ledge until he finally squeezed out the top, at the side of the crystal lens. Chime and Stoney wriggled out after him.

Back inside the now-deserted ice cave, the body of Sven Strom, whose soul had not survived, stirred, opened one eye, saw that the cave was otherwise unoccupied, and rose. Strom's body flexed its hands and arms and crawled weakly to its feet. It needed food, it needed rest, but mostly it needed a safe place to gather strength while Eve's spirit learned to manipulate it.

Toni-Marie said, "I'm sick of being treated like a foreigner. I just want to go home to AmCan."

"Haven't you ever gone back since—"

"Nope. I didn't want to know. Didn't want to see what home looked like. Never wanted to find all my friends gone. It never occurred to me that maybe they would still be hanging around on this plane too and I could see how they're doing. Maybe more people survived over there, and there are bodies to go into. I don't think we've got any great magicians, but maybe that's not such a good idea anyway, Mike. I mean, that guy back in Tibet is a magician and he just wants to use people's souls—the cost of magic might be a little high—"

"Hmph," Mike said. "Looks to me like if this is the cost of science, it was higher. But that doesn't mean it's all bad." He was willing to try anything at that point, and besides, he was curious to see what was left of the land where his mother had come from, even if he never got to tell her about it.

Toni-Marie didn't describe the place she was visualizing, and for a moment Mike lost her. He called out to her, heard her voice calling back to him to hurry up. Instead of visualizing a place, this time he visualized her and suddenly he saw her, once more hovering, over a gray blasted landscape whiskered with a few wildflowers and the barest seedlings of trees peeping up between long patches of gravel. The gravel formed ridges, mountains, valleys, and was relieved only occasionally by the steel-gray gleam of a dead-looking body of water.

"Where are we?" he asked Toni-Marie.

"I don't know. I was thinking maybe we landed in the Big Bend—"

"The what?"

"It's a desert area in South Texas. Daddy used to take us hunting there. But there's no buttes here and there weren't any mountains this size there."

"Well, it might have changed because of the bombs—the upheaval of great plates of land and the tidal waves and nuclear winter and all that kind of thing are bound to make some pretty major changes."

"I don't think a volcano could have come up in the Big Bend in the last twenty years," Toni said skeptically. "Look."

The mountain, hollowed out in somewhat the same way as Karakal had been hollowed by the great avalanche that destroyed the ancient and beautiful city of Kalapa, was steaming. What looked like an enormous mound of half-cooked bread squatted in the middle of the crater, emitting puffs of white steam while roiling clouds massed around the sides of the mountain, standing guard.

The trunks of ruined and rotting trees littered the ash-gray hillsides, a permanent logjam wallowed back and forth in the lake, and a few—a very few—trunks still stood upright, like broken bones stabbed into the earth. The rusted hulks of cars huddled against the wind sweeping the ridges.

"Let's go," Toni-Marie said. "It's livelier among other dead people."

Mike thought he heard a rumble, and turned back to look at the volcano one last time. "Toni-Marie, stop. Look," he said, pointing.

The crater was now masked with a smooth snowy dome that glistened in the sunlight, its white made brighter by the lush green trees hemming it and spreading like the skirts of a party dress to the edge of a lake. This lake was superimposed on the larger gray one and was a pristine blue, mirroring the peak in its waters. A large house stood at the edge of the lake.

From its porch an old man, sitting in a rocking chair and holding a cat on his lap, looked up at them and waved.

"I know where we are now," Toni-Marie said. "That's Fire Mountain and that old guy died during an eruption in the late twentieth century. He was a legend. This may be the worst part of this—just around the area where the volcano erupted. Come on, let's keep looking."

As they turned away, the brilliantly colored picture returned to ash, and the house, the old man, and the cat disappeared.

"So," Mike said, "where's Fire Mountain? Where are we?"

Chime and Stoney secured the spirit traps with piles of loose stones to brace them upright. When the traps were in place—one in front of her, one in back, and one to each side—Chime sat on a large flat stone with the crystal lens in front of her. She watched Stoney as he climbed down the ridge onto the outer wall of the valley, until he dropped over the side. She hoped he would remember where the plane was and would be able to have it operational soon. She hoped he was an honorable man who would not simply abandon them. Of course, if he did, where would he go? This was probably the best place around for miles. But then, that remained to be seen, and seeing what was out there was her next task. She settled herself once more into lotus position, her hands resting on her knees, her forefingers meeting her thumbs, and began to breathe deeply.

Mu Mao, purring madly, climbed into her lap. She stopped the proper breathing and looked down at him.

He sensed the break in her rhythm and looked up at her, catching her eye. "Just trying to recall how it was done again," he said, and stepped out of the circle of her legs. "Many thanks. I'll assume my own meditation position now."

"And you will guard me also?" she asked. "My body will be very vulnerable now."

"The traps will protect you."

"Cat, as you well know, some of those ghosts are very determined."

"Very well. This being is now assuming the posture of meditation *and* protection. Beware, all ye who would enter this territory." And with that he lifted his tail and sprayed a circle around both Chime and the spirit traps, then sat down at the very edge of the lens—paws daintily together, tail relaxed, eyes closed—and purred, "You may now begin."

"You mean you two know each other?" Melody asked as the two bearded older men glared at each other across Meru's teak desk.

"Don't you just love reunions?" Buzz asked. "You got any whiskey around this place, Cao Li? I'm all choked up. Think I'm in need of revivin'."

CHAPTER XXVI

"We're in the state of Washington," Toni-Marie said. "We just happened to land in an area where there have been major volcanic eruptions every hundred years or so—guess they just had another one. I think it had grown back quite a bit since the eruption that killed the old man."

"My mom is from Washington—she talks about going places with my grandmother in Tacoma and Bellingham. Can we see those places?"

Toni-Marie shrugged. "I don't see why not. Think about it."

"I don't know how," Mike admitted. "She told me about a museum in Tacoma, looking onto the sound, which she said is a little like our lake except it lets into the ocean."

The scenery shifted below him, in conformation if not content, one blasted gray vista exchanged for another. Then he and Toni-Marie came to a halt over jagged chunks of smooth stone slabs sticking up between twisted steel girders and the remnants of walls. Mike realized the jagged chunks were what was left of the paved roads of this once large city.

He wasn't all that shocked by the devastation—he just felt as if he was inside the holovid of the aftermath of the avalanche that destroyed Kalapa. A foul smell clung to the air.

"It's a good thing we're dead already," Toni-Marie said. "That smells like poison gas."

"Oh, I don't think so," Mike said. "Another thing Mom said was that a lot of times you could smell a factory or something in Tacoma. Maybe the smell just stayed in the air—hey, maybe it's the ghost of that smell."

"Either that or whatever destroyed the city destroyed the factory but released the stink," Toni-Marie said. A wind whipped up from nowhere, lifting some of the thick pall of ashes from the ground and blowing them through Mike and Toni-Marie. "Peeyew. The wind's making it even worse. Let's go on to Bellingham."

"Where is it?" he asked. They were leaving the ruins of Tacoma behind now, a mud-colored wreck against a swift-moving sky with just a spot of blue landward to the southeast.

"Bellingham's beyond Seattle, it seems to me, up closer to Canada."

But they went farther and farther north and all they saw were some very tall mountains, a lot of ash, and dirty water pustuled with white-caps.

Toni-Marie hovered above the water and scratched her head. "It's got to be around here somewhere. I just don't seem to remember there being quite so much water. There was the Pacific Ocean and then this bay and harbors and lakes and stuff, but I was only through here once, and geography was never my strong suit, but I'm almost sure there used to be mountains over there too." She pointed out to sea.

All sorts of debris and bloated organic matter Mike preferred not to think about clogged the waterways, riding the top of the wind-tortured waves in the same way that the logs had jammed the lake back by the volcano.

As they looked around them the wind pounded the water and the clouds, blowing them away from the eastern horizon.

Mike looked back toward Tacoma. A gigantic crater, hundreds of times bigger than the fire mountain they had just visited, belched steam into the patch of sky surrounding it. Seeing it dominate the southeastern section of the sky, Mike wondered how any amount of cloud could have masked it.

"My God," Toni-Marie said. "That's Mount Rainier. It's *grown*. I mean, it blew its top but it's so much *taller*. It must have been building every minute of the last twenty years. It's enormous."

Even as they watched, Rainier spewed forth a plume of ash and steam, as if the Pacific Ocean was nothing to the volcano but a spittoon.

"I think I know some of what happened to Seattle," Toni-Marie said.

"It was buried, wasn't it?" Mike asked. "Just like Shambala."

"Probably that's all that would have happened if it had been farther inland," she said. "But, uh, I think maybe if we go for a swim we'd find out for sure, only I don't want to go swimming in *that*."

"Why not?" he asked, letting himself sink feet first into the ashy waves. "You're already dead. What could hurt you?"

She sniffed, "That's no reason to neglect simple hygiene."

The water beneath them began to boil, and strangely-shaped objects suddenly poked above the surface. In a few moments, a broad white seemingly solid expanse had become exposed, topped by a smokestack and antennae and wide outer walls perforated by windows. The water poured down the windows and away as the object rose to a level even with Mike and Toni-Marie, and skulls grinned back at them from windows along the walls. At other windows they saw ectoplasmic faces like their own. About that time the deck surfaced. It was broader than the cabin, and was followed by another, barnlike level. A horn blew, sounding not unlike the great bone horns Mike and his dad had uncovered in the lower levels of Shambala.

"This ferry now departing Seattle for Bremerton. Sailing time will be approximately sixty minutes."

The barnlike level held the rusted and barnacle-wrapped chassis of dead cars and trucks. "Please clear the car deck," a weary-looking male ghost in an orange life vest told them.

They wafted back to the passenger deck and watched the boat cut through the polluted water.

"Wow, this is amazing. No cities, no people, but the ferries are still running," Toni-Marie said.

"Nah, it's still running late," said a new voice, and they turned to find a ghost in a sailor's uniform standing behind them, smoking a translucent cigarette. "And it only makes one run a day. This was the last run before the earthquake hit and the volcanoes blew all at once."

"And it just keeps doing it?" Mike asked. "Making this run back and forth across the water?"

"Old habits die hard," the sailor said, shrugging. His tone was several degrees less friendly than it had been when talking to Toni-Marie. "So every day at about 12:25, which is ten minutes after it was supposed to leave at twelve-fifteen, the Bremerton ferry surfaces from the ruins of Seattle, sails across the Sound, and sinks down to where the Bremerton dock used to be. The next day we do it all over again. Don't ask me how it gets back to Seattle without anybody noticing. That's the spooky part, I guess."

"Well, I'm relieved that something's still the same, even if it only works in one direction," Toni-Marie said, sidling up to the sailor ghost. "We've been here for hours and we saw a little bit of what was left of Tacoma but no other people—not even dead ones, till the ferry surfaced—and no city or anything. We were looking for Bellingham but we haven't even been able to find Seattle."

"Oh, you found it. You just didn't look low enough. It's all down there, under Elliot Bay, even the Space Needle. Look over there on the horizon through the mist and you can see what's left of the Olympic Mountain range sticking up out of the water."

"Those little islands over there?" Mike strained his eyes and could barely see the mounds of darkness outlined against the clouds and the mist rising from the water.

"Yep."

"Are you passengers and crew of this boat the only people left in the whole place?" Toni-Marie asked him. "Aren't there any living people left?"

"Not as such, no ma'am, not that I know. Some of the passengers, the professional folks with doctorates and briefcases who commute to work, they already reincarnated at the first possible opening. Thanks to the pollution we had up the Duwamish, and in the Hood Canal, there were already plenty of mutant marine life-forms well adapted to our current conditions. The ambitious ones just got right back in the swim of it, you might say."

"But you didn't?"

"Well, no ma'am, I'm an undersea warfare specialist for NACAF and was trained as a marine biologist. Bein' a ghost isn't as bad as bein' some things I could name." He gave them a significant look out of eyes the color of glacial crevasses.

"It must have been pretty bad here then, the day the world ended," Mike said.

"What makes you think it was any specific day?" the sailor's ghost asked. "It took several days—weeks, if you want to know—while missiles fell all around the world. We were monitoring it *real* close, I can tell you, hoping our sophisticated defenses were working—they were—hoping nothing could touch us. I am proud to say it couldn't."

"Then what happened?" Toni-Marie asked. "Obviously something destroyed the place."

"Bad vibrations, I guess the old folks might have said. Anyhow, that's what the experts thought when the San Juan fault shifted and we had the earthquake, then the tsunamis, of course. Though some of them were caused by the volcanoes all blowing at once like that."

"*What* volcanoes?" Mike said.

"Just about all of them. Mount Saint Helens, Mount Hood, Shasta down in California, then Baker, and finally, well, it was Rainier that did in Seattle and Tacoma. Tacoma just didn't get the earthquakes and the tsunamis as bad. Those last ones, from when the coast of Siberia got hit, those were what sank the peninsulas. Anyhow, that's my guess. My buddy said it was going to happen and I told him he was nuts. Then when it did happen, I was out here on this ferry, busy dying."

"But except for these natural disasters, the NAC wasn't hit?" Toni-Marie said.

"No ma'am, but what happened was a lot worse than anyone anticipated."

"Oh, I know, but it didn't happen everywhere!" she cried excitedly and threw her arms around him, dissolving them both into puddles of ectoplasm. After which she gathered herself back together, shook herself back into shape as he did, and said, "You lovely man, you have just given me terrific news. Come on, Mikey, my family's in Texas."

"But, Toni-Marie, how do you know they survived?" Mike asked.

"Some of them are bound to have. We Adairs are survivors."

Chime settled into her trance, putting from her mind the lens, the cavern, Inez and the others, the cat who guarded her, Meru and Stoney, all of the spirits who would be only too glad to take over her soulless body if they could get through her puny safeguards. One-pointed concentration was required. The point was finding survivors, finding souls—any who were left, of course—but she couldn't help entertaining a wish to direct her consciousness so it wouldn't wander around at random but would accurately seek out the most worthy spirits first.

She put the wish from her as a distraction and settled into the trance, breathing at first so slowly and deeply that all of the world centered on the air she took into her, as if by breathing deeply enough, she could inhale air from far away Shambala and exhale it into this troubled world. Then she forgot all such concerns and images and even forgot that she was breathing in a certain way, so that her breath grew shallower and slower and suddenly she was looking down at herself and at the cat, at the valley, at the mountain ranges.

The mountains melted and flowed into other mountains, different valleys, until at last she found herself regarding the ruins of a monastery set like Shambala at the foot of an enormous, ruined mountain. Living people were there too, soldiers in what was left of their uniforms. They were a miserable lot, covered with sores and with ill-healed burns and broken bones, their uniforms tattered, some with limbs gangrenous from frostbite. They were thin and starving, but they stared with concentration almost as pointed as hers at a throng of ghosts in the robes of monks.

She knew that these monks were long dead, but to her astral form they seemed almost as vivid as the soldiers.

They were weeping, sobbing as some of them broke invisible stones high above the ruins, wrecking long-demolished buildings with invisible tools. A swarm of others were centered around an invisible space, and tears gleamed on their cheeks as they beat with all their might at something in their midst that only they could see.

After a while one of the soldiers who had had enough broke into the ring of ghosts, parting them like mist, shouting, "Please, please stop, holy men! Your teacher is long dead. Stop tormenting yourselves like this!"

"Get a grip on yourself, Fu Ping, they can't hear you," another soldier said, and Chime knew it was his own sadness that made his tone harsh. He hauled Fu out from among the ghosts, and Fu argued with him, waving sticklike arms in fevered agitation.

"Of course they can. Who do you think showed us where the hidden grain stores were? You think I just fell into that by accident? Who do you think has tended our wounds, has made this place one where fear does not reach us—except for times like these?"

"Once out of every twenty-four hours isn't bad," another comrade said with a shrug. "All other places, the living nightmare plagues us all day and all night. Here, after the ghosts finish their haunting for the day, they quietly return to being good holy men and healing and caring for the sick. That's us. We were lucky to find them."

"But they're suffering so much—can't you feel it?"

"Of course I can, but I'm suffering too. So is Lin Minh, so is Huan Po, but we can't do anything about it."

He did not sound as resigned to this as his words suggested. The agitation, fear, and sorrow in the air were tangible, far more real even than the bodies of the ghosts.

Chime approached the monks. "What are you beating on?" she asked one of them.

Without pausing to look at her or wonder, one of the monks spoke to her while he continued to pound on the target in the center. "Our beloved master, Takster Rimpoche. We are beating him to death."

"There is no one there," Chime told him.

The soldier Fu Ping rushed among the monks once more, and this time his eyes boggled as he beheld Chime.

"What is it now, Fu?" another comrade asked wearily. To a man squatting beside him, he said, "Not long now and we'll be eating him too, I fear. And after he was the one who warned us all to leave Lhasa before the end."

"Maybe that's a good reason to just kill him now," another said bitterly. "I think I would rather have died."

"That can still be easily arranged."

But Fu Ping was clutching the air where Chime's astral image appeared, gazing up at her yearningly. "Make them stop. Please make them stop. I know who you are. You're black Tara, one of their saints. You're supposed to be compassionate. You must make them stop. They are not the devils Lieutenant Shih told us about. They are kind people. They have fed us and cared for us. At every hour save this hour, this place is peaceful as nowhere else I have been before, and I know it is because of them. But then once a day they come out here and tear apart their home and beat their old master to death again and I know it's because they think we are making them do it. I curse the day I came to this wretched country. Why oh why did I not remain to die with my family? I swear to you, O Tara, that I had no hand in the matter you see these ghosts act out before you."

Chime turned back to the monk. "Your master isn't there, you know."

"We know, but our acts toward Takster Rimpoche remain. Our shame at committing this act survives us. Better I should have been beaten to death *before* I beat him. It all came out to the same thing in the end. He was eighty-five years old when we killed him, and had lived for many years as a hermit until he chose to return to teach and to enlighten us. That was just before the Chinese invaded. He tried to teach us ways to strengthen ourselves and our faith, to be an armor against them, but one day the soldiers came and instead of killing him themselves, they forced us to kill him. Now we are bound to keep repeating this one act of cowardice from which there is no redemption."

"Why no redemption? All things change. Your presence comforts the living here except when you do this, in which case you share your guilt with them, although they were not here when this tragedy occurred. Takster Rimpoche is not here and so he has either reincarnated or found Nirvana. Why should you grieve for that?"

Another monk's ghost, this one of a boy who could not have been more than ten years old when he died, said, "But Lady, our wrong actions resulted in the death of a living being. We don't kill insects or animals to eat because they too are living beings, possibly friends or family members in a new form. How then can we forgive ourselves for slaying our master? You don't understand, Lady. He was an old man and the soldiers tied him to a post and made us take up sticks and rocks and beat him with all our might. He cried, Lady, and he bled a great deal. See how our robes are splattered with his blood? When I was little and I cried because I missed my home, he took me onto his lap and rocked me and made me laugh, and to repay his kindness I beat him and made him cry and bleed."

One of the other monks, this one middle-aged and heavyset, said, "Only Thondup was able to hold out against the soldiers and refuse to participate, and they beat him to death even more horribly than we beat the master."

"And where is Thondup?" Chime asked. "I do not see him here. He too has reincarnated or attained Nirvana. And yet you remain."

"They made us tear down our own monastery, Lady. And trample and burn sacred writings our monastery has protected for hundreds of years. They made us piss on the flames."

"All of these things the soldiers made you do were not of your own free will. Of your own free will, after all of these things have been done to you, you remain here and reveal food to the living and comfort them by your presence. But since they wear the uniforms of the enemy, you trouble their souls once a day with this haunting. Look carefully at these soldiers. Are they the same soldiers who forced you to do these acts?"

"No, Lady. But they are soldiers, all the same," the middle-aged monk said with a bitterness that Chime thought was unbecoming to his station. "For years our bodies wandered the countryside starving while our spirits remained here, reliving this deed, so that when we died our spirits stayed here instead of being reborn. Then suddenly no rebirths were available, and so here we remain."

"Do you not think it more productive, then, to come with me to Shambala where you may attain a good rebirth and perhaps have a chance to make amends to your master and Thondup in your next lives, and let these soldiers also come to Shambala so that they might work out their karma?"

"Lady, lead us."

"Lead us too, Lady," Fu Ping cried.

"For the living it is a long journey and extremely dangerous," Chime said. "Though others are coming who can help you if only you can make it to a certain valley I will describe."

"We'll never last that long!" one of the other guards said. Chime had not thought they could see her, but now it seemed that even here the boundaries between life and afterlife were much thinner and more permeable. "You can see for yourself that we're sick and injured."

Chime said, "I don't wish to sound callous, but if you die, the journey might be easier for you. The important thing is to keep sight of the brothers here and of me and not lose the way. Even being reborn as an insect in Shambala would be a nicer life than the one you are living." And because these were living soldiers, she had to explain about Shambala, how their wounds would be healed there and they would not age, and how, if they died on the journey, there were many life-forms reproducing all the time so that they would be able to be reborn. The place these men were from had not been Buddhist for a long time, but still they didn't seem to have too much trouble accepting what she told them. Of course, they were already asking her, an astral being, to intervene with ghosts, so perhaps it didn't take much of a leap to accept Shambala.

"I don't know," said the one with the burned face. "It sounds as if it's extremely far away."

"I don't want to be an insect," the soldier with the badly healed leg said.

"What's the matter?" Fu Ping asked with mockery harsh enough to cut through his fear. "Are you afraid someone will accuse you of social climbing? We've been in the army. Being an insect will be a promotion."

"Fu Ping, you're officer material, you know that, don't you?" another one asked, but in the end they agreed.

"Now then, I must go seek other beings who may need to go. If

I give you landmarks, do you think you can start the journey while I am gone?"

"Lady, I know how to start the journey to Shambala according to the old books," a monk said.

"Much has changed, although I believe the mountains are still there, even if some are smaller than they used to be due to avalanche and bombs, and the lakes are still roughly in the same areas, though they may have altered somewhat. I will try to meet you at Mount Kailas. Do you know the way?"

The monks nodded that they did know the way to the most holy mountain in Tibet. Chime said, "Go there, and if you do not find me, after a time continue north and east, toward the Kun Lun Mountains. When you have gone as far as you can in that direction, be alert for the hidden valley. You will know it because you will see my body sitting on top of a ridge, guarded by a lion. And there are blue-green flowers leading into the hidden valley from a broad deep plain crisscrossed with streams and without other plants or flowers."

"You have invited us, you are the Shambala being, therefore we will find it," the middle-aged monk's ghost said.

"Do we have to take them?" the boy monk's ghost asked, pointing at the soldiers.

Fu Ping fell onto his knees with his hands clasped and looked appropriately piteous.

The boy monk's ghost sighed. "Yes, I guess we do. You must have much need for insects in Shambala."

CHAPTER XXVII

"How did you know where to find us, Buzz?" Meru asked.

"I didn't. I was following that black girl, Chime. Believe me, Cao Li, if I'd known you all were here sittin' high and dry and fat and sassy, I'd have been over long before this. You been holdin' out on me, buddy."

"My work had to be secret, Buzz. I'm sure a man of your calling appreciates that occasionally one needs to employ discretion—even from one's allies. And I assumed that you were busy with your official duties and would have your own shelter, with no interest in my little covey of civilians."

"You and your people have been well hidden, good buddy, back here away from the war, away from the missiles. This is pretty slick, Cao Li."

"Meru," Meru corrected smoothly. "I am called the Guru Meru now, or simply Master."

"Oh yeah? That's real interesting, Cao Li. Now then, I want the grand tour of this place, but first I have a score to settle with that black girl. Where is she?"

"I haven't seen her this morning yet. Melody?"

"No, Master. And Inez was not at breakfast either."

"Oh, I imagine Inez is sleeping in this morning," Cao Li said with a hint of a man-to-man smile at Buzz. "Perhaps Chime is in the gardens. Come with me, Buzz, and I'll show you where we grow most of our food."

"That should be interesting," Buzz said, "though not nearly as interesting as where I grew mine."

"You do not intend to harm the girl?"

"Goodness gracious me no, but I plan to speak sternly with her and I won't have any interference, Cao Li. I saw her first."

He looked Meru full in the face, and the magician was the first one to avert his eyes. "Yes, yes, of course."

"There it is! There's Houston!" Toni-Marie cried. "And it hasn't even changed much. There's the tramway and buildings—well, some of them look a little the worse for wear, but look, people! There's people down there, Mikey."

"I don't see any other ghosts either," Mike said.

"Let's go to Daddy's office and see if he's still—you know, around. In business."

"Surely not after all these years. I mean, the end of the world was bound to be bad for most businesses."

"Maybe not. Daddy was carrying on the family tradition. He was still in the firefighting business when I left for the cruise with Richie."

The office was on the ground floor of a mirrored building. A lot of the mirrors were broken out and they could see desks sitting between the girders and people writing longhand, wiping sweat, and having meetings, looking out at the sky and the streets below. The streets weren't in very good shape, but no cars moved along them, only people moving as quickly as if the world had not essentially ended. On closer inspection, almost all of the people appeared to be men and all of them carried a minimum of one firearm slung over their shoulders or strapped to their hips.

"Daddy's name is still on the door," Toni-Marie said, her voice thrilling with affection and more excitement than Mike had heard in it before. The door said *Adair Crisis Elimination (ACE) Management Services, Ace Adair President.*

"That's your daddy? Ace Adair?" Mike asked, a little awed. He'd never seen anyone's name on a door before.

"His name's really Asa Cornelius Earp-Adair, so you can see why he might prefer Ace. Besides, it goes with the business acronym."

"Is that anything like a family crest?" Mike asked.

"Sort of. Only more commercial-like," she said. With each sentence she spoke, her words lengthened and softened and added intonations of flat sun-drenched rocks, open plains, haciendas, cattle drives, and bourbon and branch water. But she was passing through the door now to where a tall, barrel-chested gentleman with a long hawk nose, wavy white hair, and a deep reddish tan sat typing with his sausagelike forefingers on an antique manual typewriter. He was wearing a checked shirt with creased short sleeves, though sweat had already formed dark spots under the arms and in the middle of his chest.

"Oh, Daddy, you came through another one unscathed!" Toni-Marie cried. To Mike, her voice high and her drawl deepening with nervousness and excitement, she chattered, "I just knew he would. Why, after some of the scrapes he was in while we were growin' up, a little nuclear war is nothin'."

Ace Adair looked up, squinted at them as if they were bright sunlight, and asked, "What? Is somebody there?"

"It's me, Daddy. Toni-Marie. Come on, I know you can see me if you try." To Mike she said from the corner of her mouth, "He's psychic as hell. Runs in the family, I guess. On Grandpa Adair's side of the family, there's always been a lot of psychicness—Grandpa's sister, Aunt Gaia-Jean, was the best known water witch in all of southwest and south-central Texas in her lifetime. And Daddy has *had* to be psychic to survive some of the things he has. Hell, he's pulled people out of places where you couldn't see an office building this size, much less a person. He always said he just sort of sensed them." And to her father she pleaded, "So sense *me*, Daddy."

Ace blinked twice and said, "Honey? I can sort of see you but you sound like a bad connection. You're one of my girls come back from the grave, and I know it, but which one? Maybelline, who died from smoke inhalation while she was helpin' me put out the fires out in Odessa? Amy-Renee, who caught the flu and passed away with the rest of her family in Dallas? Or my little Toni-Marie, God bless her, who never returned from her last sailing trip?"

"I hope you were just savin' the best for last, Daddy, and weren't preferrin' my sisters to me even here in the afterlife," Toni-Marie answered.

The big man got up from the desk and looked around the room, his face flushing deeper red with emotion, "It is you! It is my little Toni-Marie! Let me come on over and get a look at you, punkin. You're a little on the fuzzy side."

"That's 'cause I'm a ghost, Daddy. It tends to work that way."

"A ghost? Then you *were* killed over there. We were pretty sure you had been. We grieved for you along with the others, though we didn't think we'd ever know what became of you. Ghost or no ghost, baby, it's good to have you back home where you belong. Can't you make yourself a little clearer so's I can tell how you are? I wish I could give you a hug. Have you been to see Mama yet? No, I 'spect not or she would have let me know. Besides, I guess you'd have trouble figurin' out where we live now. We've moved a few times since you left."

Chattering during periods of emotional excitement seemed to run in the family, Mike noticed.

Toni-Marie asked, "Daddy, can you see my friend, Mike?"

"Uh-huh, I think I can just make him out. Looks like a Chinese fella I used to have on one of my crews. Damn good worker too. Good to meet you, son." Ace started to stick out his hand, remembered he was talking to an incorporeal being, and withdrew it.

"Hello, sir," Mike said.

"Mike and I met in Shambala. We're trying to find a magician to send us back there, or at least to Tibet, so we can rejoin his friend Chime. She's going to help us reincarnate in Shambala."

"What's this Shambala? Some kind of music group? Listen, honey, you're back home in Texas now and this is where you belong."

Toni-Marie's mother, Dolores Adair, had similar and quite definite views on the same subject. "You know very well, Toni-Marie, that our people have never held with that reincarnation business, but since it seems to be the way things *are* done nowadays, I think you need to remember who you are and not go traipsin' back to foreign countries again. It just doesn't agree with you, honey. You're lookin' real peaked and puny."

"Mama, I'm dead, for pity's sake!"

"Be that as it may, sugar, I think you'd be a lot better off stayin' here and bein' reborn as a Texan again."

"Sure do wish you'd been home a month ago when Martha Lee, Jimmy Joe's wife, had her baby," Ace Adair said, shaking his head regretfully. "You could have been your own niece. Perfectly normal too, except for the one malformed ear. That won't show when she gets more hair, and she's an Adair carrot-top already."

Toni-Marie rolled her eyes at Mike as if to say, What can I do? They're my folks.

"Now, Father, there's no need to make the girl feel bad," Toni-Marie's mom said. "She was unavoidably detained. But she's here now and I think you ought to get in touch with one of those psychic brokers everybody's been talkin' about."

"What's a psychic broker?" Toni-Marie asked. "You guys never even read your horoscopes when I was a kid."

"Why, honey, a pyschic *bro*ker is someone with mediumistic powers who can put the livin' in touch with the dead, help match up families with an appropriate spirit for their new children, should they be so brave and potentially self-sacrificin' as to have any, and puts the dyin' in touch with rebirth opportunities—for a fee, of course."

"Ah, the NAC," Toni-Marie said, "land of opportunity."

"Now there's no need to be snooty about it, sweetie. It came as a real surprise to everybody that all the weirdos who said they'd had previous lives as Napoleon and Cleopatra might have been gettin' a tad above themselves but weren't lyin' alto*geth*er. So of course practical folks just did the sensible thing and adapted."

"Is that why there are so few ghosts around, Mrs. Adair?" Mike asked.

"Why, yes, honey. Our psychic brokers have worked day and night to find placements for everybody so that we would have to deal with folks only on one plane—the one we're used to, that is, the physical one. Since you're Toni-Marie's guest we'll try to get a placement for you too, won't we, Ace?"

"Uh, Mama," Toni-Marie said, "never mind that. Mike can only get reborn in Shambala, isn't that right, Mikey?"

Mike nodded.

"It's a political thing," Toni-Marie explained.

"If you say so, dear."

"I don't see why we have to stay hidden," Bertinelli whispered. "I'd really like a shower and a shave, and while I appreciate these raw carrots and snow peas, dear, they hardly make for an elegant dining experience."

"Sorry about that, Marco," Inez said. "I'm not sure why you need to stay hidden either except that Chime, the girl who thawed you out and plans to heal all of you, said that you should stay hidden till she says otherwise. Tell you what, I'm going to go out and reconnoiter, okay?"

"I'll come too, Inez," Full Moon Akesh said. "Sounds as if it might be dangerous."

"Not for me, I think. If I'm not back in an hour or so, I want *all* of you to come on out and get me, though. We may need reinforcements. Meanwhile, everybody should stay hidden, stay quiet, and stay calm. Unless you hear me scream bloody murder, that is, in which case you should come running."

Before anyone could object, Inez flicked on her magnesium candle and darted from the little cave room, into the main Hall of Souls, stealing past the rows of bottles, feeling as if she, as well as the people she had just left, had been newly resurrected. She made a glamorous and appealing spy, she thought, even at her age. She was rather like that woman in the films of the late twentieth century, the Dorothy Gilman character,

Emily Pollifax. That was her. A Mrs. Pollifax, spy for the twenty-first century, well, almost twenty-second century. If anyone was still counting.

The fantasy of herself in a trench coat—rather than as she was, minkless and shivering, dashing forth to save the world, which God knew was now beyond saving—kept her going. She hated the endless rows of glass bottles. They gave her the creeps in a big way. She pretended they were enemy cameras trained on her every movement until she escaped their relentless gaze by splashing into the marshy floor, littered with the occasional corpse, of what had been the hold room. Her fantasy lost its power to protect her for a moment as she thought that she too might have been pinned up there in the ice, her body naked and vulnerable, and all that was her personality—her wit, her brilliance, her talent—trapped in one of Meru's damned bottles. Ugh. To think she'd once believed that guy. Well, of course, he did have *some* kind of powers or he'd never have been able to do that to people, and Chime would never have been able to resurrect them.

The water underfoot was freezing again, and the floor beneath the puddle was as slick as glass.

She slipped and started to swear when she heard a voice from the garden say, "Damn, Cao Li. You've really done well for yourself, you sly bastard. When you were just a little Chinese flunky, I always thought you didn't look scared enough. Too fat and sassy, too healthy and too smug. And all the time you were holding out on me. On all of us. Now, explain to me how you got a garden to grow so well at this altitude. What's the secret? I want to know how all of this works."

"I'm sure you do," Meru said, and Inez detected a certain shrillness that she had never heard in his high-and-mighty tone before. "I know you, Buzz. I remember some of the betrayals and counterbetrayals you were part of—how you sold out your own wife. Whatever became of your little girl?"

"You would remember her, wouldn't you? Always had a taste for little girls, huh, Cao Li? One of the ways you and me are alike. Well, she got to be a big girl, and when I decided to move on, she got to be too much baggage. She got taken suddenly dead. She's back in the hole now."

"You should have brought her along if she was ill. I have means to preserve bodies in the next room. I'd really like to show you that room, Buzz. Several of my clients have become—ill, mostly—and I've saved their spirits in a certain way for later use and put their bodies into a state of cryogenic stasis."

"Deep freeze, huh?" Buzz asked. "Keep the meat nice and fresh." The voices were growing louder and louder, and Inez figured they were probably in the center of the cave now. She wasn't sure how to make an appearance without being connected with the damage in the room. She could concoct a story that she'd heard noises that disturbed her, and when she came out to investigate, found it like this. Trying to work up a suitably horrified emotional state wasn't too difficult when she had the Master and his new companion for inspiration.

"Yes, I showed it to Chime earlier. She was most inquisitive regarding the more esoteric aspects of our lives here. Perhaps she's back in the Hall of Souls."

"Sure is light in here," Buzz said, his voice growing fainter for a moment, then louder again, as if he was turned toward the back of the cave or craning his neck. "Did you install the skylight or was it here when you got here?"

"It's natural."

"What's that cat doing up there?"

"Cat? Oh, that silly creature. Sunning itself, no doubt. Perhaps we can investigate when I've finished showing you the hold room and the Hall of Souls." He added, his voice urging, insistent, "The cat took quite a liking to Chime. Perhaps she's with it."

"I think I'd like to go see about that right now."

"On the other hand, she could be back this way," Meru said, again trying to steer his companion toward the Hall of Souls. "You must see this. It's critical to my work." Yeah, Inez thought, and if you can freeze and bottle this Buzz guy, you won't have to worry about him killing you and the rest of us, and I can just tell by listening to you guys that he'd *love* to do that.

"*Later*. I don't like the way that animal is spying on us. I don't like anything lookin' down on me these days. How do I get up there from here?"

"From in here? Climb the wall, I suppose. The easiest way is to go around. Why are you so obsessed with the girl? She will go nowhere . . ."

Listening to the two of them made Inez shiver even more violently than the cold accounted for, and as Meru's voice and footsteps grew louder, signaling his approach, she pressed back from the doorway, against the walls of the cave. Her back touched something solid. Reaching back, she felt the unmistakable contours of a human leg. A cold human leg, naked.

She jerked her hand away in revulsion. Then the cold, naked leg, and a cold, naked foot stepped over her.

CHAPTER XXVIII

No one had lived in Lhasa for a very long time, but many dead still remained there. Here were the remnants of almost too many sad lives, so many that the death scenes constantly reenacted throughout the city seemed reduced to a series of macabre charades, as if Chime was viewing some very long, ritualistic drama.

Whole families relived their murders before her eyes—shot, beaten to death, their homes burned. Monks and nuns were publicly beaten and forced at gunpoint to copulate in public, forced to beat each other to death, forced off to the shelled-out ruins of People's Liberation Army official buildings huddled in the specious shelter of the ruined Potala. There these ghosts screamed and screamed and screamed. Now that the noise of the city was stilled, the screams were most noticeable.

These gruesome and horrible tragedies were the ones she noticed first, she supposed, because the souls taken most suddenly and agonizingly were those least likely to be able to escape the disorientation of death and negotiate the land of the dead successfully to Nirvana or rebirth. As she had done with the monks and the soldiers, she tried to enlighten the souls she met and inform them that it was now time to overcome the facts of their deaths, gain acceptance, and go on to seek the next plane of existence.

When she had spoken to them, these ghosts ceased their hauntings and settled down to wait. After a time, when she looked at the city from above, she was able to tell from the pools of calm which parts she had already dealt with and which portions still appeared the most haunted.

Three sites in particular suddenly struck her as having the most angry and agitated spirits clamoring around them.

By this time her own spirit was weary and her patience and compassion stretched further than they had ever been. "Spirit," she said to a rather undefined female entity dashing back and forth on the edge of the melee, "you are dead now, you know."

"Of course I know," the spirit snapped back. "I'm just dead, not stupid."

"In life, were you a Buddhist?" Chime decided to take another approach. Perhaps this soul knew she was dead but didn't know her options. She really was extremely hazy-looking.

"In every single one," the ghost answered promptly.

"Then why have you not sought rebirth or Nirvana, but have chosen to stay within this small section of the bardo? Are you frightened and confused?"

"Not anymore I'm not, though I was at first. Now I'm just mad as hell."

"And these others? Are they also wrathful spirits?"

"You bet they are. And with good reason. We all died in this place, and because of it have been deprived of the kind of rebirth we want."

Chime asked carefully, "And what kind is that?"

"Human, first of all, and into a nice Tibetan family. My six most recent lives have been that sort, and in the three most recent I was a very religious person—I wanted to be a nun in this life, found just the right womb, and then, just before I was ready to make my entrance, this so-called doctor tricked my mother—that's her over there, the one screaming the loudest—and forcibly aborted her instead of giving her the care she sought. She didn't survive, either, and my big brother, who was only a year old, died of neglect."

"Is that pretty much the case with all of these ghosts?" Chime asked. She remembered that this kind of thing had happened to Auntie Dolma, who had been aborted and sterilized without her consent. That was why she had never had children of her own, but had to content herself to be only everyone's auntie.

"Pretty much. We were all prevented from being born and therefore from being reborn, or else we are the mothers who were killed by the clumsy bastards who butchered us. Such are the stories of most of us. Except for the one in the middle," and here, although Chime could not clearly differentiate the ghost's features, she saw an awful smile infuse the spirit's face, a nasty vengeful smile full of deep and bitter satisfaction.

Chime's astral body passed through the ghosts as if they were smoke until she reached the center of activity. There, a form more clearly defined than that of the ghost she had been addressing knelt, staring wildly around, wielding a scalpel as if to ward off the ghosts. The figure was that of a small and skeletally thin man. He jabbed his scalpel at the ghosts and then, every few minutes or so, tried it on various arteries on his own body, with predictably unsatisfactory results since the arteries were no more corporeal than he was. His eyes bulged from his head and his mouth was gibbering, "Go away, please go away. There are no such things as ghosts. You're not real and I don't believe in you. I did nothing wrong. There are no such things as ghosts. Oh, please go away."

"Doctor," Chime said, kneeling beside him.

"Go away," he said. "I don't believe in ghosts."

"I'm not a ghost. I'm the astral projection of a living woman."

"What?" he asked, and his eyes focused on her, the first time they had been clearly focused in all the time she'd been watching him. "Oh, well. That's different. What's the matter with you? You ought to know perfectly well it's no good sending an astral projection in for medical care. I'll need a body to work on."

"Oh, no you don't, you bastard!" A woman's ghost shrieked. "No more bodies for you! No births for our children, no rebirth for you!"

The doctor's ghost quivered and for the first time forsook his bravado. "They're very angry with me, aren't they?"

"Understandably, wouldn't you say?"

"It was only population control, you know. The world is over-crowded. Tibet was overpopulated."

"Not until your government sent China's excess population to over-run us," Chime reminded him. "Come now, do you want to be reborn or not? Believe me, I haven't time to argue with you. It seems to me if you earnestly believed that what you did was right, you wouldn't still be here at the mercy of your victims."

"Who are you?"

"I am someone who can help you, but only if you are honest."

"Honest! I have forgotten what that means. I wanted to be a doctor so that I would have an honorable profession with which I could help people. I was the physician for a very important family that fell into disfavor in China. Thereafter, I was deported here to this women's clinic, where I was ordered to sterilize all ethnic Tibetan women who came in. They already had far more than their quota of children in this country, you see, and we needed to balance the population."

"Liar!" one of the mother ghosts hissed. "You wanted to wipe out Tibetans in our own country so that it would support the Chinese lie that Tibet was not and had never been more than a province of China. Admit it!"

"Madam, please!" he said, and when the ghost was no more impressed than he should have expected, said to Chime, "Well, there is much in what she says, but as for myself, I was only following orders. I was always trained to believe that population control is vital to the success of our people—I suppose it was easy to delude myself that I was helping these women."

"Even when you killed them and killed babies who could have lived?"

He hung his head.

Chime sighed. "I suppose I will have to admit you to Shambala too, to await rebirth. We have need of vermin there, and bottom-cleaning fish. I suggest in the meantime, even before you are reborn, you stop defending your actions to yourself with lies and seek to learn the lessons that will earn you spiritual advancement."

"I do not believe in such things, madam."

"You are a scientific man, are you not?"

"I am."

"Then I suggest you review your position in view of the data surrounding you. Excuse me. I must tell the others how to release themselves from this phase of afterlife and join me later for the trip to Shambala."

"Daddy, this is nuts," Toni-Marie said. "You don't *pay* somebody to help you get reborn. You choose a rebirth according to what you need to know and what's needed in the world. Right, Mikey?"

Mike nodded. He was trying to stay out of it, but he did not think his father or Chime Cincinnati would approve of such a commercialization of karmic destiny.

"Now, honey, they may not use brokers where you've been, but around here we're trying to be organized and businesslike about all this reincarnation stuff, much as it's thrown us for a loop. McCobb is supposed to be one of the best—anyway, the best in Houston, which is all I can find out about on such short notice. Our communications systems don't go beyond the city limits these days and they're gettin' more limited as time goes on."

"You mean you can't even contact Dallas anymore? Or San Antonio?" Toni-Marie asked incredulously.

Ace looked uncomfortable. "You wouldn't really want to do that, sweetie pie, even if it were possible."

"Why not? Didn't I get a card from you just before, uh, before I died, telling me that Amy-Renee had moved up to Dallas? And Maybelline was running your Austin office, wasn't she?"

Mrs. Adair looked as if she was about to cry. "Maybelline's stuck out in Odessa now. I don't know how you kids made it home, but generally speaking, most ghosts have to stay where they die until they get reborn, or maybe go to Heaven I guess. I don't think Hell could be much worse than this. We kept in touch with Dallas until the flu epidemic, but then it was quarantined off. I don't really think anybody's left up there anymore. We did hear tell about Amy-Renee and her family—" She dipped her face as if to hide her head against her own shoulder, like a bird tucking its head under its wing. Ace put his arm around her protectively. She was very frail, her skin almost transparent, and though from the front her hair was cut in a stylish gray bob, when she turned her head, the crown was bald.

After a moment she sniffed and said, "I wish we had been able to do for your sisters what we're doing for you."

"Mike, do you think if we can contact Chime, she could help them?" Toni-Marie asked. She wanted to pat her mother on the hand, but when she'd tried to kiss Mama hello, Mama had gotten goose bumps.

"Maybe. It seems to me that maybe a family member could bring them back too—"

"There's no way, son," Ace said. "Most of the livestock died in the fires that burned up the oil. We're runnin' on empty, transportationwise, except for shank's mare," he patted his leg, "and bicycles. I'm running the only foot-powered firefightin' units since the early settlers formed bucket brigades."

There was a knock at the door then. Otis McCobb, Psychic Soul-and-Body Broker, had arrived.

"Well, young lady, all I can say is I wish you had taken it into your head to come home a few years earlier," McCobb said a short time later, when he had installed himself at Toni-Marie's mama's kitchen table and was negligently sipping a cup of the preciously hoarded Tang tea that Texan hosts only brought out for very special guests—those who could not handle Old Meltdown or one of the other bootleg whiskeys whose production constituted Houston's chief postapocalypse industry.

The broker did not indulge in spiritous liquors, though of course he had to deal with spiritous everything and everybody else in order to ply his trade. Or his calling, as he referred to it.

He was a big man, tall and heavyset, the front of his head bald, with long dishwater-blond hair caught up in a braid in the back. His powder-blue eyes were bloodshot, his face flushed and sweaty over an unhealthy pallor, as if he'd been spending his day watching his beloved grandma's house burn down. He wore jeans and an ancient white T-shirt which featured skulls with top hats. Mike thought that it might be a badge of his trade.

"What abilities does he have exactly?" Mike asked Dolores Adair while McCobb went into his trance.

"Well, he can see spirits, of course, and talk to them."

"So can you—I mean, you're talking to me. And you don't need a trance to talk to Toni-Marie."

"Well, but I'm her mama and you're her friend. Mr. McCobb can see spirits who aren't kin, friends, or acquaintances even—he can talk to perfect strangers to whom he has not been properly introduced, *including* those who were some other kinda critter in their most recent life. Of course, there's not much call from mamas wantin' to know that the soul for their new little bundle of joy is a new applicant who was a catydid or a cotton plant in its last life."

Ace cut in. "See, son, the way this works is that these broker people have a network. Like right now he's not just tryin' to talk to you and Toni-Marie. He's takin' inventory of his whole operation and maybe communicatin' with other brokers. They know who and what's bein' born where to whom, so they can find their clients good placements."

Toni-Marie had grown very quiet, Mike noticed, hovering way up in a corner of the room, looking down at her parents with an expression of grief mixed with frustration and anger.

Mike joined her while her parents watched over the psychic. "What's the matter, Toni-Marie? Aren't you happy to find your parents?"

"Yeah, now if I could only talk to them," she grumbled, discontent etching its way through her face. "Dammit, Mikey, there's something wrong here. We came all this way. I was so excited to think about seeing them again, worried that they wouldn't be able to see me, and you know what?"

"No. What?"

"I was right. They don't see me."

"Of course they do, Toni-Marie—"

"No, I mean, they can make out the ectoplasm but they no more hear what I'm saying to them or care about who I am than if I was invisible. I want to help them find my sisters, Mikey. I want to ask them what happened to *them* in the war. I want to tell them what happened to me. But they're talking *at* me. I mean, jeez, after the conversations I've had with you and Chime and O'Brien and all, this just seems a little—empty. It's like they're pushing me away."

Mike considered the elderly couple sitting at the table, sipping their Tang tea while they watched the psychic breathe. Ace Adair breathed heavily, blew his nose, ran his hand through his hair, glanced at his wife, the psychic, anywhere but where Toni-Marie was, until Dolores Adair pointedly looked up at them and smiled a brief tight smile before looking quickly away again. Ace followed suit with a little wave. His hand trembled. "They're afraid, Toni-Marie."

"Get serious. Daddy has never been afraid of anything in his whole life."

"No, look at them. They are in most ways far better off than most of the people we saw in Ireland and the Middle East, but nevertheless they've suffered many shocks and the grief of losing you and your sisters. They're still in great pain, and your reappearance has dredged it all up again. Can't you see it?"

Toni-Marie studied her mother and father for a moment, the trembling hands, the eyes that quickly teared, the too-fast chattering and her mother's constant deference to her father.

Toni-Marie said, "They *are* different, and not just older. Mom is leaning on Dad a lot more, and he doesn't seem to—well, to be as in charge as he used to. And you're right. They both look as if they're about to cry. And you think it's because of me?"

Mike studied them, shaking his head slowly. "Well, they have been through the end of the world, of course, but also, not being able to care for you and your sisters after your deaths must have made it even worse. Maybe they've secretly hoped you survived. I wonder if my parents are suffering in this same way."

"I guess it would be hard, not knowing." She brightened. "But we did offer to try to find May and Amy, and I still think we should just waft up to Dallas and on out to Odessa and see if we can locate their ghosts, figure out if they or any of Amy's family has been reborn yet."

Mike was doubtful. "Maybe. But your parents didn't want us to. Maybe instead of them trying to do something for you and you trying to do something for you, you should both just stop trying to *do* something and talk with each other."

Toni-Marie made a rueful face. "You're a big help, Mikey."

Toni-Marie's mother jumped up suddenly, dumped her Tang tea cup in the sink and washed it, then sat back down, perched on the edge of her chair, her hands clasped together so that their knuckles stood out large and white.

Ace Adair patted his wife's hand reassuringly. "It'll be okay, Mama. We're a fine old Texas family and there's bound to be a real good rebirth for our little girl."

McCobb snapped out of his trance and said in an annoyed tone, as if he'd been listening to them right along, "That's generally true, but surely you must realize that the birth rate is very low these days and the death rate high. Normally ghosts of your daughter's age—that is, those who died during the great disaster or earlier, rather than of one of the plagues or during the firestorms more recently—normally someone like her would be in a very good position. But with the great forest fires in the Tropical American Parks down south of the border, well, there's been heavy traffic in quality South and Central American souls— not the peasants, mind you, but the doctors, teachers, writers, artists, religious leaders, all the people who were killed by the governments just before NAC invoked the Final Solution, as well as some of the ones who were eliminated during the conversion of residential areas to parklands."

"Why should that be happening just now?"

"Seems those souls have only just been released from their last lives as trees in the parks. The big fires freed them and they contacted Latino brokers up here."

"But those are foreigners! Our daughter is an American." Ace sounded outraged. "American bodies should go to Americans."

"Well, I certainly understand how you feel, Mr. Adair, but if you were a new mother, wouldn't you rather have your child inherit the soul of a Latin poet or martyred humanitarian than some common businessperson from the NAC?"

"Hell, no!" Ace thundered.

"No, I suppose not. But a lot of mothers seeking the best possible inner life for their children do feel that way, so as I said, there's an uncanny amount of competition right now."

"It can't be that difficult," Dolores said, her tone showing the mettle of a southern belle. "Our daughter is an Adair and she is a Texan and we want her placed here now."

"I'll see what's available and get back to you," McCobb said.

Toni-Marie and Mike rejoined the Adairs at the kitchen table. "Daddy," Toni-Marie said, "Mikey and I have had some pretty strange experiences with this rebirth stuff already and it's tricky. Let's not be too hasty here—that guy doesn't seem very competent to me."

But Ace's jaw was set and he didn't seem to hear her.

McCobb returned later that day, looking even worse than he had before. He stood well away from Ace Adair as he said, "I've located a birthing about to happen close by."

"Wonderful!" Dolores Adair said, noiselessly clapping her hands together.

"What's the catch?" Ace asked.

"Oh, there isn't one really. You can have it, and at quite a bit less than my quoted price—unless, that is, you *must* have a human rebirth?"

"Oh, yes, I think so," Dolores said nervously, looking at Ace for confirmation.

"Well, sure—"

"In that case, I'm afraid I can't help you. Even without the illegal alien souls, we were backed up forty or fifty years on the inverted birth/death ratio."

"Forty years? That long?" Toni-Marie's mom sounded as if she might faint.

"I'm afraid so."

"Well, that ain't gonna do at all, son. By that time I'll not only be unable to enjoy my grandchildren, I'll probably have kicked the bucket myself and be lookin' to be reborn *as* one of my grandchildren. Haven't you got anything else?"

"Perhaps you've heard that the Houston University animal husbandry department has been breeding longhorn stock especially to provide bodies to sort of sop up some of the extra ghosts?"

Ace nodded tightly. "I'd heard somethin' about that, though I don't see where a cow's body is any kind of life for a human being."

"Actually, scientists are beginning to believe that there has always been a strong affinity between native breeds and native peoples and that souls are reborn from one to the other as needed. It was once thought, for instance, that longhorns exemplified the Texan character possibly because association with the cattle in the same environment had a molding effect. We're beginning to think that instead, it's because the cattle and the people trade souls back and forth. However, the important thing here is that we can control to some extent the number of cattle born, whereas it naturally wouldn't be right to try to set the same limits on human beings or to force people to breed before the danger of mutation has abated."

Ace Adair was listening attentively, and Dolores Adair was nodding to show she was following the train of thought. Toni-Marie groaned and whispered to Mike. "Jesus, they *have* changed. Daddy hasn't told that creep yet that *he's* the one who's full of bull."

"But Toni-Marie, he may be right," Mike said. "O'Brien told us, and in fact the people of Tibet and Shambala have always believed, that souls may be reborn in human, animal or even, according to O'Brien, plant forms. At least two peoples I've read of believed cows in particular were sacred. And since from what you and I have been learning, that ghosts tend to stay in one region, it is very likely that the Texan and the longhorn do, as McCobb says—"

"I can't believe what I'm hearing!" Toni-Marie said.

"But it makes a certain kind of sense," Mike protested.

"I'm not feeling *that* sensible, okay? So let's just drop it."

McCobb was continuing, "The program is still getting under way, but in the near future the department there at the U. expects to build up a big enough herd to take care of the excess spiritual population. As time goes on and the human population and other life-forms start coming back, well, the lifespan of the cattle is less than that of people, and the souls will be released for rebirth again. But right now, with ladies still being so cautious about giving birth, this is your daughter's best hope of getting a body. In six months, maybe, you can pick her sex and everything."

"Our daughter can't wait six months!" Dolores said, with a little gasp in her voice but something hard in her eyes. Ace grunted agreement.

McCobb sighed, but Mike felt that he had been building up to this particular revelation all along. "Well now, at this point in time, it so happens that there *is* an opening of sorts. A cow's in labor and the calf, as it turns out, is going to be a two-headed mutation. Of course, the birth was already spoken for months ago by a state senator for his second wife, who was killed by falling glass during the earthquakes. However, since the calf is going to be a mutant, there's room for a spirit in each head, and if she hurries, your daughter might be eligible for the left-hand head."

"Why, that's the most outrageous thing I've ever heard of!" Dolores Adair sputtered. "My little girl in the left-hand head of a two-headed calf!"

"Daddy!" Toni-Marie turned to her father.

"You got to be out of your mind, McCobb," he said, and Toni-Marie relaxed, until he added, "An Adair is worth at least bein' the right-hand head."

"*Dad*dy!"

"Sorry, honey. Just jokin'. Of course you don't belong in any mutant livestock."

"I think you should reconsider this carefully, sir. It's the wave of the future to park loved ones in shorter-lived life-forms until the human birthrate increases. At least she would be a living being again, and since a mutant's life expectancy is even a little shorter than usual, maybe you could find a girl who'd be willing to conceive especially to give your daughter a new home. Or, if research continues as it's been going, we may be able to make babies in test tubes again within a few years."

Dolores was considering, her head cocked to one side and a calculating look in her eyes, as if she was getting ready to bargain for something. Finally she said, "I certainly *have* heard tell of human souls becoming animals. But we'd want to buy this calf ourselves, Mr. McCobb, and keep it here as part of the family."

"Mama!" Toni-Marie screeched. "I am *not* going to be some *cow*."

"Now, honey, you shouldn't be too hasty," her father said carefully. "Ordinarily, I'd agree with you. But these are real hard times, and sometimes—well, you have to take what you get, start at the bottom."

"That's not the bottom, Daddy, that's the pits!" she said.

"It wouldn't be so bad, honey. We wouldn't let anybody eat you."

"Well, thanks all the same but I'm just not interested. I can stick around in this form indefinitely, can't I, Mike? It's not like we rot or anything, as spirits at least. Meanwhile, I have better things to do with my time than be contaminated veal cutlets."

"But Toni-Marie," Mike said, "I thought you wanted to be reborn as soon as possible."

"Not this way. Listen, Mikey, there are a couple of other things you probably don't know about Texans and cattle, but I don't want to be a cow and I don't want to be *treated* like a cow and nobody can *make* me be a cow. Look, I think it would be better if we just both left again. I've seen that Mama and Daddy are okay and there doesn't seem to be a lot I can do for anybody else. We need to get back to tryin' to find Chime. Maybe if we both tried like goin' back to China and hollering as loud as we could, she could come fetch us? Don't *you* know any of her magic words like the ones she used on Richie and to summon that yeti, whasisname?"

"I think that only works for very holy people," Mike said.

"But you could at least try."

"Perhaps there'll be a cancellation," McCobb said, edging for the door. "We could put you on our waiting list."

"You just do that little thing, sweetie," Toni-Marie hollered after him.

To Ace Adair, McCobb handed a card saying, "Call if you change your mind. You know, if you decide it's the best thing for her, you don't need consent. I can make the arrangements."

"Kalagiya!" Mike said, suddenly remembering Chime's magic word. "Kalagiya!"

CHAPTER XXIX

The naked corpse of Sven Strom stepped over Inez and stalked toward the voices of Buzz and Meru.

Inez recovered from her surprise in time to grab for Strom's leg and hiss, "Hey, Sven, wrong way! We don't want them to know about us just yet. Come back with me. . . ."

Strom's hand reached down to strike her a glancing blow on the side of the head that sent her sliding down on her butt halfway across the icy floor of the cave room.

Oh, shit, Inez thought, just her luck that Strom would be a late sleeper and not awaken until Chime was already topside and unavailable to persuade him to cooperate with her plan.

Inez debated whether to return to the others—cowering and awaiting discovery by Meru and the nasty newcomer—or to brazen it out—using Strom as a diversionary tactic. Brazen came more naturally to her, and she was preparing her story as she emerged into the light of the garden cave.

"You can just stop right there, Cao Li," Buzz snarled. "You think I'm turnin' my back on you to go up there, you're more of a plain fool than you think I am."

Meru looked up to the crystal lens. If they climbed up there, he had little hope of escape. The air above his compound was beyond his control. Up there, above his wards, the ghosts were wild. Down here, with all of his spells and charms placed about the canyon, he controlled the dead with his apparatuses and necromancy, the living with the force of his personality. Unless, of course, a more forceful personality came along. His karma seemed to have caught up with him. Two personalities more forceful than his had entered his domain within the last two days. First Chime, now Buzz. He had been certain he could deal with Chime, but Buzz would require stronger measures. Such as a bottle judiciously applied to the skull, followed by shooting with one of the guns the man carried. The ghost he could catch and bottle as it left the body. All of that was contingent, of course, on Buzz predeceasing him, which looked increasingly unlikely since, turning to face his opponent, Meru saw that Buzz was now pointing a sidearm of some sort at him.

Meru shuddered as Buzz grinned and waggled the barrel of his gun toward the waterfall concealing the most prominent hand- and footholds. Meru considered himself primarily a creature of spirit who deplored violence . . . particularly when it was directed at him.

He crossed to the waterfall, stepped across the little stream flowing from the pool created by the cascade, and ducked beneath the falls. Climbing up the wall past the falls, he looked up to see how far he had to go.

Glittering golden eyes glared back at him. The front half of the cat protruded from the opening above the shallow ledge that supported the crystal. The beast hissed and growled at him, drawing its black lips back from sharp white teeth and quite large fangs. Meru could see the muscles in its shoulders bunching to launch the cat onto his face and tear him to pieces.

He glanced nervously down at Buzz. The man hadn't started climbing yet, but was pointing the gun in his direction.

"Don't shoot!" Meru cried, and jumped down into the stream.

At the same time, a shot rang out. Simultaneously, the cat yowled and sprang back from the opening as if jerked by a string.

Meru landed so hard it knocked the air from his lungs. For a split second he found himself staring up into Buzz's gun barrel, felt the pain in his legs and back from landing with his shins across the edge of the ditch, felt the cold water seep into his robe, and heard the cat thrash and scream above them.

Then the naked body of Sven Strom stalked past him to stand between him and Buzz's weapon.

"You shouldna left me, Pa," Strom whined to Buzz in a high nasal voice, the same voice with which Strom had pleaded not to be frozen after all, just before Meru put him on hold.

Clenching his teeth against the pain in his legs, and staring up through blurring eyes, Meru saw Strom grab Buzz's neck.

Strom seemed oblivious to the gun barrel jammed into his stomach, and before the first round thudded into his body, he bore Buzz to the ground. Buzz hadn't moved since Strom spoke, and to Meru's surprise, did not fire immediately. Strom swept the gun from the smaller man's grasp just as the shot rang out, but the shot went wild.

Inez Murdock's face, for some reason, was suddenly floating above him. "Oh, my God! Come on, Meru, don't just *lie* there. Can't you see there's something wrong with Strom?"

"Inez, help me," he cried.

But his words were lost as Strom hollered into Buzz's face. "Shouldna left me, Pa. My meat will spoil. Never waste food. We stick together. But you got to come to these top-dwellers in spite of all the food I made you. You *kilt* me to come here."

As Strom spoke he squeezed Buzz's neck and pounded his head against the floor for emphasis. Buzz kneed him in the stomach, but although the knee connected, it had no effect. He tried to bring an elbow up, but the air was being squeezed out of him. His voice wheezed out, *"Eeeeevv . . ."* but the big man kept squeezing and pounding until the body under him went limp.

For a moment Strom sat back on his haunches staring at the body in front of him as if neither Inez nor Meru had any substance, then the big man fumbled with Buzz's belt, finding the utility knife the man Eve had known as Father always carried. Calmly, Strom stripped away the clothing from Buzz's corpse and began dressing the body out.

Buzz's soul escaped his body as his killer's hands relaxed on his broken flaccid neck. Damn. Who'd have thought Evie had it in her to follow him like that, hijack some big joker's body and kill her own pa? No respect for her elders and betters, that girl.

One thing for damn sure, though, was that he had better find himself another body soon. A likely candidate was that cat. He thought maybe he'd only winged it. He'd get himself another human body ultimately, of course, but he thought he could do a lot with the cat's teeth, claws, and agility.

He did enjoy the ease with which he smoked out of the cave, leaving Evie's new male body carving up her pa's mortal remains while some hysterical woman screamed at her. Buzz saw the woman snatch up the gun he'd dropped. Ol' Meru was hollering instructions that both Evie and the woman ignored. 'Kill both of 'em, bitch, I don't give a shit,' Buzz thought as he slipped straight through the crystal lens and out of the cave, 'just so I have a chance to get into the kittycat's body first.'

He found the cat okay. It was lying across the lap of the black girl, Chime, who was just sitting up there cross-legged on top of the ridge with nothing around her but the wind and the mountaintops. The cat was bleeding all over her thighs. The only other thing up there was a couple of spiderweb-looking contraptions—ghost traps, the Tibetans had called them—busted and tangled and spotted with blood on the ground where the cat must have thrashed against them getting out of the hole.

At first he thought, 'Why isn't that girl fussing over that damned beast? She's that kind.'

The cat opened its golden eyes, bared its fangs and hissed at him. He wasn't about to evict that particular feline spirit from that particular body so he could occupy the premises any time soon, he saw. However, the girl, still sitting there oblivious to both his own ghostly presence and the spitting, hissing cat, was definitely out to lunch. The part of her that Buzz didn't need was conveniently missing, while her nubile young body sat there just waiting for him to fill it up.

The broken collection of threads and sticks on the ground had been placed there to protect her, he saw, but thanks to the cat's struggles getting out of the cave, the ghost traps were useless against him. The cat snarled and swiped at him, but since Buzz no longer had a hide to be lacerated, the cat couldn't touch him.

Laughing all the way, Buzz jumped into the girl and made himself at home. His first bodily act, he thought, would be to wring the damned cat's neck, but before he had quite gotten control of the girl's slender brown hands, the animal streaked away, leaving long burning lacerations on Buzz's smooth new thighs.

Meru, paying no attention to what Inez was bent on doing, said loudly, slowly, and very carefully. "Inez, go into the Hall of Souls and find an empty bottle and cap and hold it up to the dead man's mouth."

But Inez, shivering with disgust as she watched the soulless monster Strom had become gut the body of the man he had just murdered, instead scooped up the gun and shot Strom until he let the knife fall from his hands and fell across his victim. It wasn't as if poor Sven was really still alive—Sven would never have done such a revolting thing. She hadn't killed *Sven*. No, clearly something had gone wrong with the thawing process and something evil and alien had taken over Strom's body. She'd just . . . stopped him—it—like the heroine in one of the early twentieth century zombie movies.

As she stood looking down at the bodies, Meru whimpered, "Oh, very well, have it your way. Bring *two* bottles and caps."

Chime Cincinnati surveyed the barren wasteland in front of her, the parched earth, the bomb-pocked mountains, the once lush valleys now filled with the ash of great forests, fused rock. The smooth road that

China had built to Lhasa long ago was buckled and fissured by earthquakes, washed away by spring floods. She visited the shores of the sacred lakes and found two dry, one full of faintly glowing material the consistency of paste.

She had added the ghosts of a few guerrilla fighters, former nomads trapped in their most recent incarnations by the circumstances of their deaths. She found one deep bunker full of barely-living NACAF troops and their Indian allies. They were filthy, covered with sores and wracked by disease, foul-mouthed, parched and starving, unable to find sustenance in the sparse vegetation poking its way up from the ashes.

Everytime she found one group, it became more urgent to her to find others, similarly lost and frightened.

What good does it do to find them when, once you have located them, you simply go looking for more? her former selves asked her.

"But there are others—I have only explored a portion of our country. I have not yet begun to search China or India or to the north, in Mongolia, Russia, and those other countries."

It is time to gather the ones you've found and lead them home. The living need food and medicine. The dead have been wandering the bardo a very long time. Merely locating these people is not enough to restore order. Now you must lead them home.

"But what about the others, the ones I have not found?"

Did you think that you would make one journey and retire? Why do you think we urged you to leave Shambala when you were yet a child? This wasted earth you see before you is the work of this lifetime and many more to come. Now you must return to your physical form and fulfill your promise to these people. If you wish to return to Shambala with living beings as well as ghosts, you must return to your body and begin.

"Yes, and next time I'll bring food and medicine so that I can be of more help."

Such things are only of help to the living. The longer you delay, the more of them pass into the ghost world.

"Very well. I'll return to my body now. Except first I must find Meekay and Toni-Marie. Except I don't know how. I have found ghosts all over this land. I can find the living many miles away. But the Guru

Meru's curse must have worked, for no matter how hard I look, I cannot find my friends here."

Then it stands to reason that they are not here. Use your god eye.

"I have studied on this matter of eyes, but I can't seem to find all of mine."

Certainly you can. You have already. How do you think you have found these hidden places and people? We have had the use of all of our eyes in our former lives. It is time for you to reopen them, to extend and refine your abilities. Open our wisdom eye and seek to know what is in other minds, what there is to know. Ultimately this will lead to the reopening of Buddha eye, which sees the ultimate nature of reality.

"What about ears?"

Beg pardon?

"Ears, former selves. Do my astral ears have special metaphysical levels too? Because I hear Meekay calling me now."

"What the hell's the matter with the boy?" Ace asked his daughter's ghost.

For the last hour Mike's ghost had been doing nothing but hovering in the upper left-hand corner of the Adair kitchen alternately calling the word "Kalagiya" and Chime Cincinnati's name.

"I'm glad you brought your friend home to us, dear, but I wish you could have picked someone a little quieter," Dolores Adair said. "He's getting on my nerves."

"He wants to go home," Toni-Marie said. "So do I. To his home, I mean."

"Honey, you can't leave Texas—"

"Sure I can. Watch me. I did already. Look, I love you and all that, but there's clearly not much future for me here."

"I have it!" her mother said. "If you don't want to be a calf, how about if I plant a lovely flower in a flower box, the way I used to when your father and I were first married, before we had the garden staff back at the old house? You could be a pansy, honey, or maybe a per-ennial of some sort. They're hard to come by but perhaps the black market—"

"You could be our own little bluebonnet!" Ace said.

"Mama, Daddy, I don't want to be a two-headed calf, a bluebonnet *or* a bluebird, for that matter." Toni-Marie was perched just above a kitchen chair, wishing she could taste some of the iced Tang tea her parents were still savoring. "I think you're being a little overprotective here."

"It's not a very nice world out there."

"Tell me about it," Toni-Marie said.

"And I do believe we're the only country in the world that didn't get nuked, honey. Our soldiers did a good job of protecting us."

"Yes," Ace said. "And the Houston city legislature voted to give any of our boys who returned first crack at available rebirths."

"Oh, did many come home?"

"Not a one. I guess they're all still out there haunting battlefields and military posts in all those foreign countries we helped out. But it was a nice gesture, don't you think?" Her mother smiled.

"The point is, honey," Ace said, "that this is the place to be. There'll be another human body for you someday soon—"

Mike abruptly wafted down from the ceiling, his eyes still closed, his lips still moving. Suddenly he opened his eyes and asked, "What's the address?"

"Two thirty-three San Jacinto Drive," Ace said, raising an eyebrow questioningly. "You need the phone number too?"

Mike was murmuring something quietly, eyes closed again, then he opened them and said, "No, just the address. She couldn't pick us out among so many of the living." He sounded almost apologetic. "She's gotten used to wide open spaces with just ghosts."

A brownish cloud coalesced above the table and a rather hazy impression of Chime Cincinnati sat cross-legged in the air about six inches above the table.

"*Another* ghost?" Dolores asked fretfully as she squinted at the smoggy blob above the salt and pepper shakers. "Honey, I don't want to sound critical but don't you know any nice *living* young people anymore?"

"Chime Cincinnati is still alive," Toni-Marie said. "Or you were the last time I saw you, Chime."

"This is my astral body," Chime explained. "Meekay, I am glad you called me. I didn't know where you were."

"You heard Meru. We were banished to the ends of the earth and we finally ended up here, at Toni-Marie's parents' house, but they want her to be reborn as a calf or a flower or something and we *both* want to go back to Shambala."

"I want to be a person again, Chime," Toni-Marie said.

"I can't promise anything," Chime said. "I met many ghosts throughout Tibet, and a few living beings. I'm sure there are more to come. We will all be going back together. But once we are there and I am back in my body, I will say the Great Liberation for you and try to help guide you into a good rebirth."

"It's the best deal I've been offered so far," Toni-Marie said, casting a reproachful glance at her parents. But, looking at them, she saw how her father put his hand reassuringly around her mother's frail shoulders and how her mother reached up to pat his hand. Her mother's eyes were apprehensive, a little guilty, and her father's were also worried, but a bit less so, she thought, than they had been earlier. Using what Chime would have considered one of her nonphysical "eyes," Toni-Marie suddenly saw how old things were—her parents were older, more fragile, their belongings worn and getting shabby; and inside the cupboards, well, the cupboards had once been stocked to overflowing, but food for the living must now be exorbitant. Imagine how much more it would take if her parents were trying to support a calf as well? And yet they'd been ready, under any circumstances, to have her back because she was theirs.

"We must hurry," Chime said. "There are some sick and injured among the living who must be taken to Shambala as quickly as possible."

"Can't your friend just stay a little longer?" Toni-Marie's mother asked, and Toni-Marie heard the love and wistfulness in the voice, but also the relief and the hope that maybe her daughter's rebirth would not be one more horror with which they'd have to cope. "You haven't been here very long."

"I'm sorry, folks," Toni-Marie said gently, giving them each a kiss and as much of a hug as a ghost is able. "But I'm glad I got to come to see you're okay. I'm sorry about Maybelline and Amy-Renee and I hope they made it back as people. We got to run now, though. Bye!"

"Bye, honey, we love you," her mother called, waving as Toni-Marie and Mike blended with Chime. A little lamely she added, "Have a nice life. . . ."

"Soon, baby," Ace added grimly. "I hope it's real soon."

"Soon," his wife echoed.

CHAPTER XXX

The return journey to Tibet was almost instantaneous, so that one moment Toni-Marie was hearing her parents say good-bye, the next she was overlooking the ruined monastery with Mike and Chime. Chime pointed out the small enclave of soldiers without trying to contact them, then showed Mike and Toni-Marie the nomad encampment and the bunker where the Indian and North American soldiers lived. Last, she showed them the lifeless city of Lhasa, where only the bitter ghosts still wandered.

Mike looked sad at how little Chime had been able to find, but

Toni-Marie was happy, both to have seen her parents and to have escaped the rebirth they were willing to arrange. She was in the mood to look at everything else optimistically. "Wow. You really covered this area, didn't you, Chime? No ghosts I ever talked to knew about these people you found here. I'm impressed. And you must have some kind of great cosmic connections to be able to bring Mikey and me back here. I thought Meru kicked us out of Tibet for good."

Chime gave her a smile that was a faded imitation of her usual one. In fact, her astral body was still less well-defined than their ghost forms were. She didn't seem to be quite all there. "Meru has no control over anything outside of the valley," she said. "But he has quite a lot of power over spiritual beings within the valley. That's why I chose a place for my physical body above the valley, outside his control, before I began my astral journeys."

"Isn't that dangerous?" Mike asked. "What if Meru finds you?"

"I left Mu Mao to guard me and spirit traps around my physical being to protect it from ghosts. Still, I need to return. I've been traveling quite extensively for a first journey, I believe, and my projection is beginning to weaken. Besides, I need to regain my physical body to guide the pilot to the survivors and back to Shambala."

"You can't do that astrally?"

"I don't know. We must return to the valley now. I am having rather strange sensations—sinking spells, I would have called them in a former life. I think it is urgent that we return to my body at once."

But when they arrived at the crystal lens embedded in the ridge, all that remained was a few broken pieces of stick and twine.

Chime's astral body was a little brighter here, but her voice was shaky as she said, "I don't understand this. Where am I?"

"Chime, there you are," Inez said as the lithe black girl wiggled down from the lens, passed through the waterfall, and stood blinking, her eyes adjusting to the light inside the cave. "Did the gunshots bust you out of your trance? I'm sorry, but if you hadn't already woken the dead, what happened here would have." Inez tried to keep her voice light but her words kept piling up like a train wreck. "Do you want to stay here with Meru while I go get help, or shall I?"

"I will," Chime said. "But leave me the gun. He's dangerous."

"The—gun?" Somehow, the idea of Chime Cincinnati with the ugly little weapon Inez had tucked into her belt seemed as odd as— well, come to think of it, so many odd things had happened in the last few hours that nothing seemed all that strange anymore.

"You know, the plastic thing you're wearing where you could blow big holes in your cute little ass," Chime said. "Hand it over."

Meru was staring at Chime, abandoning his own complaints for the moment to study her. Inez hesitated as she touched the gun at her side. "Don't do it, Inez."

"Shut up, asshole," Chime said. "I wasn't talkin' to you."

"That's not Chime, Inez," Meru said. "That's Buzz Horn. The man who was just killed. He must have found some way to possess Chime."

"You're fast, Cao Li. But then, you seem to have been hiding an unexpected aptitude where dead things are concerned. I'm sure you're going to really enjoy studyin' up on them firsthand. You going to give me that gun, sugar, or do I take it away from you?"

"Kill him, Inez. Shoot him. He'll take the gun away from you and kill us all otherwise. You heard that thing that was in Sven. He's a cannibal. No form of depravity is too low. No—"

Inez made her decision. She wasn't sure she could overpower Chime's body, but she could outscream anybody and she could certainly try to outrun Chime or Buzz or whoever the hell it was. It just took her an instant to decide which direction to run. Finally she decided to sprint back into the house and alert Art and the others first. This Buzz guy probably already knew about the people in the house. No matter how this turned out, she didn't want to let Meru know about the resurrection of the other people, the ones back in the cave, until she heard from the real Chime.

She opened her mouth, took a deep breath and screeched word-lessly, letting the force of her exhalation propel her forward.

Unfortunately, she dropped the gun.

Stoney was happy again, checking out his aircraft, Stone's Pony. When Meru put him in deep freeze, Grady Stone thought he'd never see his beloved again. Up until then, he'd slipped out of the valley at least once or twice a week to check her for damage and to do maintenance on her, despite Meru's orders. Meru had harped often enough on his belief that if any of them left the valley, they were doomed to all sorts of horrible things happening to them, that their only chance of survival was to stay with him and do as he said. When Stoney hadn't obeyed, Meru had seen to it that he got radiation poisoning, just to prove the point.

Realistically, Stoney sort of thought the radiation would be around for a long time and it was up to people to start adapting. Maybe it would shorten his life. But that was okay, as long as he could have the life he preferred to live, which was working on his baby and flying her.

It had been twenty years since he flew her. At least, grounded as she was, she wasn't likely to wear out. Fortunately, the camouflaged cave he used as a hangar was dry. His last five runs had been without passengers, to bring enough heavy lubricants, more fuel, and maintenance equipment. His insistence several years ago that he needed to test-fly her to iron out any possible bugs had been what made Meru decide to clip his wings for good, he was sure.

Only it hadn't been for good, had it? The old faker actually did know a thing or two, because although Stoney had imagined that he was dying when he was shoved into the icy wall, all he remembered was dreams of being a bird, flying over calm seas and boiling seas, mountains erupting with fire and perfectly domed snow mountains, jagged ridges, rolling plains, plains filled with flame and belching ash.

Just dreams. That was all. He picked up his wrench and made an adjustment, enjoying feeling fully alive again. The Pony could hold twenty passengers, including the pilot and copilot. Even the upholstery was still in great condition inside her. He sighed with relief and with happiness. He was a happy man. He supposed maybe he wasn't sensitive or intuitive the way Meru and Inez and some of the others claimed to be. Meru had always said that the danger out here in the world was from ghosts as well as radiation. But Stoney didn't really believe in ghosts, and he sure wasn't afraid they'd hurt him. The wind whistling outside was just the wind to him. He whistled back.

"Damn," Toni-Marie said, gazing at the pilot's back. "That ol' boy is deaf as a stump when it comes to us."

"Is there no way we can make contact?" Mike asked.

"Not with him," Chime whispered, sounding as if she came from miles away.

"How's that?" Toni-Marie asked.

"Chime, you must try to stay with us," Mike said. "I can barely hear or see you, although I too am a spiritual being."

". . . body," Chime's voice said.

"What did she say?" Toni-Marie asked.

"I don't know," Mike said. "But I think the problem is that, while we are disconnected from our bodies, her essence is still attached to hers. And it has disappeared. Perhaps it's been taken over by another spirit and is now animated. That would sap her energy."

"Stay," Chime's voice said. ". . . back in."

And no more.

Mike waited, watching the pilot work, but he knew that only he, the pilot, and Toni-Marie were present in the cave now. He said so.

"She'll be back," Toni-Marie said. "She has to be back. We'll just wait for her here."

But Mike knew that they could not wait. Someone had stolen Chime's body, and until she was reunited with it, she could no longer be of any help to them. Her last words he took to mean that he and Toni-Marie were to remain with the pilot while Chime tried to find her body, but he didn't think that was going to work. What if Chime didn't come back? What would happen to the survivors she had promised to rescue? He and Toni-Marie couldn't talk to the pilot and they couldn't help Chime as long as she was inside the valley from which Meru had banished them, but maybe they could help the people Chime had left Shambala to save.

Even if he and Toni-Marie could not reenter Shambala, he thought if he could see his home again from above the mountains, he might devise a route the survivors could take—if they did not perish on the way. Chime had said they were sick. No, the plane was the only chance those people had.

"We have to take care of the living," he said. "We can't help Chime while she's in there and we don't know if she'll be able to get her body back and finish her task. We must somehow get the survivors and this pilot together and show them the way. Perhaps one of the survivors will be more receptive to us than he is, and can help me direct him to Shambala."

"That's great," Toni-Marie said. "Good plan for the survivors out there in greater metropolitan Tibet. But how about the poor dupes in Meru's valley?"

"The pilot can come back for them," Mike said. "Once he knows where to go. Although people have been known to lose their way trying to get back."

"Sounds pretty grim. But you're from Shambala too. Can't you get, like, magical help?"

"I don't think so," Mike said. "Chime Cincinnati is a special sort of being, but I'm just an ordinary fellow who happened to be born in Shambala. You saw for yourself that even though I used Chime's magic word, it didn't work for me. Only Chime came, and that was because I called her name as well. So I don't know that we can do any more for these ghosts and living beings than they have been able to do for themselves. But we have to try."

"I guess so. Mikey?"

"Yes?"

"Is there such a thing as collecting posthumous good karma?"

"It's real unhealthy to keep runnin' like that, ma'am," Buzz/Chime called to Inez, firing a short burst in the air. Inez was two feet from the door to the building and stopped in her tracks, her back still to him, her shoulder blades twitching with the desire to keep running.

"Cao Li, you're hurt pretty bad, old buddy. You're gonna need help for those legs."

"Yes, please get help."

"No, I don't want to do that. Besides, back when you worked for the PRC, you were real good at crawlin'. Why don't you show us some of that virtuoso crawlin' again. I'd like to see that. You didn't finish my tour yet, you know. I want you to show me the rest of your spread here. You, sweet thing, turn around and face me. That's right. Watch your great master here crawl. He looks like he needs encouragement."

Inez turned. Meru was on his hands and knees, his face crumpled with pain, tears streaming down his reddened cheeks. Even the top of his head was red. He had to stop to pull his robe up around his waist.

The soft trousers he wore underneath were torn, and on the side Inez faced, a piece of bone poked through the shin.

Chime's face was stretched in a manic grin. "That's a little slow, buddy. If I'm gonna see this famous deep freeze of yours and all them bottles beyond, and be back in time for lunch, you better get a move on." Chime's foot lashed out and kicked poor Meru in the backside, and though Chime was slight and her boots were soft, Meru groaned deeply and collapsed onto his elbows.

"Whoa, old man, I am really sorry. I didn't realize those legs were damaged so bad. Guess we'll have to amputate. But first, I want the tour."

If that . . . person made Meru reveal the chambers beyond, Inez thought, there was a good chance the vulnerable, newly resurrected bunch beyond the Hall of Souls would be discovered first, and they were still pretty weak and shocky. The creepy cannibal possessing Chime would no doubt consider them to be just so many half-thawed frozen dinners. No, better to steer him out front where there were a lot of healthy, strong people in their right minds.

"You mean you're not even curious?" Inez asked with a fluttering of her lashes and an innocent tone of voice that wasn't apt to fool anybody, but at least didn't sound antagonistic.

"Oh, I'm curious about a lot of things. I've seen that out there."

"Well, yes, but have you seen the end of the world yet? Chime has, I know, but then, you're not Chime and you're not any of us and we have a holo record of more places than any one person can be at once. Quite a tourist attraction, actually."

The man within Chime rubbed her chin as if he was rubbing a beard. "That might be something to see, okay. I wonder what became of the good old NAC."

"Boom," Inez said, smiling. "Very graphic, however. Lots of excruciating detail. You'll love it."

"Okay, baby, if you make the popcorn, it's a date." Meru got another boot in the behind. "Change of plan, maestro, crawl the other way."

"Well, okay," Toni-Marie said when Mike had explained his idea that they should replace Chime as guides for the survivors. "That's fine for the living, assuming somebody among them is receptive enough to see us, which they must be since they saw their own ghosts and Chime. But what about the ghosts? She said she promised those poor monks and those women and children refuge too. But there are a *lot* of ghosts around here, Mikey. How do we know which ones to take with us?"

Mike thought about it for a moment. "I don't know. But it seems to me that it doesn't matter very much which ghosts. I think Chime wants all spirits who wish to come to Shambala to be free to do so. But she has released these particular spirits from the bondage of haunting a particular place, being attached to a particular incident in their lives. So I think that if they are the ones she contacted, they will be traveling purposefully toward us. You must admit that most spirits do not seem to be traveling purposefully anywhere."

"No," Toni-Marie said. "We've been pretty exceptional that way."

"Therefore, we will go to Lhasa, and on the way we will look for this monastery, keeping a lookout for both living beings and purposeful ghosts."

They didn't have to go to Lhasa at all to find the ghosts. Like themselves, the ghosts, once freed of their habitual haunting grounds, could travel instantaneously between places. As a landmark goal for the living, Chime had chosen Mount Kailas, a mountain sacred to Tibetans. Mike had seen many pictures of it and had read and heard stories about it, so he was able to take them there. The southern face of the conical mountain was misty with ghosts already, the ghosts of monks, women, children, soldiers, and nomads, all drifting together, all waiting.

"Are you the spirits waiting to be reborn in Shambala?" Mike inquired of one of the monks.

"Where is Black Tara, she who is the Terton, to guide us to Shambala?" one monk asked in return.

"She has been detained. We will lead you to the place where she is and from there we will go to Shambala. I am called Mike. I was born in Shambala," he added, by way of establishing credentials. "Chime— the one you know as Black Tara, said there would be living beings with you."

"The living do not travel as we do," a nomad's ghost answered. "Many weeks are required for them to journey from one place to another. Once Tara released us, we were bound to no place, the pain of our deaths was erased, and the living no longer perceived us."

"Oh," Toni-Marie said. "Does that mean they're coming later?"

"That means that they are in the corporeal world and we are in the spirit world and our doings no longer concern each other."

The ghost of a very young monk spoke up. "*I* am very worried about the soldier Fu Ping. He and the other soldiers came from China only a short time before the living beings destroyed each other. They may not know of this place. We were to guide them, but found once we left our monastery that we could not do so. Will Tara be angry?"

"No, no," Mike said. "She's new at this too."

"Take us to her now," said a woman ghost whose skirt still seemed to be dripping blood.

"We'll do our best," Toni-Marie promised.

"Toni-Marie, if you will guide these spirits to the plane, I think I'd better go see if *I* can make contact with the living and help them find the way. If *you* can make contact with any other living beings more sensitive than the pilot, please do so. I will need help."

"What about Chime?"

"If Chime is able, she'll be back with us as soon as possible. If she's not, this is what she'd want us to do."

CHAPTER
XXXI

Snow filtered down from the heavens all morning, dusting the ruins of the monastery first with a light glaze, then lace, and finally gentle pearly ridges, softening the harshness of the broken masonry.

Fu Ping trembled in the ruins of his uniform and huddled closer to the other men. The time was somewhat past midday and he had grown colder as the minutes passed. He had almost persuaded himself he had not seen the vision of Black Tara, and he was beginning to believe he had imagined speaking to the monks.

Yet something had happened. The other men cast occasional furtive glances at the place where the ghost monks had daily beaten their invisible master to death and disassembled their monastery. Sergeant Minh stared fixedly, moodily, at the spot and finally spoke. "They did not come today."

"No. Perhaps they were afraid of the snow," Huan Po said, trying to make a joke.

Fu Ping cleared his throat. "They were supposed to lead us. And she said she would return."

"Perhaps it was all a delusion," said Shao. "A snow mirage or something."

"It only started snowing today," Wu-Lan pointed out.

"Well, another sort of delusion then. Ghosts, after all . . ."

"We saw them, though, and the woman," Sergeant Minh said. That gave Fu Ping courage. Sergeant Minh was a very realistic man.

Fu Ping said, "Yes. And we do not see them today. I think the woman released them."

"Yes, I got that impression too," Wu-Lan said. "In the old stories, the ones my grandmother told me before I had to turn her in for being reactionary, once the spirits are released they disappear. Perhaps once they were released they could *not* stay."

"But the girl was coming back for us."

"Perhaps she couldn't either."

Fu Ping shivered more violently as a blast of wind swept snow into his face. "She told us which direction to travel. I think we should start."

"But will she find us?"

"If she is coming, I think she will find us wherever we are. She thought to meet us anyway. She said we might all come together at Mount Kailas, which is west of here, near where they built the Fire-Bone Dragon Power Plant." He paused a moment and added, "It's a long walk, but if we are walking, we will be warmer."

"Yes," Sergeant Minh said. "There is that. Pack up the remaining food then, men, and move out."

When Chime's thoughts ceased to reach her, the old blind woman stopped, feeling even more sightless without the strong psychic signals to guide her across the valley. Locana Hoa Chung had not left her cave in years, but all those years she lived there, she knew that this day would come. She had not known that when the time came she would be blind and without Vajra to guide her, but using the *lung-gom* technique, she traveled above the surface of the ground anyway, so what she needed was a mental goal.

Chime's signals were the easiest to follow, but Mike's were also very clear. It had been Mike who caught her attention with his cry for help from far away. Fortunately, Chime had been able to respond. Dr. Chung and Vajra could not because, although they were among the beings who answered the code word "Kalagiya" with assistance, their sphere of influence was specifically within the Himalayan and Kun Lun region. Vajra had been very agitated to be unable to assist a Shambala being in distress, and Dr. Chung had tried to comfort him by saying, "It is sometimes hard to have big ears and short legs, but we must be patient." They had been, and Chime Cincinnati—whose limitations were less strict than their own—had broadened her own astral search and reeled them in.

Chime's signal was as clear as the sacred lakes of Tibet had once been, and Locana Hoa Chung had followed the girl's progress with interest.

Dr. Chung had known when the girl first set out on her astral travels, and had followed her spiritual progress in finding the monks, the ghosts of the mutilated mothers in Lhasa, the nomads and the soldiers. She and Vajra were impressed by the great surge of energy Chime had emitted to travel from Tibet and back again with her friends. Because she and Vajra had been following the girl's spiritual progress, Locana had been as unaware at first of what was happening to Chime's body as Chime had been. But the older, more experienced woman recognized the symptoms when Chime began weakening and wavering, her astral projection disturbed by the loss of its home.

She had been far more disturbed than Chime when the spirits of the three young people returned to the ledge above the crystal lens to find nothing but blood and broken spirit traps where Chime's body should have been. Chime was too young and had had too little knowledge of the dangers of astral travel to realize that the astral traveler's worst nightmare had just befallen her—her body had been taken, inhabited by another. Drawing nearer to the place where the body was, Locana sensed an evil presence, and Vajra recognized it as that emanating from the now-open hole where he had first guided Mike and Chime, not knowing that a demon, rather than a real man, dwelt there.

The demon had Chime's body, Chime's signals had faded entirely, and the two young ghosts were trying to carry out the mission of the Terton alone. Dr. Chung packed extra Spam in her backpack, pulled on her coat, hat, mittens, and boots, and picked up a soul catcher for a staff. "The time has come, Vajra," she told the yeti, and he led her down the mountain and up the next.

At the foot of the mountain where Mike had died, she cocked her big ears and heard him and Toni-Marie arguing with the ghosts near Mount Kailas. On hearing his decision to continue to find the living beings Chime had located, Dr. Chung had told Vajra, "Go. Help him. Take your secret paths and shortcuts, listen for the boy's psychic emanations and assist him." Vajra could not speak, but she knew he felt the emanations of the two Shambala people as strongly as she did. He too had big ears—and furthermore, had ways of reaching distant places that she did not, as she had learned in the past when he suddenly arrived with something they needed from a distant place.

When he left, she continued across the valley, *lung-gom* style, guided by a chaos of lower-frequency psychic mutterings, though she still could not read Chime.

After a while she heard something more useful—not with her mind this time, but with her ears. The sound was one she had heard before, a man whistling a tune she remembered from long ago the very way she remembered him whistling it before. She had asked this man about the tune, and he had told her it was a Christian gospel song, one he liked not so much because it was religious as because the tune was catchy and he liked the title, "I'll Fly Away."

The night that Mike and Toni-Marie attempted to reenter Shambala alone, Chime's parents, who had been lying awake talking after making love, broached the subject at almost the same time: of starting to search for their daughter and her friend. They agreed that it would be necessary to travel to the borders of Shambala, and maybe beyond.

"You won't mind, my husband, that when I return I will be a middle-aged woman instead of the way you see me now?" Chime's mother, Pema, asked.

George Washington Merridew, formerly a colonel in the U.S. Air Force, now the sports instructor of all of the children of Kalapa, said, "Don't be stupid, baby. I'm sixty years older than you already. She's our little Chime, and we're the ones to go after her. It's okay for Lobsang and Viv to say that she and Mike went on some big mission, that there's no signs of anybody being hurt in that cave down there, but I know she's in trouble, same as I knew it when my men were pinned down at Medog. We're the logical ones to help her. I'm in good shape and I know we can make good time. And you're young enough to survive across the border if it can be done. If you don't survive, well, then, I don't care if I do either, and we'll know our girl didn't make it. But I just have this feelin' that she did—only she needs our help."

At that moment there was a knock on their door. Lobsang Taring, Henri Thibideaux, Keith Marsh, Dolma Yangzom, Pema's parents Tsering and Samdup, and four of the other elders plus their grown children stood outside in mountain-climbing gear.

Lobsang looked a little embarrassed. "Please come with us, George, Pema. We are going to form a search party and light signal flares in the mountains," he said. "I have believed for some time that my boy was dead, but tonight I heard him call for help."

Chime had a momentary sense of panic as she slipped through the ghost hole, back inside the Hall of Souls. What if Meru had replaced the apparatus broken by Eve and Mu Mao? What if she became trapped in one of those bottles and was rendered useless for however long Meru cared to hold her there?

But when she emerged inside the hall with the familiar rows of bottles, she saw that the glass was still broken, the hole was in fact a little larger than it had been, and she was quite safe. She saw that the hold chamber once more was solid ice, though now the ice covered only the supine corpses of the three or four people whose souls had been irretrievable or whose bodies had died while in storage.

She felt a little stronger too, strong enough to check on the people hidden beyond the Hall of Souls. They were all there, resting, but Inez was not. No one stirred or seemed to sense her presence, and she saw neither Inez nor the cat.

In her weakened condition, she found it necessary to travel across the actual physical area between where she was and where she wished to go rather than using the astral shortcuts, as she had been able to do when she was stronger.

Passing through the hold room now she had the impression of something out of place, off kilter, and in the garden room she knew that the impression was not mistaken, for the plants near the waterfall were trampled and bloodied, and two bodies lay sprawled across the path, one half in the stream. A smear of blood with the marks of shoes imprinted in it was streaked all the way from the waterfall to the back door of the building.

She came abreast of the bodies and examined them. The top one she recognized as one of those that had not survived thawing in the hold room. Bloody holes pierced its back. It lay half concealing a horribly mutilated corpse. The face was averted, and much cleaner except for the blood, but she recognized the man who had murdered Mike. Neither body retained any aura whatsoever, though bodies frequently did for some time after death. Both bodies seemed so vacant, she thought that if you thumped on them they would be hollow.

Once inside the building, she learned where one of those souls was, at least. She felt a greater sense of urgency as she passed through the door, an urgency so powerful that she did not pause to wonder at the room full of nude people, bound and lying on the floor in the dining hall, shivering, swearing, and weeping. She could not help these people in her present state, and she had an overwhelming premonition that she was about to meet the entity responsible for their plight.

She was drawn to the room where she had viewed the film, where Art Murdock had cheerfully narrated the end of the world.

She heard the sound of the film running, and inside she saw there were only three people. Meru, bound and nude, was lying on the floor in front of a seated person, and Inez, also nude, ran the controls of the film. Something was wrong with Meru's legs, and the person in the chair casually leaned the barrel of a gun into Meru's upraised ear, while Inez frolicked about in the flicker of the hologram, adjusting the controls and providing commentary in a strained, small voice unlike her usual full tones.

All three parties looked up when she entered, and Chime felt much stronger than she had out in the cave. She knew why at once. Looking into the face she had seen reflected back at her from countless mirrors and still waters throughout her life, she saw it register her presence and grin at her smugly. "Well, well, well, if it ain't the wayward soul come home to roost," she heard her voice say with an unfamiliar accent. "Sorry, baby, but finders keepers, losers weepers, and I found this luscious little body and I mean to keep it."

Meru's physical voice merely groaned, but she could hear him crying, "The pain is terrible. Help us, please help us. Oh, you stupid girl, you led him straight to us."

From Chime's throat came an ugly laugh that she had never heard before, and she heard her strangely accented voice saying, "First we finish the movie. Then we have a little surgery to perform. Meru can't use those legs, and I'm feeling a little peckish. Now then, Inez, honey, I want to see what happened in the NAC again. You don't mean to tell me you've got all these pictures of other places but nothing there?"

"We don't have any record of missiles landing there, but there were a lot of natural disasters. One of the first missiles did land in TAPS— uh, the Tropical American Park Service," Inez added when Chime looked irritated and puzzled. "What used to be South and Central America."

"Oh, yeah," Chime's mouth said. "That. I've been in Asia too damned long."

"Anyway, the smoke from the burning rain forests obscured the sky," Inez continued, showing the smoke-filled holos of North and South America again. "We also registered volcanic activity, earthquakes, and tidal waves in the NAC."

"Well, that's a little better. I'd hate to think those fat cats got off without a scratch. But it looks to me like aside from that, the NAC is still the best candidate for number one vacation spot in the world. I sure would like to go back there and show those soft bastards a thing or two. Like I showed your little crew, huh, Meru?" Another jab with the gun barrel.

Chime's real self wanted to ask what had happened, how one evil being came to overpower so many people, what had become of Mu Mao, how this creature had come to be there, but she knew that he was very clever. She read Inez's fear, anger, and helplessness, and saw from her shivering that the actress was very cold, but there was no specific communication. Meru was in so much pain and so badly frightened that he too told her nothing.

She watched herself make a grab at Inez as she passed, and shook her head, smiling ruefully in spite of herself.

The being who possessed her body had seemingly dismissed her as of no consequence, but now her own face regarded her with a viciously resentful expression. "Just what have you got to smile about?"

She did not give him the satisfaction of seeing how appalled she was, but smiled even more broadly and said, "I have imagined myself in many roles in my future, but I never thought to see myself become a dirty old man."

The snow smothered the land, rendering its mountains and valleys virtually featureless except for shadows and the steep rock faces where it would not stick. Each previous year, Fu Ping and his comrades had been underground or at least in shelter when the snows fell. The first three years had been spent in their bunker, eating provisions, eating rats, eating their own excrement and worse. But the last seventeen years they had spent wandering, always looking for the safe place, the place that would keep them alive during the winter. They had lost a few of their number each winter, and the deaths of these few had helped the others continue. But now they all stood to perish for the sake of a vision. A mass hallucination. The government used to talk about that in terms of other people perpetrating such false images and ideas, denying that the government itself dealt in such forcibly induced mass hallucinations all the time.

Fu Ping's thoughts drifted with the snow and the cold broke through his clothing, freezing the marrow of his bones, pricking his face with ice needles. Shao was on his knees. With hands he could no longer feel, Fu Ping knelt and clumsily tried to raise him. He might as well have been manipulating clubs extending from his shoulders, his hands and arms felt so detached from the rest of him.

Shao glared at him through eyes crusted shut with ice, and shrugged off his help.

Sergeant Minh and the others had disappeared.

Fu Ping called into the storm, "Sergeant! Wu-Lan! Wait!" But heard no answer except the whistling wind.

He called again and again but his cries were blown back in his face until he could no more than whisper. Shao was covered completely by snow. Now they would die. The best he could hope was that perhaps the others would find him later, if they walked in circles, as he suspected perhaps they all had been doing. At least then his death and Shao's would have some use. But he did not want to die. He did not want to have lasted so long to die *this* way. And furthermore, he did not want to die with Shao, whose eyes reproached him with his folly.

He sank down onto his haunches to wait. Before he had known so many people who had frozen to death, he had read accounts of how it felt. No pain once everything went numb, and peace, maybe dreams. He thought of the black girl and tried to dream that she was coming for him after all.

His eyes would not close completely, though, and through the ice he saw the pattern of the falling snow alter slightly, seem to solidify, and a large drift of it blow directly toward him.

Then it was upon him, enveloping him, more solid and much warmer than snow had ever been. This is the freezing death, then, he thought, and gave himself up to it.

Mu Mao lay panting in the garden, within a stand of a certain plant known to staunch the flow of blood. This plant his former, less evolved self had used many times to heal the wounds of clients. After running from the demon-man who entered the girl Chime, Mu Mao had dropped back into the cave through the spirit hole and, injured even further by the fall and the broken glass below, slunk into the garden. There he passed out among the healing plants.

At length he woke again and nibbled on some Persian cat mint growing adjacent to the patch he lay in. The crystal lens offered little light now, but Mu Mao smelled a great volume of blood. Examining his wounds—that of the bullet and the cuts he had sustained from the glass—he found that he was no longer bleeding deeply. Giving his wounds a couple of careful licks, he rose painfully and limped on his three good legs to investigate.

He found the two bodies and thought that they explained most of the blood, but he also saw Meru's trail and smelled his fear still lingering in the cave.

The cat's fur bristled and he backed away. Meru was injured, was he? Someone else seemed to have won this argument. Perhaps that was what the demon-man wanted with Chime Cincinnati's body. Although in this life, as a cat, Mu Mao was by definition an extremely self-involved creature, he felt that there had been altogether too much shuffling of bodies and souls going on around here lately. And he also felt that Meru, as unenlightened a magician as any the cat had encountered in any of his previous lives, was unfit to be in control of the souls of others. If he was injured, this was a good time for Mu Mao to remedy the situation without fear of retribution.

Also, Mu Mao reflected, should his own wound prove mortal, by destroying the bottles now he would be sure he could proceed to his next eight lives as a cat unimpeded and unimprisoned.

CHAPTER XXXII

Buzz Horn was in hog heaven. Yessir, fate was finally paying him back for having to spend all those years livin' in a hole munchin' his kinfolk to stay alive. Now he had this sleek new body, young enough to give him another good sixty years, when he'd already lived seventy-odd. He had all these smug high-class people—who thought they were so smart and so much better than a poor old grunt—right where he wanted them, helpless and stark staring naked, ready for the kill or whatever else he wanted to do with them. Fortunately, he had a pretty good imagination. "You know, honey," he said to the smirking little ghost who looked down her nose at him from above the smoke-filled holo of the NAC, "I mean to take real good care of your sweet hide."

"That's reassuring," she said pleasantly. How come he could see her anyway? He'd never been able to see ghosts before. In fact, that was kind of a good thing, seeing as how he created so many. Maybe it was because he *was* in her body and she hadn't officially died yet, or maybe it was because he *had* died, so they were sort of birds of a feather now. No matter. He thought he could wipe the smile off her face.

"In the old times, in some parts of the world, people believed that you could stay young forever if you sucked the blood out of living people—especially young ones, but hell, anybody'd do in a pinch."

"Yes," she said. "Such stories occur in all myths, and my friend Meekay was for some reason very fond of the story of Count Dracula."

"Meekay. He's the one I shot, right?"

"That's correct," she said, still blandly.

"Well, I thought maybe I could just sort of use those people in there as a kind of blood bank—among other things. You seemed to get a kick out of the idea of being a dirty old man. How about being a vampire?"

"Well," she said. "Quite aside from the damage done to innocent persons, such a course might not be the best way to take care of my body. Many diseases are borne by the blood."

"You're really somethin', you know that?"

"Thank you."

Little bitch. She was so smug. He grabbed his new breasts and crotch and rubbed them suggestively. "I'm gonna go to NAC, you know. This little body ought to fetch a pretty good price on the street, and I'm going to enjoy sellin' you, honey."

"Perhaps," she said. "But you may find you feel differently than you suppose when you have to actually occupy the body while doing so. And if you intend to live in it for a good long time, take precautions against pregnancy and disease. But of course if you continue to live in my body and go to another country, these matters will no longer concern me."

" 'Cause you'll be dead, huh? I'll have your body and you'll be dead, little bitch."

"Actually, I will probably simply continue straight to Nirvana. As a bodhisattva, I've been qualified for some time. I will regret not being able to help others here, but I'm sure someone will turn up who will perform the same sort of task."

"You sound pretty goddamn cold about it."

"My faith teaches us to be willing to detach from all things."

"Oh, yeah, well, speaking of that, show's over, folks. So now I guess it's time to detach the old Master here from his worthless legs, eh, Meru?"

"Excuse me," Chime Cincinnati said, "But in former lives I was a doctor. I believe that if you simply set the bones in Mr. Meru's legs, and bandage his wounds, he will heal."

"Yeah, honey, but it's harder to eat them on the hoof. But okay, if you say so."

He knew how to get to her, then. "Inez, get your ass over here. Hold his other leg. Meru, you move, buddy, and you'll lose more than your leg."

Jamming the gun in Meru's ear, Buzz lifted the leg, keeping an iron grip on the ankle, and bit deeply into the wound. Meru jerked in spite of himself and screamed like a stuck pig. Buzz looked up at the apparition, chewed meditatively on the piece of pulpy flesh and gristle, dropped the leg and wiped his mouth. "How's that for detachment, sugar? 'Course, I only detached one bite."

"Haven't you hurt enough people? You have a chance at a whole new life—you can even go to North America if you wish."

Meru gasped, "There's a plane—"

"No shit. Tell me where. I'm a pretty good pilot."

"Leave him alone," the ghost said. He saw that he'd finally gotten to her.

"How's that? How you going to make me, bitch? Little bit of air and wind like you ain't gonna beat me."

The image of the girl's form atop the smoky hologram sighed, distorting it into waves. "Beating you is not my intention. Instead, I shall join you."

While Chime had been conversing with her body, watching the brutality and listening to the coarse boasting of the being occupying it, she had been struggling to know what to do.

Hardship and the extremities of suffering have driven humanity from this man, her former selves informed her. *In our last life, we worked with him. He was wily and cruel, but not without redeeming features. Now he has become terribly unbalanced. Depravity has taken control of him and he has taken control of our body.*

"He is like one of the wrathful blood-drinking deities referred to in the Great Liberation Through Hearing in the Bardo," Chime reflected, looking down at her own face with the blood of Meru dripping down its chin. "True, his body is not strangely colored, nor does he appear to have three heads or multiple limbs, but at this moment he bears a fearsome weapon, while Inez, like the deity's consort, holds a vessel containing blood for him to feed from."

You recognize your yidam, your teaching deity, in the guise of this perverted soul, then?

"Perhaps. I remember reading also a saying of the fourteenth Dalai Lama about the Chinese who had cast him out and kept him from his country as this being has cast me out of my body and keeps me from Shambala, who tormented his people as this being torments these people."

Ah, yes. The former selves seemed to blend with her now in agreement. In that moment a great peacefulness settled over her soul, which had been like the white water at the confluence of many mountain streams pouring into a mighty river. Now the river of her self coursed with a steady, relentless rhythm as the words of the Dalai Lama came back to her. *Tolerance can only be learned from an enemy. It cannot be learned from a spiritual teacher . . . enemies are precious in that they help us grow . . . the enemy teaches you inner strength.*

"The Great Liberation says not to be terrified or bewildered, but to recognize him as part of my own mind, and to feel longing. . . ."

Feeling the longing to understand that which was so alien to her, focusing on the grinning mouth that had once been her own, she concentrated on embracing her former body, on becoming one with it, kissing it so deeply that her whole self went into the kiss.

And tasted the salty, sticky tang of human blood, smelled through the roof of her mouth the stench of her last horrible bite, and felt the texture of the small hairs from the flesh on the tip of her tongue.

She spat and wiped her mouth on her sleeve, feeling the laughter bubbling up in her throat along with the bile of nausea. "Oh, baby, welcome welcome," the Buzz-spirit said. "I can feel the lily-white innocent virgin purity of your sweet little soul now and I'm just itchin' to dirty it up."

"Yes," she said. "Everyone else has a dark side, and in order to regain some control of this body, I decided that perhaps I could let you be mine. But did it ever occur to you that if my soul seems lily white, it is not because it is innocent and untouched but because over many lifetimes it has been scoured of wickedness by self-knowledge and discipline acquired in times of adversity? I think you will require a great deal of scouring."

CHAPTER XXXIII

Stoney jumped three feet when he felt the tap on his shoulder.

He expected to see Meru, maybe, or Inez or one of the others, but the little old lady who stood before him was in fact no one he'd ever seen before. Or had he . . . ?

The whistle on his lips died away, but for a moment he forgot to unpucker. The old lady's face was more wrinkled, and the eyes were unfocused, covered with white film, but he could almost see them as dark and dancing, full of curiosity. He recognized her voice when she spoke.

"What a pleasure it is to hear you whistle again, Mr. Stone," the old lady said. "I remember asking you about that piece when you first flew me into these mountains to study the yetis. Do you recall that flight?"

"I sure do, Dr. Chung," he said, grinning as he remembered the name of this feisty old gal. "Did you find your yetis?"

"That is why I have come to you now, Mr. Stone. I have found my yeti once, and now I must find him again, along with some stranded people. I need your help. I can guide you there."

"Well, sure, Dr. Chung, but I kinda have another commitment. There's this lady did me a big favor, and she wants me to fly some people someplace. . . ."

"My request is also part of her request, Mr. Stone. Do you believe that?"

"Aw, I trust you, Dr. Chung," he said, and he knew that he did. He had liked this lady from the first time he met her—smart as a whip, willing to take on armies to try to find her yetis. But although the dimming of her eyes did not seem to dampen the force of her personality any, it did present practical problems that maybe a little lady who'd lived out here for so long wouldn't be aware of. Keeping his voice gentle and with a little teasing humor in it, he asked, "Only, beg your pardon, ma'am, but how can you guide me anyplace with, you know, your eyes—"

"Oh, that. Don't worry about my eyes. Have you never heard that when people lose the use of one faculty they develop extraordinary acuity in others?"

And before he thought of a polite way to counter that argument, he noticed that as she stood there talking to him, her feet were clear of the ground by about two inches.

Vajra gathered the stranded men into his long, powerful arms as a girl might gather flowers, plucking them from the blinding snowstorm and depositing them in the entrance to the branch of the time cave that had brought him here.

Mike's ghost waited there, watching over the Indian and North American soldiers and the nomads Chime had contacted earlier. One of the nomads was sensitive enough to pass Mike's reassurances and occasional instructions on to the others.

Mike and Vajra had found the nomads first and, with the help of the sensitive one, who was multilingual, as nomads often were, managed to lead the Indians and the North Americans to this place.

The nomads took the frozen Chinese soldiers and started to warm them as best they could.

"I think this is all, Vajra," Mike said. "Without your help they would have died. We have to get them back to Shambala soon. Some of them are barely alive."

Vajra knew that at least one of the two he picked up in the snow could die soon. If so, the man would just have to follow the rest of his comrades as a ghost. The caves that had enabled Vajra to reach the place from which Mike's psychic distress calls emanated were only for the use of the yeti.

No human, even an unconscious one, could pass through them.

The secret of the time caves was sacred to yetis, for the magical passages had always allowed Vajra's people to make their mysterious appearances and sudden vanishings throughout the lands of snow. The mobility the caves offered made it seem as if there were many yetis, when in fact there had never been more than a few. The tracks human beings had found had always led *away* from the time caves.

Not even Locana Hoa knew Vajra's secret, and she knew much more than any mortal human being had ever known. But she did not pry. She had her secrets as he had his, and the respect for those was what had enabled them to share a cave in harmony for so many difficult years.

Vajra was wrong to bring the people to shelter in the entrance to his cave, but they had no idea where they were and it was the only shelter in the area. While they were here, however, he could not slip back through the caves to bring back the plane. Besides, the pilot would probably try to kill him instead of trying to communicate with him. No, Locana Hoa would attend to that, and if she could, she would bring help in time.

Meanwhile, the yeti could do nothing but listen as the wind moaned outside, the men moaned inside, and the snow piled up at the entrance to the cave.

•   •   •

Mu Mao the magnificent, Mu Mao the liberator, Mu Mao the wronged and wounded, Mu Mao the saboteur, Mu Mao the clever, Mu Mao the quick, Mu Mao the companion of darkness and the friend of the dead, Mu Mao the nimble-though-injured bravely limped through the garden and back across the ice and cold into the Hall of Souls, ingeniously located a box, a chair, and a table to launch himself from, and made a three-point landing on the top shelf full of soul bottles. There he commenced his revenge, there he began his holy task, there he performed with astounding grace, for one so sorely hurt, the Dance of Destruction, the Trance of Transformation, the Leap of Liberation, the Pounce of Purification. In short, he knocked every blasted one of the hated bottles in his path onto the floor and watched each break as he slapped the next down on top of it.

With each glassy crash his satisfaction grew and the pain in his shoulder increased, but his attention to it decreased with each newly freed spirit he added to his admiring audience.

In time, the Hall of Souls was smoky with swirling spirits according accolades to Mu Mao's performance. In a somewhat longer time, the people hiding beyond the Hall of Souls heard the noise and were overcome with curiosity, so that they too ventured forth to view his dance. And when they saw that he was destroying the hated bottles, the power by which the evil magician had imprisoned them, they joined the dancing cat in an ensemble orgy of smashing, and added a chorus of living laughter to the silent mirth of the ghosts.

When at last the valiant feline fell, exhausted and bleeding anew, the arms of Full Moon Akesh were there to stroke him, the hands of a gentle woman were there to bind his wounds, and all in the Hall of Souls gathered to stroke and pet and praise him. Mu Mao the magnificent, foil of foul necromancers, was exhausted but well content with his labor, and really rather hungry.

Inez did not know what the hell was going on except that she was freezing her ass off, Meru was bawling and bleeding all over her from the hunk torn out of his broken leg, and Chime Cincinnati seemed to be having one lulu of an identity crisis.

"You're sadly mistaken if you think this little trick is going to beat *me,* baby," she snarled in a nasty voice. "Now I've got you where I want you. You can't be detached if I use this body the way I want to now."

"No, I suppose I can't," she answered in another voice, her face assuming the expression of sweet calm that had drawn Inez to her to begin with. "But I can take care of other, more important matters. Inez, please take Mr. Meru into the other room, find clothing and blankets for everyone, and prepare them for our journey."

Before Chime's mind changed, Inez flung open the door. Her family and friends still lay trussed up like plucked turkeys at Thanksgiving time, but people were raising their heads or sitting up, trying to tell what was causing the terrible racket issuing from the back of the house.

"Get your butt back in here, Inez, or I shoot you and ol' Cao Li here," Chime snarled.

Inez swore under her breath and turned back toward Chime, who immediately changed tones and said, clearly arguing with herself, "Why not leave these people alone? There is no cause to torment them. If you cooperate so that I can carry through with my plan, soon we will all board an airplane and fly to Shambala. There you will have everything you could possibly want."

"I already *have* everything I could possibly want, sugar. *And* I have hostages. One more piece of interference or order out of you and I blow these two away."

The nasty voice was shouting above the racket. The noise intensified, and suddenly Full Moon Akesh sprinted into the room, carrying the cat and leading the others who had been in cold storage. Swirling all around them was a dense whitish ghost-fog.

As Inez watched, portions of the fog smeared away from the main mass and streaked through the door to wrap around Chime, who reached down, bit her own hand, and flung the gun to the far side of the room.

"Inez," Chime panted in her softer voice, "please—take the gun—throw it away—don't let him—me—find it."

Inez did not have to be asked twice. She scuttled around the edge of the room, picked up the gun by the stock and ran with it out the front door and to the lake, where she threw it as far as she could, then ran back, feet, hands, tits, and face about to freeze off.

Inside the house, the entire projection room was filled with white fog, Chime was nowhere in sight, everybody but her was pulling on clothing or had a blanket wrapped around them, and Meru was lying on the dining room table hollering gibberish at the top of his lungs.

Ghosts swarmed around Buzz, filling the air so he couldn't breathe, shrieking and wailing so he couldn't hear, crowding close to his eyes so he couldn't see, filling his mouth with a foulness even he could not stand, a foulness full of gangrene, rot, and death.

In his own body, Buzz had never seen a ghost, but he more than made up for it now. He was being smothered by ghosts.

"You're as dead as us, Pa, come out and take your medicine," Evie, twice a ghost because of him, hissed against his eardrum.

"Go to hell, Evie, you can't hurt me," he said. "Yea though I walk through the valley of the shadow of death, I shall fear no evil, 'cause I am the evilest son of a bitch in the whole valley. You got nothing to scare me with but a lot of shadows."

"I loved you, Pa. I let you do it to me and I let you eat these babies 'cause I loved you."

"You didn't love jack shit and you didn't *let* me do anything. You were mine and I used you as I saw fit. Now go back and rot, little girl, and take the brats with you."

"Oh no, Pa, like you said, I'm yours, and they're yours too. We all belong to you."

Chime's voice slipped in. "Then make breathing room for us, children, and come with us to Shambala. You can have new lives there among people who will give you the love this unfortunate being cannot."

"No. Kill 'im."

"He's dead already, children, and has turned himself into a demon. But I am alive and I alone can show you and the others the way home. Have you never wondered what it would be like with a father and mother who deserve your love, not your hatred, who do the things for you that you need them to do, who feed you and wipe your tears and rock you to sleep at night? Who clothe and shelter and protect you and tell you funny stories to give you courage when you are afraid? Who teach you wisdoms that will comfort you when they cannot aid you? Please, children, put away your righteous anger long enough to let me lead you and the others to a place where this can happen. Your lives have been short and hideous. You deserve long lives full of love and learning and happiness that would be unimaginable to you except that all beings instinctively yearn to have such lives."

"You're chokin' me up," Buzz said. "What'll we have next, the ghost of Christmas to Come?"

But her presence waited and her body held out arms to the ghosts who smothered her, and her presence and her body embraced them until they melted back into the mass of ghosts like so much butter and honey sinking into a warm cake.

Buzz was angry to feel himself quaking inside as they melted away, quaking not from their anger but from their longing. "You got no right to promise things anymore, lady. This body's mine too and I'm stronger than you."

"I don't think so. For one thing, I was born to this body, which was the one made from the biological material of my parents and my family. It knows me. It has an affinity for me. Also, I am its living soul and you are the dead soul of another being. Oh no, my friend, I wouldn't say you're stronger, but then, we're not having a rope-pull but sharing a body, trying to find our way out of a situation much more fearsome than any single being, living or dead."

"You gonna tell me you like having me here, next."

"I wouldn't go that far. You do not exactly belong here, but you've chosen to be here, and I suppose there's a reason for this to be, which I know nothing about. It is somewhat unnatural to have two complete souls in the same body, but not unheard of. I imagine when this body dies we will be reborn independently, and I will still have to do what I have to do and you will have to do what you have to do, whatever that is."

"Spare me. You say there's a plane waiting to take us away to Never-Never-Land? Then let's get out of this dump," he said. But although the thoughts he directed to her were a challenge, Buzz was worried. The bitch seemed to be right about her and her body. Every single time he had wanted to do one thing and she had wanted to do another, she had won, as if he was nothing more than a nasty whim she had no problem overcoming. The wussy little ghost he had sneered at, once inside her own body, was crushingly powerful, and he felt drowned, smothered, and overwhelmed by her. Maybe the feeling would pass in Shambala. Maybe. But the truth was, as long as he was inside her, she seemed to be the boss. He might get loose while she slept, but she was smart, and others knew about him. It would be just like her to have herself tied up or something when she slept, just to spite him.

And that Shambala place was real. He knew it was real. He had tortured prisoners, trying to find out more about it, back in the old days. And all he learned about it was that it was real and it was this great place full of treasure, but nobody who had ever seen it—not even the greediest, scummiest, whoringest, most self-seeking asshole who had ever been tortured by him—would betray anything or anyone connected with the place.

What was going to happen when that overbearing bitch who owned this body got back on her own turf? Poor old Buzz quite literally was not going to have a leg to stand on. And this concerned him. She had promised to extinguish him, and the one little demonstration he'd had of her control had made a believer out of him. She *would* bury him. For the first time in his life, he understood the term "mortal fear."

CHAPTER XXXIV

When Chime reappeared in the outer room, only those she had rescued from the hold room looked at her with any friendliness. Even Inez scrutinized her closely at first.

People now gave way before her as if she were a tank instead of a small slender girl as she walked to where Meru lay on the table. His legs were swollen, strapped to pieces of chair leg. He was drenched in sweat and very pale.

When she touched his face, he flinched.

"Soon we will be in Shambala and your wounds will heal. You

have not always done good things, and you owe an apology to all of these ghosts you have unnecessarily delayed in their spiritual quest, but you preserved all of these living people. You will be welcome."

"Chime, honey, I don't know how to break this to you but nobody wants to follow you anyplace," Inez said. "Nothing personal, but your reputation has suffered a little recently, if you know what I mean."

"Then perhaps you should tie my arms and hands so that my body cannot cause harm when the other one is in charge of it. It would be a shame if suspicion of me kept these people from finding Shambala." As soon as she said that, she twisted her head aside with a groan that Inez knew did not come from Chime. But immediately she jerked her head back to face Inez, her mouth set in a firm line.

"You got it, sister," Inez said, and started to tie her. Chime's limbs twitched and jerked as if with a seizure while she was being secured, and Inez thought, "That's old Buzz, fighting us off." But her movements were not strong enough to stop Inez from taping her hands together. Once she was bound, Chime seemed to be once more in full control of herself. "Shall we go now to the valley and see if Stoney has repaired his airplane?"

The population of Meru's community reached the valley floor with Chime in the lead while six men like pallbearers carried Meru on the tabletop. The party trailed an exhaust of ghosts behind it that filled most of the valley. However, Stoney and the plane were already gone.

Though the valley containing Kalapa was protected from severe weather, the mountains within Shambala suffered from storms like any other mountains. A blizzard all but stopped the search party half a day away from the valley.

The last time anyone had traversed the mountains had been shortly after the missiles fell, when Colonel Merridew tried to escape using Ama-La for a shield, and the old lady had sacrificed herself to show them all that they could not leave Shambala. From the grim set of Merridew's face and the way Pema kept clutching his hand, Viveka Vanachek knew that that last trip, as well as the spectre of what might be happening to Mike and Chime, was driving the colonel now.

Viv wanted to weep with frustration each time it seemed that they were making progress, only to be forced to stop at the apex of a pass and dig their way through piles of snow blocking the way. In some places the trail was no longer there and they had to backtrack and find a new trail altogether.

The memory of her dream, of Mike crying for her, was so vividly painful that although she was not extremely fit, Viv pushed herself so that she was leading the party, along with Pema and the colonel and Tea. From the way her gentle and considerate Tea drove everyone in the party, Viv knew that he too was hearing Mike's cries with every step.

At each critical pass, once a way had been found to cross it, two people stayed behind and tended signal fires.

In the old days the border took about four days to reach, but with all of the impediments, not even Dolma and Tea—who had made the trip many times—could tell exactly how far they had to go.

Finally Tea turned to the others and said through the folds of the scarf muffling his face, "Wait here. Light a fire and wait."

"What are you planning, Taring?" Merridew asked.

Tea pulled the scarf away from his face and grinned at Merridew. "It is being an ol' Native Buddhist trick, kimo sabe," he said in the silly cowboy/Tibetan accent he had affected when speaking English ever since he was a student at the Montana School of Mines. "It is called *lung-gom*. I am able to do this on accounta I am a gen-u-ine Buddhist practitioner, but it ain't for tenderfoots."

Viv put her arm around him and held him. *"Lung-gom,* like Ama-La hypnotized us to do?"

"You are getting it, little lady," he said.

She hit him on the chest. "Stop that, dammit."

"Sorry," he said in Tibetan, "but *lung-gom is* the only way to cover the ground quickly. I will go faster than you were able to go under Ama-La's spell because I am already an adept."

Merridew, who had been listening, clapped him on the shoulder and shouted into the wind, "Wish I could go too. We'll keep the home fires burnin' here, amigo. You get along now and send up the smoke signals at the border."

•   •   •

"I've heard of flying blind before, but this is ridiculous," Stoney had told the old woman. "No wonder you didn't think it would matter that you can't see. In this shit, neither can I. We're going to have to give up and go back."

"No, no. It is fine. You can land now."

"Lady, I can't even see the ground."

"Look harder," she said in the voice of his third-grade teacher. He did. And even as he looked, a particular patch of snow swept aside from the rest of the snow as if it had a mind of its own. Conditions were still close to whiteout, with nothing but snow in the sky and on the land. Then he saw that the piece of the snow he had just noticed *was* moving counter to the wind, waving something mud-colored. Looking closer, he saw that the patch of snow was instead a patch of fur. A big old white furry critter of some kind.

"Vajra will guide you in," the old lady said, as if she could see as well as he could.

"Guess you found your yeti, huh?" he said, trying not to sound as surprised as he felt.

"Oh, yes," she said simply. He set the plane down with a bump and stayed at the controls while she opened the door and acted as flight attendant while the yeti shepherded a bedraggled and half-frozen group of people out of a hole in the ground and into the plane.

While they were loading, the snow stopped, the sky cleared, and as soon as the last passenger was inside and secure, Stoney took off and headed for the valley again, the old lady still pointing the way.

Toni-Marie and her ghostly charges waited with the living for the plane to return. The ghosts who had been imprisoned in the valley mingled with the ghosts who had been haunting other places, comparing notes, seeking word of families and friends.

Chime appeared with the living a short time later. Her wrists bound with rope. She was surrounded by a great multitude of ghosts. Toni-Marie could see that there was something wrong with her aside from being tied up, but most of the time she spoke and acted like Chime, so it seemed that she had found and reoccupied her body.

"How do we know the plane is even here?" Meru demanded querulously from a litter carried by two of the other men. "That girl is not reliable. How can you follow her, knowing she is possessed by the ghost of Buzz Horn?"

So that was it, Toni-Marie thought, trying to see through all of the other ghosts.

"Don't be an ass, Meru," a tall woman with a beautiful voice demanded. "I saw Stoney thawed out myself, and Marco, Full Moon, and the others Chime rescued from your deep freeze will back us up. I don't know why the plane's gone. Maybe Stoney took it out for a test flight."

"Yes, and maybe he's deserted you while the demon inside this girl has brought you all out here to expose you to radiation and death."

Most of the ghosts were huddled around Meru and Chime, so Toni-Marie sought out the sensitives among the living and talked to them until she convinced them that she had seen the plane take off to pick up the other living people Chime had contacted. They weren't *very* sensitive, any of them, and none of them could see her or the other ghosts. They thought they were arguing among themselves instead of being the leading players in a drama with a cast of thousands. Finally, Toni-Marie said to the two young girls, "The plane is real. The plane is coming. We are all going to go to a terrific place where there will be lots of opportunities for birthin' and babies and all of the fun stuff that leads to it. Don't you think you've listened to that nasty old man long enough? There are people you know here who have *seen* the pilot go for the plane. He's real. It's real. It's on its way. Just be patient."

The girls were the only ones she could reach with whom she could make any contact, so Toni-Marie withdrew again to the fringes of the ghost hoard. To her surprise, she found that she too was suddenly being haunted by a new gaggle of curious ghostly admirers. "Boy, you sure do know how to stand up to people," said a scraggy-haired, pointed-toothed pregnant ghost girl carrying one ghost baby in her arms and another on her hip while a dozen more clung to her in other places. "Are you one of them Shambala folks like her?" She pointed an eldritch finger at Chime.

"Nah, just her and Mike are—"

"Oh, yeah. That boy. The last one Pa kilt before me."

"Uh, yeah, if you say so," Toni-Marie said. She was somewhat taken aback by this pathetic apparition but felt sorry for her too. She reminded her of some of the poor white trash on the edge of the oil fields back in Texas. "I expect Mike will be along just any time now, with the plane probably. But I'm not a Shambala person myself, not yet. I'm just their friendly spirit guide, Toni-Marie."

"I'm Evie. These are my young'uns. You sound a little like Pa. Where you from?"

"Houston, Texas," Toni-Marie answered.

"Pa was from Texas too, way back."

"If he'd stayed there, maybe you'd all still be alive," Toni-Marie said, and told the girl what she and Mike had seen back in Houston. That was when Evie opened up about her pa and what he did.

By the end of her story, when Evie told of how she had killed her father and how he had taken over Chime's body, and then how Chime had reentered her own body, the poor ghost girl and her children were so worked up they were blurry. "She's a good woman to let Pa stay in her body, Toni-Marie, but he's a hater and he's mean. He's going to hurt her and make her hurt other folks like he hurt us. You just wait."

"I don't believe I will," Toni-Marie said. She didn't know when she had ever heard anything quite so depraved or disgusting, and she'd been around a lot of depraved, disgusting things since her death. Buddhist compassion was all very well, but she was not a Buddhist and neither was Buzz Horn. They were Texans, and her kind of Texans had a whole different idea about dealing with his kind of Texans than Chime did. "Chime's got a real good heart but sometimes she's kinda naive. Look, I'm gonna try somethin', so don't you think I'm serious when I go talk to your pa, okay?"

"Okay."

The ghost hoard had thinned around Chime Cincinnati now. Chime was still bound and staring into space. Toni-Marie felt a little silly about it, but she put on her most seductive expression and moved with a very unghostly sway as she sauntered up to Chime and said, "Say there, Chime, I just want you to tell me again about Shambala. I'm beginnin' to wonder if I made the right decision about leavin' Texas."

She was hoping that the real Chime wouldn't answer first, that maybe she was saving her energies for the trip home and that the sexy come-on would convince Evie's nasty daddy to come out and play instead.

So Toni-Marie was relieved to see Chime's face altering its expression from sweet to sly, and then Chime ask in a drawl as broad as Toni's, "When did you leave Texas, sweetheart?"

"Why, just the other day. And what I want to know is, are there gonna be living folks in Shambala doing as well as they are in Texas? You know, the NAC was hardly touched at all by the war, just a few little old volcanoes and such. And everybody there has done so *well* after the war, and there's this baby boom so big they need psychic brokers like that fella McCobb my daddy hired for me. If I wasn't so crazy about you and Mikey, Chime honey, I could have been real big in the cattle industry right now. Whole new life, just like that. There is a massive breedin' program going on at the university too. Just enough folks were killed so that the entire northern continent is wide open for anybody with guts enough to take it. I guess I'm just too retirin' for somethin' like that. Never did cotton to power much myself—"

"There's a lot to be said for power." The fellow inside Chime tried to make her face look like it did when she was being reasonable, but she just looked sneaky. "How'd you get back to Texas, little lady? I thought us ghosts—meanin' you ghosts, of course—were doomed to haunt wherever we—you—died."

"Well, I got lucky. Mr. Meru banished me and Mikey to the ends of the earth, and we found out that covered just about any place we wanted to go, including Houston, so I went back to check on my folks. They had this whole new life all arranged for me just like that. Too bad that poor little bein' back home will get born without me to guide it . . . but I don't have much of a head for business and I didn't figure I'd be any good in the cattle industry."

"I'm sure you did the right thing."

"Thanks, Chime."

She passed over Meru on her way back to the ghost hoard, and he was smiling directly at her. He might be a shit, but he *was* at least a sensitive shit. A moment later she heard Chime's voice say in a phony imitation of Chime's own soft tones, "Master, I've got a real good idea.

You hate Buzz for what he did to you, and I'd really like to get rid of him. Why don't you do us both a favor and try to banish him out of me like you banished my friends that time? I know you're not feelin' well, but I don't expect you want Buzz ruinin' the neighborhood in Shambala any more than I do."

"Oh, very well, my child, if you insist," Meru said with a weakness that wasn't feigned. "However, you'll have to try to trick his spirit into peeking out your mouth so that he'll be in position to be exorcised."

Chime opened her mouth, and Toni-Marie saw Buzz's ghost come halfway out while Meru mumbled to himself a moment, then said, "Evil spirit who will not be ruled by me, go now, be banished to the ends of the earth!" And with that Buzz's ghost flew out of Chime's mouth and disappeared.

Evie and the baby ghosts watched warily. "Do you reckon he's really gone? Gone for good?"

"I do," Toni-Marie said. "And I sure do hope he likes barbecue sauce."

Stoney and Chime had to make two trips to take all of the survivors back to Shambala, but the journey was unexpectedly much easier than Chime had thought. For one thing, the shield over Shambala, from the air, had a sort of glow to it. And even before they saw the shield, they saw a flicker of fire, shining like a candle flame from the top of the first mountain they flew over. She crossed her fingers when the nose of the plane encountered the first layer of the barrier, but the plane went through it as if it was nothing more than a cloud. As they passed over the signal fire, a small dark figure waved up at them and Chime smiled and waved back at Lobsang Taring. Her dear friend had come through for her in yet one more incarnation.

Signal fires were lit on each of the other mountain passes too, and other small dark figures peered up into the plane's shadow, then hopped up and down waving hands and bits of clothing.

Lobsang Taring had been about to douse his fire and start home when Mike suddenly appeared on the other side of the fire. "Thanks, Dad," his son said with tears shining on his pale cheeks.

"My poor son," Taring said. His Buddhist calmness warred with his breaking heart. Never more would he have his boy's company down in the tunnels, for he knew immediately that this could not be Mike. This was Mike's ghost.

"I'm going to be okay now that you've helped Chime lead us back home," Mike was saying. "And I just wanted to stop and say good-bye—I mean, I expect I'll be around again soon but it may take me a while to learn to talk again. Anyhow, that's all I wanted to say. Just that I love you and, uh, please don't put out that fire yet. Chime and the pilot are going back for another load."

And at almost the same time, Viveka Vanachek picked up a handful of snow to douse the fire, only to have the snow fly from her hands. "Not yet, Mom. There's another plane coming," a voice said in her head. She turned her head slightly and there was Mike, sitting up on a rock.

Pema and Merridew were staring at him too, the snow dropping from their mittens in a little shower.

"Chime's okay. We're both bringing some other folks too." A girl in what looked like a very cold white summer outfit appeared at Mike's side.

"Time to go, Mikey. Can't you feel it? We're needed bad in the city."

"Mom, Colonel Merridew, Pema, this is my friend Toni-Marie. She and some of the other ghosts from outside are coming to be with us. That's one of the things we found out when we were out there— the ghosts really have to mingle with the living for everything to stay in balance. Toni-Marie, this is my mom and Chime's parents."

The girl ghost waggled her fingers. Viv reached up for Mike and he reached his hand down and brushed through her. "Bye, Mom, I love you. See you around," he said, using an American phrase she had once had to explain to him.

Stoney had to land in a snow meadow one valley over from Kalapa, and then they had to wait while people swarmed out of the city to investigate the strange aircraft and to help unload the weary and wounded passengers. Chime was sorry that she wouldn't get to greet her parents right away, although she had seen them waving up to her as she flew over their signal fire. She was glad, however, that she would not have to confront Mike's parents right away about his death.

A huge crowd gathered to greet the plane and to tend to the passengers, but there was something odd about the atmosphere here, for all of its beloved familiarity.

She realized suddenly that all of the noise was being made by the living, that she could no longer see, hear, or feel the ghosts any longer. She trailed behind the healthier passengers who had been in the last planeload, looking all around the valley, peering under the plane, whispering for Mike and for Toni-Marie, even for Evie, but she saw none of them, nor the ghosts of the women of Lhasa, nor the ghosts of the monks. It felt strange to be among only solid people again. It made the world feel emptier somehow, although there was one ghost in particular she did not miss. Perhaps she should have intervened when Toni-Marie and Meru tricked Buzz's ghost into being exorcised, but she really didn't think Buzz was ready for Shambala. He'd much prefer Texas, and for all of his viciousness, he was a very powerful spirit. She felt sure that somehow he would land on his hooves.

Feeling disoriented and a little lonely among mere living company, and troubled about the prospect of breaking the news of Mike's death to his family, she walked down the slope toward the sacred lake at the foot of Kalapa City. She still missed the ghosts, but now it seemed to her that the baby yaks all ran to the side of their pen to greet her when she walked by. Birds swooped down to perch on her shoulders and hands, to the delight of Mu Mao, who frightened them away with a pounce.

"Chime, I am very happy that you have brought me to this place," Mu Mao said, brushing his soft fur against her ankles. "At last I have a home worthy of me." He peered up into her face. "But something troubles you, child."

"It's the ghosts, Mu Mao," she said. "Where are they? I can't hear them or see them."

"Of course you can, girl. I just scared eight of them off your shoulders. But they're not ghosts anymore. They've all found bodies."

"Is that all!" she said, relieved finally of the last of her worries about her mission. Except for Meekay. What had become of him and how would she tell his family?

When she reached the edge of the lake, she saw Isme, her hair gleaming like butter in the sunlight, smiling and waving at her.

Well, Mike had asked that his last regards be given to Isme, after all.

"Chime Cincinnati, I was so worried about you!" Isme said, then looked around. "Are you the last? Is there no one else?" Chime shook her head and watched Isme's face fall, then they collapsed in each other's arms, weeping.

"Our parents all went out looking for you, lighting fires to guide you home. I wanted to go, but Auntie Dolma said someone should be here to welcome everyone home."

Chime hugged her and said nothing. As soon as they came to the rhododendron jungle, she joyfully lay down and rolled among the warm fragrant blossoms on the bank of the stream.

". . . see how Nyima is doing, break the news . . ." Isme was saying, but Chime was already sleeping in the blossoms before Isme finished her sentence.

Later, Isme's voice awoke her. "Come, Chime Cincinnati, you mustn't sleep out here all night. It's starting to get cold at night now. Nyima wants to see you." Isme sounded breathless with suppressed excitement, and Chime was so far infected by her tone that she managed to hurry a little on the way to Nyima's house. None of the children were playing outdoors, and even stranger in view of Chime's last memories of this house, she could hear no crying from the baby. Had she returned too late to do the poor soulless child any good?

"Don't worry," Isme said, and preceded her inside. "Something wonderful has happened."

Nyima sat cross-legged, cuddling her youngest against her, as if everything was perfectly normal. When she looked up to greet them, Chime saw that she was transformed back into the old, laughing Nyima whose name meant "sunshine." "We've been waiting for you," she said, and set the baby on her knee. The baby no longer was empty and soulless, but greeted them with questing curiosity and a gassy smile. "My children have gone to see the mothers of the other babies. They have all changed in this same fashion," Nyima said, beaming with relief.

When Isme and Chime knelt down to examine the child, he grabbed a handful of Isme's yellow hair in his tiny fist. He bounced his fist up and down for a moment, holding the hair, then let go and screwed his little face up as he turned his wide, brown, and quite familiar gaze on Chime. With a swell of affection and relief that brought tears to her eyes and a tightness to her chest and throat, Chime scooped him up, wiped and kissed his cheek, and rocked him while he bawled. "It's all right, Meekay. We're home now and it's all going to be okay. When you are a big boy again, you can come and help Chime in the outside world again. But right now I think we need to change your pants."